THE MOONSTONE

'THE DETECTIVE STORY CLUB is a clearing house
for the best detective and mystery stories chosen for
you by a select committee of experts. Only the most
ingenious crime stories will be published under the
THE DETECTIVE STORY CLUB imprint. A special
distinguishing stamp appears on the wrapper and title
page of every THE DETECTIVE STORY CLUB book—the
Man with the Gun. Always look for the Man with the Gun
when buying a Crime book.'

Wm. Collins Sons & Co. Ltd., 1929

Now the Man with the Gun is back in this series of
COLLINS CRIME CLUB reprints, and with him the
chance to experience the classic books that influenced the
Golden Age of crime fiction.

THE DETECTIVE STORY CLUB

FURTHER TITLES IN PREPARATION

THE MOONSTONE

A STORY OF CRIME

BY

WILKIE COLLINS

WITH AN INTRODUCTION BY
G.D.H. & M. COLE

COLLINS
CRIME
CLUB

COLLINS CRIME CLUB
An imprint of HarperCollins*Publishers*
1 London Bridge Street
London SE1 9GF
www.harpercollins.co.uk

This 150th Anniversary Edition 2018

2

First published in Great Britain by Tinsley Brothers 1868
Published by The Detective Story Club Ltd
for Wm Collins Sons & Co. Ltd 1931

Introduction © G.D.H. & M. Cole 1953

ISBN 978-0-00-816694-6

Typeset in Bulmer MT Std by
Palimpsest Book Production Ltd, Falkirk, Stirlingshire

Printed and bound in Great Britain by CPI Group (UK) Ltd, Croydon CRO 4YY

INTRODUCTION

In the year 1928, when the boom in 'serious' detective-novel writing which began round about the first world war was nearing its height, and the 'art and science' of it was being very seriously discussed, an eminent detective novelist, in a forty-five page introduction to a vast collection of stories, let fall the opinion that '*The Moonstone* is probably the very finest detective story ever written'. Until that date, Wilkie Collins had been slightly regarded by connoisseurs, unless they were specialists in lesser Victorian fiction—'In the British Museum catalogue,' discovered the shocked author of this encomium, 'only two critical studies of this celebrated English mystery-monger are listed: one is by an American, the other by a German.' Thereafter, however, he became great; he was almost canonised as the direct ancestor of Sherlock Holmes, Dr Thorndyke, Hercule Poirot, Lemmy Caution, and all the tribe.

It is interesting, therefore, to observe that Collins himself did not think of *The Moonstone* as a detective story at all. This was not because the *genre* had not yet come into existence. The solution of a crime by the exercise of pure ratiocination on the part of a single mind had been set out in classic form twenty years before by Edgar Allan Poe in 'The Murders in the Rue Morgue'—in which, incidentally, the character-scheme of Dupin plus adoring chronicler set the convenient pattern which was repeated in Holmes *plus* Watson, Poirot *plus* Hastings, and many other subsequent combinations. In France, also, the *roman policier* was developing fast in the hands of Gaboriau and Du Boisgobey. Collins, if he had wanted to write 'the finest detective story', had no lack of models; but he did not. What he himself thought of the intention of his own novel—and he presumably knew what he meant to do—he set out in the preface:

'The attempt made, here, is to trace the influence of character on circumstances. The conduct pursued, under a sudden emergency, by a young girl (Rachel Verinder) supplies the foundation on which I have built this book.'

He goes on to say that he has endeavoured to make his subsidiary characters behave as they would have behaved; and adds that his account of the 'physiological experiment'—the dosing of Franklin Blake with laudanum in order to induce him to repeat his sleep-walking actions on the night of the disappearance of the Moonstone—is based on a careful study of books and of living authorities. Clearly what interested the author of *The Moonstone* was not the detail of the theft of the gem and the subsequent tracking down of those responsible, but the effect of the whole series of events on the behaviour of his characters. That is to say, he was writing a novel with a plot, not a crossword puzzle.

There are, of course, elements in *The Moonstone* which have since become classic detective-story-components—so classic, indeed, that later writers seeking to avoid monotony have drawn especial attention to the fact that they are *not* using the established formulae. There is the very stupid policeman, in this case Superintendent Seegrave, who is a worthy ancestor of Lestrade, Inspector Japp, and of all the police officers whom Dr Thorndyke bewildered in his day. There is the crime brought home, after suspicion has been well distributed to the most unlikely persons; although, on the other hand, Collins is scrupulously fair and makes no attempt to confuse the reader by presenting the real criminal as a person too attractive to be mistrusted. There are some clues, notably the paint-stained nightgown, though the paint-stained nightgown does not solve the mystery; it is, in fact, not much more use to Sergeant Cuff than a blood-stained nightgown was to that unfortunate Detective Whicher whom some suppose to have been the real life model for the Sergeant. (The Constance Kent case, as a matter of fact, except for the incident of the nightgown, bears practically no resemblance to the plot of *The Moonstone*.) Finally, there is the clear attempt to build up Sergeant Cuff into a 'character', by stressing his peculiar physical appearance and his reiterated interest in the growing of roses. This might legitimately be regarded as a foreshadowing of the long array of detectives noted for personal idiosyncrasies—Sherlock Holmes above all, but including also Lord Peter Wimsey, with his collector's mania, the blind Max Carrados of Ernest Bramah, Baroness Orczy's Old Man in the Corner, who fiddled with string, and a dozen others, as well as some whose distinguishing characteristic is proudly stated to be that of possessing none whatever.

The creation of an idiosyncratic and therefore easily-memorised detective is one of the established tricks of the trade, enabling the detective to last out a course of thirty to fifty novels, and so to fix himself in the public's mind that at the circulating library counter the inveterate asks for 'the new Poirot' or whatever it may be. Sophisticated moderns may, however, observe that Sergeant Cuff's roses are rather over-stressed, and have very little relevance to the matter in hand; and, more devastatingly, that Sergeant Cuff, though doing in the course of the book some pretty detection, was quite wrong in his conclusions, and did not solve the mystery in this, his first recorded case. He does not appear, in *The Moonstone*, likely to earn his creator the modest competence which writers of detective stories expect by solving twenty or thirty problems in the future. He is no omniscient, no Great Brain—Poe's Dupin is a far more plausible prototype for the twentieth-century paladins. Sergeant Cuff is what his creator intended him to be, a character in his own right, a policeman playing a part in a story of real people with a mystery at its heart.

This type of story was extremely common in the mid-Victorian era—a fact which the sudden glorification of *The Moonstone* tends to obscure. The Victorians loved a mystery, or a crime, or both, set in the ordinary development of plot.

The greatest of them all has made his contribution in the unsolved *Mystery of Edwin Drood*; but few people appear to remember nowadays how many of the popular Victorian novels had a mystery (often involving a policeman) as their main or subsidiary plot. Leaving aside other books of Collins' own, such as *No Name* or *Armadale*, we may turn to Trollope and note, among many possible candidates, *Is He Popenjoy?*, a mystery of inheritance, the murder of Mr Bonteen, which takes up so much of the space of *Phineas Redux*, *Orley Farm*, and the theft story in the *Last Chronicle of Barset*.

Let us go a little further afield. Mrs Henry Wood is chiefly known, to this generation, for the sensational sentimentalities of *East Lynne*—itself in some sort a mystery novel. But a very much better book of hers—*The Channings*—which deserves a revival, contains within its 450 pages no fewer than three mysteries. It begins with the problem of a chorister's surplice found stained with ink, to the great disgrace of the cathedral school—it is only close to the end of the book that this ill-deed is finally brought home to the most disagreeable of a disagreeable family, Gerald Yorke. It continues with the theft of a twenty-pound note, for for which the noble Arthur Channing long bears the blame—the situation being further confused by speculation as to how Hamish Channing, Arthur's brother, was suddenly in a position to pay off his small scale creditors; and further chronicles the complete disappearance of Charley, the youngest Channing, after having been frightened by a bogus ghost in the cathedral Cloisters. It must be admitted that the eminent authoress, having landed herself with a slight over-plus of plot, shows a lamentable lack of interest in Charley Channing, only restoring him to life, with a minimum of explanation, in time for the happy reunion at the end of the book; also that Mr Butterby, the representative of the law, is exhibited as singularly incompetent. Nevertheless, *The Channings* is a novel which, like *The Moonstone*, traces 'the influence of character on circumstances', and particularly of characters in contact with crime.

The long *Johnny Ludlow* series, by the same author, is also very much concerned with crime and its detection and (or) punishment; and to enter yet more respectable precincts, it should be remembered that Charlotte Yonge, whose saga-volumes of Victorian family life now fetch such high second-hand prices, devoted the whole of one book, *The Trial*, to a murder-mystery, and that a large part even of *The Daisy Chain* turns on the questions 'who inked the school-master's book?' and 'will Norman May's character be re-established?'

The list could be extended almost indefinitely. Henry Kingsley's once very popular *Ravenshoe* is written around a mystery of parentage which dictates most of the plot. The point to realise is that the Victorian story-tellers, and the Victorian story-readers, accepted crime and punishment as things that might happen to anyone in the course of life—and made the life-story that much more readable if they did happen. But these crimes and punishments happened to real characters—or characters as real as the novelist's ability could compass. The characters were not subordinated and compelled to dance around to the exigencies of a plot which demands a body in a country-house library, a number of resident guests and servants each with their own discreditable and penetrable motives for murder, a paraphernalia of scientific instruments of detection, and a veneer of literary erudition to cover up the lack of any human interest; they were not imprisoned in a depressing mechanistic pattern. As counterbalance, of course, the Victorian novels tend to lack the puzzle fascination; they know little of the natural habitat of duck-weeds (Freeman) or the technique of electro-plating a murdered corpse so as to serve as a studio couch (Sayers). And the suspense they engender is not so much suspense about the identity of the criminal as suspense about how the innocently-accused is to be vindicated and the happy ending brought about without too many broken homes and death-beds on the way. (It must be admitted that Mrs Henry Wood over-indulged in death-beds as much as Trollope did in inheritance problems.) By all these criteria, *The Moonstone* is a Victorian novel, and not a detective story.

Not that it is any the worse for that. As a story, it is a very good one, excellently deployed, and it dispenses with any adventitious sensationalism. The death of Rosanna Spearman arises directly out of the character and past history of Rosanna Spearman; and in view of the date at which the book was written, the absence of any sentimentalising over that unfortunate girl is quite remarkable. Subsequent detective novelists—not, fortunately, Conan Doyle—were too often constrained, either by their publishers or by their own conception of what the public wanted, to insert a 'love-interest' into their novels. 'Love-interest' not fitting very well into mechanistic plots, the result was often deplorable. There is no need to particularise, only to mention that the introduction of a young lovely burning to avenge the corpse, or devoted to the chief suspect—or in any other capacity—tends seriously to hamper the activities of a detective who is working out the possible permutations of Bradshaw, or the chemical composition of a piece of tarred rope, or the significance of quotations from the works of T.S. Eliot scattered in unlikely places. It is not without significance that the English fictional detectives who have stayed the course best have been those expressly immune to amorous adventure—Sherlock Holmes, an egocentric neurotic, Dr Thorndyke, a handsome kindly 'block of teak', Father Brown, a priest, Dr Priestly, a disagreeable elderly scientist, and several policemen happily married to undistinguished wives: their French counterparts fall in and out of love with the victim, the criminal, or both—but that is Gallic levity frowned upon across the Channel.

In *The Moonstone*, however, there *is* a love-interest, that of the relations of Franklin Blake with the two women who loved him, which is both interesting and relevant to the story; and the further device of narration in turns by the people directly concerned adds to the human interest. No matter that it is not very probable that Gabriel Betteredge would ever have succeeded in putting pen to paper so as to cover the pages which he is made to cover here; this is what Gabriel, being Gabriel, would have written if he could have written it at such length. Similarly, this is what Miss Drusilla Clack would have written had she been completely frank—as, with a pen in her hand, she would probably not have been. And so with the rest. The net effect of all of which is that, though the paraphernalia of the Indian temple and the Buddhist priests is rather hastily written in, and though *The Moonstone* cannot be regarded as the master-pattern of the modern detective story, it remains something much more permanent—a thoroughly good novel.

G. D. H. AND MARGARET COLE
1953

CONTENTS

PREFACE

In some of my former novels, the object proposed has been to trace the influence of circumstances upon character. In the present story I have reversed the process. The attempt made here is to trace the influence of character on circumstances. The conduct pursued, under a sudden emergency, by a young girl, supplies the foundation on which I have built this book.

The same object has been kept in view in the handling of the other characters which appear in these pages. Their course of thought and action under the circumstances which surround them is shown to be (what it would most probably have been in real life) sometimes right and sometimes wrong. Right or wrong, their conduct, in either event, equally directs the course of those portions of the story in which they are concerned.

In the case of the physiological experiment which occupies a prominent place in the closing scenes of *The Moonstone*, the same principle has guided me once more. Having first ascertained, not only from books, but from living authorities as well, what the result of that experiment would really have been, I have declined to avail myself of the novelist's privilege of supposing something which might have happened, and have so shaped the story as to make it grow out of what actually would have happened—which, I beg to inform my readers, is also what actually does happen, in these pages.

With reference to the story of the Diamond, as here set forth, I have to acknowledge that it is founded, in some important particulars, on the stories of two of the royal diamonds of Europe. The magnificent stone which adorns the top of the Russian Imperial Sceptre was once the eye of an Indian idol. The famous Koh-i-Noor is also supposed to have been one of

1

the sacred gems of India; and, more than this, to have been the subject of a prediction, which prophesied certain misfortune to the persons who should divert it from its ancient uses.

WILKIE COLLINS
Gloucester Place, Portman Square
30th June 1868

PREFACE TO A NEW EDITION

THE circumstances under which *The Moonstone* was originally written have invested the book—in the author's mind—with an interest peculiarly its own.

While this work was still in course of periodical publication in England and in the United States, and when not more than one-third of it was completed, the bitterest affliction of my life and the severest illness from which I have ever suffered fell on me together. At the time when my mother lay dying in her little cottage in the country, I was struck prostrate, in London— crippled in every limb by the torture of rheumatic gout. Under the weight of this double calamity, I had my duty to the public still to bear in mind. My good readers in England and in America whom I had never yet disappointed, were expecting their regular weekly instalments of the new story. I held to the story—for my own sake as well as for theirs. In the intervals of grief, in the occasional remissions of pain, I dictated from my bed that portion of *The Moonstone* which has since proved most suc- cessful in amusing the public—the 'Narrative of Miss Clack'. Of the physical sacrifice which the effort cost me I shall say nothing. I only look back now at the blessed relief which my occupation (forced as it was) brought to my mind. The Art which had been always the pride and the pleasure of my life became now more than ever 'its own exceeding great reward'. I doubt if I should have lived to write another book, if the responsibility of the weekly publication of this story had not forced me to rally my sinking energies of body and mind—to dry my useless tears, and to conquer my merciless pains.

The novel completed, I awaited its reception by the public with an eagerness of anxiety which I have never felt before or since for the fate of any other writings of mine. If *The Moonstone* had failed, my mortification would have been bitter indeed. As it was, the welcome accorded to the story in England, in America, and on the Continent of Europe was instantly and universally favourable. Never have I had better reason than this work has given me to feel gratefully to novel-readers of all nations. Everywhere my characters made friends, and my story roused interest. Everywhere the public favour looked over my faults—and repaid me a hundredfold for the hard toil which these pages cost me in the dark time of sickness and grief.

I have only to add that the present edition has had the benefit of my careful revision. All that I can do towards making the book worthy of the reader's continued approval has now been done.

W.C.
May 1871

PROLOGUE

Extracted from a Family Paper

I ADDRESS these lines—written in India—to my relatives in England.

My object is to explain the motive which has induced me to refuse the right hand of friendship to my cousin, John Herncastle.

The private difference between my cousin and me took its rise in a great public event in which we were both concerned— the storming of Seringapatam, under General Baird, on the 4th of May, 1799.

In order that the circumstances may be clearly understood, I must revert for a moment to the period before the assault, and to the stories current in our camp of the treasure in jewels and gold stored up in the Palace of Seringapatam.

One of the wildest of these stories related to a Yellow Diamond—a famous gem in the native annals of India.

The earliest known traditions describe the stone as having been set in the forehead of the four-handed Indian god who typifies the Moon. Partly from its peculiar colour, partly from a superstition which represented it as feeling the influence of the deity whom it adorned, and growing and lessening in lustre with the waxing and waning of the moon, it first gained the name by which it continues to be known in India to this day— the name of THE MOONSTONE.

The adventures of the Yellow Diamond begin with the eleventh century of the Christian era.

At that date, the Mohammedan conqueror, Mahmoud of

5

Ghizni, crossed India; seized on the holy city of Somnauth; and stripped of its treasures the famous temple, which had stood for centuries—the shrine of Hindoo pilgrimage, and the wonder of the Eastern world.

Of all the deities worshipped in the temple, the moon-god alone escaped the rapacity of the conquering Mohammedans. Preserved by three Brahmins, the inviolate deity, bearing the Yellow Diamond in its forehead, was removed by night, and was transported to the second of the sacred cities of India—the city of Benares.

Here, in a new shrine—in a hall inlaid with precious stones, under a roof supported by pillars of gold—the moon-god was set up and worshipped. Here, on the night when the shrine was completed, Vishnu the Preserver appeared to the three Brahmins in a dream.

The deity breathed the breath of his divinity on the Diamond in the forehead of the god. And the Brahmins knelt and hid their faces in their robes. The deity commanded that the Moonstone should be watched, from that time forth, by three priests in turn, night and day, to the end of the generations of men. And the Brahmins heard, and bowed before his will. The deity predicted certain disaster to the presumptuous mortal who laid hands on the sacred gem, and to all of his house and name who received it after him. And the Brahmins caused the prophecy to be written over the gates of the shrine in letters of gold.

One age followed another—and still, generation after generation, the successors of the three Brahmins watched their priceless Moonstone, night and day. One age followed another until the first years of the eighteenth Christian century saw the reign of Aurungzebe, Emperor of the Moguls. At his command havoc and rapine were let loose once more among the temples of the worship of Brahmah. The shrine of the four-handed god was polluted by the slaughter of sacred animals; the images of the deities were broken in pieces; and the Moonstone was seized by an officer of rank in the army of Aurungzebe.

Powerless to recover their lost treasure by open force, the three guardian priests followed and watched it in disguise. The generations succeeded each other; the warrior who had committed the sacrilege perished miserably; the Moonstone passed (carrying its curse with it) from one lawless Mohammedan hand to another; and still, through all chances and changes, the successors of the three guardian priests kept their watch, waiting the day when the will of Vishnu the Preserver should restore to them their sacred gem. Time rolled on from the first to the last years of the eighteenth Christian century. The Diamond fell into the possession of Tippoo, Sultan of Seringapatam, who caused it to be placed as an ornament in the handle of a dagger, and who commanded it to be kept among the choicest treasures of his armoury. Even then—in the palace of the Sultan himself—the three guardian priests still kept their watch in secret. There were three officers of Tippoo's household, strangers to the rest, who had won their master's confidence by conforming, or appearing to conform, to the Mussulman faith; and to those three men report pointed as the three priests in disguise.

So, as told in our camp, ran the fanciful story of the Moonstone. It made no serious impression on any of us except my cousin—whose love of the marvellous induced him to believe it. On the night before the assault on Seringapatam, he was absurdly angry with me, and with others, for treating the whole thing as a fable. A foolish wrangle followed; and Herncastle's unlucky temper got the better of him. He declared, in his boastful way, that we should see the Diamond on his finger, if the English army took Seringapatam. The sally was saluted by a roar of laughter, and there, as we all thought that night, the thing ended.

Let me now take you on to the day of the assault.

My cousin and I were separated at the outset. I never saw him when we forded the river; when we planted the English flag in the first breach; when we crossed the ditch beyond; and, fighting every inch of our way, entered the town. It was only at dusk, when the place was ours, and after General Baird himself had found the dead body of Tippoo under a heap of the slain, that Herncastle and I met.

We were each attached to a party sent out by the general's orders to prevent the plunder and confusion which followed our conquest. The camp-followers committed deplorable excesses; and, worse still, the soldiers found their way, by an unguarded door, into the treasury of the Palace, and loaded themselves with gold and jewels. It was in the court outside the treasury that my cousin and I met, to enforce the laws of discipline on our own soldiers. Herncastle's fiery temper had been, as I could plainly see, exasperated to a kind of frenzy by the terrible slaughter through which we had passed. He was very unfit, in my opinion, to perform the duty that had been entrusted to him.

There was riot and confusion enough in the treasury, but no violence that I saw. While I was still vainly trying to establish order, I heard a frightful yelling on the other side of the court-yard, and at once ran towards the cries, in dread of finding some new outbreak of the pillage in that direction.

I got to an open door, and saw the bodies of two Indians (by their dress, as I guessed, officers of the palace) lying across the entrance, dead.

A cry inside hurried me into a room, which appeared to serve as an armoury. A third Indian, mortally wounded, was sinking at the feet of a man whose back was towards me. The man turned at the instant when I came in, and I saw John Herncastle, with a torch in one hand, and a dagger dripping with blood in the other. A stone, set like a pommel, in the end of the dagger's handle, flashed in the torchlight, as he turned on me, like a gleam of fire. The dying Indian sank to his knees, pointed to the dagger in Herncastle's hand, and said, in his native language—'The Moonstone will have its vengeance yet on you and yours!' He spoke those words, and fell dead on the floor.

Before I could stir in the matter, the men who had followed me across the courtyard crowded in. My cousin rushed to meet them, like a madman. 'Clear the room!' he shouted to me, 'and set a guard on the door!' The men fell back as he threw himself on them with his torch and his dagger. I put two sentinels of my own company, on whom I could rely, to keep the door. Through the remainder of the night, I saw no more of my cousin.

Early in the morning, the plunder still going on, General Baird announced publicly by beat of drum, that any thief detected in the fact, be he whom he might, should be hung. The provost-marshal was in attendance, to prove that the General was in earnest; and in the throng that followed the proclamation, Herncastle and I met again.

He held out his hand, as usual, and said, 'Good morning.'

I waited before I gave him my hand in return.

'Tell me first,' I said, 'how the Indian in the armoury met his death, and what those last words meant, when he pointed to the dagger in your hand.'

'The Indian met his death, as I suppose, by a mortal wound,' said Herncastle. 'What his last words meant I know no more than you do.'

I looked at him narrowly. His frenzy of the previous day had all calmed down. I determined to give him another chance.

'Is that all you have to tell me?' I asked.

He answered, 'That is all.'

I turned my back on him; and we have not spoken since.

FIRST PERIOD

THE LOSS OF THE DIAMOND (1848)

The Events related by GABRIEL BETTEREDGE, *House-Steward in the service of* JULIA, LADY VERINDER.

CHAPTER I

IN the first part of *Robinson Crusoe*, at page one hundred and twenty-nine, you will find it thus written:

'Now I saw, though too late, the Folly of beginning a Work before we count the Cost, and before we judge rightly of our own Strength to go through with it.'

Only yesterday, I opened my *Robinson Crusoe* at that place. Only this morning (May twenty-first, Eighteen hundred and fifty), came my lady's nephew, Mr Franklin Blake, and held a short conversation with me, as follows:

'Betteredge,' says Mr Franklin, 'I have been to the lawyer's about some family matters; and, among other things, we have been talking of the loss of the Indian Diamond, in my aunt's house in Yorkshire, two years since. Mr Bruff thinks as I think, that the whole story ought, in the interests of truth, to be placed on record in writing—and the sooner the better.'

Not perceiving his drift yet, and thinking it always desirable for the sake of peace and quietness to be on the lawyer's side, I said I thought so too. Mr Franklin went on.

'In this matter of the Diamond,' he said, 'the characters of innocent people have suffered under suspicion already—as you know. The memories of innocent people may suffer, hereafter, for want of a record of the facts to which those who come after us can appeal. There can be no doubt that this strange family story of ours ought to be told. And I think, Betteredge, Mr Bruff and I together have hit on the right way of telling it.'

Very satisfactory to both of them, no doubt. But I failed to see what I myself had to do with it, so far.

'We have certain events to relate,' Mr Franklin proceeded; 'and we have certain persons concerned in those events who are capable of relating them. Starting from these plain facts, the idea is that we should all write the story of the Moonstone in turn—as far as our own personal experience extends, and no farther. We must begin by showing how the Diamond first fell into the hands of my uncle Herncastle, when he was serving in India fifty years since. This prefatory narrative I have already got by me in the form of an old family paper, which relates the necessary particulars on the authority of an eye-witness. The next thing to do is to tell how the Diamond found its way into my aunt's house in Yorkshire, two years ago, and how it came to be lost in little more than twelve hours afterwards. Nobody knows as much as you do, Betteredge, about what went on in the house at that time. So you must take the pen in hand, and start the story.'

In those terms I was informed of what my personal concern was with the matter of the Diamond. If you are curious to know what course I took under the circumstances, I beg to inform you that I did what you would probably have done in my place. I modestly declared myself to be quite unequal to the task imposed upon me—and I privately felt, all the time, that I was quite clever enough to perform it, if I only gave my own abilities a fair chance. Mr Franklin, I imagine, must have seen my private sentiments in my face. He declined to believe in my modesty; and he insisted on giving my abilities a fair chance.

CHAPTER II

THE question of how I am to start the story properly I have tried to settle in two ways. First, by scratching my head, which led to nothing. Second, by consulting my daughter Penelope, which has resulted in an entirely new idea.

Penelope's notion is that I should set down what happened, regularly day by day, beginning with the day when we got the news that Mr Franklin Blake was expected on a visit to the house. When you come to fix your memory with a date in this way, it is wonderful what your memory will pick up for you upon that compulsion.

Beginning, then, on Penelope's plan, I beg to mention that I was specially called one Wednesday morning into my lady's own sitting-room, the date being the twenty-fourth of May, Eighteen hundred and forty-eight.

'Gabriel,' says my lady, 'here is news that will surprise you. Franklin Blake has come back from abroad. He has been staying with his father in London, and he is coming to us tomorrow to stop till next month, and keep Rachel's birthday.'

If I had had a hat in my hand, nothing but respect would have prevented me from throwing that hat up to the ceiling. I had not seen Mr Franklin since he was a boy, living along with us in this house. He was, out of all sight (as I remember him), the nicest boy that ever spun a top or broke a window. Miss Rachel, who was present, and to whom I made that remark, observed, in return, that *she* remembered him as the most atrocious tyrant that ever tortured a doll, and the hardest driver of an exhausted little girl in string harness that England could produce. 'I burn with indignation, and I ache with fatigue,' was the way Miss Rachel summed it up, 'when I think of Franklin Blake.'

Our nice boy didn't forget us after he went abroad. He wrote every now and then; sometimes to my lady, sometimes to Miss Rachel, and sometimes to me. We had had a transaction together, before he left, which consisted in his borrowing of me a ball of string, a four-bladed knife, and seven-and-sixpence in money—the colour of which last I have not seen, and never expect to see again. His letters to me chiefly related to borrowing more. I heard, however, from my lady, how he got on abroad, as he grew in years and stature. After he had learnt what the institutions of Germany could teach him, he gave the French a turn next, and the Italians a turn after that. They made him among them a sort of universal genius, as well as I could understand it. He wrote a little; he painted a little; he sang and played and composed a little—borrowing, as I suspect, in all these cases, just as he had borrowed from me. Twice over, he made up his mind to come back to England and see us; and twice over (saving your presence), some unmentionable woman stood in the way and stopped him. His third attempt succeeded, as you know already from what my lady told me. On Thursday the twenty-fifth of May, we were to see for the first time what our nice boy had grown to be as a man. He came of good blood; he had a high courage; and he was five-and-twenty years of age, by our reckoning. Now you know as much of Mr Franklin Blake as I did—before Mr Franklin Blake came down to our house.

The Thursday was as fine a summer's day as ever you saw: and my lady and Miss Rachel (not expecting Mr Franklin till dinner-time) drove out to lunch with some friends in the neighbourhood.

When they were gone, I went and had a look at the bedroom which had been got ready for our guest, and saw that all was straight. Then I took up my beehive chair to go out into the back court, when I was stopped by hearing a sound like the soft beating of a drum, on the terrace in front of my lady's residence.

Going round to the terrace, I found three mahogany-coloured Indians, in white linen frocks and trousers, looking up at the house.

The Indians, as I saw on looking closer, had small hand-drums slung in front of them. Behind them stood a little delicate-looking light-haired English boy carrying a bag. I judged the fellows to be strolling conjurors, and the boy with the bag to be carrying the tools of their trade. One of the three, who spoke English and who exhibited, I must own, the most elegant manners, presently informed me that my judgment was right. He requested permission to show his tricks in the presence of the lady of the house.

Now, I am not a sour old man. I am generally all for amusement, and the last person in the world to distrust another person because he happens to be a few shades darker than myself. But the best of us have our weaknesses—and my weakness, when I know a family plate-basket to be out on a pantry-table, is to be instantly reminded of that basket by the sight of a strolling stranger whose manners are superior to my own. I accordingly informed the Indian that the lady of the house was out; and I warned him and his party off the premises. He made me a beautiful bow in return; and he and his party went off the premises. On my side, I returned to my beehive chair, and set myself down on the sunny side of the court, and fell (if the truth must be owned), not exactly into a sleep, but into the next best thing to it.

I was roused up by my daughter Penelope running out at me as if the house was on fire. What do you think she wanted? She wanted to have the three Indian jugglers instantly taken up; for this reason, namely, that they knew who was coming from London to visit us, and that they meant some mischief to Mr Franklin Blake.

Mr Franklin's name roused me. I opened my eyes, and made my girl explain herself.

It appeared that Penelope had just come from our lodge, where she had been having a gossip with the lodge-keeper's daughter. The two girls had seen the Indians pass out, after I had warned them off, followed by their little boy. Taking it into their heads that the boy was ill-used by the foreigners—for no reason that I could discover, except that he was pretty and delicate-looking—the two girls had stolen along the inner side of the hedge between us and the road, and had watched the proceedings of the foreigners on the outer side. Those proceedings resulted in the performance of the following extraordinary tricks.

They first looked up the road, and down the road, and made sure that they were alone. Then they all three faced about, and stared hard in the direction of our house. Then they jabbered and disputed in their own language, and looked at each other like men in doubt. Then they all turned to their little English boy, as if they expected *him* to help them. And then the chief Indian, who spoke English, said to the boy, 'Hold out your hand.'

On hearing those dreadful words, my daughter Penelope said she didn't know what prevented her heart from flying straight out of her. I thought privately that it might have been her stays. All I said, however, was, 'You make my flesh creep.' (*Nota bene*: Women like these little compliments.)

Well, when the Indian said, 'Hold out your hand,' the boy shrunk back, and shook his head, and said he didn't like it. The Indian, thereupon, asked him (not at all unkindly), whether he would like to be sent back to London, and left where they had found him, sleeping in an empty basket in a market—a hungry, ragged, and forsaken little boy. This, it seems, ended the difficulty. The little chap unwillingly held out his hand. Upon that, the Indian took a bottle from his bosom, and poured out of it some black stuff, like ink, into the palm of the boy's hand. The Indian—first touching the boy's head, and making signs over it in the air—then said, 'Look.' The boy became quite stiff, and stood like a statue, looking into the ink in the hollow of his hand.

The Indians looked up the road and down the road once more—and then the chief Indian said these words to the boy: 'See the English gentleman from foreign parts?'

The boy said, 'I see him.'

The Indian said, 'Is it on the road to this house, and on no other, that the English gentleman will travel today?'

The boy said, 'It is on the road to this house, and on no other, that the English gentleman will travel today.'

The Indian put a second question—after waiting a little first. He said: 'Has the English gentleman got It about him?'

The boy answered—also, after waiting a little first—'Yes.'

The Indian put a third and last question: 'Will the English gentleman come here, as he has promised to come, at the close of day?'

The boy said, 'I can't tell.'

The Indian asked why.

The boy said, 'I am tired. The mist rises in my head, and puzzles me. I can see no more today.'

With that the catechism ended. The chief Indian said something in his own language to the other two, pointing to the boy, and pointing towards the town, in which (as we afterwards discovered) they were lodged. He then, after making more signs on the boy's head, blew on his forehead, and so woke him up with a start. After that, they all went on their way towards the town, and the girls saw them no more.

Most things they say have a moral, if you only look for it. What was the moral of this?

The moral was, as I thought: First, that the chief juggler had heard Mr Franklin's arrival talked of among the servants out-of-doors, and saw his way to making a little money by it. Second, that he and his men and boy (with a view to making the said money) meant to hang about till they saw my lady drive home, and then to come back, and foretell Mr Franklin's arrival by magic. Third, that Penelope had heard them rehearsing their hocus-pocus, like actors rehearsing a play. Fourth, that I should do well to have an eye, that evening, on the plate-basket. Fifth, that Penelope would do well to cool down, and leave me, her father, to doze off again in the sun.

That appeared to me to be the sensible view. If you know

anything of the ways of young women, you won't be surprised to hear that Penelope wouldn't take it. The moral of the thing was serious, according to my daughter. She particularly reminded me of the Indian's third question, Has the English gentleman got It about him? 'Oh, father!' says Penelope, clasping her hands, 'don't joke about this. What does "It" mean?'

'We'll ask Mr Franklin, my dear,' I said, 'if you can wait till Mr Franklin comes.' I winked to show I meant that in joke. Penelope took it quite seriously. My girl's earnestness tickled me. 'What on earth should Mr Franklin know about it?' I inquired. 'Ask him,' says Penelope. 'And see whether *he* thinks it a laughing matter, too.' With that parting shot, my daughter left me.

To my great surprise, Mr Franklin, like Penelope, took the thing seriously. How seriously, you will understand, when I tell you that, in his opinion, 'It' meant the Moonstone.

CHAPTER III

I WAS just stretching my legs, when out bounced another woman on me. Not my daughter again; only Nancy, the kitchen-maid, this time. I was straight in her way out; and I observed, as she asked me to let her by, that she had a sulky face—a thing which, as head of the servants, I never allow, on principle, to pass me without inquiry.

'What are you turning your back on your dinner for?' I asked. 'What's wrong now, Nancy?'

'Rosanna's late again for dinner,' says Nancy. 'And I'm sent to fetch her in. All the hard work falls on my shoulders in this house. Let me alone, Mr Betteredge!'

The person here mentioned as Rosanna was our second housemaid. Having a kind of pity for our second housemaid (why, you shall presently know), and seeing in Nancy's face, that she would fetch her fellow-servant in with more hard words than might be needful under the circumstances, it struck me that I had nothing particular to do, and that I might as well fetch Rosanna myself; giving her a hint to be punctual in future, which I knew she would take kindly from *me*.

'Where is Rosanna?' I inquired.

'At the sands, of course!' says Nancy, with a toss of her head. 'She had another of her fainting fits this morning, and she asked to go out and get a breath of fresh air. I have no patience with her.'

'Go back to your dinner, my girl,' I said. 'I have patience with her, and I'll fetch her in.'

Rosanna (to put the person before the Thing, which is but common politeness) was the only new servant in our house. About four months before the time I am writing of, my lady had been in London, and had gone over a Reformatory, intended to save forlorn women from drifting back into bad ways, after they had got released from prison. The matron, seeing my lady took an interest in the place, pointed out a girl to her, named Rosanna Spearman, and told her a most miserable story, which I haven't the heart to repeat here; for I don't like to be made wretched without any use, and no more do you. The upshot of it was, that Rosanna Spearman had been a thief, and not being of the sort that get up Companies in the City, and rob from thousands, instead of only robbing from one, the law laid hold of her, and the prison and the reformatory followed the lead of the law. The matron's opinion of Rosanna was (in spite of what she had done) that the girl was one in a thousand, and that she only wanted a chance to prove herself worthy of any Christian woman's interest in her. My lady (being a Christian woman, if ever there was one yet) said to the matron, upon that, 'Rosanna Spearman shall have her chance, in my service.' In a week afterwards, Rosanna Spearman entered this establishment as our second housemaid.

Not a soul was told the girl's story, excepting Miss Rachel and me. My lady, doing me the honour to consult me about most things, consulted me about Rosanna. Having fallen a good deal latterly into the late Sir John's way of always agreeing with my lady, I agreed with her heartily about Rosanna Spearman.

A fairer chance no girl could have had than was given to this poor girl of ours. None of the servants could cast her past life in her teeth, for none of the servants knew what it had been. She had her wages and her privileges, like the rest of them; and every now and then a friendly word from my lady, in private, to encourage her. In return, she showed herself, I am bound to say, well worthy of the kind treatment bestowed upon her. Though far from strong, and troubled occasionally with those fainting-fits already mentioned, she went about her work modestly and uncomplainingly, doing it carefully, and doing it well. But, somehow, she failed to make friends among the other women servants, excepting my daughter Penelope, who was always kind to Rosanna, though never intimate with her.

Having now told the story of Rosanna, I have only to notice one of the many queer ways of this strange girl to get on next to the story of the sands.

Our house is high up on the Yorkshire coast, and close by the sea. We have got beautiful walks all round us, in every direction but one. That one I acknowledge to be a horrid walk. It leads, for a quarter of a mile, through a melancholy plantation of firs, and brings you out between low cliffs on the loneliest and ugliest little bay on all our coast.

The sand-hills here run down to the sea, and end in two spits of rock jutting out opposite each other, till you lose sight of them in the water. One is called the North Spit, and one the South. Between the two, shifting backwards and forwards at certain seasons of the year, lies the most horrible quicksand on the shores of Yorkshire. At the turn of the tide, something goes on in the unknown deeps below, which sets the whole face of the quicksand shivering and trembling in a manner most remarkable to see, and which has given to it, among the people in our parts, the name of the Shivering Sand. A great bank, half a mile out, nigh the mouth of the bay, breaks the force of the main ocean coming in from the offing. Winter and summer, when the tide flows over the quicksand, the sea seems to leave the waves behind it on the bank, and rolls its waters in smoothly with a heave, and covers the sand in silence. A lonesome and a horrid retreat, I can tell you!

I saw no sign of the girl in the plantation. When I got out, through the sand-hills, on to the beach, there she was, in her little straw bonnet, and her plain grey cloak that she always wore to hide her deformed shoulder as much as might be—there she was, all alone, looking out on the quicksand and the sea.

She started when I came up with her, and turned her head away from me. Not looking me in the face being another of the proceedings, which, as head of the servants, I never allow, on principle, to pass without inquiry—I turned her round my way, and saw that she was crying. My bandanna handkerchief—one of six beauties given to me by my lady—was handy in my pocket. I took it out, and I said to Rosanna, 'Come and sit down, my dear, on the slope of the beach along with me. I'll dry your eyes for you first, and then I'll make so bold as to ask what you have been crying about.'

'About the years that are gone, Mr Betteredge,' says Rosanna quietly. 'My past life still comes back to me sometimes.'

'Come, come, my girl,' I said, 'your past life is all sponged out. Why can't you forget it?'

She took me by one of the lappets of my coat. I am a slovenly old man, and a good deal of my meat and drink gets splashed about on my clothes. Sometimes one of the women, and sometimes another, cleans me of my grease. The day before, Rosanna had taken out a spot for me on the lappet of my coat, with a new composition, warranted to remove anything. The grease was gone, but there was a little dull place left on the nap of the cloth where the grease had been. The girl pointed to that place, and shook her head.

'The stain is taken off,' she said. 'But the place shows, Mr Betteredge—the place shows!'

A remark which takes a man unawares by means of his own coat is not an easy remark to answer. Something in the girl herself, too, made me particularly sorry for her just then. She had nice brown eyes, plain as she was in other ways—and she looked at me with a sort of respect for my happy old age and my good character, as things for ever out of her own reach, which made my heart heavy for our second housemaid. Not feeling myself able to comfort her, there was only one other thing to do. That thing was—to take her in to dinner.

'Help me up,' I said. 'You're late for dinner, Rosanna—and I have come to fetch you in.'

'You, Mr Betteredge!' says she.

'They told Nancy to fetch you,' I said. 'But I thought you might like your scolding better, my dear, if it came from me.'

Instead of helping me up, the poor thing stole her hand into mine, and gave it a little squeeze. She tried hard to keep from crying again, and succeeded—for which I respected her. 'You're very kind, Mr Betteredge,' she said. 'I don't want any dinner today—let me bide a little longer here.'

'What makes you like to be here?' I asked. 'What is it that brings you everlastingly to this miserable place?'

'Something draws me to it,' says the girl, making images with her finger in the sand. 'I try to keep away from it, and I can't. Sometimes,' says she in a low voice, as if she was frightened at her own fancy, 'sometimes, Mr Betteredge, I think that my grave is waiting for me here.'

Here was unwholesome talk! Here was an empty stomach feeding on an unquiet mind! My answer—a pretty sharp one, in the poor girl's own interests, I promise you!—was at my tongue's end, when it was snapped short off on a sudden by a voice among the sand-hills shouting for me by my name. 'Betteredge!' cries the voice, 'where are you?' 'Here!' I shouted out in return, without a notion in my mind of who it was.

Rosanna started to her feet, and stood looking towards the voice. I was just thinking of getting on my own legs next, when I was staggered by a sudden change in the girl's face.

Her complexion turned of a beautiful red, which I had never seen in it before; she brightened all over with a kind of speechless and breathless surprise. 'Who is it?' I asked. Rosanna gave me back my own question. 'Oh! who is it?' she said softly, more to herself than to me. I twisted round on the sand and looked behind me. There, coming out on us from among the hills, was a bright-eyed young gentleman, dressed in a beautiful fawn-coloured suit, with gloves and hat to match, with a rose in his button-hole, and a smile on his face that might have set the Shivering Sand itself smiling at him in return. Before I could get on my legs, he plumped down on the sand by the side of me, put his arm round my neck, foreign fashion, and gave me a hug that fairly squeezed the breath out of my body. 'Dear old Betteredge!' says he. 'I owe you seven-and-sixpence. Now do you know who I am?'

Lord bless us and save us! Here—four good hours before we expected him—was Mr Franklin Blake!

Before I could say a word, I saw Mr Franklin, a little surprised to all appearance, look up from me to Rosanna. Following his lead, I looked at the girl too. She was blushing of a deeper red than ever, seemingly at having caught Mr Franklin's eye; and she turned and left us suddenly, in a confusion quite unaccountable to my mind, without either making her curtsey to the gentleman or saying a word to me. Very unlike her usual self: a civiller and better-behaved servant, in general, you never met with.

'That's an odd girl,' says Mr Franklin. 'I wonder what she sees in me to surprise her?'

'I suppose, sir,' I answered, drolling on our young gentleman's Continental education, 'it's the varnish from foreign parts.'

CHAPTER IV

THE first thing I did, after we were left together alone, was to make a third attempt to get up from my seat on the sand. Mr Franklin stopped me.

'There is one advantage about this horrid place,' he said; 'we have got it all to ourselves. Stay where you are, Betteredge; I have something to say to you.'

'Welcome back to the old place, Mr Franklin,' I said. 'All the more welcome, sir, that you have come some hours before we expected you.'

'I have a reason for coming before you expected me,' answered Mr Franklin. 'I suspect, Betteredge, that I have been followed and watched in London, for the last three or four days; and I have travelled by the morning instead of the afternoon train, because I wanted to give a certain dark-looking stranger the slip.'

Those words did more than surprise me. They brought back to my mind, in a flash, the three jugglers, and Penelope's notion that they meant some mischief to Mr Franklin Blake.

'Who's watching you, sir—and why?' I inquired.

'Tell me about the three Indians you have had at the house today,' says Mr Franklin, without noticing my question. 'It's just possible, Betteredge, that my stranger and your three jugglers may turn out to be pieces of the same puzzle.'

'How do you come to know about the jugglers, sir?' I asked, putting one question on the top of another, which was bad manners, I own. But you don't expect much from poor human nature—so don't expect much from me.

'I saw Penelope at the house,' says Mr Franklin; 'and Penelope told me. Your daughter promised to be a pretty girl, Betteredge, and she has kept her promise. Penelope has got a small ear and a small foot. Did the late Mrs Betteredge possess those inestimable advantages?'

'The late Mrs Betteredge possessed a good many defects, sir,' says I. 'One of them (if you will pardon my mentioning it) was never keeping to the matter in hand. She was more like a fly than a woman: she couldn't settle on anything.'

'She would just have suited me,' says Mr Franklin. 'I never settle on anything either. Betteredge, your edge is better than ever. Your daughter said as much, when I asked for particulars about the jugglers. "Father will tell you, sir. He's a wonderful man for his age; and he expresses himself beautifully." Penelope's own words—blushing divinely. Not even my respect for you prevented me from—never mind; I knew her when she was a child, and she's none the worse for it. Let's be serious. What did the jugglers do?'

I was something dissatisfied with my daughter—not for letting Mr Franklin kiss her; Mr Franklin was welcome to *that*—but for forcing me to tell her foolish story at second hand. However, there was no help for it now but to mention the circumstances. Mr Franklin's merriment all died away as I went on. He sat knitting his eyebrows, and twisting his beard. When I had done, he repeated after me two of the questions which the chief juggler had put to the boy—seemingly for the purpose of fixing them well in his mind.

'"Is it on the road to this house, and on no other, that the English gentleman will travel today?" "Has the English gentleman got It about him?" I suspect,' says Mr Franklin, pulling a little sealed paper parcel out of his pocket, 'that "It" means *this*. And "this,"Betteredge, means my uncle Herncastle's famous Diamond.'

'Good Lord, sir!' I broke out, 'how do you come to be in charge of the wicked Colonel's Diamond?'

'The wicked Colonel's will has left his Diamond as a birthday present to my cousin Rachel,' says Mr Franklin. 'And my father, as the wicked Colonel's executor, has given it in charge to me to bring down here.'

If the sea, then oozing in smoothly over the Shivering Sand, had been changed into dry land before my own eyes, I doubt if I could have been more surprised than I was when Mr Franklin spoke those words.

'The Colonel's Diamond left to Miss Rachel!' says I. 'And your father, sir, the Colonel's executor! Why, I would have laid any bet you like, Mr Franklin, that your father wouldn't have touched the Colonel with a pair of tongs!'

Mr Franklin nodded.

'I don't want to alarm my aunt without reason,' he said. 'And I don't want to leave her without what may be a needful warning. If you were in my place, Betteredge, tell me, in one word, what would you do?'

In one word, I told him: 'Wait.'

'With all my heart,' says Mr Franklin. 'How long?'

I proceeded to explain myself.

'As I understand it, sir,' I said, 'somebody is bound to put this plaguey Diamond into Miss Rachel's hands on her birthday—and you may as well do it as another. Very good. This is the twenty-fifth of May, and the birthday is on the twenty-first of June. We have got close on four weeks before us. Let's wait and see what happens in that time; and let's warn my lady, or not, as the circumstances direct us.'

'Perfect, Betteredge, as far as it goes!' says Mr Franklin. 'But between this and the birthday, what's to be done with the Diamond?'

'Put it in the safe keeping of the bank at Frizinghall.' (Frizinghall was our nearest town, and the Bank of England wasn't safer than the bank there.) 'If I were you, sir,' I added, 'I would ride straight away with it to Frizinghall before the ladies come back.'

The prospect of doing something—and, what is more, of doing that something on a horse—brought Mr Franklin up like lightning from the flat of his back. He sprang to his feet, and pulled me up, without ceremony, on to mine. 'Betteredge, you are worth your weight in gold,' he said. 'Come along, and saddle the best horse in the stables directly.'

We went back to the house in a hurry; we had the fleetest horse in the stables saddled in a hurry; and Mr Franklin rattled off in a hurry, to lodge the cursed Diamond once more in the strong-room of a bank. When I heard the last of his horse's hoofs on the drive, and when I turned about in the yard and found I was alone again, I felt half inclined to ask myself if I hadn't woke up from a dream.

CHAPTER V

WHILE I was in this bewildered frame of mind, sorely needing a little quiet time by myself to put me right again, my daughter Penelope got in my way (just as her late mother used to get in my way on the stairs), and instantly summoned me to tell her all that had passed at the conference between Mr Franklin and me. Under present circumstances, the one thing to be done was to clap the extinguisher upon Penelope's curiosity on the spot. I accordingly replied that Mr Franklin and I had both talked of foreign politics, till we could talk no longer, and had then mutually fallen asleep in the heat of the sun.

The afternoon wore on, and my lady and Miss Rachel came back.

Needless to say, how astonished they were when they heard that Mr Franklin Blake had arrived, and had gone off again on horseback. Needless also to say, that *they* asked awkward questions directly, and that the 'foreign politics' and the 'falling asleep in the sun' wouldn't serve a second time over with *them*. Being at the end of my invention, I said Mr Franklin's arrival by the early train was entirely attributable to one of Mr Franklin's freaks. Being asked, upon that, whether his galloping off again on horseback was another of Mr Franklin's freaks, I said, 'Yes, it was;' and slipped out of it—I think very cleverly—in that way.

Having got over my difficulties with the ladies, I found more difficulties waiting for me when I went back to my own room.

In came Penelope—with the natural sweetness of women—to kiss and make it up again; and—with the natural curiosity of women—to ask another question. This time she only wanted me to tell her what was the matter with our second housemaid, Rosanna Spearman.

After leaving Mr Franklin and me at the Shivering Sand, Rosanna, it appeared, had returned to the house in a very unaccountable state of mind. She had turned (if Penelope was to be believed) all the colours of the rainbow. She had been merry without reason, and sad without reason. In one breath she asked hundreds of questions about Mr Franklin Blake, and in another breath she had been angry with Penelope for presuming to suppose that a strange gentleman could possess any interest for her. She had been surprised, smiling, and scribbling Mr Franklin's name inside her workbox. She had been surprised again, crying and looking at her deformed shoulder in the glass. Had she and Mr Franklin known anything of each other before today? Quite impossible! Had they heard anything of each other? Impossible again! I could speak to Mr Franklin's astonishment as genuine, when he saw how the girl stared at him. Penelope could speak to the girl's inquisitiveness as genuine, when she asked questions about Mr Franklin. The conference between us, conducted in this way, was tiresome enough, until my daughter suddenly ended it by bursting out with what I thought the most monstrous supposition I had ever heard in my life.

'Father!' says Penelope, quite seriously, 'there's only one explanation of it. Rosanna has fallen in love with Mr Franklin Blake at first sight!'

The evening came, and the dressing-bell for dinner rang, before Mr Franklin returned from Frizinghall. I took his hot water up to his room myself, expecting to hear, after this extraordinary delay, that something had happened. To my great disappointment (and no doubt to yours also), nothing had happened. He had not met with the Indians, either going or returning. He had deposited the Moonstone in the bank—describing it merely as a valuable of great price—and he had got the receipt for it safe in his pocket. I went downstairs, feeling that this was rather a flat ending, after all our excitement about the Diamond earlier in the day.

How the meeting between Mr Franklin and his aunt and cousin went off, is more than I can tell you.

I would have given something to have waited at table that day. But, in my position in the household, waiting at dinner (except on high family festivals) was letting down my dignity in the eyes of the other servants—a thing which my lady considered me quite prone enough to do already, without seeking occasions for it. The news brought to me from the upper regions, that evening, came from Penelope and the footman. Penelope mentioned that she had never known Miss Rachel so particular about the dressing of her hair, and had never seen her look so bright and pretty as she did when she went down to meet Mr Franklin in the drawing-room. The footman's report was, that the preservation of a respectful composure in the presence of his betters, and the waiting on Mr Franklin Blake at dinner, were two of the hardest things to reconcile with each other that had ever tried his training in service. Later in the evening, we heard them singing and playing duets, Mr Franklin piping high, Miss Rachel piping higher, and my lady, on the piano, following them as it were over hedge and ditch, and seeing them safe through it in a manner most wonderful and pleasant to hear through the open windows, on the terrace at night. Later still, I went to Mr Franklin in the smoking-room, with the soda-water and brandy, and found that Miss Rachel had put the Diamond clean out of his head. 'She's the most charming girl I have seen since I came back to England!' was all I could extract from him, when I endeavoured to lead the conversation to more serious things.

Towards midnight, I went round the house to lock up, accompanied by my second in command (Samuel, the footman), as usual. When all the doors were made fast, except the side door that opened on the terrace, I sent Samuel to bed, and stepped out for a breath of fresh air before I too went to bed in my turn.

The night was still and close, and the moon was at the full in the heavens. It was so silent out of doors, that I heard from time to time, very faint and low, the fall of the sea, as the ground-swell heaved it in on the sand-bank near the mouth of our little bay. As the house stood, the terrace side was the dark side; but the broad moonlight showed fair on the gravel walk that ran along the next side to the terrace. Looking this way, after looking up at the sky, I saw the shadow of a person in the moonlight thrown forward from behind the corner of the house.

Being old and sly, I forbore to call out; but being also, unfortunately, old and heavy, my feet betrayed me on the gravel. Before I could steal suddenly round the corner, as I had proposed, I heard lighter feet than mine—and more than one pair of them as I thought—retreating in a hurry. By the time I had got to the corner, the trespassers, whoever they were, had run into the shrubbery at the off side of the walk, and were hidden from sight among the thick trees and bushes in that part of the grounds. From the shrubbery, they could easily make their way, over our fence, into the road. If I had been forty years younger, I might have had a chance of catching them before they got clear of our premises. As it was, I went back to set a-going a younger pair of legs than mine. Without disturbing anybody, Samuel and I got a couple of guns, and went all round the house and through the shrubbery. Having made sure that no persons were lurking about anywhere in our grounds, we turned back. Passing over the walk where I had seen the shadow, I now noticed, for the first time, a little bright object, lying on the clean gravel, under the light of the moon. Picking the object up, I discovered it was a small bottle, containing a thick sweet-smelling liquor, as black as ink.

I said nothing to Samuel. But, remembering what Penelope

had told me about the jugglers, and the pouring of the little pool of ink into the palm of the boy's hand, I instantly suspected that I had disturbed the three Indians, lurking about the house, and bent, in their heathenish way, on discovering the whereabouts of the Diamond that night.

CHAPTER VI

ON the twenty-ninth of the month, Miss Rachel and Mr Franklin hit on a new method of working their way together through the time which might otherwise have hung heavy on their hands. There are reasons for taking particular notice here of the occupation that amused them. You will find it has a bearing on something that is still to come.

Mr Franklin's universal genius, dabbling in everything, dabbled in what he called 'decorative painting.' He had invented, he informed us, a new mixture to moisten paint with, which he described as a 'vehicle.' What it was made of, I don't know. What it did, I can tell you in two words—it stank. Miss Rachel being wild to try her hand at the new process, Mr Franklin sent to London for the materials; mixed them up, with accompaniment of a smell which made the very dogs sneeze when they came into the room; put an apron and a bib over Miss Rachel's gown, and set her to work decorating her own little sitting-room—called, for want of English to name it in, her 'boudoir'. They began with the inside of the door. Mr Franklin scraped off all the nice varnish with pumice-stone, and made what he described as a surface to work on. Miss Rachel then covered the surface, under his directions and with his help, with patterns and devices. When they were not riding, or seeing company, or taking their meals, or piping their songs, there they were with their heads together, as busy as bees, spoiling the door. Who was the poet who said that Satan finds some mischief still for idle hands to do? If he had occupied my place in the family, and had seen Miss Rachel with her brush, and Mr Franklin with his vehicle, he could have written nothing truer of either of them than that.

The next date worthy of notice is Sunday, the fourth of June.

On that evening we, in the servants' hall, debated a domestic question for the first time, which, like the decoration of the door, has its bearing on something that is still to come.

Seeing the pleasure which Mr Franklin and Miss Rachel took in each other's society, and noting what a pretty match they were in all personal respects, we naturally speculated on the chance of their putting their heads together with other objects in view besides the ornamenting of a door. Some of us said there would be a wedding in the house before the summer was over. Others (led by me) admitted it was likely enough Miss Rachel might be married; but we doubted (for reasons which will presently appear) whether her bridegroom would be Mr Franklin Blake.

That Mr Franklin was in love, on his side, nobody who saw and heard him could doubt. The difficulty was to fathom Miss Rachel.

On June the twelfth, an invitation from my mistress was sent to a gentleman in London, to come and help to keep Miss Rachel's birthday. This was the fortunate individual on whom I believed her heart to be privately set! Like Mr Franklin, he was a cousin of hers. His name was Mr Godfrey Ablewhite.

With all his brightness and cleverness and general good qualities, Mr Franklin's chance of topping Mr Godfrey in our young lady's estimation was, in my opinion, a very poor chance indeed.

In the first place, Mr Godfrey was, in point of size, the finest man by far of the two. He stood over six feet high; he had a beautiful red and white colour; a smooth round face, shaved as bare as your hand; and a head of lovely long flaxen hair, falling negligently over the poll of his neck. But why do I try

to give you this personal description of him? If you ever
subscribed to a Ladies' Charity in London, you know Mr
Godfrey Ablewhite as well as I do. He was a barrister by profession; a ladies' man by temperament; and a good Samaritan by
choice. Female benevolence and female destitution could do
nothing without him. Maternal societies for confining poor
women; Magdalen societies for rescuing poor women; strong-
minded societies for putting poor women into poor men's
places, and leaving the men to shift for themselves; he was
vice-president, manager, referee, to them all. As a speaker at
charitable meetings the like of him for drawing your tears and
your money was not easy to find. He was quite a public character. The last time I was in London, my mistress gave me two
treats. She sent me to the theatre to see a dancing woman who
was all the rage; and she sent me to Exeter Hall to hear Mr
Godfrey. The lady did it, with a band of music. The gentleman
did it, with a handkerchief and a glass of water. Crowds at the
performance with the legs. Ditto at the performance with the
tongue. And with all this, the sweetest tempered person (I allude
to Mr Godfrey)—the simplest and pleasantest and easiest to
please—you ever met with. He loved everybody. And everybody
loved *him*. What chance had Mr Franklin—what chance had
anybody of average reputation and capacities—against such a
man as this?

On the fourteenth came Mr Godfrey's answer.

He accepted my mistress's invitation, from the Wednesday
of the birthday to the evening of Friday—when his duties to
the Ladies' Charities would oblige him to return to town. He
also enclosed a copy of verses on what he elegantly called his
cousin's 'natal day'. Miss Rachel, I was informed, joined Mr
Franklin in making fun of the verses at dinner; and Penelope,
who was all on Mr Franklin's side, asked me, in great triumph,
what I thought of that. 'Miss Rachel has led *you* off on a false
scent, my dear,' I replied; 'but *my* nose is not so easily mystified.

Wait till Mr Ablewhite's verses are followed by Mr Ablewhite himself.'

My daughter replied, that Mr Franklin might strike in, and try his luck, before the verses were followed by the poet. In favour of this view, I must acknowledge that Mr Franklin left no chance untried of winning Miss Rachel's good graces.

Though one of the most inveterate smokers I ever met with, he gave up his cigar, because she said, one day, she hated the stale smell of it in his clothes. He slept so badly, after this effort of self-denial, for want of the composing effect of the tobacco to which he was used, and came down morning after morning looking so haggard and worn, that Miss Rachel herself begged him to take to his cigars again. No! he would take to nothing again that could cause her a moment's annoyance; he would fight it out resolutely, and get back his sleep, sooner or later, by main force of patience in waiting for it. Such devotion as this, you may say (as some of them said downstairs), could never fail of producing the right effect on Miss Rachel—backed up, too, as it was, by the decorating work every day on the door.

CHAPTER VII

JUNE twenty-first, the day of the birthday, was cloudy and un-settled at sunrise, but towards noon it cleared up bravely.

After breakfast, Mr Franklin and I had a private conference on the subject of the Moonstone—the time having now come for removing it from the bank at Frizinghall, and placing it in Miss Rachel's own hands.

Whether he had been trying to make love to his cousin again, and had got a rebuff—or whether his broken rest, night after night, was aggravating the queer contradictions and uncertainties in his character—I don't know. But certain it is, that Mr Franklin failed to show himself at his best on the morning of the birthday.

He was in twenty different minds about the Diamond in as many minutes. For my part, I stuck fast by the plain facts as we knew them. Nothing had happened to justify us in alarming my lady on the subject of the jewel; and nothing could alter the legal obligation that now lay on Mr Franklin to put it in his cousin's possession. That was my view of the matter; and, twist and turn it as he might, he was forced in the end to make it his view too. We arranged that he was to ride over, after lunch, to Frizinghall, and bring the Diamond back, with Mr Godfrey and the two young ladies, in all probability, to keep him company on the way home again.

This settled, our young gentleman went back to Miss Rachel.

They consumed the whole morning, and part of the afternoon, in the everlasting business of decorating the door, Penelope standing by to mix the colours, as directed; and my lady, as luncheon time drew near, going in and out of the room, with her handkerchief to her nose (for they used a deal of Mr Franklin's vehicle that day), and trying vainly to get the two artists away from their work. It was three o'clock before they took off their aprons, and released Penelope (much the worse for the vehicle), and cleaned themselves of their mess. But they had done what they wanted—they had finished the door on the birthday, and proud enough they were of it.

Mr Franklin snatched a morsel from the luncheon-table, and rode off to Frizinghall—to escort his cousins, as he told my lady. To fetch the Moonstone, as was privately known to himself and to me.

This being one of the high festivals on which I took my place at the sideboard, in command of the attendance at table, I had plenty to occupy my mind while Mr Franklin was away. Having seen to the wine, and reviewed my men and women who were to wait at dinner, I retired to collect myself before the company came. A whiff of—you know what, and a turn at a certain book which I have had occasion to mention in these pages, composed me, body and mind. I was aroused from what I am inclined to think must have been, not a nap, but a reverie, by the clatter of horses' hoofs outside; and, going to the door, received a cavalcade comprising Mr Franklin and his three cousins, escorted by one of old Mr Ablewhite's grooms.

Mr Godfrey struck me, strangely enough, as being like Mr Franklin in this respect—that he did not seem to be in his customary spirits. He kindly shook hands with me as usual, and was most politely glad to see his old friend Betteredge wearing so well. But there was a sort of cloud over him, which I couldn't at all account for; and when I asked how he had found his father in health, he answered rather shortly, 'Much as usual.' However, the two Miss Ablewhites were cheerful enough for twenty, which more than restored the balance.

Under cover of the noise made by the young ladies, I had an opportunity of saying a private word to Mr Franklin in the hall.

'Have you got the Diamond safe, sir?'

He nodded, and tapped the breast-pocket of his coat.

'Have you seen anything of the Indians?'

'Not a glimpse.' With that answer, he asked for my lady, and, hearing she was in the small drawing-room, went there straight. The bell rang, before he had been a minute in the room, and Penelope was sent to tell Miss Rachel that Mr Franklin Blake wanted to speak to her.

Crossing the hall, about half an hour afterwards, I was brought to a sudden standstill by an outbreak of screams from the small drawing-room. I can't say I was at all alarmed; for I recognised in the screams the favourite large O of the Miss Ablewhites. However, I went in (on pretence of asking for instructions about the dinner) to discover whether anything serious had really happened.

There stood Miss Rachel at the table, like a person fascinated, with the Colonel's unlucky Diamond in her hand. There, on either side of her, knelt the two Bouncers, devouring the jewel with their eyes, and screaming with ecstasy every time it flashed on them in a new light. There, at the opposite side of the table, stood Mr Godfrey, clapping his hands like a large child, and singing out softly, 'Exquisite! exquisite!' There sat Mr Franklin in a chair by the bookcase, tugging at his beard, and looking anxiously towards the window. And there, at the window, stood the object he was contemplating—my lady, having the extract from the Colonel's Will in her hand, and keeping her back turned on the whole of the company.

She faced me, when I asked for my instructions; and I saw the family frown gathering over her eyes, and the family temper twitching at the corners of her mouth.

'Come to my room in half an hour,' she answered. 'I shall have something to say to you then.'

With those words she went out.

Before I could leave the room in my turn, Miss Rachel, always considerate to the old servant who had been in the house when she was born, stopped me. 'Look, Gabriel!' she said, and flashed the jewel before my eyes in a ray of sunlight that poured through the window.

Lord bless us! it *was* a Diamond! As large, or nearly, as a plover's egg! The light that streamed from it was like the light of the harvest moon. The Diamond laid such a hold on *me* that I burst out with as large an 'O' as the Bouncers themselves. The only one of us who kept his senses was Mr Godfrey. He put an arm round each of his sisters' waists, and, looking compassionately backwards and forwards between the Diamond and me, said, 'Carbon, Betteredge! mere carbon, my good friend, after all!'

His object, I suppose, was to instruct me. All he did, however, was to remind me of the dinner. I hobbled off to my army of waiters downstairs.

At the end of half an hour, I presented myself, as directed, in my lady's room.

What passed between my mistress and me, on this occasion, was, in the main, a repetition of what had passed between Mr

Franklin and me at the Shivering Sand—with this difference, that I took care to keep my own counsel about the jugglers, seeing that nothing had happened to justify me in alarming my lady on this head. When I received my dismissal, I could see that she took the blackest view possible of the Colonel's motives, and that she was bent on getting the Moonstone out of her daughter's possession at the first opportunity.

On my way back to my own part of the house, I was encountered by Mr Franklin. He wanted to know if I had seen anything of his cousin Rachel. I had seen nothing of her. Could I tell him where his cousin Godfrey was? I didn't know; but I began to suspect that cousin Godfrey might not be far away from cousin Rachel. Mr Franklin's suspicions apparently took the same turn. He tugged hard at his beard, and went and shut himself up in the library with a bang of the door that had a world of meaning in it.

I was interrupted no more in the business of preparing for the birthday dinner till it was time for me to smarten myself up for receiving the company. Just as I had got my white waistcoat on, Penelope presented herself at my toilet, on pretence of brushing what little hair I have got left, and improving the tie of my white cravat. My girl was in high spirits, and I saw she had something to say to me. She gave me a kiss on the top of my bald head, and whispered, 'News for you, father! Miss Rachel has refused him.'

'Who's "*him*"?' I asked.

'The ladies' committee-man, father,' says Penelope. 'I saw him take her away alone into the rose-garden,' says Penelope. 'And I waited behind the holly to see how they came back. They had gone out arm-in-arm, both laughing. They came back, walking separate, as grave as grave could be, and looking straight away from each other in a manner which there was no mistaking. I never was more delighted, father, in my life! There's one woman in the world who can resist Mr Godfrey Ablewhite, at any rate; and, if I was a lady, I should be another!

'Just on the other side of the holly,' Penelope went on, 'Mr Godfrey came to a standstill. "You prefer," says he, "that I should stop here as if nothing had happened?" Miss Rachel turned on him like lightning. "You have accepted my mother's invitation," she said; "and you are here to meet her guests. Unless you wish to make a scandal in the house, you will remain, of course!" She went on a few steps, and then seemed to relent a little. "Let us forget what has passed, Godfrey," she said, "and let us remain cousins still." She gave him her hand. He kissed it, which *I* should have considered taking a liberty, and then she left him. He waited a little by himself, with his head down, and his heel grinding a hole slowly in the gravel walk; you never saw a man look more put out in your life. "Awkward!" he said between his teeth, when he looked up, and went on to the house—"very awkward!" If that was his opinion of himself, he was quite right. Awkward enough, I'm sure. And the end of it is, father, what I told you all along,' cries Penelope, finishing me off with a last scarification, the hottest of all. 'Mr Franklin's the man!'

I got possession of the hair-brush, and opened my lips to administer the reproof which, you will own, my daughter's language and conduct richly deserved.

Before I could say a word, the crash of carriage-wheels outside struck in, and stopped me. The first of the dinner-company had come. Penelope instantly ran off. I got into the hall just in time to announce the two first of the guests. You needn't feel particularly interested about them. Only the philan-thropist's father and mother—Mr and Mrs Ablewhite.

CHAPTER VIII

ONE on top of the other, the rest of the company followed the Ablewhites, till we had the whole tale of them complete. Including the family, they were twenty-four in all. It was a noble sight to see, when they were settled in their places round the dinner-table, and the Rector of Frizinghall (with beautiful elocution) rose and said grace.

There is no need to worry you with a list of the guests. You will meet none of them a second time—in my part of the story, at any rate—with the exception of two.

Those two sat on either side of Miss Rachel, who, as queen of the day, was naturally the great attraction of the party. On this occasion she was more particularly the centre-point towards which everybody's eyes were directed; for (to my lady's secret annoyance) she wore her wonderful birthday present, which eclipsed all the rest—the Moonstone. It was without any setting when it had been placed in her hands; but that universal genius, Mr Franklin, had contrived, with the help of his neat fingers and a little bit of silver wire, to fix it as a brooch in the bosom of her white dress. Everybody wondered at the prodigious size and beauty of the Diamond, as a matter of course. But the only two of the company who said anything out of the common way about it were those two guests I have mentioned, who sat by Miss Rachel on her right hand and her left.

The guest on her left was Mr Candy, our doctor at Frizinghall.

This was a pleasant, companionable little man, with the drawback, however, I must own, of being too fond, in season and out of season, of his joke, and of his plunging in rather a headlong manner into talk with strangers, without waiting to feel his way first.

The other guest, who sat on my young lady's right hand, was an eminent public character—being no other than the celebrated Indian traveller, Mr Murthwaite, who, at risk of his life, had penetrated in disguise where no European had ever set foot before.

This was a long, lean, wiry, brown, silent man. He had a weary look, and a very steady, attentive eye. It was rumoured that he was tired of the humdrum life among the people in our parts, and longing to go back and wander off on the tramp again in the wild places of the East. Except what he said to Miss Rachel about her jewel, I doubt if he spoke six words or drank so much as a single glass of wine, all through the dinner. The Moonstone was the only object that interested him in the smallest degree. The fame of it seemed to have reached him, in some of those perilous Indian places where his wanderings had lain. After looking at it silently for so long a time that Miss Rachel began to get confused, he said to her in his cool immovable way, 'If you ever go to India, Miss Verinder, don't take your uncle's birthday gift with you. A Hindoo diamond is sometimes part of a Hindoo religion. I know a certain city, and a certain temple in that city, where, dressed as you are now, your life would not be worth five minutes' purchase.' Miss Rachel, safe in England, was quite delighted to hear of her danger in India. The Bouncers were more delighted still; they dropped their knives and forks with a crash, and burst out together vehemently, 'O! how interesting!' My lady fidgeted in her chair, and changed the subject.

As the dinner got on, I became aware, little by little, that this festival was not prospering as other like festivals had prospered before it.

Looking back at the birthday now, by the light of what happened afterwards, I am half inclined to think that the cursed Diamond must have cast a blight on the whole company. I plied them well with wine; and being a privileged character, followed the unpopular dishes round the table, and whispered to the company confidentially, 'Please to change your mind and try it; for I know it will do you good.' Nine times out of ten they changed their minds—out of regard for their old original Betteredge, they were pleased to say—but all to no purpose. There were gaps of silence in the talk, as the dinner got on, that made me feel personally uncomfortable. When they did use their tongues again, they used them innocently, in the most unfortunate manner and to the worst possible purpose. Mr Candy, the doctor, for instance, said more unlucky things than I ever knew him to say before.

A dispute between the doctor and Mr Franklin began in Mr Franklin being led—I forget how—to acknowledge that he had latterly slept very badly at night. Mr Candy thereupon told him that his nerves were all out of order and that he ought to go through a course of medicine immediately. Mr Franklin replied that a course of medicine, and a course of groping in the dark, meant, in his estimation, one and the same thing. Mr Candy, hitting back smartly, said that Mr Franklin himself was, consti-tutionally speaking, groping in the dark after sleep, and that nothing but medicine could help him to find it. Mr Franklin, keeping the ball up on his side, said he had often heard of the blind leading the blind, and now, for the first time, he knew what it meant. In this way, they kept it going briskly, cut and thrust, till they both of them got hot—Mr Candy, in particular, so completely losing his self-control, in defence of his profes-sion, that my lady was obliged to interfere, and forbid the dispute to go on. This necessary act of authority put the last extinguisher on the spirits of the company. The talk spurted up again here and there, for a minute or two at a time; but there was a miserable lack of life and sparkle in it. The Devil (or the Diamond) possessed that dinner-party; and it was a relief to everybody when my mistress rose, and gave the ladies the signal to leave the gentlemen over their wine.

I had just ranged the decanters in a row before old Mr Ablewhite (who represented the master of the house), when there came a sound from the terrace which, startled me out of my company manners on the instant. Mr Franklin and I looked at each other; it was the sound of the Indian drum. As I live by bread, here were the jugglers returning to us with the return of the Moonstone to the house!

As they rounded the corner of the terrace, and came in sight, I hobbled out to warn them off. But, as ill-luck would have it, the two Ablewhite girls were beforehand with me. They whizzed out on to the terrace like a couple of skyrockets, wild to see the

Indians exhibit their tricks. The other ladies followed; the gentlemen came out on their side. Before you could say, 'Lord bless us!' the rogues were making their salaams.

Mr Franklin got on one side of Miss Rachel, and I put myself behind her. If our suspicions were right, there she stood, innocent of all knowledge of the truth, showing the Indians the Diamond in the bosom of her dress!

I can't tell you what tricks they performed, or how they did it. What with the vexation about the dinner, and what with the provocation of the rogues coming back just in the nick of time to see the jewel with their own eyes, I own I lost my head. The first thing that I remember noticing was the sudden appearance on the scene of the Indian traveller, Mr Murthwaite. Skirting the half-circle in which the gentlefolks stood or sat, he came quietly behind the jugglers and spoke to them on a sudden in the language of their own country.

If he had pricked them with a bayonet, I doubt if the Indians could have started and turned on him with a more tigerish quickness than they did, on hearing the first words that passed his lips. The next moment they were bowing and salaaming to him in their most polite and snaky way. After a few words in the unknown tongue had passed on either side, Mr Murthwaite withdrew as quietly as he had approached. The chief Indian, who acted as interpreter, thereupon wheeled about again towards the gentlefolks. I noticed that the fellow's coffee-coloured face had turned grey since Mr Murthwaite had spoken to him. He bowed to my lady, and informed her that the exhibition was over. The Ablewhite girls, indescribably disappointed, burst out with a loud 'O!' directed against Mr Murthwaite for stopping the performance. The chief Indian laid his hand humbly on his breast, and said a second time that the juggling was over. The little boy went round with the hat. The ladies withdrew to the drawing-room; and the gentlemen (excepting Mr Franklin and Mr Murthwaite) returned to their wine. I and the footman followed the Indians, and saw them safe off the premises.

Going back by way of the shrubbery, I smelt tobacco, and found Mr Franklin and Mr Murthwaite (the latter smoking a cheroot) walking slowly up and down among the trees. Mr Franklin beckoned to me to join them.

'This,' says Mr Franklin, presenting me to the great traveller, 'is Gabriel Betteredge, the old servant and friend of our family of whom I spoke to you just now. Tell him, if you please, what you have just told me.'

Mr Murthwaite took his cheroot out of his mouth, and leaned, in his weary way, against the trunk of a tree.

'Mr Betteredge,' he began, 'those three Indians are no more jugglers than you and I are.'

Here was a new surprise! I naturally asked the traveller if he had ever met with the Indians before.

'Never,' says Mr Murthwaite; 'but I know what Indian juggling really is. All you have seen tonight is a very bad and clumsy imitation of it. Unless, after long experience, I am utterly mistaken, those men are high-caste Brahmins. I charged them with being disguised, and you saw how it told on them, clever as the Hindoo people are in concealing their feelings. There is a mystery about their conduct that I can't explain. They have doubly sacrificed their caste—first, in crossing the sea; secondly, in disguising themselves as jugglers. In the land they live in that is a tremendous sacrifice to make. There must be some very serious motive at the bottom of it, and some justification of no ordinary kind to plead for them, in recovery of their caste, when they return to their own country.'

I was struck dumb. Mr Murthwaite went on with his cheroot. Mr Franklin, after what looked to me like a little private veering about between the different sides of his character, broke the silence as follows:

'I feel some hesitation, Mr Murthwaite, in troubling you with family matters, in which you can have no interest and which I am not very willing to speak of out of our own circle. But, after what you have said, I feel bound, in the interests of Lady Verinder and her daughter, to tell you something which may possibly put the clue into your hands. I speak to you in confidence; you will oblige me, I am sure, by not forgetting that?'

With this preface, he told the Indian traveller all that he had told me at the Shivering Sand. Even the immovable Mr Murthwaite was so interested in what he heard, that he let his cheroot go out.

'Now,' says Mr Franklin, when he had done, 'what does your experience say?'

'My experience,' answered the traveller, 'says that you have had more narrow escapes of your life, Mr Franklin Blake, than I have had of mine; and that is saying a great deal.'

It was Mr Franklin's turn to be astonished now.

'Is it really as serious as that?' he asked.

'In my opinion it is,' answered Mr Murthwaite. 'I can't doubt, after what you have told me, that the restoration of the Moonstone to its place on the forehead of the Indian idol, is the motive and the justification of that sacrifice of caste which I alluded to just now. Those men will wait their opportunity with the patience of cats, and will use it with the ferocity of tigers. How you have escaped them I can't imagine,' says the eminent traveller, lighting his cheroot again, and staring hard at Mr Franklin. 'You have been carrying the Diamond backwards and forwards, here and in London, and you are still a living man! Let us try and account for it. It was daylight, both times, I suppose, when you took the jewel out of the bank in London?'

'Broad daylight,' says Mr Franklin.

'And plenty of people in the streets?'

'Plenty.'

'You settled, of course, to arrive at Lady Verinder's house at a certain time? It's a lonely country between this and the station. Did you keep your appointment?'

'No. I arrived four hours earlier than my appointment.'

'I beg to congratulate you on that proceeding! When did you take the Diamond to the bank at the town here?'

'I took it an hour after I had brought it to this house—and three hours before anybody was prepared for seeing me in these parts.'

'I beg to congratulate you again! Did you bring it back here alone?'

'No. I happened to ride back with my cousins and the groom.'

'I beg to congratulate you for the third time! If you ever feel inclined to travel beyond the civilised limits, Mr Blake, let me know, and I will go with you. You are a lucky man.'

Here I struck in. This sort of thing didn't at all square with my English ideas.

'You don't really mean to say, sir,' I asked, 'that they would have taken Mr Franklin's life, to get their Diamond, if he had given them the chance?'

'Do you smoke, Mr Betteredge?' says the traveller.

'Yes, sir.'

'Do you care much for the ashes left in your pipe when you empty it?'

'No, sir.'

'In the country those men came from, they care just as much about killing a man, as you care about emptying the ashes out of your pipe. If a thousand lives stood between them and the getting back of their Diamond—and if they thought they could destroy those lives without discovery—they would take them all. The sacrifice of caste is a serious thing in India, if you like. The sacrifice of life is nothing at all.'

I expressed my opinion upon this, that they were a set of murdering thieves. Mr Murthwaite expressed *his* opinion that they were a wonderful people. Mr Franklin, expressing no opinion at all, brought us back to the matter in hand.

'They have seen the Moonstone on Miss Verinder's dress,' he said. 'What is to be done?'

'What your uncle threatened to do,' answered Mr Murthwaite.

'Colonel Herncastle understood the people he had to deal with. Send the Diamond tomorrow (under guard of more than one man) to be cut up at Amsterdam. Make half a dozen diamonds of it, instead of one. There is an end of its sacred identity as The Moonstone—and there is an end of the conspiracy.'

Mr Franklin turned to me.

'There is no help for it,' he said. 'We must speak to Lady Verinder tomorrow.'

'What about tonight, sir?' I asked. 'Suppose the Indians come back?'

Mr Murthwaite answered me before Mr Franklin could speak.

'The Indians won't risk coming back tonight,' he said. 'The direct way is hardly ever the way they take to anything—let alone a matter like this, in which the slightest mistake might be fatal to their reaching their end.'

'But suppose the rogues are bolder than you think, sir?' I persisted.

'In that case,' says Mr Murthwaite, 'let the dogs loose. Have you got any big dogs in the yard?'

'Two, sir. A mastiff and a bloodhound.'

'They will do. In the present emergency, Mr Betteredge, the mastiff and the bloodhound have one great merit—they are not likely to be troubled with your scruples about the sanctity of human life.'

The strumming of the piano reached us from the drawing-room, as he fired that shot at me. He threw away his cheroot, and took Mr Franklin's arm, to go back to the ladies. I noticed that the sky was clouding over fast, as I followed them to the house. Mr Murthwaite noticed it too. He looked round at me, in his dry, droning way, and said:

'The Indians will want their umbrellas, Mr Betteredge, tonight!'

It was all very well for *him* to joke. But I was not an eminent traveller—and my way in this world had not led me into playing ducks and drakes with my own life, among thieves and murderers in the outlandish places of the earth. I went into my own little room, and sat down in my chair in a perspiration, and wondered helplessly what was to be done next. In this anxious frame of mind, other men might have ended by working themselves up into a fever; I ended in a different way. I lit my pipe, and took a turn at *Robinson Crusoe*.

The arrival of the carriages was the signal for the arrival of the rain. It poured as if it meant to pour all night. With the exception of the doctor, whose gig was waiting for him, the rest of the company went home snugly, under cover, in close carriages. I told Mr Candy that I was afraid he would get wet through. He told me, in return, that he wondered I had arrived at my time of life, without knowing that a doctor's skin was waterproof. So he drove away in the rain, laughing over his own little joke; and so we got rid of our dinner company.

The next thing to tell is the story of the night.

CHAPTER IX

WHEN the last of the guests had driven away, I went back into the inner hall and found Samuel at the side-table, presiding over the brandy and soda-water. My lady and Miss Rachel came out of the drawing-room, followed by the two gentlemen. Mr Godfrey had some brandy and soda-water. Mr Franklin took nothing. He sat down, looking dead tired; the talking on this birthday occasion had, I suppose, been too much for him.

My lady, turning round to wish them good-night, looked hard at the wicked Colonel's legacy shining in her daughter's dress.

'Rachel,' she asked, 'where are you going to put your Diamond tonight?'

Miss Rachel was in high good spirits, just in that humour for talking nonsense, and perversely persisting in it as if it was sense, which you may sometimes have observed in young girls, when they are highly wrought up, at the end of an exciting day. First, she declared she didn't know where to put the Diamond. Then she said, 'On her dressing-table, of course, along with her other things.' Then she remembered that the Diamond might take to shining of itself, with its awful moony light, in the dark—and that would terrify her in the dead of night. Then she bethought herself of an Indian cabinet which stood in her sitting-room; and instantly made up her mind to put the Indian diamond in the Indian cabinet, for the purpose of permitting two beautiful native productions to admire each other. Having let her little flow of nonsense run on as far as that point, her mother interposed and stopped her.

'My dear! your Indian cabinet has no lock to it,' says my lady.

'Good heavens, mamma!' cried Miss Rachel, 'is this an hotel? Are there thieves in the house?'

Without taking notice of this fantastic way of talking, my lady wished the gentlemen good-night. She next turned to Miss Rachel, and kissed her. 'Why not let *me* keep the Diamond for you tonight?' she asked.

Miss Rachel received that proposal as she might, ten years since, have received a proposal to part her from a new doll. My lady saw there was no reasoning with her that night. 'Come into my room, Rachel, the first thing tomorrow morning,' she said. 'I shall have something to say to you.' With those last words she left us slowly; thinking her own thoughts, and, to all appearance, not best pleased with the way by which they were leading her.

Miss Rachel was the next to say good-night. She shook hands first with Mr Godfrey, who was standing at the other end of the hall, looking at a picture. Then she turned back to Mr Franklin, still sitting weary and silent in a corner.

What words passed between them I can't say. But standing near the old oak frame which holds our large looking-glass, I saw her reflected in it, slyly slipping the locket which Mr Franklin had given to her, out of the bosom of her dress, and showing it to him for a moment, with a smile which certainly meant something out of the common, before she tripped off to bed. This incident staggered me a little in the reliance I had previously felt on my own judgment. I began to think that Penelope might be right about the state of her young lady's affections, after all.

As soon as Miss Rachel left him eyes to see with, Mr Franklin noticed me. His variable humour, shifting about everything, had shifted about the Indians already.

'Betteredge,' he said, 'I'm half inclined to think I took Mr Murthwaite too seriously, when we had that talk in the shrubbery. I wonder whether he has been trying any of his traveller's tales on us? Do you really mean to let the dogs loose?'

'I'll relieve them of their collars, sir,' I answered, 'and leave them free to take a turn in the night, if they smell a reason for it.'

'All right,' says Mr Franklin. 'We'll see what is to be done tomorrow. I am not at all disposed to alarm my aunt, Betteredge, without a very pressing reason for it. Good-night.'

He looked so worn and pale as he nodded to me, and took his candle to go upstairs, that I ventured to advise his having a drop of brandy-and-water, by way of night-cap. Mr Godfrey, walking towards us from the other end of the hall, backed me. He pressed Mr Franklin, in the friendliest manner, to take something, before he went to bed.

Mr Franklin declined the brandy-and-water, and went upstairs with Mr Godfrey, their rooms being next door to each other. On the landing, however, either his cousin persuaded him, or he veered about and changed his mind as usual. 'Perhaps I may want it in the night,' he called down to me. 'Send up some brandy-and-water into my room.'

About half-past seven I woke, and opened my window on a fine sunshiny day. The clock had struck eight, and I was just going out to chain up the dogs again, when I heard a sudden whisking of petticoats on the stairs behind me.

I turned about, and there was Penelope flying down after me like mad. 'Father!' she screamed, 'come upstairs, for God's sake! *The Diamond is gone!*'

'Are you out of your mind?' I asked her.

'Gone!' says Penelope. 'Gone, nobody knows how! Come up and see.'

She dragged me after her into our young lady's sitting-room, which opened into her bedroom. There, on the threshold of her bedroom door, stood Miss Rachel, almost as white in the face as the white dressing-gown that clothed her. There also stood the two doors of the Indian cabinet, wide open. One, of the drawers inside was pulled out as far as it would go.

'Look!' says Penelope. 'I myself saw Miss Rachel put the Diamond into that drawer last night.'

I went to the cabinet. The drawer was empty.

'Is this true, miss?' I asked.

With a look that was not like herself, with a voice that was not like her own, Miss Rachel answered, as my daughter had answered: 'The Diamond is gone!'

Having said those words, she withdrew into her bedroom, and shut and locked the door.

Before we knew which way to turn next, my lady came in, hearing my voice in her daughter's sitting-room, and wondering what had happened. The news of the loss of the Diamond seemed to petrify her. She went straight to Miss Rachel's bedroom, and insisted on being admitted. Miss Rachel let her in.

The alarm, running through the house like fire, caught the two gentlemen next.

Mr Godfrey was the first to come out of his room. All he did when he heard what had happened was to hold up his hands in a state of bewilderment, which didn't say much for his natural strength of mind. Mr Franklin, whose clear head I

had confidently counted on to advise us, seemed to be as helpless as his cousin when he heard the news in his turn. For a
wonder, he had had a good night's rest at last; and the unac-
customed luxury of sleep had, as he said himself, apparently
stupefied him. However, when he had swallowed his cup of
coffee—which he always took, on the foreign plan, some hours
before he ate any breakfast—his brains brightened; the clear-
headed side of him turned up, and he took the matter in hand,
resolutely and cleverly, much as follows:

He first sent for the servants, and told them to leave all the
lower doors and windows (with the exception of the front door,
which I had opened) exactly as they had been left when we
locked up overnight. He next proposed to his cousin and to
me to make quite sure, before we took any further steps, that
the Diamond had not accidentally dropped somewhere out of
sight—say at the back of the cabinet, or down behind the table
on which the cabinet stood. Having searched in both places,
and found nothing—having also questioned Penelope, and
discovered from her no more than the little she had already
told me—Mr Franklin suggested next extending our inquiries
to Miss Rachel, and sent Penelope to knock at her bedroom
door.

My lady answered the knock, and closed the door behind
her. The moment after, we heard it locked inside by Miss Rachel.
My mistress came out among us, looking sorely puzzled and
distressed. 'The loss of the Diamond seems to have quite overwhelmed Rachel,' she said, in reply to Mr Franklin. 'She shrinks,
in the strangest manner, from speaking of it, even to *me*. It is
impossible you can see her for the present.'

Having added to our perplexities by this account of Miss
Rachel, my lady, after a little effort, recovered her usual composure, and acted with her usual decision.

'I suppose there is no help for it?' she said, quietly. 'I suppose
I have no alternative but to send for the police?'

'And the first thing for the police to do,' added Mr Franklin, catching her up, 'is to lay hands on the Indian jugglers who performed here last night.'

My lady and Mr Godfrey (not knowing what Mr Franklin and I knew) both started, and both looked surprised.

'I can't stop to explain myself now,' Mr Franklin went on. 'I can only tell you that the Indians have certainly stolen the Diamond. Give me a letter of introduction,' says he, addressing my lady, 'to one of the magistrates at Frizinghall—merely telling him that I represent your interests and wishes, and let me ride off with it instantly. Our chance of catching the thieves may depend on our not wasting one unnecessary minute.'

A little before eleven, Mr Franklin came back. The resolute side of him had, to all appearance, given way, in the interval since his departure, under the stress that had been laid on it. He had left us at a gallop; he came back to us at a walk. When he went away, he was made of iron. When he returned, he was stuffed with cotton, as limp as limp could be.

'Well,' says my lady, 'are the police coming?'

'Yes,' says Mr Franklin; 'they said they would follow me in a fly. Superintendent Seegrave, of your local police force, and two of his men. A mere form! The case is hopeless.'

'What! have the Indians escaped, sir?' I asked.

'The poor ill-used Indians have been most unjustly put in prison,' says Mr Franklin. 'They are as innocent as the babe unborn. My idea that one of them was hidden in the house has ended, like all the rest of my ideas, in smoke. It's been proved,' says Mr Franklin, dwelling with great relish on his own incapacity, 'to be simply impossible.'

After astonishing us by announcing this totally new turn in the matter of the Moonstone, our young gentleman, at his aunt's request, took a seat, and explained himself.

It appeared that the resolute side of him had held out as far as Frizinghall. He had put the whole case plainly before the magistrate, and the magistrate had at once sent for the police. The first inquiries instituted about the Indians showed that they had not so much as attempted to leave the town. Further questions addressed to the police, proved that all three had been seen returning to Frizinghall with their boy, on the previous night between ten and eleven—which (regard being had to hours and distances) also proved that they had walked straight back after performing on our terrace. Later still, at midnight, the police, having occasion to search the common lodging-house where they lived, had seen them all three again, and their little boy with them, as usual. Soon after midnight I myself had safely shut up the house. Plainer evidence than this, in favour of the Indians, there could not well be. The magistrate said there was not even a case of suspicion against them so far. But, as it was just possible, when the police came to investigate the matter, that discoveries affecting the jugglers might be made, he would contrive, by committing them as rogues and vagabonds, to keep them at our disposal, under lock and key, for a week. They had ignorantly done something (I forget what) in the town, which barely brought them within the operation of the law. Every human institution (justice included) will stretch a little, if you only pull it the right way. The worthy magistrate was an old friend of my lady's, and the Indians were 'committed' for a week, as soon as the court opened that morning.

Such was Mr Franklin's narrative of events at Frizinghall. The Indian clue to the mystery of the lost jewel was now, to all appearance, a clue that had broken in our hands. If the jugglers were innocent, who, in the name of wonder, had taken the Moonstone out of Miss Rachel's drawer?

Ten minutes later, to our infinite relief, Superintendent Seegrave arrived at the house. He began by going round the premises, outside and in; the result of that investigation proving to him that no thieves had broken in upon us from outside, and that the robbery, consequently, must have been committed by some person in the house. I leave you to imagine the state the servants were in when this official announcement first reached their ears. The Superintendent decided to begin by examining the boudoir, and, that done, to examine the servants next. At the same time, he posted one of his men on the stair-case which led to the servants' bedrooms, with instructions to let nobody in the house pass in, till further orders.

At this latter proceeding, the weaker half of the human family went distracted on the spot. They bounced out of their corners, whisked upstairs in a body to Miss Rachel's room (Rosanna Spearman being carried away among them this time), burst in on Superintendent Seegrave, and, all looking equally guilty, summoned him to say which of them he suspected, at once.

Mr Superintendent proved equal to the occasion; he looked at them with his resolute eye, and he cowed them with his military voice.

'Now, then, you women, go downstairs again, every one of you; I won't have you here. Look!' says Mr Superintendent, suddenly pointing to a little smear of the decorative painting on Miss Rachel's door, at the outer edge, just under the lock. 'Look what mischief the petticoats of some of you have done already. Clear out! clear out!' Rosanna Spearman, who was nearest to him, and nearest to the little smear on the door, set the example of obedience, and slipped off instantly to her work. The rest followed her out. The Superintendent finished his examination of the room, and, making nothing of it, asked me who had first discovered the robbery. My daughter had first discovered it. My daughter was sent for.

Mr Superintendent proved to be a little too sharp with Penelope at starting. 'Now, young woman, attend to me, and mind you speak the truth.' Penelope fired up instantly. 'I've never been taught to tell lies, Mr Policeman!—and if father can stand there and hear me accused of falsehood and thieving, and my own bedroom shut against me, and my character taken away, which is all a poor girl has left, he's not the good father I take him for!' A timely word from me put Justice and Penelope on a pleasanter footing together. The questions and answers went swimmingly, and ended in nothing worth mentioning. My daughter had seen Miss Rachel put the Diamond in the drawer of the cabinet the last thing at night. She had gone in with Miss Rachel's cup of tea at eight the next morning, and had found the drawer open and empty. Upon that, she had alarmed the house—and there was an end of Penelope's evidence.

Mr Superintendent next asked to see Miss Rachel herself. Penelope mentioned his request through the door. The answer reached us by the same road: 'I have nothing to tell the police-man—I can't see anybody.' Our experienced officer looked equally surprised and offended when he heard that reply. I told him my young lady was ill, and begged him to wait a little and see her later. We thereupon went downstairs again, and were met by Mr Godfrey and Mr Franklin crossing the hall.

The two gentlemen, being inmates of the house, were summoned to say if they could throw any light on the matter. Neither of them knew anything about it. Had they heard any suspicious noises during the previous night? They had heard nothing but the pattering of the rain. Had I, lying awake longer than either of them, heard nothing either? Nothing! Released from examination, Mr Franklin, still sticking to the helpless view of our difficulty, whispered to me: 'That man will be of no earthly use to us. Superintendent Seegrave is an ass.' Released in his turn, Mr Godfrey whispered to me—'Evidently a most competent person. Betteredge, I have the greatest faith in him!' Many men, many opinions, as one of the ancients said, before my time.

Mr Superintendent's next proceeding took him back to the 'boudoir' again, with my daughter and me at his heels. His object was to discover whether any of the furniture had been moved, during the night, out of its customary place—his previous investigation in the room having, apparently, not gone quite far enough to satisfy his mind on this point.

Having ferreted about all over the 'boudoir', without making any discoveries among the furniture, our experienced officer applied to me to know, whether the servants in general were or were not acquainted with the place in which the Diamond had been put for the night.

'I knew where it was put, sir,' I said, 'to begin with. Samuel, the footman, knew also—for he was present in the hall, when they were talking about where the Diamond was to be kept that night. My daughter knew, as she has already told you. She or Samuel may have mentioned the thing to the other servants—or the other servants may have heard the talk for themselves, through the side-door of the hall, which might have been open to the back staircase. For all I can tell, everybody in the house may have known where the jewel was, last night.'

My answer presenting rather a wide field for Mr Superintendent's suspicions to range over, he tried to narrow it by asking about the servants' characters next.

I thought directly of Rosanna Spearman. But it was neither my place nor my wish to direct suspicion against a poor girl, whose honesty had been above all doubt as long as I had known her. The matron at the Reformatory had reported her to my lady as a sincerely penitent and thoroughly trustworthy girl. It was the Superintendent's business to discover reason for suspecting her first—and then, and not till then, it would be my duty to tell him how she came into my lady's service. 'All our people have excellent characters,' I said. 'And all have deserved the trust their mistress has placed in them.' After that, there was but one thing left for Mr Seegrave to do—namely, to set to work, and tackle the servants' characters himself.

One after another, they were examined. One after another, they proved to have nothing to say—and said it (so far as the women were concerned) at great length, and with a very angry sense of the embargo laid on their bedrooms.

The next and last step in the investigation brought matters, as they say, to a crisis. The officer had an interview (at which I was present) with my lady. After informing her that the Diamond *must* have been taken by somebody in the house, he requested permission for himself and his men to search the servants' rooms and boxes on the spot. My good mistress, like the generous high-bred woman she was, refused to let us be treated like thieves. 'I will never consent to make such a return as that,' she said, 'for all I owe to the faithful servants who are employed in my house.'

Mr Superintendent made his bow, with a look in my direction, which said plainly, 'Why employ me, if you are to tie my hands in this way?' As head of the servants, I felt directly that we were bound, in justice to all parties, not to profit by our mistress's generosity. 'We gratefully thank your ladyship,' I said; 'but we ask your permission to do what is right in this matter by giving up our keys. When Gabriel Betteredge sets the example,' says I, stopping Superintendent Seegrave at the door, 'the rest of the servants will follow, I promise you. There are my keys, to begin with!' My lady took me by the hand, and thanked me with the tears in her eyes. Lord! what would I not have given, at that moment, for the privilege of knocking Superintendent Seegrave down!

As I had promised for them, the other servants followed my lead, sorely against the grain, of course, but all taking the view that I took. The women were a sight to see, while the police officers were rummaging among their things. The cook looked as if she could grill Mr Superintendent alive on a furnace, and the other women looked as if they could eat him when he was done.

The search over, and no Diamond or sign of a Diamond being found, of course, anywhere, Superintendent Seegrave retired to my little room to consider with himself what he was to do next. He and his men had now been hours in the house, and had not advanced us one inch towards a discovery of how the Moonstone had been taken, or of whom we were to suspect as the thief.

While the police officer was still pondering in solitude, I was sent for to see Mr Franklin in the library. To my unutterable astonishment, just as my hand was on the door, it was suddenly opened from the inside, and out walked Rosanna Spearman!

After the library had been swept and cleaned in the morning, neither first nor second housemaid had any business in that room at any later period of the day. I stopped Rosanna Spearman, and charged her with a breach of domestic discipline on the spot.

'What might you want in the library at this time of day?' I inquired.

'Mr Franklin Blake dropped one of his rings upstairs,' says Rosanna; 'and I have been into the library to give it to him.' The girl's face was all in a flush as she made me that answer; and she walked away with a toss of her head and a look of self-importance which I was quite at a loss to account for. The proceedings in the house had doubtless upset all the women-servants more or less; but none of them had gone clean out of their natural characters, as Rosanna, to all appearance, had now gone out of hers.

I found Mr Franklin writing at the library table. He asked for a conveyance to the railway station the moment I entered the room. The first sound of his voice informed me that we now had the resolute side of him uppermost once more. The man made of cotton had disappeared; and the man made of iron sat before me again.

'Going to London, sir?' I asked.

'Going to telegraph to London,' says Mr Franklin. 'I have convinced my aunt that we must have a cleverer head than Superintendent Seegrave's to help us; and I have got her permission to despatch a telegram to my father. He knows the Chief Commissioner of Police, and the Commissioner can lay his hand on the right man to solve the mystery of the Diamond. Talking of mysteries, by-the-bye,' says Mr Franklin, dropping his voice, 'I have another word to say to you before you go to the stables. Don't breathe a word of it to anybody as yet; but either Rosanna Spearman's head is not quite right, or I am afraid she knows more about the Moonstone than she ought to know.'

I can hardly tell whether I was more startled or distressed at hearing him say that. If I had been younger, I might have confessed as much to Mr Franklin. But when you are old, you acquire one excellent habit. In cases where you don't see your way clearly, you hold your tongue.

'She came in here with a ring I dropped in my bedroom,' Mr Franklin went on. 'When I had thanked her, of course I expected her to go. Instead of that, she stood opposite to me at the table, looking at me in the oddest manner—half frightened, and half familiar—I couldn't make it out. "This is a strange thing about the Diamond, sir," she said, in a curiously sudden, headlong way. I said, "Yes, it was," and wondered what was coming next. Upon my honour, Betteredge, I think she must be wrong in the head! She said, "They will never find the Diamond, sir, will they? No! nor the person who took it—I'll answer for that." She actually nodded and smiled at me! Before I could ask her what she meant, we heard your step outside. I suppose she was afraid of your catching her here. At any rate, she changed colour, and left the room. What on earth does it mean?'

I could not bring myself to tell him the girl's story, even then. It would have been almost as good as telling him that she was the thief. Besides, even if I had made a clean breast of it, and even supposing she was the thief, the reason why she should let out her secret to Mr Franklin, of all the people in the world, would have been still as far to seek as ever.

'I can't bear the idea of getting the poor girl into a scrape, merely because she has a flighty way with her, and talks very strangely,' Mr Franklin went on. 'And yet if she had said to the Superintendent what she said to me, fool as he is, I'm afraid—' He stopped there, and left the rest unspoken.

'The best way, sir,' I said, 'will be for me to say two words privately to my mistress about it at the first opportunity. My lady has a very friendly interest in Rosanna; and the girl may only have been forward and foolish, after all. When there's a mess of any kind in a house, sir, the women-servants like to look at the gloomy side—it gives the poor wretches a kind of importance in their own eyes. If there's anybody ill, trust the women for prophesying that the person will die. If it's a jewel lost, trust them for prophesying that it will never be found again.'

This view (which I am bound to say, I thought a probable view myself, on reflection) seemed to relieve Mr Franklin mightily: he folded up his telegram, and dismissed the subject. On my way to the stables, to order the pony-chaise, I looked in at the servants' hall, where they were at dinner. Rosanna Spearman was not among them. On inquiry, I found that she had been suddenly taken ill, and had gone upstairs to her own room to lie down.

'Curious! She looked well enough when I saw her last,' I remarked.

Penelope followed me out. 'Don't talk in that way before the rest of them, father,' she said. 'You only make them harder on Rosanna than ever. The poor thing is breaking her heart about Mr Franklin Blake.'

I saw the pony harnessed myself. In the infernal network of mysteries and uncertainties that now surrounded us, I declare it was a relief to observe how well the buckles and straps understood each other! When you had seen the pony backed into the shafts of the chaise, you had seen something there was no doubt about. And that, let me tell you, was becoming a treat of the rarest kind in our household.

Going round with the chaise to the front door, I found not only Mr Franklin, but Mr Godfrey and Superintendent Seegrave also waiting for me on the steps.

Mr Superintendent's reflections (after failing to find the Diamond in the servants' rooms or boxes) had led him, it appeared, to an entirely new conclusion. Still sticking to his first text, namely, that somebody in the house had stolen the jewel, our experienced officer was now of the opinion that the thief (he was wise enough not to name poor Penelope, whatever he might privately think of her!) had been acting in concert with the Indians; and he accordingly proposed shifting his inquiries to the jugglers in the prison at Frizinghall. Hearing of this new move, Mr Franklin had volunteered to take the Superintendent back to the town, from which he could tele-graph to London as easily as from our station. Mr Godfrey, still devoutly believing in Mr Seegrave, and greatly interested in witnessing the examination of the Indians, had begged leave to accompany the officer to Frizinghall. One of the two inferior policemen was to be left at the house, in case anything happened. The other was to go back with the Superintendent to the town. So the four places in the pony-chaise were just filled.

Before he took the reins to drive off, Mr Franklin walked me away a few steps out of hearing of the others.

'I will wait to telegraph to London,' he said, 'till I see what comes of our examination of the Indians. My own conviction is, that this muddle-headed local police officer is as much in the dark as ever, and is simply trying to gain time. The idea of any of the servants being in league with the Indians is a prepos-terous absurdity, in my opinion. Keep about the house, Betteredge, till I come back, and try what you can make of Rosanna Spearman. I don't ask you to do anything degrading to your own self-respect, or anything cruel towards the girl. I only ask you to exercise your observation more carefully than usual. We will make as light of it as we can before my aunt—but this is a more important matter than you may suppose.'

CHAPTER X

THE Thursday night passed, and nothing happened. With the Friday morning came two pieces of news.

Item the first: the baker's man declared he had met Rosanna Spearman, on the previous afternoon, with a thick veil on, walking towards Frizinghall by the foot-path way over the moor. It seemed strange that anybody should be mistaken about Rosanna, whose shoulder marked her out pretty plainly, poor thing—but mistaken the man must have been; for Rosanna, as you know, had been all the Thursday afternoon ill upstairs in her room.

Item the second came through the postman. Worthy Mr Candy had said one more of his many unlucky things, when he drove off in the rain on the birthday night, and told me that a doctor's skin was waterproof. In spite of his skin, the wet had got through him. He had caught a chill that night, and was now down with a fever. The last accounts, brought by the postman, represented him to be light-headed—talking nonsense as glibly, poor man, in his delirium as he often talked it in his sober senses. We were all sorry for the little doctor; but Mr Franklin appeared to regret his illness, chiefly on Miss Rachel's account. From what he said to my lady, while I was in the room at breakfast-time, he appeared to think that Miss Rachel— if the suspense about the Moonstone was not soon set at rest—might stand in urgent need of the best medical advice at our disposal.

Breakfast had not been over long, when a telegram from Mr Blake, the elder, arrived, in answer to his son. It informed us that he had laid hands (by help of his friend, the Commissioner) on the right man to help us. The name of him was Sergeant Cuff; and the arrival of him from London might be expected by the morning train.

At reading the name of the new police officer, Mr Franklin gave a start. It seems that he had heard some curious anecdotes about Sergeant Cuff, from his father's lawyer, during his stay in London.

'I begin to hope we are seeing the end of our anxieties already,' he said. 'If half the stories I have heard are true, when it comes to unravelling a mystery, there isn't the equal in England of Sergeant Cuff!'

When the time came for the Sergeant's arrival, I went down to the gate to look out for him.

A fly from the railway drove up as I reached the lodge; and out got a grizzled, elderly man, so miserably lean that he looked as if he had not got an ounce of flesh on his bones in any part of him. He was dressed all in decent black, with a white cravat round his neck. His face was as sharp as a hatchet, and the skin of it was as yellow and dry and withered as an autumn leaf. His eyes, of a steely light grey, had a very disconcerting trick, when they encountered your eyes, of looking as if they expected something more from you than you were aware of yourself. His walk was soft; his voice was melancholy; his long lanky fingers were hooked like claws. He might have been a parson, or an undertaker—or anything else you like, except what he really was. A more complete opposite to Superintendent Seegrave than Sergeant Cuff, and a less comforting officer to look at, for a family in distress, I defy you to discover, search where you may.

'Is this Lady Verinder's?' he asked.

'Yes, sir.'

'I am Sergeant Cuff.'

'This way, sir, if you please.'

Why Superintendent Seegrave should have appeared to be several sizes smaller than life, on being presented to Sergeant Cuff, I can't undertake to explain. I can only state the fact. They retired together; and remained a weary long time shut up from all mortal intrusion. When they came out, Mr Superintendent was excited, and Mr Sergeant was yawning.

'The Sergeant wishes to see Miss Verinder's sitting-room,' says Mr Seegrave, addressing me with great pomp and eagerness. 'The Sergeant may have some questions to ask. Attend the Sergeant, if you please!'

While I was being ordered about in this way, I looked at the great Cuff. The great Cuff, on his side, looked at Superintendent Seegrave in that quietly expecting way which I have already noticed. I can't affirm that he was on the watch for his brother officer's speedy appearance in the character of an Ass—I can only say that I strongly suspected it.

I led the way upstairs. The Sergeant went softly all over the Indian cabinet and all round the 'boudoir'; asking questions (occasionally only of Mr Superintendent, and continually of me), the drift of which I believe to have been equally unintelligible to both of us. In due time, his course brought him to the door, and put him face to face with the decorative painting that you know of. He laid one lean inquiring finger on the small smear, just under the lock, which Superintendent Seegrave had already noticed, when he reproved the women-servants for all crowding together into the room.

'That's a pity,' says Sergeant Cuff. 'How did it happen?'

He put the question to me. I answered that the women-servants had crowded into the room on the previous morning, and that some of their petticoats had done the mischief, 'Superintendent Seegrave ordered them out, sir,' I added, 'before they did any more harm.'

'Right!' says Mr Superintendent in his military way. 'I ordered them out. The petticoats did it, Sergeant—the petticoats did it.'

'Did you notice which petticoat did it?' asked Sergeant Cuff, still addressing himself, not to his brother-officer, but to me.

'No, sir.'

He turned to Superintendent Seegrave upon that, and said, '*You* noticed, I suppose?'

Mr Superintendent looked a little taken aback; but he made the best of it. 'I can't charge my memory, Sergeant,' he said, 'a mere trifle—a mere trifle.'

Sergeant Cuff looked at Mr Seegrave, as he had looked at the gravel walks in the rosery, and gave us, in his melancholy way, the first taste of his quality which we had had yet.

'I made a private inquiry last week, Mr Superintendent,' he said. 'At one end of the inquiry there was a murder, and at the other end there was a spot of ink on a table cloth that nobody could account for. In all my experience along the dirtiest ways of this dirty little world, I have never met with such a thing as a trifle yet. Before we go a step further in this business we must see the petticoat that made the smear, and we must know for certain when that paint was wet.'

Mr Superintendent—taking his set-down rather sulkily—asked if he should summon the women. Sergeant Cuff, after considering a minute, sighed, and shook his head.

'No,' he said, 'we'll take the matter of the paint first. It's a question of Yes or No with the paint—which is short. It's a question of petticoats with the women—which is long. What o'clock was it when the servants were in this room yesterday morning? Eleven o'clock—eh? Is there anybody in the house who knows whether that paint was wet or dry, at eleven yesterday morning?'

'Her ladyship's nephew, Mr Franklin Blake, knows,' I said.

'Is the gentleman in the house?'

Mr Franklin was as close at hand as could be—waiting for his first chance of being introduced to the great Cuff. In half a minute he was in the room, and was giving his evidence as follows:

'That door, Sergeant,' he said, 'has been painted by Miss Verinder, under my inspection, with my help, and in a vehicle of my own composition. The vehicle dries whatever colours may be used with it, in twelve hours.'

'Do you remember when the smeared bit was done, sir?' asked the Sergeant.

'Perfectly,' answered Mr Franklin. 'That was the last morsel of the door to be finished. We wanted to get it done, on Wednesday last—and I myself completed it by three in the afternoon, or soon after.'

'Today is Friday,' said Sergeant Cuff, addressing himself to

Superintendent Seegrave. 'Let us reckon back, sir. At three on the Wednesday afternoon, that bit of the painting was completed. The vehicle dried it in twelve hours—that is to say, dried it by three o'clock on Thursday morning. At eleven on Thursday morning you held your inquiry here. Take three from eleven, and eight remains. That paint had been *eight hours dry*, Mr Superintendent, when you supposed that the women-servants' petticoats smeared it.'

Having settled the question of the paint, Sergeant Cuff, from that moment, gave his brother-officer up as a bad job—and addressed himself to Mr Franklin, as the more promising assistant of the two.

'It's quite on the cards, sir,' he said, 'that you have put the clue into our hands.'

As the words passed his lips, the bedroom door opened, and Miss Rachel came out among us suddenly.

She addressed herself to the Sergeant, without appearing to notice (or to heed) that he was a perfect stranger to her.

'Did you say,' she asked, pointing to Mr Franklin, 'that *he* had put the clue into your hands?'

('This is Miss Verinder,' I whispered, behind the Sergeant.)

'That gentleman, miss,' says the Sergeant—with his steely-grey eyes carefully studying my young lady's face—'has possibly put the clue into our hands.'

She turned for one moment, and tried to look at Mr Franklin. I say, tried, for she suddenly looked away again before their eyes met. There seemed to be some strange disturbance in her mind. She coloured up, and then she turned pale again. With the paleness, there came a new look into her face—a look which it startled me to see.

'Having answered your question, miss,' says the Sergeant, 'I beg leave to make an inquiry in my turn. There is a smear on the painting of your door, here. Do you happen to know when it was done? or who did it?'

Instead of making any reply, Miss Rachel went on with her

questions, as if he had not spoken, or as if she had not heard him.

'Are you another police officer?' she asked.

'I am Sergeant Cuff, miss, of the Detective Police.'

'Do you think a young lady's advice worth having?'

'I shall be glad to hear it, miss.'

'Do your duty by yourself—and don't allow Mr Franklin Blake to help you!'

She said those words so spitefully, so savagely, with such an extraordinary outbreak of ill-will towards Mr Franklin, in her voice and in her look, that—though I had known her from a baby, though I loved and honoured her next to my lady herself—I was ashamed of Miss Rachel for the first time in my life.

Sergeant Cuff's immovable eyes never stirred from off her face. 'Thank you, miss,' he said. 'Do you happen to know anything about the smear? Might you have done it by accident yourself?'

'I know nothing about the smear.'

With that answer, she turned away, and shut herself up again in her bedroom. This time, I heard her—as Penelope had heard her before—burst out crying as soon as she was alone again.

I couldn't bring myself to look at the Sergeant—I looked at Mr Franklin, who stood nearest to me. He seemed to be even more sorely distressed at what had passed than I was.

'I told you I was uneasy about her,' he said. 'And now you see why.'

'A young lady's tongue is a privileged member, sir,' says the Sergeant to Mr Franklin. 'Let us forget what has passed, and go straight on with this business. Thanks to you, we know when the paint was dry. The next thing to discover is when the paint was last seen without that smear. *You* have got a head on your shoulders—and you understand what I mean.'

Mr Franklin composed himself, and came back with an effort from Miss Rachel to the matter in hand.

'I think I do understand,' he said. 'The more we narrow the question of time, the more we also narrow the field of inquiry.'

'That's it, sir,' said the Sergeant. 'Did you notice your work here, on the Wednesday afternoon, after you had done it?'

Mr Franklin shook his head, and answered, 'I can't say I did.'

'Did *you*?' inquired Sergeant Cuff, turning to me.

'I can't say I did either, sir.'

'Who was the last person in the room, the last thing on Wednesday night?'

'Miss Rachel, I suppose, sir.'

Mr Franklin struck in there, 'Or possibly your daughter, Betteredge.' He turned to Sergeant Cuff, and explained that my daughter was Miss Verinder's maid.

'Mr Betteredge, ask your daughter to step up. Stop!' says the Sergeant, taking me away to the window, out of earshot. 'Your Superintendent here,' he went on, in a whisper, 'has made a pretty full report to me of the manner in which he has managed this case. Among other things, he has, by his own confession, set the servants' backs up. It's very important to smooth them down again. Tell your daughter, and tell the rest of them, these two things, with my compliments: First, that I have no evidence before me, yet, that the Diamond has been stolen; I only know that the Diamond has been lost. Second, that *my* business here with the servants is simply to ask them to lay their heads together and help me to find it.'

My experience of the women-servants, when Superintendent Seegrave laid his embargo on their rooms, came in handy here.

'May I make so bold, Sergeant, as to tell the women a third thing?' I asked. 'Are they free (with your compliments) to fidget up and downstairs, and whisk in and out of their bedrooms, if the fit takes them?'

'Perfectly free,' said the Sergeant.

'*That* will smooth them down, sir,' I remarked, 'from the cook to the scullion.'

'Go, and do it at once, Mr Betteredge.'

The Sergeant seemed to approve of Penelope. He became a trifle less dreary; and he looked much as he had looked when he noticed the white musk rose in the flower-garden. Here is my daughter's evidence, as drawn off from her by the Sergeant. She gave it, I think, very prettily—but, there! she is my child all over: nothing of her mother in her; Lord bless you, nothing of her mother in her!

Penelope examined: Took a lively interest in the painting on the door, having helped to mix the colours. Noticed the bit of work under the lock, because it was the last bit done. Had seen it, some hours afterwards, without a smear. Had left it, as late as twelve at night, without a smear. Had, at that hour, wished her young lady good night in the bedroom; had heard the clock strike in the 'boudoir'; had her hand at the time on the handle of the painted door; knew the paint was wet (having helped to mix the colours, as aforesaid); took particular pains not to touch it; could swear that she held up the skirts of her dress, and that there was no smear on the paint then; could *not* swear that her dress mightn't have touched it accidentally in going out; remembered the dress she had on, because it was new, a present from Miss Rachel; her father remembered, and could speak to it, too; could, and would, and did fetch it; dress recognised by her father as the dress she wore that night; skirts examined, a long job from the size of them; not the ghost of a paint-stain discovered anywhere. End of Penelope's evidence—and very pretty and convincing, too. Signed, Gabriel Betteredge.

The Sergeant's next proceeding was to question me about any large dogs in the house who might have got into the room, and done the mischief with a whisk of their tails. Hearing that this was impossible, he next sent for a magnifying-glass, and tried how the smear looked, seen that way. No skin-mark (as of a human hand) printed off on the paint. All the signs visible— signs which told that the paint had been smeared by some loose article of somebody's dress touching it in going by. That somebody (putting together Penelope's evidence and Mr Franklin's evidence) must have been in the room, and done the mischief, between midnight and three o'clock on the Thursday morning.

Having brought his investigation to this point, Sergeant Cuff discovered that such a person as Superintendent Seegrave was still left in the room, upon which he summed up the proceedings for his brother-officer's benefit, as follows:

'This trifle of yours, Mr Superintendent,' says the Sergeant, pointing to the place on the door, 'has grown a little in importance since you noticed it last. At the present stage of the inquiry there are, as I take it, three discoveries to make, starting from that smear. Find out (first) whether there is any article of dress in this house with the smear of the paint on it. Find out (second) who that dress belongs to. Find out (third) how the person can account for having been in this room, and smeared the paint, between midnight and three in the morning. If the person can't satisfy you, you haven't far to look for the hand that has got the Diamond. I'll work this by myself, if you please, and detain you no longer from your regular business in the town. You have got one of your men here, I see. Leave him here at my disposal, in case I want him—and allow me to wish you good morning.'

Turning from the window, after a minute or two, the Sergeant walked into the middle of the room, and stopped there, deep in thought, with his eyes on Miss Rachel's bedroom door. After a little he roused himself, nodded his head, as much as to say, 'That will do,' and, addressing me, asked for ten minutes' conversation with my mistress, at her ladyship's earliest convenience.

Leaving the room with this message, I heard Mr Franklin ask the Sergeant a question, and stopped to hear the answer also at the threshold of the door.

'Can you guess yet,' inquired Mr Franklin, 'who has stolen the Diamond?'

'*Nobody has stolen the Diamond,*' answered Sergeant Cuff.

We both started at that extraordinary view of the case, and both earnestly begged him to tell us what he meant.

'Wait a little,' said the Sergeant. 'The pieces of the puzzle are not all put together yet.'

CHAPTER XI

I FOUND my lady in her own sitting room. She started and looked annoyed when I mentioned that Sergeant Cuff wished to speak to her.

'If I must see him, I must,' she said. 'But I can't prevail on myself to see him alone. Bring him in, Gabriel, and stay here as long as he stays.'

This was the first attack of the megrims that I remembered in my mistress since the time when she was a young girl. I went back to the 'boudoir'. Mr Franklin strolled out into the garden, and joined Mr Godfrey, whose time for departure was now drawing near. Sergeant Cuff and I went straight to my mistress's room.

'I have already formed an opinion on this case,' says Sergeant Cuff, 'which I beg your ladyship's permission to keep to myself for the present. My business now is to mention what I have discovered upstairs in Miss Verinder's sitting-room, and what I have decided (with your ladyship's leave) on doing next.'

He then went into the matter of the smear on the paint, and stated the conclusions he drew from it—just as he had stated them (only with greater respect of language) to Superintendent Seegrave. 'One thing,' he said, in conclusion, 'is certain. The Diamond is missing out of the drawer in the cabinet. Another thing is next to certain. The marks from the smear on the door must be on some article of dress belonging to somebody in this house. We must discover that article of dress before we go a step further.'

'And that discovery,' remarked my mistress, 'implies, I presume, the discovery of the thief?'

'I beg your ladyship's pardon—I don't say the Diamond is stolen. I only say, at present, that the Diamond is missing. The discovery of the stained dress may lead the way to finding it.'

'How do you propose to discover the stained dress?' inquired my mistress, addressing herself once more to the Sergeant. 'My good servants, who have been with me for years, have, I am ashamed to say, had their boxes and rooms searched already by the other officer. I can't and won't permit them to be insulted in that way a second time!'

(There was a mistress to serve! There was a woman in ten thousand, if you like!)

'That is the very point I was about to put to your ladyship,' said the Sergeant. 'The other officer has done a world of harm to this inquiry, by letting the servants see that he suspected them. If I give them cause to think themselves suspected a second time, there's no knowing what obstacles they may not throw in my way—the women especially. At the same time, their boxes *must* be searched again—for this plain reason, that the first investigation only looked for the Diamond, and that the second investigation must look for the stained dress. I quite agree with you, my lady, that the servants' feelings ought to be consulted. But I am equally clear that the servants' wardrobes ought to be searched.'

This looked very like a deadlock. My lady said so, in choicer language than mine.

'I have got a plan to meet the difficulty,' said Sergeant Cuff, 'if your ladyship will consent to it. I propose explaining the case to the servants.'

'The women will think themselves suspected directly,' I said, interrupting him.

'The women won't, Mr Betteredge,' answered the Sergeant, 'if I can tell them I am going to examine the wardrobes of *everybody*—from her ladyship downwards—who slept in the house on Wednesday night. It's a mere formality,' he added, with a side look at my mistress; 'but the servants will accept it as even dealing between them and their betters; and, instead of hindering the investigation, they will make a point of honour of assisting it.'

I saw the truth of that. My lady, after her first surprise was over, saw the truth of it also.

'You are certain the investigation is necessary?' she said.

'It's the shortest way that I can see, my lady, to the end we have in view.'

My mistress rose to ring the bell for her maid. 'You shall speak to the servants,' she said, 'with the keys of my wardrobe in your hand.'

Sergeant Cuff stopped her by a very unexpected question.

'Hadn't we better make sure first,' he asked, 'that the other ladies and gentlemen in the house will consent, too?'

'The only other lady in the house is Miss Verinder,' answered my mistress, with a look of surprise. 'The only gentlemen are my nephews, Mr Blake and Mr Ablewhite. There is not the least fear of a refusal from any of the three.'

I reminded my lady here that Mr Godfrey was going away. As I said the words, Mr Godfrey himself knocked at the door to say good-bye, and was followed in by Mr Franklin, who was going with him to the station. My lady explained the difficulty. Mr Godfrey settled it directly. He called to Samuel, through the window, to take his portmanteau upstairs again, and he then put the key himself into Sergeant Cuff's hand. 'My baggage can follow me to London,' he said, 'when the inquiry is over.'

My lady's unaccountable objection to the Sergeant seemed to make our conference more distasteful to her than ever, as soon as we were left alone again. 'If I send you down Miss Verinder's keys,' she said to him, 'I presume I shall have done all you want of me for the present?'

'I beg your ladyship's pardon,' said Sergeant Cuff. 'Before

we begin, I should like, if convenient, to have the washing-book. The stained article of dress may be an article of linen. If the search leads to nothing, I want to be able to account next for all the linen in the house, and for all the linen sent to the wash. If there is an article missing, there will be at least a presumption that it has got the paint-stain on it, and that it has been purposely made away with, yesterday or today, by the person owning it. Superintendent Seegrave,' added the Sergeant, turning to me, 'pointed the attention of the women-servants to the smear, when they all crowded into the room on Thursday morning. That *may* turn out, Mr Betteredge, to have been one more of Superintendent Seegrave's many mistakes.'

My lady desired me to ring the bell, and order the washing-book. She remained with us until it was produced, in case Sergeant Cuff had any further request to make of her after looking at it.

The washing-book was brought in by Rosanna Spearman. The girl had come down to breakfast that morning miserably pale and haggard, but sufficiently recovered from her illness of the previous day to do her usual work. Sergeant Cuff looked attentively at our second housemaid—at her face, when she came in; at her crooked shoulder, when she went out.

The great Cuff opened the washing-book, understood it perfectly in half a minute, and shut it up again. 'I venture to trouble your ladyship with one last question,' he said. 'Has the young woman who brought us this book been in your employment as long as the other servants?'

'Why do you ask?' said my lady.

'The last time I saw her,' answered the Sergeant, 'she was in prison for theft.'

After that, there was no help for it, but to tell him the truth. My mistress dwelt strongly on Rosanna's good conduct in her service, and on the high opinion entertained of her by the matron at the reformatory. 'You don't suspect her, I hope?' my lady added, in conclusion, very earnestly.

'I have already told your ladyship that I don't suspect any person in the house of thieving—up to the present time.'

After that answer, my lady rose to go upstairs, and ask for Miss Rachel's keys. The Sergeant was beforehand with me in opening the door for her. He made a very low bow. My lady shuddered as she passed him.

We waited, and waited, and no keys appeared. Sergeant Cuff made no remark to me. He turned his melancholy face to the window; he put his lanky hands into his pockets; and he whistled 'The Last Rose of Summer' softly to himself.

At last, Samuel came in, not with the keys, but with a morsel of paper for me. I got at my spectacles, with some fumbling and difficulty, feeling the Sergeant's dismal eyes fixed on me all the time. There were two or three lines on the paper, written in pencil by my lady. They informed me that Miss Rachel flatly refused to have her wardrobe examined. Asked for her reasons, she had burst out crying. Asked again, she had said: 'I won't, because I won't. I must yield to force if you use it, but I will yield to nothing else.' I understood my lady's disinclination to face Sergeant Cuff with such an answer from her daughter as that. If I had not been too old for the amiable weaknesses of youth, I believe I should have blushed at the notion of facing him myself.

'Any news of Miss Verinder's keys?' asked the Sergeant.

'My young lady refuses to have her wardrobe examined.'

'Ah!' said the Sergeant.

His voice was not quite in such a perfect state of discipline as his face. When he said 'Ah!' he said it in the tone of a man who had heard something which he expected to hear. He half angered and half frightened me—why, I couldn't tell, but he did it.

'Must the search be given up?' I asked.

'Yes,' said the Sergeant, 'the search must be given up, because your young lady refuses to submit to it like the rest. We must examine all the wardrobes in the house or none. Send Mr

Ablewhite's portmanteau to London by the next train, and return the washing-book, with my compliments and thanks, to the young woman who brought it in.'

He laid the washing-book on the table, and taking out his penknife, began to trim his nails.

'You don't seem to be much disappointed,' I said.

'No,' said Sergeant Cuff; 'I am not much disappointed.'

I tried to make him explain himself.

'Why should Miss Rachel put an obstacle in your way?' I inquired. 'Isn't it her interest to help you?'

'Come out into the garden,' he said, 'and let's have a look at the roses.'

CHAPTER XII

THE nearest way to the garden, on going out of my lady's sitting-room, was by the shrubbery path, which you already know of. For the sake of your better understanding of what is now to come, I may add to this, that the shrubbery path was Mr Franklin's favourite walk. When he was out in the grounds, and when we failed to find him anywhere else, we generally found him here.

I am afraid I must own that I am rather an obstinate old man. The more firmly Sergeant Cuff kept his thoughts shut up from me, the more firmly I persisted in trying to look in at them. As we turned into the shrubbery path, I attempted to circumvent him in another way.

'We won't enter into your young lady's motives,' the Sergeant said; 'we will only say it's a pity she declines to assist me, because, by so doing, she makes this investigation more difficult than it might otherwise have been. We must now try to solve the mystery of the smear on the door—which, you may take my word for it, means the mystery of the Diamond also— in some other way. I have decided to see the servants, and to search their thoughts and actions, Mr Betteredge, instead of searching their wardrobes. Before I begin, however, I want to ask you a question or two. You are an observant man—did you notice anything strange in any of the servants (making due allowance, of course, for fright and fluster), after the loss of the Diamond was found out? Any particular quarrel among them? Any one of them not in his or her usual spirits? Unexpectedly out of temper, for instance? or unexpectedly taken ill?'

I had just time to think of Rosanna Spearman's sudden illness at yesterday's dinner—but not time to make any answer—when I saw Sergeant Cuff's eyes suddenly turn aside towards the shrubbery; and I heard him say softly to himself, 'Hullo!'

'What's the matter?' I asked.

'A touch of the rheumatism in my back,' said the Sergeant, in a loud voice, as if he wanted some third person to hear us. 'We shall have a change in the weather before long.'

A few steps further brought us to the corner of the house. Turning off sharp to the right, we entered on the terrace, and went down, by the steps in the middle, into the garden below. Sergeant Cuff stopped there, in the open space, where we could see round us on every side.

'About that young person, Rosanna Spearman?' he said. 'It isn't very likely, with her personal appearance, that she has got a lover. But, for the girl's own sake, I must ask you at once whether *she* has provided herself with a sweetheart, poor wretch, like the rest of them?'

What on earth did he mean, under present circumstances, by putting such a question to me as that? I stared at him, instead of answering him.

'I saw Rosanna Spearman hiding in the shrubbery as we went by,' said the Sergeant.

'When you said "Hullo"?'

'Yes—when I said "Hullo!" If there's a sweetheart in the case, the hiding doesn't much matter. If there isn't—as things are in this house—the hiding is a highly suspicious circumstance, and it will be my painful duty to act on it accordingly.'

What, in God's name, was I to say to him? I knew the shrubbery was Mr Franklin's favourite walk; I knew he would most likely turn that way when he came back from the station; I knew that Penelope had over and over again caught her fellow-servant hanging about there, and had always declared to me that Rosanna's object was to attract Mr Franklin's attention. If my daughter was right, she might well have been lying in wait for Mr Franklin's return when the Sergeant noticed her. I was put between the two difficulties of mentioning Penelope's fanciful notion as if it was mine, or of leaving an unfortunate creature to suffer the consequences, the very serious consequences, of exciting the suspicion of Sergeant Cuff. Out of pure pity for the girl—on my soul and my character, out of pure pity for the girl—I gave the Sergeant the necessary explanations, and told him that Rosanna had been mad enough to set her heart on Mr Franklin Blake.

Sergeant Cuff never laughed. On the few occasions when anything amused him, he curled up a little at the corners of the lips, nothing more. He curled up now.

'Hadn't you better say she's mad enough to be an ugly girl and only a servant?' he asked. 'The falling in love with a gentleman of Mr Franklin Blake's manners and appearance doesn't seem to *me* to be the maddest part of her conduct by any means.

'Can you give me a little information about the country round here?' went on the Sergeant.

I couldn't well object to improve Sergeant Cuff in his geography.

'Is there any path, in that direction, leading to the sea-beach from this house?' asked the Sergeant. He pointed, as he spoke, to the fir-plantation which led to the Shivering Sand.

'Yes,' I said, 'there is a path.'

'Show it to me.'

Side by side, in the grey of the summer evening, Sergeant Cuff and I set forth for the Shivering Sand.

CHAPTER XIII

THE Sergeant remained silent, thinking his own thoughts, till we entered the plantation of firs which led to the quicksand. There he roused himself, like a man whose mind was made up, and spoke to me again.

'Mr Betteredge,' he said, 'as you have honoured me by taking an oar in my boat, and as you may, I think, be of some assistance to me before the evening is out, I see no use in our mystifying one another any longer, and I propose to set you an example of plain speaking on my side. You are determined to give me no information to the prejudice of Rosanna Spearman, because she has been a good girl to *you*, and because you pity her heartily. Those humane considerations do you a world of credit, but they happen in this instance to be humane considerations clean thrown away. Rosanna Spearman is not in the slightest danger of getting into trouble—no, not if I fix her with being concerned in the disappearance of the Diamond, on evidence which is as plain as the nose on your face!'

'Do you mean that my lady won't prosecute?' I asked.

'I mean that your lady *can't* prosecute,' said the Sergeant. 'Rosanna Spearman is simply an instrument in the hands of another person, and Rosanna Spearman will be held harmless for that other person's sake.'

He spoke like a man in earnest—there was no denying that. Still, I felt something stirring uneasily against him in my mind. 'Can't you give that other person a name?' I said.

'Can't *you*, Mr Betteredge?'

'No.'

Sergeant Cuff stood stock-still, and surveyed me with a look of melancholy interest.

'It's always a pleasure to me to be tender towards human infirmity,' he said. 'I feel particularly tender at the present moment, Mr Betteredge, towards you. And you, with the same excellent motive, feel particularly tender towards Rosanna Spearman, don't you? Do you happen to know whether she has had a new outfit of linen lately?'

What he meant by slipping in this extraordinary question unawares, I was at a total loss to imagine. Seeing no possible injury to Rosanna if I owned the truth, I answered that the girl had come to us rather sparely provided with linen, and that my lady, in recompense for her good conduct (I laid a stress on her good conduct), had given her a new outfit not a fortnight since.

'This is a miserable world,' says the Sergeant. 'Human life, Mr Betteredge, is a sort of target—misfortune is always firing at it, and always hitting the mark. But for that outfit, we should have discovered a new nightgown or petticoat among Rosanna's things, and have nailed her in that way. You're not at a loss to follow me, are you? You have examined the servants yourself, and you know what discoveries two of them made outside Rosanna's door. Surely you know what the girl was about yesterday, after she was taken ill? You can't guess? Oh, dear me, it's as plain as that strip of light there, at the end of the trees. At eleven, on Thursday morning, Superintendent Seegrave (who is a mass of human infirmity) points out to all the women servants the smear on the door. Rosanna has her own reasons for suspecting her own things; she takes the first opportunity of getting to her room, finds the paint-stain on her nightgown, or petticoat, or what not, shams ill and slips away to the town, gets the materials for making a new petticoat or nightgown, makes it alone in her room on the Thursday night, lights a fire (not to destroy it; two of her fellow-servants are prying outside her door, and she knows better than to make a smell of burning, and to have a lot of tinder to get rid of)—lights a fire, I say, to dry and iron the substitute dress after wringing it out, keeps the stained dress hidden (probably *on* her), and is at this moment occupied in making away with it, in some convenient place, on that lonely bit of beach ahead of us. I have traced her this evening to your fishing village, and to one particular cottage, which we may possibly have to visit, before we go back. She stopped in the cottage for some time, and she came out with (as I believe) something hidden under her cloak. A cloak (on a woman's back) is an emblem of charity—it covers a multitude of sins. I saw her set off northwards along the coast, after leaving the cottage. Is your seashore here considered a fine specimen of marine landscape, Mr Betteredge?'

I answered, 'Yes,' as shortly as might be.

'Tastes differ,' says Sergeant Cuff. 'Looking at it from my point of view, I never saw a marine landscape that I admired less. If you happen to be following another person along your sea-coast, and if that person happens to look round, there isn't a scrap of cover to hide you anywhere. I had to choose between taking Rosanna in custody on suspicion, or leaving her, for the time being, with her little game in her own hands. For reasons which I won't trouble you with, I decided on making any sacrifice rather than give the alarm as soon as tonight to a certain person who shall be nameless between us. I came back to the house to ask you to take me to the north end of the beach by another way. Sand—in respect of its printing off people's footsteps—is one of the best detective officers I know. If we don't meet with Rosanna Spearman by coming round on her in this way, the sand may tell us what she has been at, if the light only lasts long enough. Here *is* the sand. If you will excuse my suggesting it—suppose you hold your tongue, and let me go first?'

If there is such a thing known at the doctor's shop as a *detective-fever*, that disease had now got fast hold of your humble servant. Sergeant Cuff went on between the hillocks of sand, down to the beach. I followed him (with my heart in my mouth); and waited at a little distance for what was to happen next.

The last of the evening light was fading away; and over all the desolate place there hung a still and awful calm. The heave of the main ocean on the great sandbank out in the bay, was a heave that made no sound. The inner sea lay lost and dim, without a breath of wind to stir it. Patches of nasty ooze floated, yellow-white, on the dead surface of the water. Scum and slime shone faintly in certain places, where the last of the light still caught them on the two great spits of rock jutting out, north and south, into the sea. It was now the time of the turn of the tide: and even as I stood there waiting, the broad brown face of the quicksand began to dimple and quiver—the only moving thing in all the horrid place.

I saw the Sergeant start as the shiver of the sand caught his eye. After looking at it for a minute or so, he turned and came back to me.

'A treacherous place, Mr Betteredge,' he said; 'and no signs of Rosanna Spearman anywhere on the beach, look where you may.'

He took me down lower on the shore, and I saw for myself that his footsteps and mine were the only footsteps printed off on the sand.

'How does the fishing village bear, standing where we are now?' asked Sergeant Cuff.

'Cobb's Hole,' I answered (that being the name of the place), 'bears as near as may be, due south.'

'I saw the girl this evening, walking northward along the shore, from Cobb's Hole,' said the Sergeant. 'Consequently, she must have been walking towards this place. Is Cobb's Hole on the other side of that point of land there? And can we get to it—now it's low water—by the beach?'

I answered, 'Yes,' to both those questions.

'If you'll excuse my suggesting it, we'll step out briskly,' said the Sergeant. 'I want to find the place where she left the shore, before it gets dark.'

We had walked, I should say, a couple of hundred yards

towards Cobb's Hole, when Sergeant Cuff suddenly went down on his knees on the beach, to all appearance seized with a sudden frenzy for saying his prayers.

'There's something to be said for your marine landscape here, after all,' remarked the Sergeant. 'Here are a woman's footsteps, Mr Betteredge! Let us call them Rosanna's footsteps, until we find evidence to the contrary that we can't resist. Very confused footsteps, you will please to observe—purposely confused, I should say. Ah, poor soul, she understands the detective virtues of sand as well as I do! But hasn't she been in rather too great a hurry to tread out the marks thoroughly? I think she has. Here's one footstep going *from* Cobb's Hole; and here is another going back to it. Isn't that the toe of her shoe pointing straight to the water's edge? And don't I see two heel-marks further down the beach, close at the water's edge also? I don't want to hurt your feelings, but I'm afraid Rosanna is sly. It looks as if she had determined to get to that place you and I have just come from, without leaving any marks on the sand to trace her by. Shall we say that she walked through the water from this point till she got to that ledge of rocks behind us, and came back the same way, and then took to the beach again where those two heel marks are still left? Yes, we'll say that. It seems to fit in with my notion that she had something under her cloak, when she left the cottage. No! not something to destroy—for, in that case, where would have been the need of all these precautions to prevent my tracing the place at which her walk ended? Something to hide is, I think, the better guess of the two. Perhaps, if we go on to the cottage, we may find out what that something is?'

At this proposal, my detective-fever suddenly cooled. 'You don't want me,' I said. 'What good can I do?'

'The longer I know you, Mr Betteredge,' said the Sergeant, 'the more virtues I discover. Modesty—oh dear me, how rare modesty is in this world! and how much of that rarity you possess! If I go alone to the cottage, the people's tongues will be tied at the first question I put to them. If I go with you, I go introduced by a justly respected neighbour, and a flow of conversation is the necessary result. It strikes me in that light; how does it strike you?'

Not having an answer of the needful smartness as ready as I could have wished, I tried to gain time by asking him what cottage he wanted to go to.

On the Sergeant describing the place, I recognised it as a cottage inhabited by a fisherman named Yolland, with his wife and two grown-up children, a son and a daughter. If you will look back, you will find that, in first presenting Rosanna Spearman to your notice, I have described her as occasionally varying her walk to the Shivering Sand, by a visit to some friends of hers at Cobb's Hole. Those friends were the Yollands—respectable, worthy people, a credit to the neighbourhood. Rosanna's acquaintance with them had begun by means of the daughter, who was afflicted with a misshapen foot, and who was known in our parts by the name of Limping Lucy. The two deformed girls had, I suppose, a kind of fellow-feeling for each other. Anyway, the Yollands and Rosanna always appeared to get on together, at the few chances they had of meeting, in a pleasant and friendly manner. The fact of Sergeant Cuff having traced the girl to *their* cottage, set the matter of my helping his inquiries in quite a new light. Rosanna had merely gone where she was in the habit of going; and to show that she had been in company with the fisherman and his family was as good as to prove that she had been innocently occupied so far, at any rate. It would be doing the girl a service, therefore, instead of an injury, if I allowed myself to be convinced by Sergeant Cuff's logic. I professed myself convinced by it accordingly.

We went on to Cobb's Hole, seeing the footsteps on the sand, as long as the light lasted.

On reaching the cottage, the fisherman and his son proved to be out in the boat; and Limping Lucy, always weak and weary, was resting on her bed upstairs. Good Mrs Yolland received us alone in her kitchen. When she heard that Sergeant Cuff was a celebrated character in London, she clapped a bottle of Dutch gin and a couple of clean pipes on the table, and stared as if she could never see enough of him.

I sat quiet in a corner, waiting to hear how the Sergeant would find his way to the subject of Rosanna Spearman. His usual roundabout manner of going to work proved, on this occasion, to be more roundabout than ever. How he managed it is more than I could tell at the time, and more than I can tell now. But this is certain, he began with the Royal Family, the Primitive Methodists, and the price of fish; and he got from that (in his dismal, underground way) to the loss of the Moonstone, the spitefulness of our first housemaid, and the hard behaviour of the women-servants generally towards Rosanna Spearman. Having reached his subject in this fashion, he described himself as making his inquiries about the lost Diamond, partly with a view to find it, and partly for the purpose of clearing Rosanna from the unjust suspicions of her enemies in the house. In about a quarter of an hour from the time when we entered the kitchen, good Mrs Yolland was persuaded that she was talking to Rosanna's best friend, and was pressing Sergeant Cuff to comfort his stomach and revive his spirits out of the Dutch bottle.

Being firmly persuaded that the Sergeant was wasting his breath to no purpose on Mrs Yolland, I sat enjoying the talk between them, much as I have sat, in my time, enjoying a stage play. The great Cuff showed a wonderful patience; trying his luck drearily this way and that way, and firing shot after shot, as it were, at random, on the chance of hitting the mark. Everything to Rosanna's credit, nothing to Rosanna's prejudice—that was how it ended, try as he might; with Mrs Yolland talking nineteen to the dozen, and placing the most entire confidence in him. His last effort was made, when we had looked at our watches, and had got on our legs previous to taking leave.

'I shall now wish you good-night, ma'am,' says the Sergeant.

'And I shall only say, at parting, that Rosanna Spearman has a sincere well-wisher in myself, your obedient servant. But, oh dear me! she will never get on in her present place; and my advice to her is—leave it.'

'Bless your heart alive! she is *going* to leave it!' cries Mrs Yolland. Rosanna Spearman going to leave us! I pricked up my ears at that.

'So she means to leave?' says the Sergeant. 'What is she to do when she does leave? Sad, sad! The poor creature has got no friends in the world, except you and me.'

'Ah, but she has though!' says Mrs Yolland. 'She came in here, as I told you, this evening; and, after sitting and talking a little with my girl Lucy and me she asked to go upstairs by herself, into Lucy's room. It's the only room in our place where there's pen and ink. "I want to write a letter to a friend," she says "and I can't do it for the prying and peeping of the servants up at the house." Who the letter was written to I can't tell you: it must have been a mortal long one, judging by the time she stopped upstairs over it. I offered her a postage-stamp when she came down. She hadn't got the letter in her hand, and she didn't accept the stamp. A little close, poor soul (as you know), about herself and her doings. But a friend she has got somewhere, I can tell you; and to that friend you may depend upon it, she will go.'

'Soon?' asked the Sergeant.

'As soon as she can.' says Mrs Yolland.

Here I stepped in again from the door. As chief of my lady's establishment, I couldn't allow this sort of loose talk about a servant of ours going, or not going, to proceed any longer in my presence, without noticing it.

'You must be mistaken about Rosanna Spearman,' I said. 'If she had been going to leave her present situation, she would have mentioned it, in the first place, to *me*.'

'Mistaken?' cries Mrs Yolland. 'Why, only an hour ago she bought some things she wanted for travelling—of my own self,

Mr Betteredge, in this very room. And that reminds me,' says the wearisome woman, suddenly beginning to feel in her pocket, 'of something I have got it on my mind to say about Rosanna and her money. Are you either of you likely to see her when you go back to the house?'

'I'll take a message to the poor thing, with the greatest pleasure,' answered Sergeant Cuff, before I could put in a word edgewise.

Mrs Yolland produced out of her pocket, a few shillings and sixpences, and counted them out with a most particular and exasperating carefulness in the palm of her hand. She offered the money to the Sergeant, looking mighty loth to part with it all the while.

'Might I ask you to give this back to Rosanna, with my love and respects?' says Mrs Yolland. 'She insisted on paying me for the one or two things she took a fancy to this evening—and money's welcome enough in our house, I don't deny it. Still, I'm not easy in my mind about taking the poor thing's little savings. And to tell you the truth, I don't think my man would like to hear that I had taken Rosanna Spearman's money, when he comes back tomorrow morning from his work. Please say she's heartily welcome to the things she bought of me—as a gift. And don't leave the money on the table,' says Mrs Yolland, putting it down suddenly before the Sergeant, as if it burnt her fingers—'don't, there's a good man! For times are hard, and flesh is weak; and I *might* feel tempted to put it back in my pocket again.'

'Come along!' I said, 'I can't wait any longer: I must go back to the house.'

'I'll follow you directly,' says Sergeant Cuff.

For the second time, I went to the door; and, for the second time, try as I might, I couldn't cross the threshold.

'It's a delicate matter, ma'am,' I heard the Sergeant say, 'giving money back. You charged her cheap for the things, I'm sure?'

'Cheap!' says Mrs Yolland. 'Come and judge for yourself.'

She took up the candle and led the Sergeant to a corner of the kitchen. For the life of me, I couldn't help following them. Shaken down in the corner was a heap of odds and ends (mostly old metal), which the fisherman had picked up at different times from wrecked ships, and which he hadn't found a market for yet, to his own mind. Mrs Yolland dived into this rubbish, and brought up an old japanned tin case, with a cover to it, and a hasp to hang it up by—the sort of thing they use, on board ship, for keeping their maps and charts, and such-like, from the wet.

'There!' says she. 'When Rosanna came in this evening, she bought the fellow to that. "It will just do," she says, "to put my cuffs and collars in, and keep them from being crumpled in my box." One and ninepence, Mr Cuff. As I live by bread, not a halfpenny more!'

'Dirt cheap!' says the Sergeant, with a heavy sigh.

He weighed the case in his hand. I thought I heard a note or two of 'The Last Rose of Summer' as he looked at it. There was no doubt now! He had made another discovery to the prejudice of Rosanna Spearman, in the place of all others where I thought her character was safest, and all through me! I leave you to imagine what I felt, and how sincerely I repented having been the medium of introduction between Mrs Yolland and Sergeant Cuff.

'That will do,' I said. 'We really must go.'

Without paying the least attention to me, Mrs Yolland took another dive into the rubbish, and came up out of it, this time, with a dog-chain.

'Weigh it in your hand, sir,' she said to the Sergeant. 'We had three of these; and Rosanna has taken two of them. "What can you want, my dear, with a couple of dog's chains?" says I. "If I join them together they'll go round my box nicely," says she. "Rope's cheapest," says I. "Chain's surest," says she. "Who ever heard of a box corded with chain?" says I. "Oh, Mrs Yolland, don't make objections!" says she; "let me have my chains!" A strange girl, Mr Cuff—good as gold, and kinder than a sister to my Lucy—but always a little strange. There! I humoured her. Three and sixpence. On the word of an honest woman, three *and* sixpence, Mr Cuff!'

'Each?' says the Sergeant.

'Both together!' says Mrs Yolland. 'Three and sixpence for the two.'

'Given away, ma'am,' says the Sergeant, shaking his head. 'Clean given away!'

'There's the money,' says Mrs Yolland, getting back sideways to the little heap of silver on the table, as if it drew her in spite of herself. 'The tin case and the dog chains were all she bought, and all she took away. One and ninepence and three and sixpence—total, five and three. With my love and respects—and I can't find it in my conscience to take a poor girl's savings, when she may want them herself.'

'I can't find it in *my* conscience, ma'am, to give the money back,' says Sergeant Cuff. 'You have as good as made her a present of the things—you have indeed.'

'Is that your sincere opinion, sir?' says Mrs Yolland brightening up wonderfully.

'There can't be a doubt about it,' answered the Sergeant. 'Ask Mr Betteredge.'

It was no use asking *me*. All they got out of *me* was, 'Goodnight.'

This time, I not only went to the door, but went fairly out on the road back. Explain it how you may, I felt as if one or both of them had mortally offended me. Before I had taken three steps down the village, I heard the Sergeant behind me.

'Thank you for your introduction, Mr Betteredge,' he said. 'I am indebted to the fisherman's wife for an entirely new sensation. Mrs Yolland has puzzled me.

'Yes,' says the Sergeant, as if he was actually reading my thoughts in the dark. 'Instead of putting me on the scent, it may console you to know, Mr Betteredge (with your interest in Rosanna), that you have been the means of throwing me off. What the girl has done, tonight, is clear enough, of course. She has joined the two chains, and has fastened them to the hasp in the tin case. She has sunk the case, in the water or in the quicksand. She has made the loose end of the chain fast to some place under the rocks, known only to herself. And she will leave the case secure at its anchorage till the present proceedings have come to an end; after which she can privately pull it up again out of its hiding-place, at her own leisure and convenience. All perfectly plain, so far. But,' says the Sergeant, with the first tone of impatience in his voice that I had heard yet, 'the mystery is—what the devil has she hidden in the tin case?'

I thought to myself, 'The Moonstone!' But I only said to Sergeant Cuff, 'Can't you guess?'

'It's not the Diamond,' says the Sergeant. 'The whole experience of my life is at fault, if Rosanna Spearman has got the Diamond.'

On hearing those words, the infernal detective-fever began, I suppose, to burn in me again. At any rate, I forgot myself in the interest of guessing this new riddle. I said rashly, 'The stained dress!'

Sergeant Cuff stopped short in the dark, and laid his hand on my arm.

'Is anything thrown into that quicksand of yours, ever thrown up on the surface again?' he asked.

'Never,' I answered. 'Light or heavy whatever goes into the Shivering Sand is sucked down, and seen no more.'

'Does Rosanna Spearman know that?'

'She knows it as well as I do.'

'Then,' said the Sergeant, 'what on earth has she got to do but to tie up a bit of stone in the stained dress and throw it into the quicksand? There isn't the shadow of a reason why she should have hidden it—and yet she must have hidden it. Query,' says the Sergeant, walking on again, 'is the paint-stained dress a petticoat or a night-gown? Or is it something else which there is a reason for preserving at any risk? Mr Betteredge, if nothing occurs to prevent it, I must go to Frizinghall tomorrow, and discover what she bought in the town, when she privately got the materials for making the substitute dress. It's a risk to leave the house, as things are now—but it's a worse risk still to stir another step in this matter in the dark. Excuse my being a little out of temper; I'm degraded in my own estimation—I have let Rosanna Spearman puzzle me.'

When we got back, the servants were at supper. The first person we saw in the outer yard was the policeman whom Superintendent Seegrave had left at the Sergeant's disposal. The Sergeant asked if Rosanna Spearman had returned. Yes. When? Nearly an hour since. What had she done? She had gone upstairs to take off her bonnet and cloak—and she was now at supper quietly with the rest.

Without making any remark, Sergeant Cuff walked on, sinking lower and lower in his own estimation, to the back of the house. Missing the entrance in the dark, he went on (in spite of my calling to him) till he was stopped by a wicket-gate which led into the garden. When I joined him to bring him back by the right way, I found that he was looking up attentively at one particular window, on the bedroom floor, at the back of the house.

Looking up, in my turn, I discovered that the object of his contemplation was the window of Miss Rachel's room, and that lights were passing backwards and forwards there as if something unusual was going on.

'Isn't that Miss Verinder's room?' asked Sergeant Cuff.

I replied that it was, and invited him to go in with me to supper. The Sergeant remained in his place, and said something about enjoying the smell of the garden at night. I left him to his enjoyment. Just as I was turning in at the door, I heard 'The Last Rose of Summer' at the wicket-gate. Sergeant Cuff had made another discovery! And my young lady's window was at the bottom of it this time!

The latter reflection took me back again to the Sergeant, with a polite intimation that I could not find it in my heart to leave him by himself. 'Is there anything you don't understand up there?' I added, pointing to Miss Rachel's window.

Judging by his voice, Sergeant Cuff had suddenly risen again to the right place in his own estimation. 'You are great people for betting in Yorkshire, are you not?' he asked.

'Well?' I said. 'Suppose we are?'

'If I was a Yorkshireman,' proceeded the Sergeant, taking my arm, 'I would lay you an even sovereign, Mr Betteredge, that your young lady has suddenly resolved to leave the house. If I won on that event, I should offer to lay another sovereign, that the idea has occurred to her within the last hour.'

The first of the Sergeant's guesses startled me. The second mixed itself up somehow in my head with the report we had heard from the policeman, that Rosanna Spearman had returned from the sands with in the last hour. The two together had a curious effect on me as we went in to supper. I shook off Sergeant Cuff's arm, and, forgetting my manners, pushed by him through the door to make my own inquiries for myself.

Samuel, the footman, was the first person I met in the passage.

'Her ladyship is waiting to see you and Sergeant Cuff,' he said, before I could put any questions to him.

'How long has she been waiting?' asked the Sergeant's voice behind me.

'For the last hour, sir.'

There it was again! Rosanna had come back; Miss Rachel had taken some resolution out of the common; and my lady had been waiting to see the Sergeant—all within the last hour! It was not pleasant to find these very different persons and things linking themselves together in this way. I went on upstairs, without looking at Sergeant Cuff, or speaking to him. My hand took a sudden fit of trembling as I lifted it to knock at my mistress's door.

'I shouldn't be surprised,' whispered the Sergeant over my

shoulder, 'if a scandal was to burst up in the house tonight. Don't be alarmed! I have put the muzzle on worse family difficulties than this, in my time.'

As he said the words, I heard my mistress's voice calling to us to come in.

CHAPTER XIV

WE found my lady with no light in the room but the reading-lamp. The shade was screwed down so as to overshadow her face. Instead of looking up at us in her usual straightforward way, she sat close at the table, and kept her eyes fixed obstinately on an open book.

'Officer,' she said, 'is it important to the inquiry you are conducting, to know beforehand if any person now in this house wishes to leave it?'

'Most important, my lady.'

'I have to tell you, then, that Miss Verinder proposes going to stay with her aunt, Mrs Ablewhite, of Frizinghall. She has arranged to leave us the first thing tomorrow morning.'

Sergeant Cuff looked at me. I made a step forward to speak to my mistress—and, feeling my heart fail me (if I must own it), took a step back again, and said nothing.

'May I ask your ladyship *when* Miss Verinder informed you that she was going to her aunt's?' inquired the Sergeant.

'About an hour since,' answered my mistress.

Sergeant Cuff looked at me once more. They say old people's hearts are not very easily moved. *My* heart couldn't have thumped much harder than it did now, if I had been five-and-twenty again!

'I have no claim, my lady,' says the Sergeant, 'to control Miss Verinder's actions. All I can ask you to do is to put off her departure, if possible, till later in the day. I must go to Frizinghall myself tomorrow morning—and I shall be back by two o'clock, if not before. If Miss Verinder can be kept here till that time, I should wish to say two words to her—unexpectedly—before she goes.'

My lady directed me to give the coachman her orders, that the carriage was not to come for Miss Rachel until two o'clock. 'Have you more to say?' she asked of the Sergeant, when this had been done.

'Only one thing, your ladyship. If Miss Verinder is surprised at this change in the arrangements, please not to mention me as being the cause of putting off her journey.'

My mistress lifted her head suddenly from her book as if she was going to say something—checked herself by a great effort—and, looking back again at the open page, dismissed us with a sign of her hand.

'That's a wonderful woman,' said Sergeant Cuff, when we were out in the hall again. 'But for her self-control, the mystery that puzzles you, Mr Betteredge, would have been at an end tonight.'

At those words, the truth rushed at last into my stupid old head. For the moment, I suppose I must have gone clean out of my senses. I seized the Sergeant by the collar of his coat, and pinned him against the wall.

'Damn you!' I cried out, 'there's something wrong about Miss Rachel—and you have been hiding it from me all this time!'

Sergeant Cuff looked up at me—flat against the wall—without stirring a hand, or moving a muscle of his melancholy face.

'Ah,' he said, 'you've guessed it at last.'

My hand dropped from his collar, and my head sunk on my breast. Please to remember, as some excuse for my breaking out as I did, that I had served the family for fifty years. Miss Rachel had climbed upon my knees, and pulled my whiskers, many and many a time when she was a child. Miss Rachel, with all her faults, had been, to my mind, the dearest and prettiest and best young mistress that ever an old servant waited on, and loved. I begged Sergeant's Cuff's pardon, but I am afraid I did it with watery eyes, and not in a very becoming way.

'Don't distress yourself, Mr Betteredge,' says the Sergeant, with more kindness than I had any right to expect from him. 'In my line of life, if we were quick at taking offence, we shouldn't be worth salt to our porridge. If it's any comfort to you, collar me again. You don't in the least know how to do it; but I'll overlook your awkwardness in consideration of your feelings.'

He curled up at the corners of his lips, and, in his own dreary way, seemed to think he had delivered himself of a very good joke.

I led him into my own little sitting-room, and closed the door.

'Tell me the truth, Sergeant,' I said. 'What do you suspect? It's no kindness to hide it from me now.'

'I don't suspect,' said Sergeant Cuff. 'I know.'

My unlucky temper began to get the better of me again.

'Do you mean to tell me, in plain English,' I said, 'that Miss Rachel has stolen her own Diamond?'

'Yes,' says the Sergeant; 'that is what I mean to tell you, in so many words. Miss Verinder has been in secret possession of the Moonstone from first to last; and she has taken Rosanna Spearman into her confidence, because she has calculated on our suspecting Rosanna Spearman of the theft. There is the whole case in a nutshell. Collar me again, Mr Betteredge. If it's any vent to your feelings, collar me again.'

God help me! My feelings were not to be relieved in that way. 'Give me your reasons!' That was all I could say to him.

'You shall hear my reasons tomorrow,' said the Sergeant. 'If Miss Verinder refuses to put off her visit to her aunt (which you will find Miss Verinder will do), I shall be obliged to lay the whole case before your mistress tomorrow. And, as I don't know what may come of it, I shall request you to be present, and to hear what passes on both sides. Let the matter rest for tonight. No, Mr Betteredge, you don't get a word more on the subject of the Moonstone out of me. There is your table spread for supper. That's one of the many human infirmities which I always treat tenderly. If you will ring the bell, I'll say grace. "For what we are going to receive—"'

'I wish you a good appetite to it, Sergeant,' I said. '*My* appetite is gone. I'll wait and see you served, and then I'll ask you to excuse me, if I go away, and try to get the better of this by myself.'

I saw him served with the best of everything—and I shouldn't have been sorry if the best of everything had choked him. The head gardener (Mr Begbie) came in at the same time, with his weekly account. The Sergeant got on the subject of roses and the merits of grass walks and gravel walks immediately. I left the two together, and went out with a heavy heart.

In the passage, I met Penelope hanging about, and asked what she was waiting for.

She was waiting for her young lady's bell, when her young lady chose to call her back to go on with the packing for the next day's journey. Further inquiry revealed to me, that Miss Rachel had given it as a reason for wanting to go to her aunt at Frizinghall, that the house was unendurable to her, and that she could bear the odious presence of a policeman under the same roof with herself no longer. On being informed, half an hour since, that her departure would be delayed till two in the afternoon, she had flown into a violent passion. My lady, present at the time, had severely rebuked her, and then (having apparently something to say, which was reserved for her daughter's private ear) had sent Penelope out of the room. My girl was in wretchedly low spirits about the changed state of things in the house. 'Nothing goes right, father; nothing is like what it used to be. I feel as if some dreadful misfortune was hanging over us all.'

That was my feeling too. But I put a good face on it, before my daughter. Miss Rachel's bell rang while we were talking.

Penelope ran up the back stairs to go on with the packing. I went by the other way to the hall, to see what the glass said about the change in the weather.

Just as I approached the swing-door leading into the hall from the servants' offices, it was violently opened from the other side, and Rosanna Spearman ran by me, with a miserable look of pain in her face, and one of her hands pressed hard over her heart, as if the pang was in that quarter. 'What's the matter, my girl?' I asked, stopping her. 'Are you ill?' 'For God's sake, don't speak to me,' she answered, and twisted herself out of my hands, and ran on towards the servants' staircase. I called to the cook (who was within hearing) to look after the poor girl. Two other persons proved to be within hearing, as well as the cook. Sergeant Cuff darted softly out of my room, and asked what was the matter. I answered, 'Nothing.' Mr Franklin, on the other side, pulled open the swing-door, and beckoning me into the hall, inquired if I had seen anything of Rosanna Spearman.

'She has just passed me, sir, with a very disturbed face, and in a very odd manner.'

'I am afraid I am innocently the cause of that disturbance, Betteredge.'

'You, sir!'

'I can't explain it,' says Mr Franklin; 'but, if the girl *is* concerned in the loss of the Diamond, I do really believe she was on the point of confessing everything—to me, of all the people in the world—not two minutes since.'

Looking towards the swing-door, as he said those last words, I fancied I saw it opened a little way from the inner side.

Was there anybody listening? The door fell to, before I could get to it. Looking through, the moment after, I thought I saw the tails of Sergeant Cuff's respectable black coat disappearing round the corner of the passage. He knew, as well as I did, that he could expect no more help from me, now that I had discovered the turn which his investigations were really taking. Under those circumstances, it was quite in his character to help himself, and to do it by the underground way.

Not feeling sure that I had really seen the Sergeant—and not desiring to make needless mischief, where, Heaven knows, there was mischief enough going on already—I told Mr Franklin that I thought one of the dogs had got into the house—and then begged him to describe what had happened between Rosanna and himself.

'Were you passing through the hall, sir?' I asked. 'Did you meet her accidentally, when she spoke to you?'

Mr Franklin pointed to the billiard-table.

'I was knocking the balls about,' he said, 'and trying to get this miserable business of the Diamond out of my mind. I happened to look up—and there stood Rosanna Spearman at the side of me, like a ghost! Her stealing on me in that way was so strange, that I hardly knew what to do at first. Seeing a very anxious expression in her face, I asked her if she wished to speak to me. She answered, "Yes, if I dare." Knowing what suspicion attached to her, I could only put one construction on such language as that. I confess it made me uncomfortable. I had no wish to invite the girl's confidence. At the same time, in the difficulties that now beset us, I could hardly feel justified in refusing to listen to her, if she was really bent on speaking to me. It was an awkward position; and I dare say I got out of it awkwardly enough. I said to her, "I don't quite understand you. Is there anything you want me to do?" Mind, Betteredge, I didn't speak unkindly! The poor girl can't help being ugly—I felt that, at the time. The cue was still in my hand, and I went on knocking the balls about, to take off the awkwardness of the thing. As it turned out, I only made matters worse still. I'm afraid I mortified her without meaning it! She suddenly turned away. "He looks at the billiard balls," I heard her say. "Anything rather than look at *me*!" Before I could stop her, she had left the hall. I am not quite easy about it, Betteredge. Would you mind telling Rosanna that I meant no unkindness? I have been a little hard on her, perhaps, in my own thoughts—I have almost hoped that the loss of the Diamond might be traced to *her*. Not from any ill-will to the poor girl; but—' He stopped there, and going back to the billiard-table, began to knock the balls about once more.

CHAPTER XV

I HAD expected the Sergeant to set off for Frizinghall the first thing in the morning. He waited about, however, as if he had something else to do first. I left him to his own devices; and going into the grounds shortly after, met Mr Franklin on his favourite walk by the shrubbery side.

Before we had exchanged two words, the Sergeant unexpectedly joined us. He made up to Mr Franklin, who received him, I must own, haughtily enough. 'Have you anything to say to me?' was all the return he got for politely wishing Mr Franklin good morning.

'I have something to say to you, sir,' answered the Sergeant, 'on the subject of the inquiry I am conducting here. You detected the turn that inquiry was really taking, yesterday. Naturally enough, in your position, you are shocked and distressed. Naturally enough, also, you visit your own angry sense of your own family scandal upon me.'

'What do you want?' Mr Franklin broke in, sharply enough.

'I want to remind you, sir, that I have at any rate, thus far, not been *proved* to be wrong. Bearing that in mind, be pleased to remember, at the same time, that I am an officer of the law acting here under the sanction of the mistress of the house. Under these circumstances, is it, or is it not, your duty as a good citizen, to assist me with any special information which you may happen to possess?'

'I possess no special information,' says Mr Franklin.

Sergeant Cuff put that answer by him, as if no answer had been made.

'You may save my time, sir, from being wasted on an inquiry at a distance,' he went on, 'if you choose to understand me and speak out.'

'I don't understand you,' answered Mr Franklin; 'and I have nothing to say.'

'One of the female servants (I won't mention names) spoke to you privately, sir, last night.'

Once more Mr Franklin cut him short; once more Mr Franklin answered, 'I have nothing to say.'

Standing by in silence, I thought of the movement in the swing-door on the previous evening, and of the coat-tails which I had seen disappearing down the passage. Sergeant Cuff had, no doubt, just heard enough, before I interrupted him, to make him suspect that Rosanna had relieved her mind by confessing something to Mr Franklin Blake.

This notion had barely struck me—when who should appear at the end of the shrubbery walk but Rosanna Spearman in her own proper person! She was followed by Penelope, who was evidently trying to make her retrace her steps to the house. Seeing that Mr Franklin was not alone, Rosanna came to a standstill, evidently in great perplexity what to do next. Penelope waited behind her. Mr Franklin saw the girls as soon as I saw them. The Sergeant, with his devilish cunning, took on not to have noticed them at all. All this happened in an instant. Before either Mr Franklin or I could say a word, Sergeant Cuff struck in smoothly, with an appearance of continuing the previous conversation.

'You needn't be afraid of harming the girl, sir,' he said to Mr Franklin, speaking in a loud voice, so that Rosanna might hear him. 'On the contrary, I recommend you to honour me with your confidence, if you feel any interest in Rosanna Spearman.'

Mr Franklin instantly took on not to have noticed the girls either. He answered, speaking loudly on his side:

'I take no interest whatever in Rosanna Spearman.'

I looked towards the end of the walk. All I saw at the distance was that Rosanna suddenly turned round, the moment Mr Franklin had spoken. Instead of resisting Penelope, as she had done the moment before, she now let my daughter take her by the arm and lead her back to the house.

The breakfast-bell rang as the two girls disappeared—and even Sergeant Cuff was now obliged to give it up as a bad job! He said to me quietly, 'I shall go to Frizinghall, Mr Betteredge; and I shall be back before two.' He went his way without a word more—and for some few hours we were well rid of him.

'You must make it right with Rosanna,' Mr Franklin said to me, when we were alone. 'I seem to be fated to say or do something awkward, before that unlucky girl. You must have seen yourself that Sergeant Cuff laid a trap for both of us. If he could confuse *me*, or irritate *her* into breaking out, either she or I might have said something which would answer his purpose. On the spur of the moment, I saw no better way out of it than the way I took. It stopped the girl from saying anything, and it showed the Sergeant that I saw through him. He was evidently listening, Betteredge, when I was speaking to you last night.'

He had done worse than listen, as I privately thought to myself. He had remembered my telling him that the girl was in love with Mr Franklin; and he had calculated on *that*, when he appealed to Mr Franklin's interest in Rosanna—in Rosanna's hearing.

'As to listening, sir,' I remarked (keeping the other point to myself), 'we shall all be rowing in the same boat if this sort of thing goes on much longer. Prying, and peeping, and listening are the natural occupations of people situated as we are. In another day or two, Mr Franklin, we shall all be struck dumb together—for this reason, that we shall all be listening to surprise each other's secrets, and all know it. Excuse my breaking out, sir. The horrid mystery hanging over us in this house gets into my head like liquor, and makes me wild. I won't forget what you have told me. I'll take the first opportunity of making it right with Rosanna Spearman.'

'You haven't said anything to her yet about last night, have you?' Mr Franklin asked.

'No, sir.'

'Then say nothing now. I had better not invite the girl's confidence, with the Sergeant on the look-out to surprise us together. My conduct is not very consistent, Betteredge—is it? I see no way out of this business, which isn't dreadful to think of, unless the Diamond is traced to Rosanna. And yet I can't, and won't, help Sergeant Cuff to find the girl out.'

CHAPTER XVI

GOING down to the front door, I met the Sergeant on the steps; he had just returned from Frizinghall.

It went against the grain with me, after what had passed between us, to show him that I felt any sort of interest in his proceedings. In spite of myself, however, I felt an interest that there was no resisting. My sense of dignity sank from under me, and out came the words: 'What news from Frizinghall?'

'I have seen the Indians,' answered Sergeant Cuff. 'And I have found out what Rosanna bought privately in the town, on Thursday last. The Indians will be set free on Wednesday in next week. There isn't a doubt on my mind, and there isn't a doubt on Mr Murthwaite's mind, that they came to this place to steal the Moonstone. Their calculations were all thrown out, of course, by what happened in the house on Wednesday night; and they have no more to do with the actual loss of the jewel than you have. But I can tell you one thing, Mr Betteredge—if *we* don't find the Moonstone, *they* will. You have not heard the last of the three jugglers yet.'

Mr Franklin came back from his walk as the Sergeant said those startling words. Governing his curiosity better than I had governed mine, he passed us without a word, and went on into the house.

As for me, having already dropped my dignity, I determined to have the whole benefit of the sacrifice. 'So much for the Indians,' I said. 'What about Rosanna next?'

Sergeant Cuff shook his head.

'The mystery in that quarter is thicker than ever,' he said. 'I have traced her to a shop at Frizinghall, kept by a linen-draper named Maltby. She bought nothing whatever at any of the other drapers' shops, or at any milliners' or tailors' shops; and she bought nothing at Maltby's but a piece of long cloth. She was very particular in choosing a certain quality. As to quantity, she bought enough to make a nightgown.'

'Whose nightgown?' I asked.

'Her own, to be sure. Between twelve and three, on the Thursday morning, she must have slipped down to your young lady's room, to settle the hiding of the Moonstone while all the rest of you were in bed. In going back to her own room, her nightgown must have brushed the wet paint on the door. She couldn't wash out the stain; and she couldn't safely destroy the nightgown without first providing another like it, to make the inventory of her linen complete.'

'What proves that it was Rosanna's nightgown?' I objected.

'The material she bought for making the substitute dress,' answered the Sergeant. 'If it had been Miss Verinder's nightgown, she would have had to buy lace, and frilling, and Lord knows what besides; and she wouldn't have had time to make it in one night. Plain long cloth means a plain servant's nightgown. No, no, Mr Betteredge—all that is clear enough. The pinch of the question is—why, after having provided the substitute dress, does she hide the smeared nightgown, instead of destroying it? If the girl won't speak out, there is only one way of settling the difficulty. The hiding-place at the Shivering Sand must be searched—and the true state of the case will be discovered there.'

'How are you to find the place?' I inquired.

'I am sorry to disappoint you,' said the Sergeant—'but that's a secret which I mean to keep to myself.'

(Not to irritate your curiosity, as he irritated mine, I may here inform you that he had come back from Frizinghall provided with a search-warrant. His experience in such matters told him that Rosanna was in all probability carrying about her a memorandum of the hiding-place, to guide her, in case she returned to it, under changed circumstances and after a lapse of time. Possessed of this memorandum, the Sergeant would be furnished with all that he could desire.)

'Now, Mr Betteredge,' he went on, 'suppose we drop speculation, and get to business. I told Joyce to have an eye on Rosanna. Where is Joyce?'

Joyce was the Frizinghall policeman, who had been left by Superintendent Seegrave at Sergeant Cuff's disposal. The clock struck two, as he put the question; and, punctual to the moment, the carriage came round to take Miss Rachel to her aunt's.

'One thing at a time,' said the Sergeant, stopping me as I was about to send in search of Joyce. 'I must attend to Miss Verinder first.'

As the rain was still threatening, it was the closed carriage that had been appointed to take Miss Rachel to Frizinghall. Sergeant Cuff beckoned Samuel to come down to him from the rumble behind.

'You will see a friend of mine waiting among the trees, on this side of the lodge gate,' he said. 'My friend, without stopping the carriage, will get up into the rumble with you. You have nothing to do but to hold your tongue, and shut your eyes. Otherwise, you will get into trouble.'

With that advice, he sent the footman back to his place. What Samuel thought I don't know. It was plain, to my mind, that Miss Rachel was to be privately kept in view from the time when she left our house—if she did leave it. A watch set on my young lady! A spy behind her in the rumble of her mother's carriage! I could have cut my own tongue out for having forgotten myself so far as to speak to Sergeant Cuff.

The first person to come out of the house was my lady. She

stood aside, on the top step, posting herself there to see what happened. Not a word did she say, either to the Sergeant or to me. With her lips closed, and her arms folded in the light garden cloak which she had wrapped round her on coming into the air, there she stood, as still as a statue, waiting for her daughter to appear.

In a minute more, Miss Rachel came downstairs. Her eyes were brighter and fiercer than I liked to see; and her lips had so completely lost their colour and their smile that I hardly knew them again. She kissed her mother in a hasty and sudden manner on the cheek. She said, 'Try to forgive me, mamma'—and then pulled down her veil over her face so vehemently that she tore it. In another moment she had run down the steps, and had rushed into the carriage as if it was a hiding-place.

Sergeant Cuff was just as quick on his side. He put Samuel back, and stood before Miss Rachel, with the open carriage-door in his hand, at the instant when she settled herself in her place.

'What do you want?' says Miss Rachel, from behind her veil.

'I want to say one word to you, miss,' answered the Sergeant, 'before you go. I can't presume to stop your paying a visit to your aunt. I can only venture to say that your leaving us, as things are now, puts an obstacle in the way of my recovering your Diamond. Please to understand that; and now decide for yourself whether you go or stay.'

Miss Rachel never even answered him. 'Drive on, James!' she called out to the coachman.

Without another word, the Sergeant shut the carriage-door. Just as he closed it, Mr Franklin came running down the steps. 'Good-bye, Rachel,' he said, holding out his hand.

'Drive on!' cried Miss Rachel, louder than ever, and taking no more notice of Mr Franklin than she had taken of Sergeant Cuff.

Mr Franklin stepped back thunderstruck, as well he might be. The coachman, not knowing what to do, looked towards my lady, still standing immovable on the top step. My lady, with anger and sorrow and shame all struggling together in her face, made him a sign to start the horses, and then turned back hastily into the house. Mr Franklin, recovering the use of his speech, called after her, as the carriage drove off, 'Aunt! you were quite right. Accept my thanks for all your kindness—and let me go.'

My lady turned as though to speak to him. Then, as if distrusting herself, waved her hand kindly. 'Let me see you, before you leave us, Franklin,' she said, in a broken voice—and went on to her own room.

'Do me a last favour, Betteredge,' says Mr Franklin, turning to me, with the tears in his eyes. 'Get me away to the train as soon as you can!'

He too went his way into the house. For the moment, Miss Rachel had completely unmanned him. Judge from that, how fond he must have been of her!

Sergeant Cuff and I were left face to face, at the bottom of the steps. The Sergeant stood with his face set towards a gap in the trees, commanding a view of one of the windings of the drive which led from the house. He had his hands in his pockets, and he was softly whistling 'The Last Rose of Summer' to himself.

'There's a time for everything,' I said savagely enough. 'This isn't a time for whistling.'

At that moment, the carriage appeared in the distance, through the gap, on its way to the lodge gate. There was another man, besides Samuel, plainly visible in the rumble behind.

'All right!' said the Sergeant to himself. He turned round to me. 'It's no time for whistling, Mr Betteredge, as you say. It's time to take this business in hand, now, without sparing anybody. We'll begin with Rosanna Spearman. Where is Joyce?'

We both called for Joyce, and received no answer. I sent one of the stable-boys to look for him.

'You heard what I said to Miss Verinder?' remarked the Sergeant, while we were waiting. 'And you saw how she received it? I tell her plainly that her leaving us will be an obstacle in the way of my recovering her Diamond—and she leaves, in the face of that statement! Your young lady has got a travelling companion in her mother's carriage, Mr Betteredge—and the name of it is, the Moonstone.'

I said nothing. I only held on like death to my belief in Miss Rachel.

The stable-boy came back, followed—very unwillingly, as it appeared to me—by Joyce.

'Where is Rosanna Spearman?' asked Sergeant Cuff.

'I can't account for it, sir,' Joyce began; 'and I am very sorry. But somehow or other—'

'Before I went to Frizinghall,' said the Sergeant, cutting him short, 'I told you to keep your eyes on Rosanna Spearman, without allowing her to discover that she was being watched. Do you mean to tell me that you have let her give you the slip?'

'I am afraid, sir,' says Joyce, beginning to tremble, 'that I was perhaps a little *too* careful not to let her discover me. There are such a many passages in the lower parts of this house—'

'How long is it since you missed her?'

'Nigh on an hour since, sir.'

'You can go back to your regular business at Frizinghall,' said the Sergeant, speaking just as composedly as ever, in his usual quiet and dreary way. 'I don't think your talents are at all in our line, Mr Joyce. Your present form of employment is a trifle beyond you. Good morning.'

The man slunk off. I find it very difficult to describe how I was affected by the discovery that Rosanna Spearman was missing. I seemed to be in fifty different minds about it, all at the same time. In that state, I stood staring at Sergeant Cuff—and my powers of language quite failed me.

'No, Mr Betteredge,' said the Sergeant, as if he had discovered the uppermost thought in me, and was picking it out to be answered, before all the rest. 'Your young friend, Rosanna, won't slip through my fingers so easy as you think. As long as I know where Miss Verinder is, I have the means at my disposal of tracing Miss Verinder's accomplice. I prevented them from communicating last night. Very good. They will get together at Frizinghall, instead of getting together here. The present inquiry must be simply shifted (rather sooner than I had anticipated) from this house, to the house at which Miss Verinder is visiting. In the meantime, I'm afraid I must trouble you to call the servants together again.'

I went round with him to the servants' hall. It is very disgraceful, but it is not the less true, that I had another attack of the detective-fever, when he said those last words. I forgot that I hated Sergeant Cuff. I seized him confidentially by the arm. I said, 'For goodness' sake, tell us what you are going to do with the servants now?'

The great Cuff stood stock still, and addressed himself in a kind of melancholy rapture to the empty air.

'If this man,' said the Sergeant (apparently meaning me), 'only understood the growing of roses he would be the most completely perfect character on the face of creation!' After that strong expression of feeling, he sighed, and put his arm through mine. 'This is how it stands,' he said, dropping down again to business. 'Rosanna has done one of two things. She has either gone direct to Frizinghall (before I can get there), or she has gone first to visit her hiding-place at the Shivering Sand. The first thing to find out is, which of the servants saw the last of her before she left the house.'

On instituting this inquiry, it turned out that the last person who had set eyes on Rosanna was Nancy, the kitchen-maid.

Nancy had seen her slip out with a letter in her hand, and stop the butcher's man who had just been delivering some meat at the back door. Nancy had heard her ask the man to post the letter when he got back to Frizinghall. The man had looked at the address, and had said it was a roundabout way of delivering a letter directed to Cobb's Hole, to post it at Frizinghall—and that, moreover, on a Saturday, which would prevent the letter from getting to its destination until Monday morning, Rosanna had answered that the delivery of the letter being delayed till Monday was of no importance. The only thing she wished to be sure of was that the man would do what she told him. The man had promised to do it, and had driven away. Nancy had been called back to her work in the kitchen. And no other person had seen anything afterwards of Rosanna Spearman.

'Well?' I asked, when we were alone again.

'Well,' says the Sergeant. 'I must go to Frizinghall.'

'About the letter, sir?'

'Yes. The memorandum of the hiding-place is in that letter. I must see the address at the post-office. If it is the address I suspect, I shall pay our friend, Mrs Yolland, another visit on Monday next.'

I went with the Sergeant to order the pony-chaise. In the stable-yard we got a new light thrown on the missing girl.

CHAPTER XVII

The news of Rosanna's disappearance had, as it appeared, spread among the out-of-door servants. They too had made their inquiries; and they had just laid hands on a quick little imp, nicknamed 'Duffy'—who was occasionally employed in weeding the garden, and who had seen Rosanna Spearman as lately as half-an-hour since. Duffy was certain that the girl had passed him in the fir-plantation, not walking, but *running*, in the direction of the seashore.

'Does this boy know the coast hereabouts?' asked Sergeant Cuff.

'He has been born and bred on the coast,' I answered.

'Duffy!' says the Sergeant, 'do you want to earn a shilling? If you do, come along with me. Keep the pony-chaise ready, Mr Betteredge, till I come back.'

He started for the Shivering Sand, at a rate that my legs

(though well enough preserved for my time of life) had no hope of matching. Little Duffy, as the way is with the young savages in our parts when they are in high spirits, gave a howl, and trotted off at the Sergeant's heels.

Here again, I find it impossible to give anything like a clear account of the state of my mind in the interval after Sergeant Cuff had left us. A curious and stupefying restlessness got possession of me. I did a dozen different needless things in and out of the house, not one of which I can now remember. I don't even know how long it was after the Sergeant had gone to the sands, when Duffy came running back with a message for me. Sergeant Cuff had given the boy a leaf torn out of his pocket-book, on which was written in pencil, 'Send me one of Rosanna Spearman's boots, and be quick about it.'

I despatched the first woman-servant I could find to Rosanna's room; and I sent the boy back to say that I myself would follow him with the boot.

This, I am well aware, was not the quickest way to take of obeying the directions which I had received. But I was resolved to see for myself what new mystification was going on before I trusted Rosanna's boot in the Sergeant's hands. My old notion of screening the girl, if I could, seemed to have come back on me again, at the eleventh hour. This state of feeling (to say nothing of the detective-fever) hurried me off, as soon as I had got the boot, at the nearest approach to a run which a man turned seventy can reasonably hope to make.

As I got near the shore, the clouds gathered black, and the rain came down, drifting in great white sheets of water before the wind. I heard the thunder of the sea on the sand-bank at the mouth of the bay. A little further on, I passed the boy crouching for shelter under the lee of the sand hills. Then I saw the raging sea, and the rollers tumbling in on the sand-bank, and the driven rain sweeping over the waters like a flying garment, and the yellow wilderness of the beach with one solitary black figure standing on it—the figure of Sergeant Cuff.

He waved his hand towards the north, when he first saw me. 'Keep on that side!' he shouted. 'And come on down here to me!'

I went down to him, choking for breath, with my heart leaping as if it was like to leap out of me. I was past speaking. I had a hundred questions to put to him; and not one of them would pass my lips. His face frightened me. I saw a look in his eyes which was a look of horror. He snatched the boot out of my hand, and set it in a footmark on the sand, bearing south from us as we stood, and pointing straight towards the rocky ledge called the South Spit. The mark was not yet blurred out by the rain—and the girl's boot fitted it to a hair.

The Sergeant pointed to the boot in the footmark, without saying a word.

I caught at his arm, and tried to speak to him, and failed as I had failed when I tried before. He went on, following the footsteps down and down to where the rocks and the sand joined. The South Spit was just awash with the flowing tide; the waters heaved over the hidden face of the Shivering Sand. Now this way, and now that, with an obstinate patience that was dreadful to see, Sergeant Cuff tried the boot in the footsteps, and always found it pointing the same way—straight to the rocks. Hunt as he might, no sign could he find anywhere of the footsteps walking *from* them.

He gave it up at last. Still keeping silence, he looked again at me; and then he looked out at the waters before us, heaving in deeper and deeper over the quicksand. I looked where he looked—and I saw his thought in his face. A dreadful dumb trembling crawled all over me on a sudden. I fell upon my knees on the beach.

'She has been back at the hiding-place,' I heard the Sergeant say to himself. 'Some fatal accident has happened to her on those rocks.'

The girl's altered looks, and words, and actions—the numbed, deadened way in which she listened to me, and spoke to me—when I had found her sweeping the corridor but a few hours since, rose up in my mind, and warned me, even as the Sergeant spoke, that his guess was wide of the dreadful truth. I tried to tell him of the fear that had frozen me up. I tried to say, 'The death she has died, Sergeant, was a death of her own seeking.' No! the words wouldn't come. The dumb trembling held me in its grip. I couldn't feel the driving rain. I couldn't see the rising tide. As in the vision of a dream, the poor lost creature came back before me. I saw her again as I had seen her in the past time—on the morning when I went to fetch her into the house. I heard her again, telling me that the Shivering Sand seemed to draw her to it against her will, and wondering whether her grave was waiting for her *there*. The horror of it struck at me, in some unfathomable way, through my own child. My girl was just her age. My girl, tried as Rosanna was tried, might have lived that miserable life, and died this dreadful death.

The Sergeant kindly lifted me up, and turned me away from the sight of the place where she had perished.

At the sand-hillocks we were met by the under-groom, running to us from the house. The lad is a good lad, and has an honest respect for me. He handed me a little note, with a decent sorrow in his face. 'Penelope sent me with this, Mr Betteredge,' he said. 'She found it in Rosanna's room.'

It was her last farewell word to the old man who had done his best—thank God, always done his best—to befriend her.

'You have often forgiven me, Mr Betteredge, in past times. When you next see the Shivering Sand, try to forgive me once more. I have found my grave where my grave was waiting for me. I have lived, and died, sir, grateful for your kindness.'

There was no more than that. Little as it was, I hadn't manhood enough to hold up against it. Your tears come easy, when you're young, and beginning the world. Your tears come easy, when you're old, and leaving it. I burst out crying.

Sergeant Cuff took a step nearer to me—meaning kindly, I

don't doubt. I shrank back from him. 'Don't touch me,' I said. 'It's the dread of you, that has driven her to it.'

'You are wrong, Mr Betteredge,' he answered, quietly. 'But there will be time enough to speak of it when we are indoors again.'

I followed the rest of them, with the help of the groom's arm. Through the driving rain we went back—to meet the trouble and the terror that were waiting for us at the house.

CHAPTER XVIII

THOSE in front had spread the news before us. We found the servants in a state of panic. As we passed my lady's door, it was thrown open violently from the inner side. My mistress came out among us (with Mr Franklin following, and trying vainly to compose her), quite beside herself with the horror of the thing.

'You are answerable for this!' she cried out, threatening the Sergeant wildly with her hand. 'Gabriel! give that wretch his money—and release me from the sight of him!'

The Sergeant was the only one among us who was fit to cope with her—being the only one among us who was in possession of himself.

'I am no more answerable for this distressing calamity, my lady, than you are,' he said. 'If, in half an hour from this, you still insist on my leaving the house, I will accept your ladyship's dismissal, but not your ladyship's money.'

It was spoken very respectfully, but very firmly at the same time—and it had its effect on my mistress as well as on me. She suffered Mr Franklin to lead her back into the room.

At the end of the half-hour, my mistress's bell rang.

On my way to answer it, I met Mr Franklin coming out of his aunt's sitting-room. He mentioned that her ladyship was ready to see Sergeant Cuff—in my presence as before—and he added that he himself wanted to say two words to the Sergeant first. On our way back to my room, he stopped, and looked at the railway time-table in the hall.

'Are you really going to leave us, sir?' I asked. 'Miss Rachel will surely come right again, if you only give her time?'

'She will come right again,' answered Mr Franklin, 'when she hears that I have gone away, and that she will see me no more.'

What he had to say to the Sergeant was spoken in my presence. He described her ladyship as willing to acknowledge that she had spoken over-hastily. And he asked if Sergeant Cuff would consent—in that case—to accept his fee, and to leave the matter of the Diamond where the matter stood now. The Sergeant answered, 'No, sir. My fee is paid me for doing my duty. I decline to take it, until my duty is done.'

'I don't understand you,' says Mr Franklin.

'I'll explain myself, sir,' says the Sergeant. 'When I came here, I undertook to throw the necessary light on the matter of the missing Diamond. I am now ready, and waiting to redeem my pledge. When I have stated the case to Lady Verinder as the case now stands, and when I have told her plainly what course of action to take for the recovery of the Moonstone, the responsibility will be off my shoulders. Let her ladyship decide, after that, whether she does, or does not, allow me to go on. I shall then have done what I undertook to do—and I'll take my fee.'

In those words Sergeant Cuff reminded us that, even in the Detective Police, a man may have a reputation to lose.

The view he took was so plainly the right one, that there was no more to be said. As I rose to conduct him to my lady's room, he asked if Mr Franklin wished to be present. Mr Franklin answered, 'Not unless Lady Verinder desires it.' He added, in a whisper to me, as I was following the Sergeant out, 'I know what that man is going to say about Rachel; and I am too fond of her to hear it, and keep my temper. Leave me by myself.'

CHAPTER XIX

THE first words, when we had taken our seats, were spoken by my lady.

'Sergeant Cuff,' she said, 'there was perhaps some excuse for the inconsiderate manner in which I spoke to you half an hour since. I have no wish, however, to claim that excuse. I say, with perfect sincerity, that I regret it, if I wronged you.'

The grace of voice and manner with which she made him that atonement had its due effect on the Sergeant. He requested permission to justify himself—putting his justification as an act of respect to my mistress. It was impossible, he said, that he could be in any way responsible for the calamity, which had shocked us all, for this sufficient reason, that his success in bringing his inquiry to its proper end depended on his neither saying nor doing anything that could alarm Rosanna Spearman. He appealed to me to testify whether he had, or had not, carried that object out. I could, and did, bear witness that he had. And there, as I thought, the matter might have been judiciously left to come to an end.

Sergeant Cuff, however, took it a step further, evidently (as you shall now judge) with the purpose of forcing the most painful of all possible explanations to take place between her ladyship and himself.

'I have heard a motive assigned for the young woman's suicide,' said the Sergeant, 'which may possibly be the right one. It is a motive quite unconnected with the case which I am conducting here. I am bound to add, however, that my own opinion points the other way. Some unbearable anxiety in connexion with the missing Diamond, has, I believe, driven the poor creature to her own destruction. I don't pretend to know what that unbearable anxiety may have been. But I think (with your ladyship's permission) I can lay my hand on a person who is capable of deciding whether I am right or wrong.'

'Is the person now in the house?' my mistress asked, after waiting a little.

'The person has left the house, my lady.'

That answer pointed as straight to Miss Rachel as straight could be. A silence dropped on us which I thought would never come to an end. Lord! how the wind howled, and how the rain drove at the window, as I sat there waiting for one or other of them to speak again!

'Be so good as to express yourself plainly,' said my lady. 'Do you refer to my daughter?'

'I do,' said Sergeant Cuff, in so many words.

My mistress had her cheque-book on the table when we entered the room—no doubt to pay the Sergeant his fee. She now put it back in the drawer. It went to my heart to see how her poor hand trembled—the hand that had loaded her old servant with benefits; the hand that, I pray God, may take mine, when my time comes, and I leave my place for ever!

'I had hoped,' said my lady, very slowly and quietly, 'to have recompensed your services, and to have parted with you without Miss Verinder's name having been openly mentioned between us as it has been mentioned now. My nephew has probably said something of this, before you came into my room?'

'Mr Blake gave his message, my lady. And I gave Mr Blake a reason—'

'It is needless to tell me your reason. After what you have just said, you know as well as I do that you have gone too far to go back. I owe it to myself, and I owe it to my child, to insist on your remaining here, and to insist on your speaking out.'

The Sergeant looked at his watch.

'If there had been time, my lady,' he answered, 'I should have preferred writing my report, instead of communicating it by word of mouth. But, if this inquiry is to go on, time is of too much importance to be wasted in writing. I am ready to go into the matter at once. It is a very painful matter for me to speak of, and for you to hear—'

There my mistress stopped him once more.

'I may possibly make it less painful to you, and to my good servant and friend here,' she said, 'if I set the example of speaking boldly, on my side. You suspect Miss Verinder of deceiving us all, by secreting the Diamond for some purpose of her own? Is that true?'

'Quite true, my lady.'

'Very well. Now, before you begin, I have to tell you, as Miss Verinder's mother, that she is *absolutely incapable* of doing what you suppose her to have done. Your knowledge of her character dates from a day or two since. My knowledge of her character dates from the beginning of her life. State your suspicion of her as strongly as you please—it is impossible that you can offend me by doing so. I am sure, beforehand, that (with all your experience) the circumstances have fatally misled you in this case. Mind! I am in possession of no private information. I am as absolutely shut out of my daughter's confidence as you are. My one reason for speaking positively, is the reason you have heard already. I know my child.'

She turned to me, and gave me her hand. I kissed it in silence. 'You may go on,' she said, facing the Sergeant again as steadily as ever.

Sergeant Cuff bowed. My mistress had produced but one effect on him. His hatchet-face softened for a moment, as if he was sorry for her. As to shaking him in his own conviction, it was plain to see that she had not moved him by a single inch. He settled himself in his chair; and he began his vile attack on Miss Rachel's character in these words:

'I must ask your ladyship,' he said, 'to look this matter in the face, from my point of view as well as from yours. Will you please to suppose yourself coming down here, in my place, and with my experience? and will you allow me to mention very briefly what that experience has been?'

My mistress signed to him that she would do this. The Sergeant went on:

'For the last twenty years,' he said, 'I have been largely employed in cases of family scandal, acting in the capacity of confidential man. The one result of my domestic practice which has any bearing on the matter now in hand, is a result which I may state in two words. It is well within my experience, that young ladies of rank and position do occasionally have private debts which they dare not acknowledge to their nearest relatives and friends. Sometimes, the milliner and the jeweller are at the bottom of it. Sometimes, the money is wanted for purposes which I don't suspect in this case, and which I won't shock you by mentioning. Bear in mind what I have said, my lady—and now let us see how events in this house have forced me back on my own experience, whether I liked it or not!'

He considered with himself for a moment, and went on—with a horrid clearness that obliged you to understand him; with an abominable justice that favoured nobody.

'My first information relating to the loss of the Moonstone,' said the Sergeant, 'came to me from Superintendent Seegrave. He proved to my complete satisfaction that he was perfectly incapable of managing the case. The one thing he said which struck me as worth listening to, was this—that Miss Verinder had declined to be questioned by him, and had spoken to him with a perfectly incomprehensible rudeness and contempt. I thought this curious—but I attributed it mainly to some clumsiness on the Superintendent's part which might have offended the young lady. After that, I put it by in my mind, and applied myself, single-handed, to the case. It ended, as you are aware, in the discovery of the smear on the door, and in Mr Franklin Blake's evidence satisfying me, that this same smear, and the loss of the Diamond, were pieces of the same puzzle. So far, if I suspected anything, I suspected that the Moonstone had been stolen, and that one of the servants might prove to be the thief. Very good. In this state of things, what happens? Miss Verinder suddenly comes out of her room, and speaks to me. I observe three suspicious appearances in that young lady. She is still violently agitated, though more than four-and-twenty hours have passed since the Diamond was lost. She treats me as she has already treated Superintendent Seegrave. And she is mortally offended with Mr Franklin Blake. Very good again. Here (I say to myself) is a young lady who has lost a valuable jewel—a young lady, also, as my own eyes and ears inform me, who is of an impetuous temperament. Under these circumstances, and with that character, what does she do? She betrays an incomprehensible resentment against Mr Blake, Mr Superintendent, and myself—otherwise, the very three people who have all, in their different ways, been trying to help her to recover her lost jewel. Having brought my inquiry to that point—*then*, my lady, and not till then, I begin to look back into my own mind for my own experience. My own experience explains Miss Verinder's otherwise incomprehensible conduct. It associates her with those other young ladies that I know of. It tells me she has debts she daren't acknowledge, that must be paid. And it sets me asking myself, whether the loss of the Diamond may not mean—that the Diamond must be secretly pledged to pay them. That is the conclusion which my experience draws from plain facts. What does your ladyship's experience say against it?'

'What I have said already,' answered my mistress. 'The circumstances have misled you.'

Sergeant Cuff went on:

'Right or wrong, my lady,' he said, 'having drawn my conclusion, the next thing to do was to put it to the test. I suggested to your ladyship the examination of all the wardrobes in the house. It was a means of finding the article of dress which had, in all probability, made the smear; and it was a means of putting my conclusion to the test. How did it turn out? Your ladyship consented; Mr Blake consented; Mr Ablewhite consented. Miss Verinder alone stopped the whole proceeding by refusing point-blank. That result satisfied me that my view was the right one. If your ladyship and Mr Betteredge persist in not agreeing with me, you must be blind to what happened before you this very day. In your hearing, I told the young lady that her leaving the house (as things were then) would put an obstacle in the way of my recovering her jewel. You saw yourselves that she drove off in the face of that statement. You saw yourself that, so far from forgiving Mr Blake for having done more than all the rest of you to put the clue into my hands, she publicly insulted Mr Blake, on the steps of her mother's house. What do these things mean? If Miss Verinder is not privy to the suppression of the Diamond, what do these things mean?'

Finding that I made no remark, and that my mistress made no remark, Sergeant Cuff proceeded. Lord! how it did enrage me to notice that he was not in the least put out by our silence!

'What I have to say next,' answered Sergeant Cuff, 'relates to Rosanna Spearman. I recognised the young woman, as your ladyship may remember, when she brought the washing-book into this room. Up to that time I was inclined to doubt whether Miss Verinder had trusted her secret to any one. When I saw Rosanna, I altered my mind. I suspected her at once of being privy to the suppression of the Diamond. The poor creature has met her death by a dreadful end, and I don't want your ladyship to think, now she's gone, that I was unduly hard on her. If this had been a common case of thieving, I should have given Rosanna the benefit of the doubt just as freely as I should have given it to any of the other servants in the house. Our experience of the Reformatory woman is, that when tried in service—and when kindly and judiciously treated—they prove themselves in the majority of cases to be honestly penitent, and honestly worthy of the pains taken with them. But this was not a common case of thieving. It was a case—in my mind—of a deeply planned fraud, with the owner of the Diamond at the bottom of it. Holding this view, the first consideration which naturally presented itself to me, in connection with Rosanna, was this: Would Miss Verinder be satisfied (begging your ladyship's pardon) with leading us all to think that the Moonstone was merely lost? Or would she go a step further, and delude us into believing that the Moonstone was stolen? In the latter event there was Rosanna Spearman—with the character of a thief—ready to her hand; the person of all others to lead your ladyship off, and to lead me off, on a false scent.'

Was it possible (I asked myself) that he could put his case against Miss Rachel and Rosanna in a more horrid point of view than this? It *was* possible, as you shall now see.

'I had another reason for suspecting the deceased woman,' he said, 'which appears to me to have been stronger still. Who would be the very person to help Miss Verinder in raising money privately on the Diamond? Rosanna Spearman. No young lady in Miss Verinder's position could manage such a risky matter as that by herself. A go-between she must have, and who so fit, I ask again, as Rosanna Spearman? Your lady-ship's deceased housemaid was at the top of her profession when she was a thief. She had relations, to my certain knowl-edge, with one of the few men in London (in the money-lending line) who would advance a large sum on such a notable jewel as the Moonstone, without asking awkward questions, or insisting on awkward conditions. Bear this in mind, my lady; and now let me show you how my suspicions have been justi-fied by Rosanna's own acts, and by the plain inferences to be drawn from them.'

He thereupon passed the whole of Rosanna's proceedings under review. You are already as well acquainted with those proceedings as I am; and you will understand how unanswer-ably this part of his report fixed the guilt of being concerned in the disappearance of the Moonstone on the memory of the poor dead girl. Even my mistress was daunted by what he said now. She made him no answer when he had done. It didn't seem to matter to the Sergeant whether he was answered or not. On he went (devil take him!), just as steady as ever.

'Having stated the whole case as I understand it,' he said, 'I have only to tell your ladyship, now, what I propose to do next. I see two ways of bringing this inquiry successfully to an end.

'My way,' said the Sergeant, going on as easy as ever, 'is to try that bold experiment to which I have alluded. I think I have formed a pretty correct estimate of Miss Verinder's temperament. She is quite capable (according to my belief) of committing a daring fraud. But she is too hot and impetuous in temper, and too little accustomed to deceit as a habit, to act the hypocrite in small things, and to restrain herself under all provocations. Her feelings, in this case, have repeatedly got beyond her control, at the very time when it was plainly her interest to conceal them. It is on this peculiarity in her character that I now propose to act. I want to give her a great shock suddenly, under circumstances that will touch her to the quick. In plain English, I want to tell Miss Verinder, without a word of warning, of Rosanna's death—on the chance that her own better feelings will hurry her into making a clean breast of it. Does your ladyship accept *that* alternative?'

My mistress astonished me beyond all power of expression. She answered him on the instant:

'Yes; I do.'

'The pony-chaise is ready,' said the Sergeant. 'I wish your ladyship good morning.'

My lady held up her hand, and stopped him at the door.

'My daughter's better feelings shall be appealed to, as you propose,' she said. 'But I claim the right, as her mother, of putting her to the test myself. You will remain here, if you please; and I will go to Frizinghall.'

For once in his life, the great Cuff stood speechless with amazement, like an ordinary man.

My mistress rang the bell, and ordered her waterproof things. It was still pouring with rain; and the close carriage had gone, as you know, with Miss Rachel to Frizinghall. I tried to dissuade her ladyship from facing the severity of the weather. Quite useless! I asked leave to go with her, and hold the umbrella.

She wouldn't hear of it. The pony-chaise came round, with the groom in charge. 'You may rely on two things,' she said to Sergeant Cuff, in the hall. 'I will try the experiment on Miss Verinder as boldly as you could try it yourself. And I will inform you of the result, either personally or by letter, before the last train leaves for London tonight.'

With that, she stepped into the chaise, and, taking the reins herself, drove off to Frizinghall.

CHAPTER XX

THE pony-chaise returned a good half-hour before I had ventured to expect it. My lady had decided to remain for the present, at her sister's house. The groom brought two letters from his mistress; one addressed to Mr Franklin, and the other to me.

Mr Franklin's letter I sent to him in the library—into which refuge his driftings had now taken him for the second time. My own letter, I read in my own room. A cheque, which dropped out when I opened it, informed me (before I had mastered the contents) that Sergeant Cuff's dismissal from the inquiry after the Moonstone was now a settled thing.

I sent to the conservatory to say that I wished to speak to the Sergeant directly. He appeared, with his mind full of the gardener and the dog-rose, declaring that the equal of Mr Begbie for obstinacy never had existed yet, and never would exist again. I requested him to dismiss such wretched trifling as this from our conversation, and to give his best attention to a really serious matter. Upon that he exerted himself sufficiently to notice the letter in my hand. 'Ah!' he said in a weary way, 'you have heard from her ladyship. Have I anything to do with it, Mr Betteredge?'

'You shall judge for yourself, Sergeant.' I thereupon read him the letter (with my best emphasis and discretion), in the following words:

'My Good Gabriel,—I request that you will inform Sergeant Cuff, that I have performed the promise I made to him; with this result, so far as Rosanna Spearman is concerned. Miss Verinder solemnly declares, that she has never spoken a word in private to Rosanna, since that unhappy woman first entered my house. They never met, even accidentally, on the night when the Diamond was lost; and no communication of any sort whatever took place between them, from the Thursday morning when the alarm was first raised in the house, to this present Saturday afternoon, when Miss Verinder left us. After telling my daughter suddenly, and in so many words, of Rosanna Spearman's suicide—this is what has come of it.'

Having reached that point, I looked up, and asked Sergeant Cuff what he thought of the letter, so far.

'I should only offend you if I expressed *my* opinion,' answered the Sergeant. 'Go on, Mr Betteredge,' he said, with the most exasperating resignation, 'go on.'

When I remembered that this man had had the audacity to complain of our gardener's obstinacy, my tongue itched to 'go on' in other words than my mistress's. This time, however, my Christianity held firm. I proceeded steadily with her ladyship's letter:

'Having appealed to Miss Verinder in the manner which the officer thought most desirable, I spoke to her next in the manner which I myself thought most likely to impress her. On two different occasions, before my daughter left my roof, I privately warned her that she was exposing herself to suspicion of the most unendurable and most degrading kind. I have now told her, in the plainest terms, that my apprehensions have been realised.

'Her answer to this, on her own solemn affirmation, is as plain as words can be. In the first place, she owes no money privately to any living creature. In the second place, the Diamond is not now, and never has been, in her possession, since she put it into her cabinet on Wednesday night.

'The confidence which my daughter has placed in me goes no further than this. She maintains an obstinate silence, when I ask her if she can explain the disappearance of the Diamond. She refuses, with tears, when I appeal to her to speak out for my sake. "The day will come when you will know why I am careless about being suspected, and why I am silent even to *you*. I have done much to make my mother pity me—nothing to make my mother blush for me." Those are my daughter's own words.

'After what has passed between the officer and me, I think—stranger as he is—that he should be made acquainted with what Miss Verinder has said, as well as you. Read my letter to him, and then place in his hands the cheque which I enclose. In resigning all further claim on his services, I have only to say that I am convinced of his honesty and his intelligence; but I am more firmly persuaded than ever, that the circumstances, in this case, have fatally misled him.'

There the letter ended. Before presenting the cheque, I asked Sergeant Cuff if he had any remark to make.

'It's no part of my duty, Mr Betteredge,' he answered, 'to make remarks on a case, when I have done with it.'

I tossed the cheque across the table to him. 'Do you believe in *that* part of her ladyship's letter?' I said, indignantly.

The Sergeant looked at the cheque, and lifted up his dismal eyebrows in acknowledgment of her ladyship's liberality.

'This is such a generous estimate of the value of my time,' he said, 'that I feel bound to make some return for it. I'll bear in mind the amount in this cheque, Mr Betteredge, when the occasion comes round for remembering it.'

'What do you mean?' I asked.

'Her ladyship has smoothed matters over for the present very cleverly,' said the Sergeant. 'But *this* family scandal is of the sort that bursts up again when you least expect it. We shall have more detective-business on our hands, sir, before the Moonstone is many months older.'

If those words meant anything, and if the manner in which he spoke them meant anything—it came to this. My mistress's letter had proved, to his mind, that Miss Rachel was hardened enough to resist the strongest appeal that could be addressed to her, and that she had deceived her own mother (good God, under what circumstances!) by a series of abominable lies. How other people, in my place, might have replied to the Sergeant, I don't know. I answered what he said in these plain terms:

'Sergeant Cuff, I consider your last observation as an insult to my lady and her daughter!'

'Mr Betteredge, consider it as a warning to yourself, and you will be nearer the mark.'

Hot and angry as I was, the infernal confidence with which he gave me that answer closed my lips.

I walked to the window to compose myself. The rain had given over; and, who should I see in the court-yard, but Mr Begbie, the gardener, waiting outside to continue the dog-rose controversy with Sergeant Cuff.

'My compliments to the Sairgent,' said Mr Begbie, the moment he set eyes on me. 'If he's minded to walk to the station, I'm agreeable to go with him.'

'What!' cries the Sergeant, behind me, 'are you not convinced yet?'

'The de'il a bit I'm convinced!' answered Mr Begbie.

'Then I'll walk to the station!' says the Sergeant.

'Then I'll meet you at the gate!' says Mr Begbie.

I was angry enough, as you know—but how was any man's anger to hold out against such an interruption as this? Sergeant Cuff noticed the change in me, and encouraged it by a word in season. 'Come! come!' he said, 'why not treat my view of the case as her ladyship treats it? Why not say, the circumstances have fatally misled me?'

To take anything as her ladyship took it was a privilege worth enjoying—even with the disadvantage of its having been offered to me by Sergeant Cuff. I cooled slowly down to my customary level. I regarded any other opinion of Miss Rachel, than my lady's opinion or mine, with a lofty contempt. The only thing I could *not* do, was to keep off the subject of the Moonstone! My own good sense ought to have warned me, I know, to let the matter rest—but, there! the virtues which distinguish the present generation were not invented in my time. Sergeant Cuff had hit me on the raw, and, though I did look down upon him with contempt, the tender place still tingled for all that. The end of it was that I perversely led him back to the subject of her ladyship's letter. 'I am quite satisfied myself,' I said. 'But never mind that! Go on, as if I was still open to conviction. You think Miss Rachel is not to be believed on her word; and you say we shall hear of the Moonstone again. Back your opinion, Sergeant,' I concluded, in an airy way. 'Back your opinion.'

Instead of taking offence, Sergeant Cuff seized my hand, and shook it till my fingers ached again.

'I declare to heaven,' says this strange officer solemnly, 'I would take to domestic service tomorrow, Mr Betteredge, if I had a chance of being employed along with *you*! To say you are as transparent as a child, sir, is to pay the children a compliment which nine out of ten of them don't deserve. There! there! we won't begin to dispute again. You shall have it out of me on easier terms than that. I won't say a word more about her ladyship, or about Miss Verinder—I'll only turn prophet, for once in a way, and for your sake. I have warned you already that you haven't done with the Moonstone yet. Very well. Now I'll tell you, at parting, of three things which will happen in the future, and which, I believe, will force themselves on your attention, whether you like it or not.'

'Go on!' I said, quite unabashed, and just as airy as ever.

'First,' said the Sergeant, 'you will hear something from the Yollands—when the postman delivers Rosanna's letter at Cobb's Hole, on Monday next.'

If he had thrown a bucket of cold water over me, I doubt if I could have felt it much more unpleasantly than I felt those words. Miss Rachel's assertion of her innocence had left Rosanna's conduct—the making the new nightgown, the hiding the smeared nightgown, and all the rest of it—entirely without explanation. And this had never occurred to me, till Sergeant Cuff forced it on my mind all in a moment!

'In the second place,' proceeded the Sergeant, 'you will hear of the three Indians again. You will hear of them in the neighbourhood, if Miss Rachel remains in the neighbourhood. You will hear of them in London, if Miss Rachel goes to London.'

Having lost all interest in the three jugglers, and having thoroughly convinced myself of my young lady's innocence, I took this second prophecy easily enough. 'So much for two of the three things that are going to happen,' I said. 'Now for the third!'

'Third, and last,' said Sergeant Cuff, 'you will, sooner or later, hear something of that money-lender in London, whom I have twice taken the liberty of mentioning already. Give me your pocket-book, and I'll make a note for you of his name and address—so that there may be no mistake about it if the thing really happens.'

He wrote accordingly on a blank leaf: 'Mr Septimus Luker, Middlesex Place, Lambeth, London.'

'There,' he said, pointing to the address, 'are the last words, on the subject of the Moonstone, which I shall trouble you with for the present. Time will show whether I am right or wrong. In the meanwhile, sir, I carry away with me a sincere personal liking for you, which I think does honour to both of us. If we don't meet again before my professional retirement takes place, I hope you will come and see me in a little house near London, which I have got my eye on. There will be grass walks, Mr Betteredge, I promise you, in *my* garden. And as for the white moss rose—'

CHAPTER XXI

I HAD kept the pony chaise ready, in case Mr Franklin persisted in leaving us by the train that night. The appearance of the luggage, followed downstairs by Mr Franklin himself, informed me plainly enough that he had held firm to a resolution for once in his life.

'So you have really made up your mind, sir?' I said, as we met in the hall. 'Why not wait a day or two longer, and give Miss Rachel another chance?'

The foreign varnish appeared to have all worn off Mr Franklin, now that the time had come for saying good-bye. Instead of replying to me in words, he put the letter which her ladyship had addressed to him into my hand. The greater part of it said over again what had been said already in the other communication received by me. But there was a bit about Miss Rachel added at the end, which will account for the steadiness of Mr Franklin's determination, if it accounts for nothing else.

'You will wonder, I dare say' (her ladyship wrote), 'at my allowing my own daughter to keep me perfectly in the dark. A Diamond worth twenty thousand pounds has been lost—and I am left to infer that the mystery of its disappearance is no mystery to Rachel, and that some incomprehensible obligation of silence has been laid on her, by some person or persons utterly unknown to me, with some object in view at which I cannot even guess. Is it conceivable that I should allow myself to be trifled with in this way? It is quite conceivable, in Rachel's present state. She is in a condition of nervous agitation pitiable to see. I dare not approach the subject of the Moonstone again until time has done something to quiet her. To help this end,

I have not hesitated to dismiss the police officer. The mystery which baffles us, baffles him too. This is not a matter in which any stranger can help us. He adds to what I have to suffer; and he maddens Rachel if she only hears his name.

'My plans for the future are as well settled as they can be. My present idea is to take Rachel to London—partly to relieve her mind by a complete change, partly to try what may be done by consulting the best medical advice. Can I ask you to meet us in town? My dear Franklin, you, in your way, must imitate my patience, and wait, as I do, for a fitter time. The valuable assistance which you rendered to the inquiry after the lost jewel is still an unpardoned offence, in the present dreadful state of Rachel's mind. Moving blindfold in this matter, you have added to the burden of anxiety which she has had to bear, by innocently threatening her secret with discovery, through your exertions. It is impossible for me to excuse the perversity that holds you responsible for consequences which neither you nor I could imagine or foresee. She is not to be reasoned with—she can only be pitied. I am grieved to have to say it, but for the present, you and Rachel are better apart. The only advice I can offer you is, to give her time.'

I handed the letter back, sincerely sorry for Mr Franklin, for I knew how fond he was of my young lady; and I saw that her mother's account of her had cut him to the heart. 'You know the proverb, sir,' was all I said to him. 'When things are at the worst, they're sure to mend. Things can't be much worse, Mr Franklin, than they are now.'

I followed him down the steps. It was very miserable to see him leaving the old place, where he had spent the happiest years of his life, in this way. Penelope (sadly upset by all that had happened in the house) came round crying, to bid him good-bye. Mr Franklin kissed her. I waved my hand as much as to say, 'You're heartily welcome, sir.' Some of the other female servants appeared, peeping after him round the corner. He was one of those men whom the women all like. At the last moment,

I stopped the pony chaise, and begged as a favour that he would let us hear from him by letter. He didn't seem to heed what I said—he was looking round from one thing to another, taking a sort of farewell of the old house and grounds. 'Tell us where you are going to, sir!' I said, holding on by the chaise, and trying to get at his future plans in that way. Mr Franklin pulled his hat down suddenly over his eyes. 'Going?' says he, echoing the word after me. 'I am going to the devil!' The pony started at the word, as if he had felt a Christian horror of it. 'God bless you, sir, go where you may!' was all I had time to say, before he was out of sight and hearing.

On the next day (Sunday), the close carriage, which had been kept at Mr Ablewhite's, came back to us empty. The coachman brought a message for me, and written instructions for my lady's own maid and for Penelope.

The message informed me that my mistress had determined to take Miss Rachel to her house in London, on the Monday. The written instructions informed the two maids of the clothing that was wanted, and directed them to meet their mistresses in town at a given hour. Most of the other servants were to follow. My lady had found Miss Rachel so unwilling to return to the house, after what had happened in it, that she had decided on going to London direct from Frizinghall. I was to remain in the country, until further orders, to look after things indoors and out. The servants left with me were to be put on board wages.

How the Monday affected the rest of the household I don't know. The Monday gave *me* a good shake up. The first of Sergeant Cuff's prophecies of what was to happen—namely, that I should hear from the Yollands—came true on that day.

I had seen Penelope and my lady's maid off in the railway with the luggage for London, and was pottering about the grounds, when I heard my name called. Turning round, I found myself face to face with the fisherman's daughter, Limping Lucy. Bating her lame foot and her leanness (this last a horrid drawback to a woman, in my opinion), the girl had some pleasing qualities in the eye of a man. A dark, keen, clever face, and a nice clear voice, and a beautiful brown head of hair counted among her merits. A crutch appeared in the list of her misfortunes. And a temper reckoned high in the sum total of her defects.

'Well, my dear,' I said, 'what do you want with me?'

'Where's the man you call Franklin Blake?' says the girl, fixing me with a fierce look, as she rested herself on her crutch.

'That's not a respectful way to speak of any gentleman,' I answered. 'If you wish to inquire for my lady's nephew, you will please to mention him as Mr Franklin Blake.'

She limped a step nearer to me, and looked as if she could have eaten me alive. '*Mr* Franklin Blake?' she repeated after me. 'Murderer Franklin Blake would be a fitter name for him.'

My practice with the late Mrs Betteredge came in handy here. Whenever a woman tries to put *you* out of temper, turn the tables, and put *her* out of temper instead. They are generally prepared for every effort you can make in your own defence, but that. One word does it as well as a hundred; and one word did it with Limping Lucy. I looked her pleasantly in the face; and I said—'Pooh!'

The girl's temper flamed out directly. She poised herself on her sound foot, and she took her crutch, and beat it furiously three times on the ground. 'He's a murderer! he's a murderer! he's a murderer! He has been the death of Rosanna Spearman!' She screamed that answer out at the top of her voice. One or two of the people at work in the grounds near us looked up— saw it was Limping Lucy—knew what to expect from that quarter—and looked away again.

'He has been the death of Rosanna Spearman?' I repeated. 'What makes you say that, Lucy?'

'What do you care? What does any man care? Oh! If she had only thought of the men as I think, she might have been living now!'

'She always thought kindly of *me*, poor soul,' I said; 'and, to the best of my ability, I always tried to act kindly by *her*.'

I spoke those words in as comforting a manner as I could. The truth is, I hadn't the heart to irritate the girl by another of my smart replies. I had only noticed her temper at first. I noticed her wretchedness now—and wretchedness is not uncommonly insolent, you will find, in humble life. My answer melted Limping Lucy. She bent her head down, and laid it on the top of her crutch.

'I loved her,' the girl said softly. 'She had lived a miserable life, Mr Betteredge—vile people had ill-treated her and led her wrong—and it hadn't spoiled her sweet temper. She was an angel. She might have been happy with me. I had a plan for our going to London together like sisters, and living by our needles. That man came here, and spoilt it all. He bewitched her. Don't tell me he didn't mean it, and didn't know it. He ought to have known it. He ought to have taken pity on her. "I can't live without him—and, oh, Lucy, he never even looks at me." That's what she said. Cruel, cruel, cruel. I said, "No man is worth fretting for in that way." And she said, "There are men worth dying for, Lucy, and he is one of them." I had saved up a little money. I had settled things with father and mother. I meant to take her away from the mortification she was suffering here. We should have had a little lodging in London, and lived together like sisters. She had a good education, sir, as you know, and she wrote a good hand. She was quick at her needle. I have a good education, and I write a good hand. I am not as quick at my needle as she was—but I could have done. We might have got our living nicely. And, oh! what happens this morning? What happens this morning? Her letter comes and tells me that she has done with the burden of her life. Her letter comes, and bids me good-bye for ever. Where is he?' cries the girl, lifting her head from the crutch, and flaming out again through her tears. 'Where's this gentleman that I mustn't speak of, except with respect? Ha, Mr Betteredge, the day is not far off when the poor will rise against the rich. I pray Heaven they may begin with *him*. I pray Heaven they may begin with *him*.'

Here was another of your average good Christians, and here was the usual break-down, consequent on that same average Christianity being pushed too far! The parson himself (though I own this is saying a great deal) could hardly have lectured the girl in the state she was in now. All I ventured to do was to keep her to the point—in the hope of something turning up which might be worth hearing.

'What do you want with Mr Franklin Blake?' I asked.

'I want to see him.'

'For anything particular?'

'I have got a letter to give him.'

'From Rosanna Spearman?'

'Yes.'

'Sent to you in your own letter?'

'Yes.'

Was the darkness going to lift? Were all the discoveries that I was dying to make, coming and offering themselves to me of their own accord? I was obliged to wait a moment. Sergeant Cuff had left his infection behind him. Certain signs and tokens, personal to myself, warned me that the detective-fever was beginning to set in again.

'You can't see Mr Franklin,' I said.

'I must, and will, see him.'

'He went to London last night.'

Limping Lucy looked me hard in the face, and saw that I was speaking the truth. Without a word more, she turned about again instantly towards Cobb's Hole.

'Stop!' I said. 'I expect news of Mr Franklin Blake tomorrow. Give me your letter, and I'll send it on to him by the post.'

Limping Lucy steadied herself on her crutch and looked back at me over her shoulder.

'I am to give it from my hands into his hands,' she said. 'And I am to give it to him in no other way.'

'Shall I write, and tell him what you have said?'

'Tell him I hate him. And you will tell him the truth.'

'Yes, yes. But about the letter?'

'If he wants the letter, he must come back here, and get it from me.'

With those words she limped off on the way to Cobb's Hole. The detective-fever burnt up all my dignity on the spot. I followed her, and tried to make her talk. All in vain. It was my misfortune to be a man—and Limping Lucy enjoyed disappointing me. Later in the day, I tried my luck with her mother. Good Mrs Yolland could only cry, and recommend a drop of comfort out of the Dutch bottle. I found the fisherman on the beach. He said it was 'a bad job', and went on mending his net. Neither father nor mother knew more than I knew. The one way left to try was the chance, which might come with the morning, of writing to Mr Franklin Blake.

Saturday, the last day of the week, is also the last day in my narrative.

The morning's post brought me a surprise in the shape of a London newspaper. The handwriting on the direction puzzled me. I compared it with the money-lender's name and address as recorded in my pocket-book, and identified it at once as the writing of Sergeant Cuff.

Looking through the paper eagerly enough, after this discovery, I found an ink-mark drawn round one of the police reports. Here it is, at your service. Read it as I read it, and you will set the right value on the Sergeant's polite attention in sending me the news of the day:

'LAMBETH—Shortly before the closing of the court, Mr Septimus Luker, the well-known dealer in ancient gems, carvings, intagli, etc., etc., applied to the sitting magistrate for advice. The applicant stated that he had been annoyed, at intervals throughout the day, by the proceedings of some of those strolling Indians who infest the streets. The

persons complained of were three in number. After having
been sent away by the police, they had returned again and
again, and had attempted to enter the house on pretence
of asking for charity. Warned off in the front, they had
been discovered again at the back of the premises. Besides
the annoyance complained of, Mr Luker expressed himself
as being under some apprehension that robbery might be
contemplated. His collection contained many unique
gems, both classical and Oriental, of the highest value. He
had only the day before been compelled to dismiss a
skilled workman in ivory carving from his employment (a
native of India, as we understood), on suspicion of
attempted theft; and he felt by no means sure that this
man and the street jugglers of whom he complained, might
not be acting in concert. It might be their object to collect
a crowd, and create a disturbance in the street, and, in
the confusion thus caused, to obtain access to the house.
In reply to the magistrate, Mr Luker admitted that he had
no evidence to produce of any attempt at robbery being
in contemplation. He could speak positively to the annoyance and interruption caused by the Indians, but not to
anything else. The magistrate remarked that, if the annoyance were repeated, the applicant could summon the
Indians to that court, where they might easily be dealt
with under the Act. As to the valuables in Mr Luker's
possession, Mr Luker himself must take the best measures
for their safe custody. He would do well perhaps to
communicate with the police, and to adopt such additional
precautions as their experience might suggest. The applicant thanked his worship, and withdrew.'

One of the wise ancients is reported (I forget on what occasion) as having recommended his fellow-creatures to 'look to
the end'. Looking to the end of these pages of mine, and
wondering for some days past how I should manage to write

SECOND PERIOD

THE DISCOVERY OF THE TRUTH (1848–1849)

FIRST NARRATIVE

Contributed by MISS CLACK, *niece of the late*
SIR JOHN VERINDER

CHAPTER I

I AM indebted to my dear parents (both now in heaven) for having had habits of order and regularity instilled into me at a very early age.

In that happy bygone time, I was taught to keep my hair tidy at all hours of the day and night, and to fold up every article of my clothing carefully, in the same order, on the same chair, in the same place at the foot of the bed, before retiring to rest. An entry of the day's events in my little diary invariably preceded the folding up. This habit has enabled poor me to serve the caprice of a wealthy member of the family into which my late uncle married. I am fortunate enough to be useful to Mr Franklin Blake.

I have been cut off from all news of my relatives by marriage for some time past. When we are isolated and poor, we are not infrequently forgotten. I am now living, for economy's sake, in a little town in Brittany, inhabited by a select circle of serious English friends, and possessed of the inestimable advantages of a Protestant clergyman and a cheap market.

In this retirement—a Patmos amid the howling ocean of Popery that surrounds us—a letter from England has reached

me at last. I find my insignificant existence suddenly remembered by Mr Franklin Blake. My wealthy relative—would that
I could add my spiritually-wealthy relative!—writes, without
even an attempt at disguising that he wants something of me.
The whim has seized him to stir up the deplorable scandal of
the Moonstone; and I am to help him by writing the account
of what I myself witnessed while visiting at Aunt Verinder's
house in London. Pecuniary remuneration is offered to me—
with the want of feeling peculiar to the rich. I am to re-open
wounds that Time has barely closed; I am to recall the most
intensely painful remembrances—and this done, I am to feel
myself compensated by a new laceration, in the shape of Mr
Blake's cheque. My nature is weak. It cost me a hard struggle,
before Christian humility conquered sinful pride, and self-
denial accepted the cheque.

Without my diary, I doubt—pray let me express it in the
grossest terms!—if I could have honestly earned my money.
With my diary, the poor labourer (who forgives Mr Blake for
insulting her) is worthy of her hire. Nothing escaped me at the
time I was visiting dear Aunt Verinder. Everything was entered
(thanks to my early training) day by day as it happened; and
everything, down to the smallest particular, shall be told here.
My sacred regard for truth is (thank God) far above my respect
for persons.

My diary informs me, that I was accidentally passing Aunt
Verinder's house in Montagu Square, on Monday, 3rd July,
1848.

Seeing the shutters opened, and the blinds drawn up, I felt
that it would be an act of polite attention to knock, and make
inquiries. The person who answered the door, informed me
that my aunt and her daughter (I really cannot call her my
cousin!) had arrived from the country a week since, and medi-
tated making some stay in London. I sent up a message at once,
declining to disturb them, and only begging to know whether
I could be of any use.

The person who answered the door, took my message in insolent silence, and left me standing in the hall.

'My lady is much obliged, and begs you will come and lunch tomorrow at two.'

We had a meeting that evening of the Select Committee of the Mothers'-Small-Clothes-Conversion-Society. The object of this excellent Charity is—as all serious people know—to rescue unredeemed fathers' trousers from the pawnbroker, and to prevent their resumption, on the part of the irreclaimable parent, by abridging them immediately to suit the proportions of the innocent son. I was a member, at that time, of the select committee; and I mention the Society here, because my precious and admirable friend, Mr Godfrey Ablewhite, was associated with our work of moral and material usefulness. I had expected to see him in the boardroom, on the Monday evening of which I am now writing, and had proposed to tell him, when we met, of dear Aunt Verinder's arrival in London. To my great disappointment he never appeared. On my expressing a feeling of surprise at his absence, my sisters of the Committee all looked up together from their trousers (we had a great pressure of business that night), and asked in amazement, if I had not heard the news. I acknowledged my ignorance, and was then told, for the first time, of an event which forms, so to speak, the starting-point of this narrative. On the previous Friday, two gentlemen—occupying widely-different positions in society—had been the victims of an outrage which had startled all London. One of the gentlemen was Mr Septimus Luker, of Lambeth. The other was Mr Godfrey Ablewhite.

The date—thanks to my dear parents, no dictionary that ever was written can be more particular than I am about dates—was Friday, June 30th, 1848.

Early on that memorable day, our gifted Mr Godfrey happened to be cashing a cheque at a banking-house in Lombard Street. On gaining the door, he encountered a gentleman—a perfect stranger to him—who was accidentally leaving the office exactly at the same time as himself. A momentary contest of politeness ensued between them as to who should be the first to pass through the door of the bank. The stranger insisted on making Mr Godfrey precede him; Mr Godfrey said a few civil words; they bowed, and parted in the street.

Thoughtless and superficial people may say, Here is surely a very trumpery little incident related in an absurdly circumstantial manner. Oh, my young friends and fellow-sinners! beware of presuming to exercise your poor carnal reason. Oh, be morally tidy. Let your faith be as your stockings, and your stockings as your faith. Both ever spotless, and both ready to put on at a moment's notice!

I beg a thousand pardons. I have fallen insensibly into my Sunday-school style. Most inappropriate in such a record as this. Let me try to be worldly—let me say that trifles, in this case as in many others, led to terrible results. Merely premising that the polite stranger was Mr Luker, of Lambeth, we will now follow Mr Godfrey home to his residence at Kilburn.

He found waiting for him, in the hall, a poorly clad but delicate and interesting-looking little boy. The boy handed him a letter, merely mentioning that he had been entrusted with it by an old lady whom he did not know, and who had given him no instructions to wait for an answer. Such incidents as these were not uncommon in Mr Godfrey's large experience as a promoter of public charities. He let the boy go, and opened the letter.

The handwriting was entirely unfamiliar to him. It requested his attendance, within an hour's time, at a house in Northumberland Street, Strand, which he had never had occasion to enter before. The object sought was to obtain from the worthy manager certain details on the subject of the Mothers'-Small-Clothes-Conversion-Society, and the information was wanted by an elderly lady who proposed adding largely to the resources of the charity, if her questions were met by satisfactory replies.

She mentioned her name, and she added that the shortness of her stay in London prevented her from giving any longer notice to the eminent philanthropist whom she addressed.

Ordinary people might have hesitated before setting aside their own engagements to suit the convenience of a stranger. The Christian hero never hesitates where good is to be done. Mr Godfrey instantly turned back, and proceeded to the house in Northumberland Street. A most respectable though somewhat corpulent man answered the door, and, on hearing Mr Godfrey's name, immediately conducted him into an empty apartment at the back, on the drawing-room floor. He noticed two unusual things on entering the room. One of them was a faint odour of musk and camphor. The other was an ancient Oriental manuscript, richly illuminated with Indian figures and devices, that lay open to inspection on a table.

He was looking at the book, the position of which caused him to stand with his back turned towards the closed folding doors communicating with the front room, when, without the slightest previous noise to warn him, he felt himself suddenly seized round the neck from behind. He had just time to notice that the arm round his neck was naked and of a tawny-brown colour, before his eyes were bandaged, his mouth was gagged, and he was thrown helpless on the floor by (as he judged) two men. A third rifled his pockets, and—if, as a lady, I may venture to use such an expression—searched him, without ceremony, through and through to his skin.

Here I should greatly enjoy saying a few cheering words on the devout confidence which could alone have sustained Mr Godfrey in an emergency so terrible as this. Perhaps, however, the position and appearance of my admirable friend at the culminating period of the outrage (as above described) are hardly within the proper limits of female discussion. Let me pass over the next few moments, and return to Mr Godfrey at the time when the odious search of his person had been completed. The outrage had been perpetrated throughout in dead silence. At the end of it some words were exchanged, among the invisible wretches, in a language which he did not understand, but in tones which were plainly expressive (to his cultivated ear) of disappointment and rage. He was suddenly lifted from the ground, placed in a chair, and bound there hand and foot. The next moment he felt the air flowing in from the open door, listened, and concluded that he was alone again in the room.

An interval elapsed, and he heard a sound below like the rustling sound of a woman's dress. It advanced up the stairs, and stopped. A female scream rent the atmosphere of guilt. A man's voice below exclaimed 'Hullo!' A man's feet ascended the stairs. Mr Godfrey felt Christian fingers unfastening his bandage, and extracting his gag. He looked in amazement at two respectable strangers, and faintly articulated, 'What does it mean?' The two respectable strangers looked back, and said, 'Exactly the question we were going to ask *you*.'

It appeared from the statement of the landlord and landlady of the house (persons of good repute in the neighbourhood), that their first and second floor apartments had been engaged, on the previous day, for a week certain, by a most respectable-looking gentleman—the same who has been already described as answering the door to Mr Godfrey's knock. The gentleman had paid the week's rent and all the week's extras in advance, stating that the apartments were wanted for three Oriental noblemen, friends of his, who were visiting England for the first time. Early on the morning of the outrage, two of the Oriental strangers, accompanied by their respectable English friend, took possession of the apartments. The third was expected to join them shortly; and the luggage (reported as very bulky) was announced to follow when it had passed through the Custom-house, late in the afternoon. Not more than ten minutes previous to Mr Godfrey's visit, the third foreigner had arrived. Nothing out of the common had happened, to the knowledge of the landlord and landlady downstairs, until within the last five minutes—when they had seen the three foreigners, accompanied by their respectable English friend, all leave the house together, walking quietly in the direction of the Strand. Remembering that a visitor had called, and not having seen the visitor also leave the house, the landlady had thought it rather strange that the gentleman should be left by himself upstairs. After a short discussion with her husband, she had considered it advisable to ascertain whether anything was wrong. The result had followed, as I have already attempted to describe it; and there the explanation of the landlord and the landlady came to an end.

An investigation was next made in the room. Dear Mr Godfrey's property was found scattered in all directions. When the articles were collected, however, nothing was missing; his watch, chain, purse, keys, pocket-handkerchief, note-book, and all his loose papers had been closely examined, and had then been left unharmed to be resumed by the owner. In the same way, not the smallest morsel of property belonging to the proprietors of the house had been abstracted. The Oriental noblemen had removed their own illuminated manuscript, and had removed nothing else.

What did it mean? Taking the worldly point of view, it appeared to mean that Mr Godfrey had been the victim of some incomprehensible error, committed by certain unknown men.

I could write pages of affectionate warning on this one theme, but (alas!) I am not permitted to improve—I am condemned to narrate. My wealthy relative's cheque—henceforth, the incubus of my existence—warns me that I have not done with this record of violence yet. We must leave Mr Godfrey to recover in Northumberland Street, and must follow the proceedings of Mr Luker at a later period of the day.

After leaving the bank, Mr Luker had visited various parts of London on business errands. Returning to his own residence, he found a letter waiting for him, which was described as having been left a short time previously by a boy. In this case, as in

Mr Godfrey's case, the handwriting was strange; but the name mentioned was the name of one of Mr Luker's customers. His correspondent announced (writing in the third person—apparently by the hand of a deputy) that he had been unexpectedly summoned to London. He had just established himself in lodgings in Alfred Place, Tottenham Court Road; and he desired to see Mr Luker immediately, on the subject of a purchase which he contemplated making. The gentleman was an enthusiastic collector of Oriental antiquities, and had been for many years a liberal patron of the establishment in Lambeth. Oh, when shall we wean ourselves from the worship of Mammon! Mr Luker called a cab, and drove off instantly to his liberal patron.

Exactly what had happened to Mr Godfrey in Northumberland Street now happened to Mr Luker in Alfred Place. The one point of difference between the two cases occurred when the scattered contents of Mr Luker's pockets were being collected from the floor. His watch and purse were safe, but (less fortunate than Mr Godfrey) one of the loose papers that he carried about him had been taken away. The paper in question acknowledged the receipt of a valuable of great price which Mr Luker had that day left in the care of his bankers. This document would be useless for purposes of fraud, inasmuch as it provided that the valuable should only be given up on the personal application of the owner. As soon as he recovered himself, Mr Luker hurried to the bank, on the chance that the thieves who had robbed him might ignorantly present themselves with the receipt. Nothing had been seen of them when he arrived at the establishment, and nothing was seen of them afterwards. Their respectable English friend had (in the opinion of the bankers) looked the receipt over before they attempted to make use of it, and had given them the necessary warning in good time.

I was punctual to the luncheon hour on Tuesday. Reference to my diary shows this to have been a chequered day—much in it to be devoutly regretted, much in it to be devoutly thankful for.

Dear Aunt Verinder received me with her usual grace and kindness. But I noticed, after a little while, that something was wrong. Certain anxious looks escaped my aunt, all of which took the direction of her daughter. I never see Rachel myself without wondering how it can be that so insignificant-looking a person should be the child of such distinguished parents as Sir John and Lady Verinder. On this occasion, however, she not only disappointed—she really shocked me. There was an absence of all lady-like restraint in her language and manner most painful to see. She was possessed by some feverish excitement which made her distressingly loud when she laughed, and sinfully wasteful and capricious in what she ate and drank at lunch. I felt deeply for her poor mother, even before the true state of the case had been confidentially made known to me.

Luncheon over, my aunt said: 'Remember what the doctor told you, Rachel, about quieting yourself with a book after taking your meals.'

'I'll go into the library, mamma,' she answered. 'But if Godfrey calls, mind I am told of it. I am dying for more news of him, after his adventure in Northumberland Street.' She kissed her mother on the forehead, and looked my way. 'Good-bye, Clack,' she said, carelessly. Her insolence roused no angry feeling in me; I only made a private memorandum to pray for her.

When we were left by ourselves, my aunt told me the whole horrible story of the Indian Diamond, which, I am happy to know, it is not necessary to repeat here. She did not conceal from me that she would have preferred keeping silence on the subject. But when her own servants all knew of the loss of the Moonstone, and when some of the circumstances had actually found their way into the newspapers—when strangers were speculating whether there was any connection between what had happened at Lady Verinder's country-house, and what had happened in Northumberland Street and Alfred Place—conceal-ment was not to be thought of; and perfect frankness became a necessity as well as a virtue.

As she was ending the tale, a servant opened the door, and announced Mr Godfrey Ablewhite.

CHAPTER II

'Go to Miss Verinder,' said my aunt, addressing the servant, 'and tell her Mr Ablewhite is here.'

We both inquired after his health. We both asked him together whether he felt like himself again, after his terrible adventure of the past week. With perfect tact, he contrived to answer us at the same moment. Lady Verinder had his reply in words. I had his charming smile.

'What,' he cried, with infinite tenderness, 'have I done to deserve all this sympathy? My dear aunt! My dear Miss Clack! I have merely been mistaken for somebody else. I have only been blindfolded; I have only been strangled; I have only been thrown flat on my back, on a very thin carpet, covering a particularly hard floor. Just think how much worse it might have been! I might have been murdered; I might have been robbed. What have I lost? Nothing but Nervous Force—which the law doesn't recognise as property; so that, strictly speaking, I have lost nothing at all. If I could have had my own way, I would have kept my adventure to myself—I shrink from all this fuss and publicity. But Mr Luker made *his* injuries public, and *my* injuries, as the necessary consequence, have been proclaimed in their turn. I have become the property of the newspapers, until the gentle reader gets sick of the subject. I am very sick indeed of it myself. May the gentle reader soon be like me! And how is dear Rachel? Still enjoying the gaieties of London? So glad to hear it! Miss Clack, I need all your indulgence. I am sadly behind-hand with my Committee Work and my dear Ladies. But I really do hope to look in at the Mothers'-Small-Clothes next week. Did you make cheering progress at Monday's Committee? Was the Board hopeful about future prospects? And are we nicely off for trousers?'

The heavenly gentleness of his smile made his apologies irresistible. The richness of his deep voice added its own indescribable charm to the interesting business question which he had just addressed to me. In truth, we were almost *too* nicely off for trousers; we were quite overwhelmed by them. I was just about to say so, when the door opened again, and an element of worldly disturbance entered the room, in the person of Miss Verinder.

She approached dear Mr Godfrey at a most unladylike rate of speed, with her hair shockingly untidy, and her face, what *I* should call unbecomingly flushed.

'I am charmed to see you, Godfrey,' she said, addressing him, I grieve to add, in the off-hand manner of one young man talking to another. 'I wish you had brought Mr Luker with you. You and he (as long as our present excitement lasts) are the two most interesting men in all London. It's morbid to say this; it's unhealthy; it's all that a well-regulated mind like Miss Clack's most instinctively shudders at. Never mind that. Tell me the whole of the Northumberland Street story directly. I know the newspapers have left some of it out.'

'Dearest Rachel,' he said, in the same voice which had thrilled me when he spoke of our prospects and our trousers, 'the newspapers have told you everything—and they have told it much better than I can.'

'Godfrey thinks we all make too much of the matter,' my aunt remarked. 'He has just been saying that he doesn't care to speak of it.'

'Why?' She put the question with a sudden flash in her eyes, and a sudden look up into Mr Godfrey's face. On his side, he looked down at her with an indulgence so injudicious and so ill-deserved, that I really felt called on to interfere.

'Rachel, darling!' I remonstrated gently, 'true greatness and true courage are ever modest.'

'You are a very good fellow in your way, Godfrey,' she said— not taking the smallest notice, observe, of me, and still speaking to her cousin as if she was one young man addressing another. 'But I am quite sure you are not great; I don't believe you possess any extraordinary courage; and I am firmly persuaded—if you ever had any modesty—that your lady-worshippers relieved you of that virtue a good many years since. You have some private reason for not talking of your adventure in Northumberland Street; and I mean to know it.'

'My reason is the simplest imaginable, and the most easily acknowledged,' he answered, still bearing with her. 'I am tired of the subject.'

'You are tired of the subject? My dear Godfrey, I am going to make a remark.'

'What is it?'

'You live a great deal too much in the society of women. And you have contracted two very bad habits in consequence. You have learnt to talk nonsense seriously, and you have got into a way of telling fibs for the pleasure of telling them. You can't go straight with your lady-worshippers. I mean to make you go straight with me. Come, and sit down. I am brimful of downright questions; and I expect you to be brimful of down-right answers.'

In the meantime, Rachel had settled herself at the window with our amiable and forbearing—our too forbearing—Mr Godfrey. She began the string of questions with which she had threatened him, taking no more notice of her mother, or of myself, than if we had not been in the room.

'Have the police done anything, Godfrey?'

'Nothing whatever.'

'It is certain, I suppose, that the three men who laid the trap for you were the same three men who afterwards laid the trap for Mr Luker?'

'Humanly speaking, my dear Rachel, there can be no doubt of it.'

'And not a trace of them has been discovered?'

'Not a trace.'

'It is thought—is it not?—that these three men are the three Indians who came to our house in the country.'

'Some people think so.'

'Do you think so?'

'My dear Rachel, they blindfolded me before I could see their faces. I know nothing whatever of the matter. How can I offer an opinion on it?'

Even the angelic gentleness of Mr Godfrey was, you see, beginning to give way at last under the persecution inflicted on him. Whether unbridled curiosity, or ungovernable dread, dictated Miss Verinder's questions I do not presume to inquire. I only report that, on Mr Godfrey's attempting to rise, after giving her the answer just described, she actually took him by the two shoulders, and pushed him back into his chair—Oh, don't say this was immodest! don't even hint that the recklessness of guilty terror could alone account for such conduct as I have described! We must not judge others. My Christian friends, indeed, indeed, indeed, we must not judge others!

She went on with her questions, unabashed. Earnest Biblical students will perhaps be reminded—as I was reminded—of the blinded children of the devil, who went on with their orgies, unabashed, in the time before the Flood.

'I want to know something about Mr Luker, Godfrey.'

'I am again unfortunate, Rachel. No man knows less of Mr Luker than I do.'

'You never saw him before you and he met accidentally at the bank?'

'Never.'

'You have seen him since?'

'Yes. We have been examined together, as well as separately, to assist the police.'

'Mr Luker was robbed of a receipt which he had got from his banker's—was he not? What was the receipt for?'

'For a valuable gem which he had placed in the safe keeping of the bank.'

'That's what the newspapers say. It may be enough for the general reader; but it is not enough for me. The banker's receipt must have mentioned what the gem was?'

'The banker's receipt, Rachel—as I have heard it described—mentioned nothing of the kind! A valuable gem, belonging to Mr Luker; deposited by Mr Luker; sealed with Mr Luker's seal; and only to be given up on Mr Luker's personal application. That was the form, and that is all I know about it.'

She waited a moment, after he had said that. She looked at her mother, and sighed. She looked back again at Mr Godfrey, and went on.

'Some of our private affairs, at home,' she said, 'seem to have got into the newspapers?'

'I grieve to say, it is so.'

'And some idle people, perfect strangers to us, are trying to trace a connection between what happened at our house in Yorkshire and what has happened since, here in London?'

'The public curiosity, in certain quarters, is, I fear, taking that turn.'

'The people who say that the three unknown men who ill-used you and Mr Luker are the three Indians, also say that the valuable gem—'

There she stopped. She had become gradually, within the last few moments, whiter and whiter in the face. The extraordinary blackness of her hair made this paleness, by contrast, so ghastly to look at, that we all thought she would faint, at the moment when she checked herself in the middle of her question. Dear Mr Godfrey made a second attempt to leave his chair. My aunt entreated her to say no more. I followed my aunt with a modest medicinal peace-offering, in the shape of a bottle of salts. We none of us produced the slightest effect on her. 'Godfrey, stay where you are. Mamma, there is not the least reason to be alarmed about me. Clack, you're dying to hear the end of it—I won't faint, expressly to oblige *you*.'

Those were the exact words she used—taken down in my

diary the moment I got home. But, oh, don't let us judge! My Christian friends, don't let us judge!

She turned once more to Mr Godfrey. With an obstinacy dreadful to see, she went back again to the place where she had checked herself, and completed her question in these words:

'I spoke to you, a minute since, about what people were saying in certain quarters. Tell me plainly, Godfrey, do they any of them say that Mr Luker's valuable gem is—the Moonstone?'

As the name of the Indian Diamond passed her lips, I saw a change come over my admirable friend. His complexion deepened. He lost the genial suavity of manner which is one of his greatest charms. A noble indignation inspired his reply.

'They *do* say it,' he answered. 'There are people who don't hesitate to accuse Mr Luker of telling a falsehood to serve some private interests of his own. He has over and over again solemnly declared that, until this scandal assailed him, he had never even heard of the Moonstone. And these vile people reply, without a shadow of proof to justify them, He has his reasons for concealment; we decline to believe him on his oath. Shameful! Shameful!'

Rachel looked at him very strangely—I can't well describe how—while he was speaking. When he had done, she said:

'Considering that Mr Luker is only a chance acquaintance of yours, you take up his cause, Godfrey, rather warmly.'

My gifted friend made her one of the most truly evangelical answers I ever heard in my life.

'I hope, Rachel, I take up the cause of all oppressed people rather warmly,' he said.

The tone in which those words were spoken might have melted a stone. But, oh dear, what is the hardness of stone? Nothing, compared to the hardness of the unregenerate human heart! She sneered. I blush to record it—she sneered at him to his face.

'Keep your noble sentiments for your Ladies' Committees, Godfrey. I am certain that the scandal which has assailed Mr Luker, has not spared you.'

Even my aunt's torpor was roused by those words.

'My dear Rachel,' she remonstrated, 'you have really no right to say that!'

'I mean no harm, mamma—I mean good. Have a moment's patience with me, and you will see.'

She looked back at Mr Godfrey, with what appeared to be a sudden pity for him. She went the length—the very unladylike length—of taking him by the hand.

'I am certain,' she said, 'that I have found out the true reason of your unwillingness to speak of this matter before my mother and before me. An unlucky accident has associated you in people's minds with Mr Luker. You have told me what scandal says of *him*. What does scandal say of *you*?'

Even at the eleventh hour, dear Mr Godfrey—always ready to return good for evil—tried to spare her.

'Don't ask me!' he said. 'It's better forgotten, Rachel—it is, indeed.'

'I *will* hear it!' she cried out fiercely, at the top of her voice.

'Tell her, Godfrey!' entreated my aunt. 'Nothing can do her such harm as your silence is doing now!'

Mr Godfrey's fine eyes filled with tears. He cast one last appealing look at her—and then he spoke the fatal words:

'If you will have it, Rachel—scandal says that the Moonstone is in pledge to Mr Luker, and that I am the man who has pawned it.'

She started to her feet with a scream. She looked backwards and forwards from Mr Godfrey to my aunt, and from my aunt to Mr Godfrey, in such a frantic manner that I really thought she had gone mad.

'Don't speak to me! Don't touch me!' she exclaimed, shrinking back from all of us (I declare like some hunted animal!) into a corner of the room. 'This is my fault! I must set it right. I have sacrificed myself—I had a right to do that, if I liked. But to let an innocent man be ruined; to keep a secret which destroys his character for life—Oh, good God, it's too horrible! I can't bear it!'

My aunt half rose from her chair, then suddenly sat down again. She called to me faintly, and pointed to a little phial in her work-box.

'Quick!' she whispered. 'Six drops, in water. Don't let Rachel see.'

Under other circumstances, I should have thought this strange. There was no time now to think—there was only time to give the medicine. Dear Mr Godfrey unconsciously assisted me in concealing what I was about from Rachel, by speaking composing words to her at the other end of the room.

'Indeed, indeed, you exaggerate,' I heard him say. 'My reputation stands too high to be destroyed by a miserable passing scandal like this. It will be all forgotten in another week. Let us never speak of it again.' She was perfectly inaccessible, even to such generosity as this. She went on from bad to worse.

'I must, and will, stop it,' she said. 'Mamma! hear what I say. Miss Clack! hear what I say. I know the hand that took the Moonstone. I know—' she laid a strong emphasis on the words; she stamped her foot in the rage that possessed her—'*I know that Godfrey Ablewhite is innocent.* Take me to the magistrate, Godfrey! Take me to the magistrate, and I will swear it!'

My aunt caught me by the hand, and whispered, 'Stand between us for a minute or two. Don't let Rachel see me.' I noticed a bluish tinge in her face which alarmed me. She saw I was startled. 'The drops will put me right in a minute or two,' she said, and so closed her eyes, and waited a little.

While this was going on, I heard dear Mr Godfrey still gently remonstrating.

'You must not appear publicly in such a thing as this,' he said. '*Your* reputation, dearest Rachel, is something too pure and too sacred to be trifled with.'

'*My* reputation!' She burst out laughing. 'Why, I am accused, Godfrey, as well as you. The best detective officer in England declares that I have stolen my own Diamond. Ask him what he thinks—and he will tell you that I have pledged the Moonstone to pay my private debts!' She stopped, ran across the room—and fell on her knees at her mother's feet. 'Oh mamma! mamma! mamma! I must be mad—mustn't I?—not to own the truth *now*?' She was too vehement to notice her mother's condition—she was on her feet again, and back with Mr Godfrey, in an instant. 'I won't let you—I won't let any innocent man—be accused and disgraced through my fault. If you won't take me before the magistrate, draw out a declaration of your innocence on paper, and I will sign it. Do as I tell you, Godfrey, or I'll write it to the newspapers I'll go out, and cry it in the streets!'

We will not say this was the language of remorse—we will say it was the language of hysterics. Indulgent Mr Godfrey pacified her by taking a sheet of paper, and drawing out the declaration. She signed it in a feverish hurry. 'Show it everywhere—don't think of *me*,' she said, as she gave it to him. 'I am afraid, Godfrey, I have not done you justice, hitherto, in my thoughts. You are more unselfish—you are a better man than I believed you to be. Come here when you can, and I will try and repair the wrong I have done you.'

She gave him her hand. Alas, for our fallen nature! Alas, for Mr Godfrey! He not only forgot himself so far as to kiss her hand—he adopted a gentleness of tone in answering her which, in such a case, was little better than a compromise with sin. 'I will come, dearest,' he said, 'on condition that we don't speak of this hateful subject again.' Never had I seen and heard our Christian hero to less advantage than on this occasion.

Before another word could be said by anybody, a thundering knock at the street door startled us all. I looked through the window, and saw the World, the Flesh, and the Devil waiting before the house—as typified in a carriage and horses, a powdered footman, and three of the most audaciously dressed women I ever beheld in my life.

Rachel started, and composed herself. She crossed the room to her mother.

'They have come to take me to the flower-show,' she said. 'One word, mamma, before I go. I have not distressed you, have I?'

(Is the bluntness of moral feeling which could ask such a question as that, after what had just happened, to be pitied or condemned? I like to lean towards mercy. Let us pity it.)

The drops had produced their effect. My poor aunt's complexion was like itself again. 'No, no, my dear,' she said. 'Go with your friends, and enjoy yourself.'

Her daughter stooped, and kissed her. I had left the window, and was near the door, when Rachel approached it to go out. Another change had come over her—she was in tears. I looked with interest at the momentary softening of that obdurate heart. I felt inclined to say a few earnest words. Alas! my well-meant sympathy only gave offence. 'What do you mean by pitying me?' she asked in a bitter whisper, as she passed to the door. 'Don't you see how happy I am? I'm going to the flower-show, Clack; and I've got the prettiest bonnet in London.' She completed the hollow mockery of that address by blowing me a kiss—and so left the room.

I wish I could describe in words the compassion I felt for this miserable and misguided girl. But I am almost as poorly provided with words as with money. Permit me to say—my heart bled for her.

Returning to my aunt's chair, I observed dear Mr Godfrey searching for something softly, here and there, in different parts of the room. Before I could offer to assist him he had found what he wanted. He came back to my aunt and me, with his declaration of innocence in one hand, and with a box of matches in the other.

'Dear aunt, a little conspiracy!' he said. 'Dear Miss Clack, a pious fraud which even your high moral rectitude will excuse! Will you leave Rachel to suppose that I accept the generous self-sacrifice which has signed this paper? And will you kindly bear witness that I destroy it in your presence, before I leave the house?' He kindled a match, and, lighting the paper, laid it to burn in a plate on the table. 'Any trifling inconvenience that I may suffer is as nothing,' he remarked, 'compared with the importance of preserving that pure name from the contaminating contact of the world. There! We have reduced it to a little harmless heap of ashes; and our dear impulsive Rachel will never know what we have done! How do you feel? My precious friends, how do you feel? For my poor part, I am as light-hearted as a boy!'

He beamed on us with his beautiful smile; he held out a hand to my aunt, and a hand to me. I was too deeply affected by his noble conduct to speak. I closed my eyes; I put his hand, in a kind of spiritual self-forgetfulness, to my lips. He murmured a soft remonstrance. Oh, the ecstasy, the pure, unearthly ecstasy of that moment! I sat—I hardly know on what—quite lost in my own exalted feelings. When I opened my eyes again, it was like descending from heaven to earth. There was nobody but my aunt in the room. He had gone.

I should like to stop here—I should like to close my narrative with the record of Mr Godfrey's noble conduct. Unhappily there is more, much more, which the unrelenting pecuniary pressure of Mr Blake's cheque obliges me to tell. The painful disclosures which were to reveal themselves in my presence, during that Tuesday's visit to Montagu Square, were not at an end yet.

Finding myself alone with Lady Verinder, I turned naturally to the subject of her health; touching delicately on the strange anxiety which she had shown to conceal her indisposition, and the remedy applied to it, from the observation of her daughter.

My aunt's reply greatly surprised me.

'Drusilla,' she said (if I have not already mentioned that my Christian name is Drusilla, permit me to mention it now), 'you are touching quite innocently, I know—on a very distressing subject.'

I rose immediately. Delicacy left me but one alternative—the alternative, after first making my apologies, of taking my leave. Lady Verinder stopped me, and insisted on my sitting down again.

'You have surprised a secret,' she said, 'which I had confided to my sister Mrs Ablewhite, and to my lawyer Mr Bruff, and to no one else. I can trust in their discretion; and I am sure, when I tell you the circumstances, I can trust in yours. Have you any pressing engagement, Drusilla? Or is your time your own this afternoon?'

It is needless to say that my time was entirely at my aunt's disposal.

'Keep me company then,' she said, 'for another hour. I have something to tell you which I believe you will be sorry to hear. And I shall have a service to ask of you afterwards, if you don't object to assist me.'

It is again needless to say that, so far from objecting, I was all eagerness to assist her.

'You can wait here,' she went on, 'till Mr Bruff comes at five. And you can be one of the witnesses, Drusilla, when I sign my Will.'

Her Will! I thought of the drops which I had seen in her work-box. I thought of the bluish tinge which I had noticed in her complexion. A light which was not of this world—a light shining prophetically from an unmade grave—dawned on my mind. My aunt's secret was a secret no longer—she was seriously ill.

CHAPTER III

THE signing of the Will was a much shorter matter than I had anticipated. It was hurried over, to my thinking, in indecent haste. Samuel, the footman, was sent for to act as second witness—and the pen was put at once into my aunt's hand. I felt strongly urged to say a few appropriate words on this solemn occasion. But Mr Bruff's manner convinced me that it was wisest to check the impulse while he was in the room. In less than two minutes it was all over—and Samuel (unbenefited by what I might have said) had gone downstairs again.

Mr Bruff folded up the Will, and then looked my way; apparently wondering whether I did or did not mean to leave him alone with my aunt. I had my mission of mercy to fulfil, and my bag of precious publications ready on my lap. He might as well have expected to move St. Paul's Cathedral by looking at it, as to move me. There was one merit about him (due no doubt to his worldly training) which I have no wish to deny. He was quick at seeing things. I appeared to produce almost the same impression on him which I had produced on the cabman. *He* too uttered a profane expression, and withdrew in a violent hurry, and left me mistress of the field.

As soon as we were alone, my aunt reclined on the sofa, and then alluded, with some appearance of confusion, to the subject of her Will.

'I hope you won't think yourself neglected, Drusilla,' she said. 'I mean to *give* you your little legacy, my dear, with my own hand.'

Here was a golden opportunity! I seized it on the spot. In other words, I instantly opened my bag, and took out the top publication. It proved to be an early edition—only the twenty-fifth—of the famous anonymous work (believed to be by precious Miss Bellows), entitled *The Serpent at Home*. The design of the book—with which the worldly reader may not be acquainted—is to show how the Evil One lies in wait for us in all the most apparently innocent actions of our daily lives. The chapters best adapted to female perusal are 'Satan in the Hair Brush'; 'Satan behind the Looking Glass'; 'Satan under the Tea Table'; 'Satan out of the Window'; and many others.

'Give your attention, dear aunt, to this precious book—and you will give me all I ask.' With those words, I handed it to her open, at a marked passage—one continuous burst of burning eloquence! Subject: Satan among the Sofa Cushions.

Poor Lady Verinder (reclining thoughtlessly on her own sofa cushions) glanced at the book, and handed it back to me looking more confused than ever.

'I'm afraid, Drusilla,' she said, 'I must wait till I am a little better, before I can read that. The doctor tells me that I am not so well today. He forbids me to see any strangers; and he orders me, if I read at all, only to read the lightest and the most amusing books. "Do nothing, Lady Verinder, to weary your head, or to quicken your pulse"—those were his last words, Drusilla, when he left me today.'

There was no help for it but to yield again—for the moment only, as before. Any open assertion of the infinitely superior importance of such a ministry as mine, compared with the ministry of the medical man, would only have provoked the doctor to practise on the human weakness of his patient, and to threaten to throw up the case. Happily, there are more ways than one of sowing the good seed, and few persons are better versed in those ways than myself.

'You might feel stronger, dear, in an hour or two,' I said. 'Or you might wake, tomorrow morning, with a sense of something wanting, and even this unpretending volume might be able to supply it. You will let me leave the book, aunt? The doctor can hardly object to that!'

I slipped it under the sofa cushions, half in, and half out, close by her handkerchief, and her smelling-bottle. Every time her hand searched for either of these, it would touch the book; and, sooner or later (who knows?) the book might touch *her*. After making this arrangement, I thought it wise to withdraw. 'Let me leave you to repose, dear aunt; I will call again tomorrow.' I looked accidentally towards the window as I said that. It was full of flowers, in boxes and pots. Lady Verinder was extravagantly fond of these perishable treasures, and had a habit of rising every now and then, and going to look at them and smell them. A new idea flashed across my mind. 'Oh! may I take a flower?' I said—and got to the window unsuspected, in that way. Instead of taking away a flower, I added one, in the shape of another book from my bag, which I left, to surprise my aunt, among the geraniums and roses. The happy thought followed, 'Why not do the same for her, poor dear, in every other room that she enters?' I immediately said good-bye; and, crossing the hall, slipped into the library. Samuel, coming up to let me out, and supposing I had gone, went downstairs again. On the library table I noticed two of the 'amusing books' which the infidel doctor had recommended. I instantly covered them from sight with two of my own precious publications. In the breakfast-room I found my aunt's favourite canary singing in his cage. She was always in the habit of feeding the bird herself. Some groundsel was strewed on a table which stood immediately under the cage. I put a book among the groundsel. In the drawing-room I found more cheering opportunities of emptying my bag. My aunt's favourite musical pieces were on the piano. I slipped in two more books among the music. I disposed of another in the back drawing-room, under some unfinished embroidery, which I knew to be of Lady Verinder's working. A third little room opened out of the back drawing-room, from which it was shut off by curtains instead of a door. My aunt's plain old-fashioned fan was on the chimney-piece. I opened my ninth book at a very special passage, and put the fan in as a marker, to keep the place. The question then came, whether I should go higher still, and try the bedroom floor—at the risk, undoubtedly, of being insulted, if the person with the cap-ribbons happened to be in the upper regions of the house, and to find me out. But oh, what of that? It is a poor Christian that is afraid of being insulted. I went upstairs, prepared to bear anything. All was silent and solitary—it was the servants' tea-time, I suppose. My aunt's room was in front. The miniature of my late dear uncle, Sir John, hung on the wall opposite the bed. It seemed to smile at me; it seemed to

say, 'Drusilla! deposit a book.' There were tables on either side
of my aunt's bed. She was a bad sleeper, and wanted, or thought
she wanted, many things at night. I put a book near the matches
on one side, and a book under the box of chocolate drops on
the other. Whether she wanted a light, or whether she wanted
a drop, there was a precious publication to meet her eye, or
to meet her hand, and to say with silent eloquence, in either
case, 'Come, try me! try me!' But one book was now left at the
bottom of my bag, and but one apartment was still unex-
plored—the bathroom, which opened out of the bedroom. I
peeped in; and the holy inner voice that never deceives, whispered to me, 'You have met her, Drusilla, everywhere else;
meet her at the bath, and the work is done.' I observed a
dressing-gown thrown across a chair. It had a pocket in it, and
in that pocket I put my last book. Can words express my
exquisite sense of duty done, when I had slipped out of the
house, unsuspected by any of them, and when I found myself
in the street with my empty bag under my arm? Oh, my worldly
friends, pursuing the phantom, Pleasure, through the guilty
mazes of Dissipation, how easy it is to be happy, if you will
only be good!

When I folded up my things that night—when I reflected
on the *true* riches which I had scattered with such a lavish
hand, from top to bottom of the house of my wealthy aunt—I
declare I felt as free from all anxiety as if I had been a child
again. I was so light-hearted that I sang a verse of the Evening
Hymn. I was so light-hearted that I fell asleep before I could
sing another. Quite like a child again! quite like a child again!

So I passed that blissful night. On rising the next morning,
how young I felt! I might add, how young I looked, if I were
capable of dwelling on the concerns of my own perishable body.
But I am not capable—and I add nothing.

Towards luncheon time—not for the sake of the creature-
comforts, but for the certainty of finding dear aunt—I put on
my bonnet to go to Montagu Square. Just as I was ready, the

maid at the lodgings in which I then lived looked in at the door, and said, 'Lady Verinder's servant, to see Miss Clack.'

I occupied the parlour-floor, at that period of my residence in London. The front parlour was my sitting-room. Very small, very low in the ceiling, very poorly furnished—but, oh, so neat! I looked into the passage to see which of Lady Verinder's servants had asked for me. It was the young footman, Samuel—a civil fresh-coloured person, with a teachable look and a very obliging manner. I had always felt a spiritual interest in Samuel, and a wish to try him with a few serious words. On this occasion, I invited him into my sitting-room.

He came in, with a large parcel under his arm. When he put the parcel down, it appeared to frighten him. 'My lady's love, Miss; and I was to say that you would find a letter inside.' Having given that message, the fresh-coloured young footman surprised me by looking as if he would have liked to run away.

I detained him to make a few kind inquiries. Could I see my aunt, if I called in Montagu Square? No; she had gone out for a drive. He ran as he said the words—and I found myself alone again, with some anxious thoughts to occupy me.

On finding myself alone in my room, I naturally turned my attention to the parcel which appeared to have so strangely intimidated the fresh-coloured young footman. Had my aunt sent me my promised legacy? and had it taken the form of cast-off clothes, or worn-out silver spoons, or unfashionable jewellery, or anything of that sort? Prepared to accept all, and to resent nothing, I opened the parcel—and what met my view? The twelve precious publications which I had scattered through the house, on the previous day; all returned to me by the doctor's orders! Well might the youthful Samuel shrink when he brought his parcel into my room! Well might he run when he had performed his miserable errand! As to my aunt's letter, it simply amounted, poor soul, to this—that she dare not disobey her medical man.

What was to be done now? With my training and my principles, I never had a moment's doubt.

In the case of my misguided aunt, the form which pious perseverance was next to take revealed itself to me plainly enough.

Preparation by clerical friends had failed, owing to Lady Verinder's own reluctance. Preparation by books had failed, owing to the doctor's infidel obstinacy. So be it! What was the next thing to try? The next thing to try was—Preparation by Little Notes. In other words, the books themselves having been sent back, select extracts from the books, copied by different hands, and all addressed as letters to my aunt, were, some to be sent by post, and some to be distributed about the house on the plan I had adopted on the previous day. As letters they would excite no suspicion; as letters they would be opened—and, once opened, might be read. Some of them I wrote myself. 'Dear aunt, may I ask your attention to a few lines?' etc. 'Dear aunt, I was reading last night, and I chanced on the following passage,' etc. Other letters were written for me by my valued fellow-workers, the sisterhood at the Mothers'-Small-Clothes. 'Dear madam, pardon the interest taken in you by a true, though humble, friend.' 'Dear madam, may a serious person surprise you by saying a few cheering words?' Using these and other similar forms of courteous appeal, we reintroduced all my precious passages under a form which not even the doctor's watchful materialism could suspect. Before the shades of evening had closed around us, I had a dozen awakening letters for my aunt, instead of a dozen awakening books. Six I made immediate arrangements for sending through the post, and six I kept in my pocket for personal distribution in the house the next day.

Soon after two o'clock I was again on the field of pious conflict, addressing more kind inquiries to Samuel at Lady Verinder's door.

The footman came to the door. His ruddy colour was all gone. He said, 'Please to come downstairs, Miss! My lady has fainted, and we can't bring her to again.'

In a moment more I was alone, and free to go downstairs in my turn, quite unobserved.

Mr Godfrey passed me in the hall, hurrying out, to fetch the doctor. 'Go in, and help them!' he said, pointing to the room. I found Rachel on her knees by the sofa, with her mother's head on her bosom. One look at my aunt's face (knowing what I knew) was enough to warn me of the dreadful truth. I kept my thoughts to myself till the doctor came in. It was not long before he arrived. He began by sending Rachel out of the room—and then he told the rest of us that Lady Verinder was no more. Serious persons, in search of proofs of hardened scepticism, may be interested in hearing that he showed no signs of remorse when he looked at me.

At a later hour I peeped into the breakfast-room, and the library. My aunt had died without opening one of the letters which I had addressed to her. I was so shocked at this, that it never occurred to me, until some days afterwards, that she had also died without giving me my little legacy.

SECOND NARRATIVE

Contributed by MATHEW BRUFF, *Solicitor,*
of Gray's Inn Square

CHAPTER I

My fair friend, Miss Clack, having laid down the pen, there are two reasons for my taking it up next, in my turn.

About a week or ten days after Lady Verinder died, one of my clerks entered the private room at my office, with a card in his hand, and informed me that a gentleman was below, who wanted to speak to me.

I looked at the card. There was a foreign name written on it, which has escaped my memory. It was followed by a line written in English at the bottom of the card, which I remember perfectly well:

'Recommended by Mr Septimus Luker.'

The audacity of a person in Mr Luker's position presuming to recommend anybody to me, took me so completely by surprise, that I sat silent for the moment, wondering whether my own eyes had not deceived me. The clerk, observing my bewilderment, favoured me with the result of his own observation of the stranger who was waiting downstairs.

'He is rather a remarkable-looking man, sir. So dark in the complexion that we all set him down in the office for an Indian, or something of that sort.'

Associating the clerk's idea with the line inscribed on the card in my hand, I thought it possible that the Moonstone might be at the bottom of Mr Luker's recommendation, and of the stranger's visit at my office. To the astonishment of my clerk, I at once decided on granting an interview to the gentleman below.

In justification of the highly unprofessional sacrifice to mere curiosity which I thus made, permit me to remind anybody who may read these lines, that no living person (in England, at any rate) can claim to have had such an intimate connexion with the romance of the Indian Diamond as mine has been. I was trusted with the secret of Colonel Herncastle's plan for escaping assassination. I received the Colonel's letters, periodically reporting himself a living man. I drew his Will, leaving the Moonstone to Miss Verinder. I persuaded his executor to act, on the chance that the jewel might prove to be a valuable acquisition to the family. And, lastly, I combated Mr Franklin Blake's scruples, and induced him to be the means of transporting the Diamond to Lady Verinder's house. If anyone can claim a prescriptive right of interest in the Moonstone, and in everything connected with it, I think it is hardly to be denied that I am the man.

The moment my mysterious client was shown in, I felt an inner conviction that I was in the presence of one of the three Indians—probably of the chief. He was carefully dressed in European costume. But his swarthy complexion, his long lithe figure, and his grave and graceful politeness of manner were enough to betray his Oriental origin to any intelligent eyes that looked at him.

I pointed to a chair, and begged to be informed of the nature of his business with me.

After first apologising—in an excellent selection of English words—for the liberty which he had taken in disturbing me, the Indian produced a small parcel, the outer covering of which was of cloth of gold. Removing this and a second wrapping of some silken fabric, he placed a little box, or casket, on my table, most beautifully and richly inlaid in jewels, on an ebony ground.

'I have come, sir,' he said, 'to ask you to lend me some money. And I leave this as an assurance to you that my debt will be paid back.'

I pointed to his card. 'And you apply to me,' I rejoined, 'at Mr Luker's recommendation?'

The Indian bowed.

'May I ask how it is that Mr Luker himself did not advance the money that you require?'

'Mr Luker informed me, sir, that he had no money to lend.'

'And so he recommended you to come to me?'

The Indian, in his turn, pointed to the card. 'It is written there,' he said.

Briefly answered, and thoroughly to the purpose! If the Moonstone had been in my possession, this Oriental gentleman would have murdered me, I am well aware, without a moment's hesitation. At the same time, and barring that slight drawback, I am bound to testify that he was the perfect model of a client. He might not have respected my life. But he did what none of my own countrymen had ever done, in all my experience of them—he respected my time.

'I am sorry,' I said, 'that you should have had the trouble of coming to me. Mr Luker is quite mistaken in sending you here. I am trusted, like other men in my profession, with money to lend. But I never lend it to strangers, and I never lend it on such a security as you have produced.'

Far from attempting, as other people would have done, to induce me to relax my own rules, the Indian only made me another bow, and wrapped up his box in its two coverings without a word of protest. He rose—this admirable assassin rose to go, the moment I had answered him!

'Will your condescension towards a stranger, excuse my asking one question,' he said, 'before I take my leave?'

I bowed on my side. Only one question at parting! The average in my experience was fifty.

'Supposing, sir, it had been possible (and customary) for

you to lend me the money,' he said, 'in what space of time would it have been possible (and customary) for me to pay it back?'

'According to the usual course pursued in this country,' I answered, 'you would have been entitled to pay the money back (if you liked) in one year's time from the date at which it was first advanced to you.'

The Indian made me a last bow, the lowest of all—and suddenly and softly walked out of the room.

It was done in a moment, in a noiseless, supple, cat-like way, which a little startled me, I own. As soon as I was composed enough to think, I arrived at one distinct conclusion in reference to the otherwise incomprehensible visitor who had favoured me with a call.

His face, voice, and manner—while I was in his company—were under such perfect control that they set all scrutiny at defiance. But he had given me one chance of looking under the smooth outer surface of him, for all that. He had not shown the slightest sign of attempting to fix anything that I had said to him in his mind, until I mentioned the time at which it was customary to permit the earliest repayment, on the part of a debtor, of money that had been advanced as a loan. When I gave him that piece of information, he looked me straight in the face, while I was speaking, for the first time. The inference I drew from this was—that he had a special purpose in asking me his last question, and a special interest in hearing my answer to it. The more carefully I reflected on what had passed between us, the more shrewdly I suspected the production of the casket, and the application for the loan, of having been mere formalities, designed to pave the way for the parting inquiry addressed to me.

I had satisfied myself of the correctness of this conclusion—and was trying to get on a step further, and penetrate the Indian's motives next—when a letter was brought to me, which proved to be from no less a person than Mr Septimus Luker himself. He asked my pardon in terms of sickening servility, and assured me that he could explain matters to my satisfaction, if I would honour him by consenting to a personal interview.

I made another unprofessional sacrifice to mere curiosity. I honoured him by making an appointment at my office, for the next day.

Mr Luker was, in every respect, such an inferior creature to the Indian—he was so vulgar, so ugly, so cringing, and so prosy—that he is quite unworthy of being reported, at any length, in these pages. The substance of what he had to tell me may be fairly stated as follows:

The day before I had received the visit of the Indian, Mr Luker had been favoured with a call from that accomplished gentleman. In spite of his European disguise, Mr Luker had instantly identified his visitor with the chief of the three Indians, who had formerly annoyed him by loitering about his house, and who had left him no alternative but to consult a magistrate. From this startling discovery he had rushed to the conclusion (naturally enough I own) that he must certainly be in the company of one of the three men, who had blindfolded him, gagged him, and robbed him of his banker's receipt. The result was that he became quite paralysed with terror, and that he firmly believed his last hour had come.

On his side, the Indian preserved the character of a perfect stranger. He produced the little casket, and made exactly the same application which he had afterwards made to me. As the speediest way of getting rid of him, Mr Luker had at once declared that he had no money. The Indian had thereupon asked to be informed of the best and safest person to apply to for the loan he wanted. Mr Luker had answered that the best and safest person, in such cases, was usually a respectable solicitor. Asked to name some individual of that character and profession, Mr Luker had mentioned me—for the one simple reason that, in the extremity of his terror, mine was the first name which occurred to him. 'The perspiration was pouring off me like rain, sir,' the wretched creature concluded. 'I didn't know what I was talking about. And I hope you'll look over it, Mr Bruff, sir, in consideration of my having been really and truly frightened out of my wits.'

I excused the fellow graciously enough. It was the readiest way of releasing myself from the sight of him. Before he left me, I detained him to make one inquiry.

Had the Indian said anything noticeable, at the moment of quitting Mr Luker's house?

Yes! The Indian had put precisely the same question to Mr Luker, at parting, which he had put to me; receiving of course, the same answer as the answer which I had given him.

What did it mean? Mr Luker's explanation gave me no assistance towards solving the problem. My own unaided ingenuity, consulted next, proved quite unequal to grapple with the difficulty. I had a dinner engagement that evening; and I went upstairs, in no very genial frame of mind, little suspecting that the way to my dressing-room and the way to discovery, meant, on this particular occasion, one and the same thing.

CHAPTER II

THE prominent personage among the guests at the dinner party I found to be Mr Murthwaite.

'If I am not mistaken, Mr Murthwaite,' I began, as soon as I had the opportunity of speaking to him alone, 'you were acquainted with the late Lady Verinder, and you took some interest in the strange succession of events which ended in the loss of the Moonstone?'

The eminent traveller did me the honour of waking up in an instant, and asking me who I was.

I informed him of my professional connection with the Herncastle family, not forgetting the curious position which I had occupied towards the Colonel and his Diamond in the bygone time.

Mr Murthwaite shifted round in his chair, so as to put the rest of the company behind him (Conservatives and Liberals alike), and concentrated his whole attention on plain Mr Bruff, of Gray's Inn Square.

'Have you heard anything lately of the Indians?' he asked.

'I have every reason to believe,' I answered, 'that one of them had an interview with me in my office yesterday.'

Mr Murthwaite was not an easy man to astonish; but that last answer of mine completely staggered him. I described what had happened to Mr Luker, and what had happened to myself, exactly as I have described it here. 'It is clear that the Indian's parting inquiry had an object,' I added. 'Why should he be so anxious to know the time at which a borrower of money is usually privileged to pay the money back?'

'Is it possible that you don't see his motive, Mr Bruff?'

'I am ashamed of my stupidity, Mr Murthwaite—but I certainly don't see it.'

The great traveller became quite interested in sounding the immense vacuity of my dullness to its lowest depths.

'Let me ask you one question,' he said. 'In what position does the conspiracy to seize the Moonstone now stand?'

'I can't say,' I answered. 'The Indian plot is a mystery to me.'

'The Indian plot, Mr Bruff, can only be a mystery to you, because you have never seriously examined it. Shall we run over it together, from the time when you drew Colonel Herncastle's Will, to the time when the Indian called at your office? In your position, it may be of very serious importance to the interests of Miss Verinder, that you should be able to take a clear view of this matter in case of need. Tell me, bearing that in mind, whether you will penetrate the Indian's motive for yourself? Or whether you wish me to save you the trouble of making any inquiry into it?'

It is needless to say that I thoroughly appreciated the practical purpose which I now saw that he had in view, and that the first of the two alternatives was the alternative I chose.

'Very good,' said Mr Murthwaite. 'We will take the question of the ages of the three Indians first. I can testify that they all look much about the same age—and you can decide for yourself, whether the man whom you saw was, or was not, in the prime of life. Not forty, you think? My idea too. We will say not forty. Now look back to the time when Colonel Herncastle came to England, and when you were concerned in the plan he adopted to preserve his life. I don't want you to count the years. I will only say, it is clear that these present Indians, at their age, must be the successors of three other Indians (high caste Brahmins all of them, Mr Bruff, when they left their native country!) who followed the Colonel to these shores. Very well. These present men of ours have succeeded to the men who were here before them. If they had only done that, the matter would not have been worth inquiring into. But they have done more. They have succeeded to the organisation which their predecessors established in this country. Don't start! The organisation is a very trumpery affair, according to our ideas, I have no doubt. I should reckon it up as including the command of money; the services, when needed, of that shady sort of Englishman, who lives in the byways of foreign life in London; and, lastly, the secret sympathy of such few men of their own country, and (formerly, at least) of their own religion, as happen to be employed in ministering to some of the multitudinous wants of this great city. Nothing very formidable, as you see! But worth notice at starting, because we *may* find occasion to refer to this modest little Indian organisation as we go on. Having now cleared the ground, I am going to ask you a question; and I expect your experience to answer it. What was the event which gave the Indians their first chance of seizing the Diamond?'

I understood the allusion to my experience.

'The first chance they got,' I replied, 'was clearly offered to them by Colonel Herncastle's death. They would be aware of his death, I suppose, as a matter of course?'

'As a matter of course. And his death, as you say, gave them their first chance. Up to that time the Moonstone was safe in the strong-room of the bank. You drew the Colonel's Will leaving his jewel to his niece; and the Will was proved in the usual way. As a lawyer, you can be at no loss to know what course the Indians would take (under English advice) after *that*.'

'They would provide themselves with a copy of the Will from Doctors' Commons,' I said.

'Exactly. One or other of those shady Englishmen to whom I have alluded, would get them the copy you have described. That copy would inform them that the Moonstone was bequeathed to the daughter of Lady Verinder, and that Mr Blake the elder, or some person appointed by him, was to place it in her hands. You will agree with me that the necessary information about persons in the position of Lady Verinder and Mr Blake, would be perfectly easy information to obtain. The one difficulty for the Indians would be to decide whether they should make their attempt on the Diamond when it was in course of removal from the keeping of the bank, or whether they should wait until it was taken down to Yorkshire to Lady Verinder's house. The second way would be manifestly the safest way—and there you have the explanation of the appearance of the Indians at Frizinghall, disguised as jugglers, and waiting their time. In London, it is needless to say, they had their organisation at their disposal to keep them informed of events. Two men would do it. One to follow anybody who went from Mr Blake's house to the bank. And one to treat the lower menservants with beer, and to hear the news of the house. These commonplace precautions would readily inform them that Mr Franklin Blake had been to the bank, and that Mr Franklin Blake was the only person in the house who was going to visit Lady Verinder. What actually followed upon that discovery, you remember, no doubt, quite as correctly as I do.'

I remembered that Franklin Blake had detected one of the spies in the street—that he had, in consequence, advanced the time of his arrival in Yorkshire by some hours—and that (thanks to old Betteredge's excellent advice) he had lodged the Diamond in the bank at Frizinghall, before the Indians were so much as prepared to see him in the neighbourhood. All perfectly clear so far. But the Indians being ignorant of the precautions thus taken, how was it that they had made no attempt on Lady Verinder's house (in which they must have supposed the Diamond to be) through the whole of the interval that elapsed before Rachel's birthday?

In putting this difficulty to Mr Murthwaite, I thought it right to add that I had heard of the little boy, and the drop of ink, and the rest of it, and that any explanation based on the theory of clairvoyance was an explanation which would carry no conviction whatever with it, to *my* mind.

'Nor to mine either,' said Mr Murthwaite. 'The clairvoyance in this case is simply a development of the romantic side of the Indian character. It would be refreshment and an encouragement to those men—quite inconceivable, I grant you, to the English mind—to surround their wearisome and perilous errand in this country with a certain halo of the marvellous and the supernatural. Their boy is unquestionably a sensitive subject to the mesmeric influence—and, under that influence, he has no doubt reflected what was already in the mind of the person mesmerising him. I have tested the theory of clairvoyance—and I have never found the manifestations get beyond that point. The Indians don't investigate the matter in this way; the Indians look upon their boy as a Seer of things invisible to their eyes—and, I repeat, in that marvel they find the source of a new interest in the purpose that unites them. I only notice this as offering a curious view of human character, which must be quite new to you. We have nothing whatever to do with clairvoyance, or with mesmerism, or with anything else that is hard of belief to a practical man, in the inquiry that we are now pursuing. My object in following the Indian plot, step by step, is to trace results back, by rational means, to natural causes. Have I succeeded to your satisfaction so far?'

'Not a doubt of it, Mr Murthwaite! I am waiting, however, with some anxiety, to hear the rational explanation of the difficulty which I have just had the honour of submitting to you.'

Mr Murthwaite smiled. 'It's the easiest difficulty to deal with of all,' he said. 'Permit me to begin by admitting your statement of the case as a perfectly correct one. The Indians were undoubtedly not aware of what Mr Franklin Blake had done with the Diamond—for we find them making their first mistake, on the first night of Mr Blake's arrival at his aunt's house.'

'Their first mistake?' I repeated.

'Certainly! The mistake of allowing themselves to be surprised, lurking about the terrace at night, by Gabriel Betteredge. However, they had the merit of seeing for themselves that they had taken a false step—for, as you say, again, with plenty of time at their disposal, they never came near the house for weeks afterwards.'

'Why, Mr Murthwaite? That's what I want to know! Why?'

'Because no Indian, Mr Bruff, ever runs an unnecessary risk. The clause you drew in Colonel Herncastle's Will, informed them (didn't it?) that the Moonstone was to pass absolutely into Miss Verinder's possession on her birthday. Very well. Tell me which was the safest course for men in their position? To make their attempt on the Diamond while it was under the control of Mr Franklin Blake, who had shown already that he could suspect and outwit them? Or to wait till the Diamond was at the disposal of a young girl, who would innocently delight in wearing the magnificent jewel at every possible opportunity? Perhaps you want a proof that my theory is correct? Take the conduct of the Indians themselves as the proof. They appeared at the house, after waiting all those weeks, on Miss Verinder's birthday; and they were rewarded for the patient accuracy of their calculations by seeing the Moonstone in the bosom of her dress! When I heard the story of the Colonel and the Diamond, later in the evening, I felt so sure about the risk Mr Franklin Blake had run (they would have certainly attacked him, if he had not happened to ride back to Lady Verinder's in the company of other people); and I was so strongly convinced of the worse risks still, in store for Miss Verinder, that I recommended following the Colonel's plan, and destroying the identity of the gem by having it cut into separate stones. How its extraordinary disappearance that night, made my advice useless, and utterly defeated the Hindoo plot—and how all further action on the part of the Indians was paralysed the next day by their confinement in prison as rogues and vagabonds— you know as well as I do. The first act in the conspiracy closes there. Before we go on to the second, may I ask whether I have met your difficulty, with an explanation which is satisfactory to the mind of a practical man?'

It was impossible to deny that he had met my difficulty fairly; thanks to his superior knowledge of the Indian character—and thanks to his not having had hundreds of other Wills to think of since Colonel Herncastle's time!

'So far, so good,' resumed Mr Murthwaite. 'The first chance the Indians had of seizing the Diamond was a chance lost, on the day when they were committed to the prison at Frizinghall. When did the second chance offer itself? The second chance offered itself—as I am in a condition to prove—while they were still in confinement.'

He took out his pocket-book, and opened it at a particular leaf, before he went on.

'I was staying,' he resumed, 'with some friends at Frizinghall, at the time. A day or two before the Indians were set free (on a Monday, I think), the governor of the prison came to me with a letter. It had been left for the Indians by one Mrs Macann, of whom they had hired the lodging in which they lived; and it had been delivered at Mrs Macann's door, in ordinary course of post, on the previous morning. The prison authorities had noticed that the postmark was "Lambeth", and that the address on the outside, though expressed in correct English, was, in form, oddly at variance with the customary method of directing a letter. On opening it, they had found the contents to be written in a foreign language, which they rightly guessed at as Hindustani. Their object in coming to me was, of course, to have the letter translated to them. I took a copy in my pocket-book of the original, and of my translation—and there they are at your service.'

He handed me the open pocket-book. The address on the letter was the first thing copied. It was all written in one paragraph, without any attempt at punctuation, thus: 'To the three Indian men living with the lady called Macann at Frizinghall in Yorkshire.' The Hindoo characters followed; and the English translation appeared at the end, expressed in these mysterious words:

'In the name of the Regent of the Night, whose seat is on the Antelope, whose arms embrace the four corners of the earth.

'Brothers, turn your faces to the south, and come to me in the street of many noises, which leads down to the muddy river.

'The reason is this.

'My own eyes have seen it.'

There the letter ended, without either date or signature. I handed it back to Mr Murthwaite, and owned that this curious specimen of Hindoo correspondence rather puzzled me.

'I can explain the first sentence to you,' he said; 'and the conduct of the Indians themselves will explain the rest. The god of the moon is represented, in the Hindoo mythology, as a four-armed deity, seated on an antelope; and one of his titles is the regent of the night. Here, then, to begin with, is something which looks suspiciously like an indirect reference to the Moonstone. Now, let us see what the Indians did, after the prison authorities had allowed them to receive their letter. On the very day when they were set free they went at once to the railway station, and took their places in the first train that started for London. We all thought it a pity at Frizinghall that their proceedings were not privately watched. But, after Lady Verinder had dismissed the police officer, and had stopped all further inquiry into the loss of the Diamond, no one else could presume to stir in the matter. The Indians were free to go to London, and to London they went. What was the next news we heard of them, Mr Bruff?'

'They were annoying Mr Luker,' I answered, 'by loitering about the house at Lambeth.'

'Did you read the report of Mr Luker's application to the magistrate?'

'Yes.'

'In the course of his statement he referred, if you remember, to a foreign workman in his employment, whom he had just dismissed on suspicion of attempted theft, and whom he also distrusted as possibly acting in collusion with the Indians who had annoyed him. The inference is pretty plain, Mr Bruff, as to who wrote that letter which puzzled you just now, and as to which of Mr Luker's Oriental treasures the workman had attempted to steal.'

The inference (as I hastened to acknowledge) was too plain to need being pointed out. I had never doubted that the Moonstone had found its way into Mr Luker's hands, at the time Mr Murthwaite alluded to. My only question had been, How had the Indians discovered the circumstance? This question (the most difficult to deal with of all, as I had thought) had now received its answer, like the rest. Lawyer as I was, I began to feel that I might trust Mr Murthwaite to lead me blindfold through the last windings of the labyrinth, along which he had guided me thus far. I paid him the compliment of telling him this, and found my little concession very graciously received.

'You shall give me a piece of information in your turn before we go on,' he said. 'Somebody must have taken the Moonstone from Yorkshire to London. And somebody must have raised money on it, or it would never have been in Mr Luker's possession. Has there been any discovery made of who that person was?'

'None that I know of.'

'There was a story (was there not?) about Mr Godfrey Ablewhite. I am told he is an eminent philanthropist—which is decidedly against him, to begin with.'

I heartily agreed in this with Mr Murthwaite. At the same time, I felt bound to inform him (without, it is needless to say, mentioning Miss Verinder's name) that Mr Godfrey Ablewhite had been cleared of all suspicion, on evidence which I could answer for as entirely beyond dispute.

'Very well,' said Mr Murthwaite, quietly, 'let us leave it to time to clear the matter up. In the meanwhile, Mr Bruff, we must get back again to the Indians, on your account. Their journey to London simply ended in their becoming the victims of another defeat. The loss of their second chance of seizing the Diamond is mainly attributable, as I think, to the cunning and foresight of Mr Luker—who doesn't stand at the top of the prosperous and ancient profession of usury for nothing! By the prompt dismissal of the man in his employment, he deprived the Indians of the assistance which their confederate would have rendered them in getting into the house. By the prompt transport of the Moonstone to his banker's, he took the conspirators by surprise before they were prepared with a new plan for robbing him. How the Indians, in this latter case, suspected what he had done, and how they contrived to possess themselves of his banker's receipt, are events too recent to need dwelling on. Let it be enough to say that they know the Moonstone to be once more out of their reach; deposited (under the general description of "a valuable of great price") in a banker's strong room. Now, Mr Bruff, what is their third chance of seizing the Diamond? And when will it come?'

As the question passed his lips, I penetrated the motive of the Indian's visit to my office at last!

'I see it!' I exclaimed. 'The Indians take it for granted, as we do, that the Moonstone has been pledged; and they want to be certainly informed of the earliest period at which the pledge can be redeemed—because that will be the earliest period at which the Diamond can be removed from the safe keeping of the bank!'

'I told you you would find it out for yourself, Mr Bruff, if I only gave you a fair chance. In a year from the time when the Moonstone was pledged, the Indians will be on the watch for their third chance. Mr Luker's own lips have told them how long they will have to wait, and your respectable authority has satisfied them that Mr Luker has spoken the truth. When do we suppose, at a rough guess, that the Diamond found its way into the money-lender's hands?'

'Towards the end of last June,' I answered, 'as well as I can reckon it.'

'And we are now in the year 'forty-eight. Very good. If the unknown person who has pledged the Moonstone can redeem it in a year, the jewel will be in that person's possession again at the end of June, 'forty-nine. I shall be thousands of miles from England and English news at that date. But it may be worth *your* while to take a note of it, and to arrange to be in London at the time.'

'You think something serious will happen?' I said.

'I think I shall be safer,' he answered, 'among the fiercest fanatics of Central Asia than I should be if I crossed the door of the bank with the Moonstone in my pocket. The Indians have been defeated twice running, Mr Bruff. It's my firm belief that they won't be defeated a third time.'

Those were the last words he said on the subject. The coffee came in; the guests rose, and dispersed themselves about the room; and we joined the ladies of the dinner-party upstairs.

I made a note of the date, and it may not be amiss if I close my narrative by repeating that note here:

June, 'forty-nine. Expect news of the Indians towards the end of the month.

And that done, I hand the pen, which I have now no further claim to use, to the writer who follows me next.

THIRD NARRATIVE

Contributed by FRANKLIN BLAKE

CHAPTER I

In the spring of the year eighteen hundred and forty-nine I was wandering in the East, and had then recently altered the travelling plans which I had laid out some months before, and which I had communicated to my lawyer and my banker in London.

This change made it necessary for me to send one of my servants to obtain my letters and remittances from the English consul in a certain city, which was no longer included as one of my resting-places in my new travelling scheme. The man was to join me again at an appointed place and time. An accident, for which he was not responsible, delayed him on his errand. For a week I and my people waited, encamped on the borders of a desert. At the end of that time the missing man made his appearance, with the money and the letters, at the entrance of my tent.

'I am afraid I bring you bad news, sir,' he said, and pointed to one of the letters, which had a mourning border round it, and the address on which was in the handwriting of Mr Bruff.

I know nothing, in a case of this kind, so unendurable as suspense. The letter with the mourning border was the letter that I opened first.

It informed me that my father was dead, and that I was heir to his great fortune. The wealth which had thus fallen into my hands brought its responsibilities with it, and Mr Bruff entreated me to lose no time in returning to England.

By daybreak the next morning, I was on my way back to my own country.

I went abroad, resolved—if change and absence could help me—to forget her. It is, I am persuaded, no true view of human nature which denies that change and absence *do* help a man under these circumstances; they force his attention away from the exclusive contemplation of his own sorrow. I never forgot her; but the pang of remembrance lost its worst bitterness, little by little, as time, distance, and novelty interposed themselves more and more effectually between Rachel and me.

On the other hand, it is no less certain that, with the act of turning homeward, the remedy which had gained its ground so steadily, began now, just as steadily, to drop back. The nearer I drew to the country which she inhabited, and to the prospect of seeing her again, the more irresistibly her influence began to recover its hold on me. On leaving England she was the last person in the world whose name I would have suffered to pass my lips. On returning to England, she was the first person I inquired after, when Mr Bruff and I met again.

She was living under the care of a widowed sister of the late Sir John Verinder—one Mrs Merridew—whom her mother's executors had requested to act as guardian, and who had accepted the proposal. They were reported to me as getting on together admirably well, and as being now established, for the season, in Mrs Merridew's house in Portland Place.

Half an hour after receiving this information, I was on my way to Portland Place—without having had the courage to own it to Mr Bruff!

The man who answered the door was not sure whether Miss Verinder was at home or not. I sent him upstairs with my card, as the speediest way of setting the question at rest. The man came down again with an impenetrable face, and informed me that Miss Verinder was out.

I might have suspected other people of purposely denying

themselves to me. But it was impossible to suspect Rachel. I left word that I would call again at six o'clock that evening.

At six o'clock I was informed for the second time that Miss Verinder was not at home. Had any message been left for me. No message had been left for me. Had Miss Verinder not received my card? The servant begged my pardon—Miss Verinder *had* received it.

The inference was too plain to be resisted. Rachel declined to see me.

On my side, I declined to be treated in this way, without making an attempt, at least, to discover a reason for it. I sent up my name to Mrs Merridew, and requested her to favour me with a personal interview at any hour which it might be most convenient to her to name.

Mrs Merridew made no difficulty about receiving me at once. I was shown into a comfortable little sitting-room, and found myself in the presence of a comfortable little elderly lady. She was so good as to feel great regret and much surprise, entirely on my account. She was at the same time, however, not in a position to offer me any explanation, or to press Rachel on a matter which appeared to relate to a question of private feeling alone. This was said over and over again, with a polite patience that nothing could tire; and this was all I gained by applying to Mrs Merridew.

My last chance was to write to Rachel. My servant took a letter to her the next day, with strict instructions to wait for an answer.

The answer came back, literally in one sentence.

'Miss Verinder begs to decline entering into any correspondence with Mr Franklin Blake.'

Fond as I was of her, I felt indignantly the insult offered to me in that reply. Mr Bruff came in to speak to me on business, before I had recovered possession of myself. I dismissed the business on the spot, and laid the whole case before him. He proved to be as incapable of enlightening me as Mrs Merridew herself. I asked him if any slander had been spoken of me in

Rachel's hearing. Mr Bruff was not aware of any slander of which I was the object. Had she referred to me in any way while she was staying under Mr Bruff's roof? Never. Had she not so much as asked, during all my long absence, whether I was living or dead? No such question had ever passed her lips. I took out of my pocket-book the letter which poor Lady Verinder had written to me from Frizinghall, on the day when I left her house in Yorkshire. And I pointed Mr Bruff's attention to these two sentences in it:

'The valuable assistance which you rendered to the inquiry after the lost jewel is still an unpardoned offence, in the present dreadful state of Rachel's mind. Moving blindfold in this matter, you have added to the burden of anxiety which she has had to bear, by innocently threatening her secret with discovery through your exertions.'

'Is it possible,' I asked, 'that the feeling towards me which is there described, is as bitter as ever against me now?'

Mr Bruff looked unaffectedly distressed.

'If you insist on an answer,' he said, 'I own I can place no other interpretation on her conduct than that.'

I rang the bell, and directed my servant to pack my portmanteau, and to send out for a railway guide. Mr Bruff asked, in astonishment, what I was going to do.

'I am going to Yorkshire,' I answered, 'by the next train.'

'May I ask for what purpose?'

'Mr Bruff, the assistance I innocently rendered to the inquiry after the Diamond was an unpardoned offence, in Rachel's mind, nearly a year since; and it remains an unpardoned offence still. I won't accept that position! I am determined to find out the secret of her silence towards her mother, and her enmity towards *me*. If time, pains, and money can do it, I will lay my hand on the thief who took the Moonstone!'

The worthy old gentleman attempted to remonstrate—to induce me to listen to reason—to do his duty towards me, in short. I was deaf to everything that he could urge. No earthly consideration would, at that moment, have shaken the resolution that was in me.

'I shall take up the inquiry again,' I went on, 'at the point where I dropped it; and I shall follow it onwards, step by step, till I come to the present time. There are missing links in the evidence, as *I* left it, which Gabriel Betteredge can supply, and to Gabriel Betteredge I go!'

Towards sunset that evening I stood again on the well-remembered terrace, and looked once more at the peaceful old country house. The gardener was the first person whom I saw in the deserted grounds. He had left Betteredge, an hour since, sunning himself in the customary corner of the back yard. I knew it well; and I said I would go and seek him myself.

I walked round by the familiar paths and passages, and looked in at the open gate of the yard.

There he was—the dear old friend of the happy days that were never to come again—there he was in the old corner, on the old beehive chair, with his pipe in his mouth, and his *Robinson Crusoe* on his lap, and his two friends, the dogs, dozing on either side of him! In the position in which I stood, my shadow was projected in front of me by the last slanting rays of the sun. Either the dogs saw it, or their keen scent informed them of my approach; they started up with a growl. Starting in his turn, the old man quieted them by a word, and then shaded his failing eyes with his hand, and looked inquiringly at the figure at the gate.

My own eyes were full of tears. I was obliged to wait a moment before I could trust myself to speak to him.

CHAPTER II

'BETTEREDGE!' I said, pointing to the well-remembered book on his knee, 'has *Robinson Crusoe* informed you, this evening, that you might expect to see Franklin Blake?'

'By the lord Harry, Mr Franklin!' cried the old man, 'that's exactly what *Robinson Crusoe* has done!'

He struggled to his feet with my assistance, and stood for a moment, looking backwards and forwards between *Robinson Crusoe* and me, apparently at a loss to discover which of us had surprised him most. The verdict ended in favour of the book. Holding it open before him in both hands, he surveyed the wonderful volume with a stare of unutterable anticipation—as if he expected to see Robinson Crusoe himself walk out of the pages, and favour us with a personal interview.

'Here's the bit, Mr Franklin!' he said, as soon as he had recovered the use of his speech. 'As I live by bread, sir, here's the bit I was reading, the moment before you came in! Page one hundred and fifty-six as follows: "I stood like one Thunderstruck, or as if I had seen an Apparition." If that isn't as much as to say: "Expect the sudden appearance of Mr Franklin Blake"—there's no meaning in the English language!' said Betteredge, closing the book with a bang, and getting one of his hands free at last to take the hand which I offered him.

I had expected him, naturally enough under the circumstances, to overwhelm me with questions. But no—the hospitable impulse was the uppermost impulse in the old servant's mind, when a member of the family appeared (no matter how!) as a visitor at the house.

'Walk in, Mr Franklin,' he said, opening the door behind him, with his quaint old-fashioned bow. 'I'll ask what brings you here afterwards—I must make you comfortable first. There have been sad changes, since you went away. The house is shut up, and the servants are gone. Never mind that! I'll cook your dinner; and the gardener's wife will make your bed—and if there's a bottle of our famous Latour claret left in the cellar, down your throat, Mr Franklin, that bottle shall go. I bid you welcome, sir! I bid you heartily welcome!' said the poor old fellow, fighting manfully against the gloom of the deserted house, and receiving me with the sociable and courteous attention of the bygone time.

It vexed me to disappoint him. But the house was Rachel's house, now. Could I eat in it, or sleep in it, after what had happened in London? The commonest sense of self-respect forbade me—properly forbade me—to cross the threshold.

I took Betteredge by the arm, and led him out into the garden. There was no help for it. I was obliged to tell him the truth. Between his attachment to Rachel, and his attachment to me, he was sorely puzzled and distressed at the turn things had taken. His opinion, when he expressed it, was given in his usual downright manner, and was agreeably redolent of the most positive philosophy I know—the philosophy of the Betteredge school.

'I am heartily sorry for this,' he said. 'I had hoped, Mr Franklin, to hear that things were all smooth and pleasant again between you and Miss Rachel. If you must have your own way, sir,' he continued, after a moment's reflection, 'there is no need to go to Frizinghall tonight for a bed. It's to be had nearer than that. There's Hotherstone's Farm, barely two miles from here. You can hardly object to *that* on Miss Rachel's account,' the old man added slyly. 'Hotherstone lives, Mr Franklin, on his own freehold.'

I remembered the place the moment Betteredge mentioned it. The farm-house stood in a sheltered inland valley, on the banks of the prettiest stream in that part of Yorkshire: and the farmer had a spare bedroom and parlour, which he was accustomed to let to artists, anglers, and tourists in general. A more agreeable place of abode, during my stay in the neighbourhood, I could not have wished to find.

'Are the rooms to let?' I inquired.

'Mrs Hotherstone herself, sir, asked for my good word to recommend the rooms, yesterday.'

'I'll take them, Betteredge, with the greatest pleasure.'

'If it's no secret, sir,' said Betteredge suddenly, 'I'm burning to know what's brought you down here, if you please, in this sudden way.'

'What brought me here before?' I asked.

'The Moonstone, Mr Franklin. But what brings you now, sir?'

'The Moonstone again, Betteredge.'

Betteredge's last-left obscurity vanished at that.

'If I am doing wrong to help you, Mr Franklin,' he exclaimed, 'all I can say is—I am as innocent of seeing it as the babe unborn! I can put you on the road to discovery, if you can only go on by yourself. You remember that poor girl of ours—Rosanna Spearman?'

'Of course!'

'You always thought she had some sort of confession in regard to this matter of the Moonstone, which she wanted to make to you?'

'I certainly couldn't account for her strange conduct in any other way.'

'You may set that doubt at rest, Mr Franklin, whenever you please.'

It was my turn to come to a standstill now. I tried vainly, in the gathering darkness, to see his face. In the surprise of the moment, I asked a little impatiently what he meant.

'Steady, sir!' proceeded Betteredge. 'I mean what I say. Rosanna Spearman left a sealed letter behind her—a letter addressed to *you.*'

'Where is it?'

'In the possession of a friend of hers, at Cobb's Hole. You must have heard tell, when you were here last, sir, of Limping Lucy—a lame girl with a crutch.'

'The fisherman's daughter?'

'The same, Mr Franklin.'

'Why wasn't the letter forwarded to me?'

'Limping Lucy has a will of her own, sir. She wouldn't give it into any hands but yours. And you had left England before I could write to you.'

'Let's go back, Betteredge, and get it at once!'

'Too late, sir, tonight. They're great savers of candles along our coast; and they go to bed early at Cobb's Hole.'

'Nonsense! We might get there in half an hour.'

'*You* might, sir. And when you did get there, you would find the door locked.' He pointed to a light, glimmering below us; and, at the same moment, I heard through the stillness of the evening the bubbling of a stream. "There's the Farm, Mr Franklin! Make yourself comfortable for tonight, and come to me tomorrow morning—if you'll be so kind?"'

'You will go with me to the fisherman's cottage?'

'Yes, sir.'

'Early?'

'As early, Mr Franklin, as you like.'

We descended the path that led to the Farm.

CHAPTER III

I HAVE only the most indistinct recollection of what happened at Hotherstone's Farm.

It had been arranged over-night with Betteredge, that I was to call for him, on our way to Cobb's Hole, as early as I liked—which, interpreted by my impatience to get possession of the letter, meant as early as I could. Without waiting for breakfast at the Farm, I took a crust of bread in my hand, and set forth, in some doubt whether I should not surprise the excellent Betteredge in his bed. To my great relief he proved to be quite as excited about the coming event as I was. I found him ready, and waiting for me, with his stick in his hand.

'How are you this morning, Betteredge?'

'Very poorly, sir.'

'Sorry to hear it. What do you complain of?'

'I complain of a new disease, Mr Franklin, of my own inventing. I don't want to alarm you, but you're certain to catch it before the morning is out.'

'The devil I am!'

'Do you feel an uncomfortable heat at the pit of your stomach, sir? And a nasty thumping at the top of your head? Ah! not yet? It will lay hold of you at Cobb's Hole, Mr Franklin. I call it the detective-fever; and I first caught it in the company of Sergeant Cuff.'

'Aye! aye! and the cure in this instance is to open Rosanna Spearman's letter, I suppose? Come along, and let's get it.'

Early as it was, we found the fisherman's wife astir in her kitchen. On my presentation by Betteredge, good Mrs Yolland performed a social ceremony, strictly reserved (as I afterwards learnt) for strangers of distinction. She put a bottle of Dutch gin and a couple of clean pipes on the table, and opened the conversation by saying, 'What news from London, sir?'

Before I could find an answer to this immensely comprehensive question, an apparition advanced towards me, out of a dark corner of the kitchen. A wan, wild, haggard girl, with remarkably beautiful hair, and with a fierce keenness in her eyes, came limping up on a crutch to the table at which I was sitting, and looked at me as if I was an object of mingled interest and horror, which it quite fascinated her to see.

'Mr Betteredge,' she said, without taking her eyes off me, 'mention his name again, if you please.'

'This gentleman's name,' answered Betteredge (with a strong emphasis on *gentleman*), 'is Mr Franklin Blake.'

The girl turned her back on me, and suddenly left the room. Good Mrs Yolland—as I believe—made some apologies for her daughter's odd behaviour, and Betteredge (probably) translated them into polite English. I speak of this in complete uncertainty. My attention was absorbed in following the sound of the girl's crutch. Thump-thump, up the wooden stairs; thump-thump across the room above our heads; thump-thump down the stairs again—and there stood the apparition at the open door, with a letter in its hand, beckoning me out!

I left more apologies in course of delivery behind me, and

followed this strange creature—limping on before me, faster and faster—down the slope of the beach. She led me behind some boats, out of sight and hearing of the few people in the fishing-village, and then stopped, and faced me for the first time.

'Stand there,' she said, 'I want to look at you.'

There was no mistaking the expression on her face. I inspired her with the strongest emotions of abhorrence and disgust. Let me not be vain enough to say that no woman had ever looked at me in this manner before. I will only venture on the more modest assertion that no woman had ever let me perceive it yet. There is a limit to the length of the inspection which a man can endure, under certain circumstances. I attempted to direct Limping Lucy's attention to some less revolting object than my face.

'I think you have got a letter to give me,' I began. 'Is it the letter there, in your hand?'

'Say that again,' was the only answer I received.

I repeated the words, like a good child learning its lesson.

'No,' said the girl, speaking to herself, but keeping her eyes still mercilessly fixed on me. 'I can't find out what she saw in his face. I can't guess what she heard in his voice.' She suddenly looked away from me, and rested her head wearily on the top of her crutch. 'Oh, my poor dear!' she said, in the first soft tones which had fallen from her, in my hearing. 'Oh, my lost darling! what could you see in this man?' She lifted her head again fiercely, and looked at me once more. 'Can you eat and drink?' she asked.

I did my best to preserve my gravity, and answered, 'Yes.'

'Can you sleep?'

'Yes.'

'When you see a poor girl in service, do you feel no remorse?'

'Certainly not. Why should I?'

She abruptly thrust the letter (as the phrase is) into my face. 'Take it!' she exclaimed furiously. 'I never set eyes on you before. God Almighty forbid I should ever set eyes on you again.'

With those parting words she limped away from me at the top of her speed. The one interpretation that I could put on her conduct has, no doubt, been anticipated by everybody. I could only suppose that she was mad.

Having reached that inevitable conclusion, I turned to the more interesting object of investigation which was presented to me by Rosanna Spearman's letter. The address was written as follows: '*For Franklin Blake, Esq. To be given into his own hands (and not to be trusted to any one else), by Lucy Yolland.*'

I broke the seal. The envelope contained a letter: and this, in its turn, contained a slip of paper. I read the letter first:

'Sir,—If you are curious to know the meaning of my behaviour to you, whilst you were staying in the house of my mistress, Lady Verinder, do what you are told to do in the memorandum enclosed with this—and do it without any person being present to overlook you. Your humble servant,

'Rosanna Spearman.'

I turned to the slip of paper next. Here is the literal copy of it, word for word:

'*Memorandum.*—To go to the Shivering Sand at the turn of the tide. To walk out on the South Spit, until I get the South Spit Beacon, and the flagstaff at the Coast-guard station above Cobb's Hole in a line together. To lay down on the rocks, a stick, or any straight thing to guide my hand, exactly in the line of the Beacon and the flagstaff. To take care, in doing this, that one end of the stick shall be at the edge of the rocks, on the side of them which overlooks the quicksand. To feel along the stick, among the seaweed (beginning from the end of the stick which points towards the Beacon), for the Chain. To run my hand along the Chain, when found, until I come to the part of it which stretches over the edge of the rocks, down into the quicksand. *And then, to pull the Chain.*'

Just as I had read the last words—underlined in the original—I heard the voice of Betteredge behind me. The inventor of the detective-fever had completely succumbed to that irresistible malady. 'I can't stand it any longer, Mr Franklin. What does her letter say? For mercy's sake, sir, tell us, what does her letter say?'

I handed him the letter, and the memorandum. He read the first without appearing to be much interested in it. But the second—the memorandum—produced a strong impression on him.

'The Sergeant said it!' cried Betteredge. 'From first to last, sir, the Sergeant said she had got a memorandum of the hiding-place. And here it is! Lord save us, Mr Franklin, here is the secret that puzzled everybody, from the great Cuff downwards, ready and waiting, as one may say, to show itself to *you*! It's the ebb now, sir, as anybody may see for themselves. How long will it be till the turn of the tide?' He looked up, and observed a lad at work, at some little distance from us, mending a net. 'Tammie Bright!' he shouted at the top of his voice.

'I hear you!' Tammie shouted back.

'When's the turn of the tide?'

'In an hour's time.'

We both looked at our watches.

'We can go round by the coast, Mr Franklin,' said Betteredge; 'and get to the quicksand in that way with plenty of time to spare. What do you say, sir?'

'Come along!'

With Betteredge's help, I soon stood in the right position to see the Beacon and the Coast-guard flagstaff in a line together. Following the memorandum as our guide, we next laid my stick in the necessary direction, as neatly as we could, on the uneven surface of the rocks. And then we looked at our watches once more.

It wanted nearly twenty minutes yet of the turn of the tide. I suggested waiting through this interval on the beach, instead of on the wet and slippery surface of the rocks. Having reached the dry sand, I prepared to sit down; and, greatly to my surprise, Betteredge prepared to leave me.

'What are you going away for?' I asked.

'Look at the letter again, sir, and you will see.'

A glance at the letter reminded me that I was charged, when I made my discovery, to make it alone.

'It's hard enough for me to leave you, at such a time as this,' said Betteredge. 'But she died a dreadful death, poor soul—and I feel a kind of call on me, Mr Franklin, to humour that fancy of hers. Besides,' he added, confidentially, 'there's nothing in the letter against your letting out the secret afterwards. I'll hang about in the fir plantation, and wait till you pick me up. Don't be longer than you can help, sir. The detective-fever isn't an easy disease to deal with, under *these* circumstances.'

With that parting caution, he left me.

The interval of expectation, short as it was when reckoned by the measure of time, assumed formidable proportions when reckoned by the measure of suspense. This was one of the occasions on which the invaluable habit of smoking becomes especially precious and consolatory. I lit a cigar, and sat down on the slope of the beach.

The turn of the tide came before my cigar was finished. I saw the preliminary heaving of the sand, and then the awful shiver that crept over its surface—as if some spirit of terror lived and moved and shuddered in the fathomless deeps beneath. I threw away my cigar, and went back again to the rocks.

My directions in the memorandum instructed me to feel along the line traced by the stick, beginning with the end which was nearest to the Beacon.

I advanced, in this manner, more than half way along the stick, without encountering anything but the edges of the rocks. An inch or two further on, however, my patience was rewarded. In a narrow little fissure, just within reach of my forefinger, I felt the chain. Attempting, next, to follow it, by touch, in the direction of the quicksand, I found my progress stopped by a thick growth of seaweed—which had fastened itself into the fissure, no doubt, in the time that had elapsed since Rosanna Spearman had chosen her hiding-place.

It was equally impossible to pull up the seaweed, or to force my hand through it. After marking the spot indicated by the end of the stick which was placed nearest to the quicksand, I determined to pursue the search for the chain on a plan of my own. My idea was to 'sound' immediately under the rocks, on the chance of recovering the lost trace of the chain at the point at which it entered the sand. I took up the stick, and knelt down on the brink of the South Spit.

In this position, my face was within a few feet of the surface of the quicksand. The sight of it so near me, still disturbed at intervals by its hideous shivering fit, shook my nerves for the moment. A horrible fancy that the dead woman might appear on the scene of her suicide, to assist my search—an unutterable dread of seeing her rise through the heaving surface of the sand, and point to the place—forced itself into my mind, and turned me cold in the warm sunlight. I own I closed my eyes at the moment when the point of the stick first entered the quicksand.

The instant afterwards, before the stick could have been submerged more than a few inches, I was free from the hold of my own superstitious terror, and was throbbing with excitement from head to foot. Sounding blindfold, at my first attempt—at that first attempt I had sounded right! The stick struck the chain.

Taking a firm hold of the roots of the seaweed with my left hand, I laid myself down over the brink, and felt with my right hand under the overhanging edges of the rock. My right hand found the chain.

I drew it up without the slightest difficulty. And there was the japanned tin case fastened to the end of it.

The action of the water had so rusted the chain that it was impossible for me to unfasten it from the hasp which attached it to the case. Putting the case between my knees and exerting my utmost strength, I contrived to draw off the cover. Some white substance filled the whole interior when I looked in. I put in my hand, and found it to be linen.

In drawing out the linen, I also drew out a letter crumpled up with it. After looking at the direction, and discovering that it bore my name, I put the letter in my pocket, and completely removed the linen. It came out in a thick roll, moulded, of course, to the shape of the case in which it had been so long confined, and perfectly preserved from any injury by the sea.

I carried the linen to the dry sand of the beach, and there unrolled and smoothed it out. There was no mistaking it as an article of dress. It was a nightgown.

The uppermost side, when I spread it out, presented to view innumerable folds and creases, and nothing more. I tried the undermost side, next—and instantly discovered the smear of the paint from the door of Rachel's boudoir!

My eyes remained riveted on the stain, and my mind took me back at a leap from present to past. The very words of Sergeant Cuff recurred to me, as if the man himself was at my side again, pointing to the unanswerable inference which he drew from the smear on the door.

'Find out whether there is any article of dress in this house with the stain of paint on it. Find out who that dress belongs to. Find out how the person can account for having been in the room, and smeared the paint between midnight and three in the morning. If the person can't satisfy you, you haven't far to look for the hand that took the Diamond.'

One after another those words travelled over my memory, repeating themselves again and again with a wearisome, mechanical reiteration. I was roused from what felt like a trance of many hours—from what was really, no doubt, the pause of a few moments only—by a voice calling to me. I looked up, and saw that Betteredge's patience had failed him at last. He was just visible between the sandhills, returning to the beach.

The old man's appearance recalled me, the moment I perceived it, to my sense of present things, and reminded me that the inquiry which I had pursued thus far still remained incomplete. I had discovered the smear on the nightgown. To whom did the nightgown belong?

My first impulse was to consult the letter in my pocket—the letter which I had found in the case.

As I raised my hand to take it out, I remembered that there was a shorter way to discovery than this. The nightgown itself would reveal the truth, for, in all probability, the nightgown was marked with its owner's name.

I took it up from the sand, and looked for the mark.

I found the mark, and read—My Own Name.

There were the familiar letters which told me that the nightgown was mine. I looked up from them. There was the sun; there were the glittering waters of the bay; there was old Betteredge, advancing nearer and nearer to me. I looked back again at the letters. My own name. Plainly confronting me—my own name.

'If time, pains, and money can do it, I will lay my hand on the thief who took the Moonstone.' I had left London, with those words on my lips. I had penetrated the secret which the quicksand had kept from every other living creature. And, on the unanswerable evidence of the paint-stain, I had discovered Myself as the Thief.

CHAPTER IV

I HAVE not a word to say about my own sensations.

My impression is that the shock inflicted on me completely suspended my thinking and feeling power. I certainly could not have known what I was about when Betteredge joined me—for I have it on his authority that I laughed, when he asked what was the matter, and putting the nightgown into his hands, told him to read the riddle for himself.

Of what was said between us on the beach, I have not the faintest recollection. The first place in which I can now see myself again plainly is the plantation of firs. Betteredge and I are walking back together to the house; and Betteredge is telling me that I shall be able to face it, and he will be able to face it, when we have had a glass of grog.

The scene shifts from the plantation, to Betteredge's little sitting-room. My resolution not to enter Rachel's house is forgotten. I feel gratefully the coolness and shadiness and quiet of the room. I drink the grog (a perfectly new luxury to me, at that time of day), which my good old friend mixes with icy-cold water from the well. Under any other circumstances, the drink would simply stupefy me. As things are, it strings up my nerves. I begin to 'face it' as Betteredge has predicted. And Betteredge, on his side, begins to 'face it' too.

The picture which I am now presenting of myself, will, I suspect, be thought a very strange one, to say the least of it. Placed in a situation which may, I think, be described as entirely without parallel, what is the first proceeding to which I resort? Do I seclude myself from all human society? Do I set my mind to analyse the abominable impossibility which, nevertheless, confronts me as an undeniable fact? Do I hurry back to London by the first train to consult the highest authorities, and to set a searching inquiry on foot immediately? No. I accept the shelter of a house which I had resolved never to degrade myself by entering again; and I sit, tippling spirits and water in the company of an old servant, at ten o'clock in the morning. Is this the conduct that might have been expected from a man placed in my horrible position? I can only answer that the sight of old Betteredge's familiar face was an inexpressible comfort to me, and that the drinking of old Betteredge's grog helped me, as I believe nothing else would have helped me, in the state of complete bodily and mental prostration into which I had fallen. I can only offer this excuse for myself; and I can only admire that invariable preservation of dignity, and that strictly logical consistency of conduct which distinguish every man and woman who may read these lines, in every emergency of their lives from the cradle to the grave.

'Now, Mr Franklin, there's one thing certain, at any rate,' said Betteredge, throwing the nightgown down on the table between us, and pointing to it as if it was a living creature that could hear him. '*He's* a liar, to begin with.'

This comforting view of the matter was not the view that presented itself to my mind.

'I am as innocent of all knowledge of having taken the Diamond as you are,' I said. 'But there is the witness against me! The paint on the nightgown, and the name on the nightgown are facts.'

Betteredge lifted my glass, and put it persuasively into my hand.

'Facts?' he repeated. 'Take a drop more grog, Mr Franklin, and you'll get over the weakness of believing in facts! Foul play, sir!' he continued, dropping his voice confidentially. 'That is how I read the riddle. Foul play somewhere—and you and I must find it out. Was there nothing else in the tin case, when you put your hand into it?'

The question instantly reminded me of the letter in my pocket. I took it out, and opened it. It was a letter of many pages, closely written. I looked impatiently for the signature at the end. 'Rosanna Spearman.'

As I read the name, a sudden remembrance illuminated my mind, and a sudden suspicion rose out of the new light.

'Stop!' I exclaimed. 'Rosanna Spearman came to my aunt out of a reformatory? Rosanna Spearman had once been a thief?'

'There's no denying that, Mr Franklin. What of it now, if you please?'

'What of it now? How do we know she may not have stolen the Diamond after all? How do we know she may not have smeared my nightgown purposely with the paint—?'

Betteredge laid his hand on my arm, and stopped me before I could say any more.

'You will be cleared of this, Mr Franklin, beyond all doubt. But I hope you won't be cleared in *that* way. See what the letter says, sir. In justice to the girl's memory, see what it says.'

I felt the earnestness with which he spoke—felt it as a friendly rebuke to me. 'You shall form your own judgment on her letter,' I said. 'I will read it out.'

I began—and read these lines:

'SIR—I have something to own to you. A confession which means much misery, may sometimes be made in very few words. This confession can be made in three words. I love you.'

The letter dropped from my hand. I looked at Betteredge. 'In the name of Heaven,' I said, 'what does it mean?'

He seemed to shrink from answering the question.

'You and Limping Lucy were alone together this morning, sir,' he said. 'Did she say nothing about Rosanna Spearman?'

'She never mentioned Rosanna Spearman's name.'

'Please to go back to the letter, Mr Franklin. I tell you plainly, I can't find it in my heart to distress you, after what you have had to bear already. Let her speak for herself, sir. And get on with your grog. For your own sake, get on with your grog.'

I resumed the reading of the letter.

'It would be very disgraceful to me to tell you this, if I was a living woman when you read it. I shall be dead and gone, sir, when you find my letter. It is that which makes me bold. Not even my grave will be left to tell of me. I may own the truth—with the quicksand waiting to hide me when the words are written.

'Besides, you will find your nightgown in my hiding-place, with the smear of the paint on it; and you will want to know how it came to be hidden by me? and why I said nothing to you about it in my life-time? I have only one reason to give. I did these strange things, because I loved you.

'Do you remember when you came out on us from among the sand hills, that morning, looking for Mr Betteredge? You were like a prince in a fairy-story. You were like a lover in a dream. You were the most adorable human creature I had ever seen. Something that felt like the happy life I had never led yet, leapt up in me at the instant I set eyes on you. Don't laugh at this if you can help it. Oh, if I could only make you feel how serious it is to *me*!

'I was so aggravated by the foolish talk among the women servants, all wondering who was to be suspected first; and I was so angry with you (knowing no better at that time) for the pains you took in hunting for the jewel, and sending for the police, that I kept as much as possible away by myself, until later in the day, when the officer from Frizinghall came to the house.

'Mr Seegrave began, as you may remember, by setting a guard on the women's bedrooms; and the women all followed him upstairs in a rage, to know what he meant by the insult he had put on them. I went with the rest, because if I had done anything different from the rest, Mr Seegrave was the sort of man who would have suspected me directly. We found him in Miss Rachel's room. He told us he wouldn't have a lot of women there; and he pointed to the smear on the painted door, and said some of our petticoats had done the mischief, and sent us all downstairs again.

'After leaving Miss Rachel's room, I stopped a moment on one of the landings, by myself, to see if I had got the paint-stain by any chance on *my* gown. Penelope Betteredge (the only one of the women with whom I was on friendly terms) passed, and noticed what I was about.

'"You needn't trouble yourself, Rosanna," she said. "The paint on Miss Rachel's door has been dry for hours. If Mr Seegrave hadn't set a watch on our bedrooms, I might have told him as much. I don't know what *you* think—*I* was never so insulted before in my life!"

'Penelope was a hot-tempered girl. I quieted her, and brought her back to what she had said about the paint on the door having been dry for hours.

'"How do you know that?" I asked.

'"I was with Miss Rachel, and Mr Franklin, all yesterday morning," Penelope said, "mixing the colours, while they finished the door. I heard Miss Rachel ask whether the door would be dry that evening, in time for the birthday company to see it. And Mr Franklin shook his head, and said it wouldn't be dry in less than twelve hours. It was long past luncheon-time—it was three o'clock before they had done. What does your arithmetic say, Rosanna? Mine says the door was dry by three this morning."

'"Did some of the ladies go upstairs yesterday evening to see it?" I asked. "I thought I heard Miss Rachel warning them to keep clear of the door."

'"None of the ladies made the smear," Penelope answered. "I left Miss Rachel in bed at twelve last night. And I noticed the door, and there was nothing wrong with it then."

'"Oughtn't you to mention this to Mr Seegrave, Penelope?"

'"I wouldn't say a word to help Mr Seegrave for anything that could be offered to me!"

'She went to her work, and I went to mine.'

'My work, sir, was to make your bed, and to put your room tidy. It was the happiest hour I had in the whole day. I used to kiss the pillow on which your head had rested all night. No matter who has done it since, you have never had your clothes folded as nicely as I folded them for you. Of all the little knick-knacks in your dressing-case, there wasn't one that had so much as a speck on it. You never noticed it, any more than you noticed me. I beg your pardon; I am forgetting myself. I will make haste, and go on again.

'Well, I went in that morning to do my work in your room. There was your nightgown tossed across the bed, just as you had thrown it off. I took it up to fold it—and I saw the stain of the paint from Miss Rachel's door!

'I was so startled by the discovery that I ran out with the nightgown in my hand, and made for the back stairs, and locked myself into my own room, to look at it in a place where nobody could intrude and interrupt me.

'As soon as I got my breath again, I called to mind my talk with Penelope, and I said to myself, "Here's the proof that he was in Miss Rachel's sitting-room between twelve last night and three this morning!"

'I shall not tell you in plain words what was the first suspicion that crossed my mind, when I had made that discovery. You would only be angry—and, if you were angry, you might tear my letter up and read no more of it.

'Let it be enough, if you please, to say only this. After thinking it over to the best of my ability, I made it out that the thing wasn't likely, for a reason that I will tell you. If you had been in Miss Rachel's sitting-room, at that time of night, with Miss Rachel's knowledge (and if you had been foolish enough to forget to take care of the wet door) *she* would have reminded you—*she* would never have let you carry away such a witness against her, as the witness I was looking at now! At the same time, I own I was not completely certain in my own mind that I had proved my own suspicion to be wrong. You will not have forgotten that I have owned to hating Miss Rachel. Try to think, if you can, that there was a little of that hatred in all this. It ended in my determining to keep the nightgown, and to wait, and watch, and see what use I might make of it. At that time, please to remember, not the ghost of an idea entered my head that *you* had stolen the Diamond.'

There, I broke off in the reading of the letter for the second time.

I had read those portions of the miserable woman's confession which related to myself, with unaffected surprise, and, I can honestly add, with sincere distress. I had regretted, truly regretted, the aspersion which I had thoughtlessly cast on her memory, before I had seen a line of her letter. But when I had advanced as far as the passage which is quoted above, I own I felt my mind growing bitterer and bitterer against Rosanna Spearman as I went on. 'Read the rest for yourself,' I said, handing the letter to Betteredge across the table. 'If there is anything in it that I *must* look at, you can tell me as you go on.'

'I understand you, Mr Franklin,' he answered. 'It's natural, sir, in *you*. And, God help us all!' he added, in a lower tone, 'it's no less natural in *her*.'

I proceed to copy the continuation of the letter from the original, in my own possession:

'Having determined to keep the nightgown, and to see what use my love, or my revenge (I hardly know which) could turn it to in the future, the next thing to discover was how to keep it without the risk of being found out.

'There was only one way—to make another nightgown exactly like it, before Saturday came, and brought the laundry-woman and her inventory to the house.

'When I got back to the servants' hall, the bell was

going for our dinner. Afternoon already! and the materials for making the new nightgown were still to be got! There was but one chance of getting them. I shammed ill at dinner; and so secured the whole of the interval from then till tea-time to my own use.

'What I was about, while the household believed me to be lying down in my own room; and how I spent the night, after shamming ill again at tea-time, and having been sent up to bed, there is no need to tell you. Sergeant Cuff discovered that much, if he discovered nothing more. And I can guess how. I was detected (though I kept my veil down) in the draper's shop at Frizinghall. There was a glass in front of me, at the counter where I was buying the longcloth; and—in that glass—I saw one of the shop-men point to my shoulder and whisper to another. At night again, when I was secretly at work, locked into my room, I heard the breathing of the women servants who suspected me, outside my door.

'It didn't matter then; it doesn't matter now. On the Friday morning, hours before Sergeant Cuff entered the house, there was the new nightgown—to make up your number in place of the nightgown that I had got—made, wrung out, dried, ironed, marked, and folded as the laundry woman folded all the others, safe in your drawer. There was no fear (if the linen in the house was examined) of the newness of the nightgown betraying me. All your underclothing had been renewed, when you came to our house—I suppose on your return home from foreign parts.

'The next thing was the arrival of Sergeant Cuff; and the next great surprise was the announcement of what *he* thought about the smear on the door.

'I had believed you to be guilty (as I have owned), more because I wanted you to be guilty than for any other reason. And now, the Sergeant had come round by a totally different way to the same conclusion (respecting the nightgown) as mine! And I had got the dress that was the only proof against you! And not a living creature knew it—yourself included! I am afraid to tell you how I felt when I called these things to mind—you would hate my memory for ever afterwards.'

At that place, Betteredge looked up from the letter.

'Not a glimmer of light so far, Mr Franklin,' said the old man, taking off his heavy tortoiseshell spectacles, and pushing Rosanna Spearman's confession a little away from him. 'Have you come to any conclusion, sir, in your own mind, while I have been reading?'

'Finish the letter first, Betteredge; there may be something to enlighten us at the end of it. I shall have a word or two to say to you after that.'

'Very good, sir. I'll just rest my eyes, and then I'll go on again. In the meantime, Mr Franklin—I don't want to hurry you—but would you mind telling me, in one word, whether you see your way out of this dreadful mess yet?'

'I see my way back to London,' I said, 'to consult Mr Bruff. If he can't help me—'

'Yes, sir?'

'And if the Sergeant won't leave his retirement at Dorking—'

'He won't, Mr Franklin!'

'Then, Betteredge—as far as I can see now—I am at the end of my resources. After Mr Bruff and the Sergeant, I don't know of a living creature who can be of the slightest use to me.'

As the words passed my lips, some person outside knocked at the door of the room.

Betteredge looked surprised as well as annoyed by the interruption.

'Come in,' he called out, irritably, 'whoever you are!'

The door opened, and there entered to us, quietly, the most remarkable-looking man that I had ever seen. Judging him by his figure and his movements, he was still young. Judging him by his face, and comparing him with Betteredge, he looked the elder of the two. His complexion was of a gipsy darkness; his fleshless cheeks had fallen into deep hollows, over which the bone projected like a pent-house. His nose presented the fine shape and modelling so often found among the ancient people of the East, so seldom visible among the newer races of the West. His forehead rose high and straight from the brow. His marks and wrinkles were innumerable. From this strange face, eyes, stranger still, of the softest brown—eyes dreamy and mournful, and deeply sunk in their orbits—looked out at you, and (in my case, at least) took your attention captive at their will. Add to this a quantity of thick closely-curling hair, which, by some freak of Nature, had lost its colour in the most startlingly partial and capricious manner. Over the top of his head it was still of the deep black which was its natural colour. Round the sides of his head—without the slightest gradation of grey to break the force of the extraordinary contrast—it had turned completely white. The line between the two colours preserved no sort of regularity. At one place, the white hair ran up into the black; at another, the black hair ran down into the white. I looked at the man with a curiosity which, I am ashamed to say, I found it quite impossible to control. His soft brown eyes looked back at me gently; and he met my involuntary rudeness in staring at him, with an apology which I was conscious that I had not deserved.

'I beg your pardon,' he said. 'I had no idea that Mr Betteredge was engaged.' He took a slip of paper from his pocket, and handed it to Betteredge. 'The list for next week,' he said. His eyes just rested on me again—and he left the room as quietly as he had entered it.

'Who is that?' I asked.

'Mr Candy's assistant,' said Betteredge. 'By the bye, Mr Franklin, you will be sorry to hear that the little doctor has never recovered that illness he caught, going home from the birthday dinner. He's pretty well in health; but he lost his memory in the fever, and he has never recovered more than the wreck of it since. The work all falls on his assistant. Not much of it now, except among the poor. *They* can't help themselves, you know. *They* must put up with the man with the piebald hair, and the gipsy complexion—or they would get no doctoring at all.'

'You don't seem to like him, Betteredge?'

'Nobody likes him, sir.'

'Why is he so unpopular?'

'Well, Mr Franklin, his appearance is against him, to begin with. And then there's a story that Mr Candy took him with a very doubtful character. Nobody knows who he is—and he hasn't a friend in the place. How can you expect one to like him, after that?'

'Quite impossible, of course! May I ask what he wanted with you, when he gave you that bit of paper?'

'Only to bring me the weekly list of the sick people about here, sir, who stand in need of a little wine. My lady always had a regular distribution of good sound port and sherry among the infirm poor; and Miss Rachel wishes the custom to be kept up. Times have changed! Times have changed! I remember when Mr Candy himself brought the list to my mistress. Now it's Mr Candy's assistant who brings the list to me. I'll go on with the letter, if you will allow me, sir,' said Betteredge, drawing Rosanna Spearman's confession back to him. 'It isn't lively reading, I grant you. But, there! it keeps me from getting sour with thinking of the past.' He put on his spectacles, and wagged his head gloomily. 'There's a bottom of good sense, Mr Franklin, in our conduct to our mothers, when they first start us on the journey of life. We are all of us more or less unwilling to be brought into the world. And we are all of us right.'

Mr Candy's assistant had produced too strong an impression on me to be immediately dismissed from my thoughts. I passed over the last unanswerable utterance of the Betteredge philosophy; and returned to the subject of the man with the piebald hair.

'What is his name?' I asked.

'As ugly a name as need be,' Betteredge answered gruffly.
'Ezra Jennings.'

CHAPTER V

HAVING told me the name of Mr Candy's assistant, Betteredge
appeared to think that we had wasted enough of our time on
an insignificant subject. He resumed the perusal of Rosanna
Spearman's letter.

'You have no need to be angry, Mr Franklin, even if I did
feel some little triumph at knowing that I held all your
prospects in life in my own hands. Anxieties and fears
soon came back to me. With the view Sergeant Cuff took
of the loss of the Diamond, he would be sure to end in
examining our linen and our dresses. There was no place
in my room—there was no place in the house—which I
could feel satisfied would be safe from him. How to hide
the nightgown so that not even the Sergeant could find
it? and how to do that without losing one moment of
precious time?—these were not easy questions to answer.
My uncertainties ended in my taking a way that may make
you laugh. I undressed, and put the nightgown on me.
You had worn it—and I had another little moment of
pleasure in wearing it after you.

'The next news that reached us in the servants' hall
showed that I had not made sure of the nightgown a moment
too soon. Sergeant Cuff wanted to see the washing-book.

'I found it, and took it to him in my lady's sitting-room.
The Sergeant and I had come across each other more
than once in former days. I was certain he would know
me again—and I was *not* certain of what he might do when
he found me employed as servant in a house in which a

valuable jewel had been lost. In this suspense, I felt it would be a relief to me to get the meeting between us over, and to know the worst of it at once.

'He looked at me as if I was a stranger, when I handed him the washing-book; and he was very specially polite in thanking me for bringing it. I thought those were both bad signs. There was no knowing what he might say of me behind my back; there was no knowing how soon I might not find myself taken in custody on suspicion, and searched. It was then time for your return from seeing Mr Godfrey Ablewhite off by the railway; and I went to your favourite walk in the shrubbery, to try for another chance of speaking to you—the last chance, for all I knew to the contrary, that I might have.

'You never appeared; and, what was worse still, Mr Betteredge and Sergeant Cuff passed by the place where I was hiding—and the Sergeant saw me.

'I had no choice, after that, but to return to my proper place and my proper work, before more disasters happened to me. Just as I was going to step across the path, you came back from the railway. You were making straight for the shrubbery, when you saw me—I am certain, sir, you saw me—and you turned away as if I had got the plague, and went into the house.*

'I made the best of my way indoors again, returning by the servants' entrance. There was nobody in the laundry-room at that time; and I sat down there alone. I have told you already of the thoughts which the Shivering Sand

---

* NOTE by Franklin Blake.—The writer is entirely mistaken, poor creature. I never noticed her. My intention was certainly to have taken a turn in the shrubbery. But, remembering at the same moment that my aunt might wish to see me, after my return from the railway, I altered my mind, and went into the house.

put into my head. Those thoughts came back to me now. I wondered in myself which it would be harder to do, if things went on in this manner—to bear Mr Franklin Blake's indifference to me, or to jump into the quicksand and end it for ever in that way?

'As soon as possible, I made the first excuse that came into my head, and got leave to go out for a breath of fresh air. I went straight to Cobb's Hole, to Mr Yolland's cottage. His wife and daughter were the best friends I had. Don't suppose I trusted them with your secret—I have trusted nobody. All I wanted was to write this letter to you, and to have a safe opportunity of taking the nightgown off me. Suspected as I was, I could do neither of those things with any sort of security, up at the house.

'And now I have nearly got through my long letter, writing it alone in Lucy Yolland's bedroom. When it is done, I shall go downstairs with the nightgown rolled up, and hidden under my cloak. I shall find the means I want for keeping it safe and dry in its hiding-place, among the litter of old things in Mrs Yolland's kitchen. And then I shall go to the Shivering Sand—don't be afraid of my letting my footmarks betray me!—and hide the nightgown down in the sand, where no living creature can find it without being first let into the secret by myself.

'And, when that's done, what then?

'Then, Mr Franklin, I shall have two reasons for making another attempt to say the words to you which I have not said yet. If you leave the house, as Penelope believes you will leave it, and if I haven't spoken to you before that, I shall lose my opportunity forever. That is one reason. Then, again, there is the comforting knowledge—if my speaking does make you angry—that I have got the night-gown ready to plead my cause for me as nothing else can. That is my other reason. If these two together don't harden my heart against the coldness which has hitherto frozen it up (I mean the coldness of your treatment of me), there will be the end of my efforts—and the end of my life.

'Yes. If I miss my next opportunity—if you are as cruel as ever, and if I feel it again as I have felt it already—good-bye to the world which has grudged me the happiness that it gives to others. Good-bye to life, which nothing but a little kindness from *you* can ever make pleasurable to me again. Don't blame yourself, sir, if it ends in this way. But try—do try—to feel some forgiving sorrow for me! I shall take care that you find out what I have done for you, when I am past telling you of it myself. Will you say something kind of me then—in the same gentle way that you have when you speak to Miss Rachel? If you do that, and if there are such things as ghosts, I believe my ghost will hear it, and tremble with the pleasure of it.

'It's time I left off. I am making myself cry. How am I to see my way to the hiding-place if I let these useless tears come and blind me?

'Besides, why should I look at the gloomy side? Why not believe, while I can, that it will end well after all? I may find you in a good humour tonight—or, if not, I may succeed better tomorrow morning. I shan't improve my plain face by fretting—shall I? Who knows but I may have filled all these weary long pages of paper for nothing? They will go, for safety's sake (never mind now for what other reason) into the hiding-place along with the night-gown. It has been hard, hard work writing my letter. Oh! if we only end in understanding each other, how I shall enjoy tearing it up!

'I beg to remain, sir, your true lover and humble servant,
                              'ROSANNA SPEARMAN.'

'Betteredge,' I said, 'is there any hint to guide me at the end of the letter?' He looked up with a heavy sigh.

'There is nothing to guide you, Mr Franklin,' he answered. 'If you take my advice you will keep the letter in the cover till these present anxieties of yours have come to an end. It will sorely distress you, whenever you read it. Don't read it now.'

I put the letter away in my pocket-book.

A glance back at the fourteenth and fifteenth chapters of Betteredge's Narrative will show that there really was a reason for my thus sparing myself, at a time when my fortitude had been already cruelly tried. Twice over, the unhappy woman had made her last attempt to speak to me. And twice over, it had been my misfortune (God knows how innocently!) to repel the advances she had made to me. On the Friday night, as Betteredge truly describes it, she had found me alone at the billiard-table. Her manner and language suggested to me and would have suggested to any man, under the circumstances—that she was about to confess a guilty knowledge of the disappearance of the Diamond. For her own sake, I had purposely shown no special interest in what was coming; for her own sake, I had purposely looked at the billiard-balls, instead of looking at *her*—and what had been the result? I had sent her away from me, wounded to the heart! On the Saturday again—on the day when she must have foreseen, after what Penelope had told her, that my departure was close at hand—the same fatality still pursued us. She had once more attempted to meet me in the shrubbery walk, and she had found me there in company with Betteredge and Sergeant Cuff. In her hearing, the Sergeant, with his own underhand object in view, had appealed to my interest in Rosanna Spearman. Again for the poor creature's own sake, I had met the police officer with a flat denial, and had declared—loudly declared, so that she might hear me too—that I felt 'no interest whatever in Rosanna Spearman'. At those words, solely designed to warn her against attempting to gain my private ear, she had turned away and left the place: cautioned of her danger, as I then believed; self-doomed to destruction, as I know now. From that point, I have already traced the succession of events which led me to the astounding discovery at the quicksand. The retrospect is now complete. I may leave the miserable story of Rosanna Spearman—to which, even at this distance of time, I cannot revert without a pang of distress—to suggest for itself all that is here purposely left unsaid. I may pass from the suicide at the Shivering Sand, with its strange and terrible influence on my present position and future prospects, to interests which concern the living people of this narrative, and to events which were already paving my way for the slow and toilsome journey from the darkness to the light.

CHAPTER VI

'BEFORE I go back to Hotherstone's,' I began, 'I have two questions to ask you. They relate to myself, and I believe they will rather surprise you.'

'If they will put that poor creature's letter out of my head, Mr Franklin, they may do anything else they like with me. Please to begin surprising me, sir, as soon as you can.'

'My first question, Betteredge, is this. Was I drunk on the night of Rachel's birthday?'

'*You* drunk!' exclaimed the old man. 'Why it's the great defect of your character, Mr Franklin that you only drink with your dinner, and never touch a drop of liquor afterwards!'

'But the birthday was a special occasion. I might have abandoned my regular habits, on that night of all others.'

Betteredge considered for a moment.

'You did go out of your habits, sir,' he said. 'And I'll tell you how. You looked wretchedly ill—and we persuaded you to have a drop of brandy and water to cheer you up a little.'

'I am not used to brandy and water. It is quite possible—'

'Wait a bit, Mr Franklin. I knew you were not used, too. I poured you out half a wineglassful of our fifty-year-old Cognac; and (more shame for me!) I drowned that noble liquor in nigh on a tumblerful of cold water. A child couldn't have got drunk on it—let alone a grown man!'

I knew I could depend on his memory, in a matter of this kind. It was plainly impossible that I could have been intoxicated. I passed on to the second question.

'Before I was sent abroad, Betteredge, you saw a great deal of me when I was a boy? Now tell me plainly, do you remember anything strange of me, after I had gone to bed at night? Did you ever discover me walking in my sleep?'

Betteredge stopped, looked at me for a moment, nodded his head, and walked on again.

'I see your drift now, Mr Franklin!' he said 'You're trying to account for how you got the paint on your nightgown, without knowing it yourself. It won't do, sir. You're miles away still from getting at the truth. Walk in your sleep? You never did such a thing in your life!'

Here again, I felt that Betteredge must be right. Neither at home nor abroad had my life ever been of the solitary sort. If I had been a sleep-walker, there were hundreds on hundreds of people who must have discovered me, and who, in the interest of my own safety, would have warned me of the habit, and have taken precautions to restrain it.

Still, admitting all this, I clung—with an obstinacy which was surely natural and excusable, under the circumstances—to one or other of the only two explanations that I could see which accounted for the unendurable position in which I then stood. Observing that I was not yet satisfied, Betteredge shrewdly adverted to certain later events in the history of the Moonstone; and scattered both my theories to the wind at once and for ever.

'Let's try it another way, sir,' he said. 'Keep your own opinion, and see how far it will take you towards finding out the truth. If we are to believe the nightgown—which I don't for one—you not only smeared off the paint from the door, without knowing it, but you also took the Diamond without knowing it. Is that right, so far?'

'Quite right. Go on.'

'Very good, sir. We'll say you were drunk, or walking in your sleep, when you took the jewel. That accounts for the night and morning, after the birthday. But how does it account for what has happened since that time? The Diamond has been taken to London, since that time. The Diamond has been pledged to Mr Luker, since that time. Did you do those two things, without knowing it, too? Were you drunk when I saw you off in the pony-chaise on that Saturday evening? And did you walk in your sleep to Mr Luker's, when the train had brought you to your journey's end? Excuse me for saying it, Mr Franklin, but this business has so upset you, that you're not fit yet to judge for yourself.'

CHAPTER VII

THE next person who was of any material help in the elucidating of this terrible tangle was, strangely enough, Ezra Jennings—the assistant to Mr Candy.

I called on Mr Candy with the forlorn idea of finding if he could throw any new light on the happenings at the birthday dinner. I was distressed, however, to discover that he had completely lost his memory. I was leaving the house when I met Ezra Jennings. Pouring brightly into the hall, the morning light fell full on the face of Mr Candy's assistant when I turned, and looked at him.

'Are you walking my way, Mr Jennings?' I said, observing that he held his hat in his hand. 'I am going to call on my aunt, Mrs Ablewhite.'

Ezra Jennings replied that he had a patient to see, and that he was walking my way.

We left the house together. I observed that the pretty servant girl—who was all smiles and amiability when I wished her good morning on my way out—received a modest little message from

Ezra Jennings, relating to the time at which he might be expected to return, with pursed-up lips, and with eyes which ostentatiously looked anywhere rather than look in his face. The poor wretch was evidently no favourite in the house. Out of the house, I had Betteredge's word for it that he was unpopular everywhere. 'What a life!' I thought to myself, as we descended the doctor's doorsteps.

Having already referred to Mr Candy's illness on his side, Ezra Jennings now appeared determined to leave it to me to resume the subject. His silence said significantly, 'It's your turn now.' I, too, had my reasons for referring to the doctor's illness: and I readily accepted the responsibility of speaking first.

'Judging by the change I see in him,' I began, 'Mr Candy's illness must have been far more serious than I had supposed?'

'It is almost a miracle,' said Ezra Jennings, 'that he lived through it.'

'Is his memory never any better than I have found it today? He has been trying to speak to me—'

'Of something which happened before he was taken ill?' asked the assistant, observing that I hesitated.

'Yes.'

'His memory of events, at that past time, is hopelessly enfeebled,' said Ezra Jennings. 'It is almost to be deplored, poor fellow, that even the wreck of it remains. While he remembers dimly plans that he formed—things, here and there, that he had to say or do before his illness—he is perfectly incapable of recalling what the plans were, or what the thing was that he had to say or do. He is painfully conscious of his own deficiency, and painfully anxious, as you must have seen, to hide it from observation. If he could only have recovered in a complete state of oblivion as to the past, he would have been a happier man. Perhaps we should all be happier,' he added, with a sad smile, 'if we could but completely forget!'

'There are some events surely in all men's lives,' I replied, 'the memory of which they would be unwilling entirely to lose?'

'That is, I hope, to be said of most men, Mr Blake. I am afraid it cannot truly be said of *all*. Have you any reason to suppose that the lost remembrance which Mr Candy tried to recover—while you were speaking to him just now—was a remembrance which it was important to *you* that he should recall?'

In saying those words, he had touched, of his own accord, on the very point upon which I was anxious to consult him. The interest I felt in this strange man had impelled me, in the first instance, to give him the opportunity of speaking to me; reserving what I might have to say, on my side, in relation to his employer, until I was first satisfied that he was a person in whose delicacy and discretion I could trust. The little that he had said, thus far, had been sufficient to convince me that I was speaking to a gentleman. He had what I may venture to describe as the *unsought self-possession* which is a sure sign of good breeding, not in England only, but everywhere else in the civilised world. Whatever the object which he had in view, in putting the question that he had just addressed to me, I felt no doubt that I was justified—so far—in answering him without reserve.

'I believe I have a strong interest,' I said, 'in tracing the lost remembrance which Mr Candy was unable to recall. May I ask whether you can suggest to me any method by which I might assist his memory?'

Ezra Jennings looked at me, with a sudden flash of interest in his dreamy brown eyes.

'Mr Candy's memory is beyond the reach of assistance,' he said. 'I have tried to help it often enough since his recovery, to be able to speak positively on that point.'

This disappointed me; and I owned it.

'I confess you led me to hope for a less discouraging answer than that,' I said.

Ezra Jennings smiled. 'It may not, perhaps, be a final answer, Mr Blake. It may be possible to trace Mr Candy's lost recollection, without the necessity of appealing to Mr Candy himself.'

'Indeed? Is it an indiscretion, on my part, to ask how?'

'You have heard, I dare say, of the original cause of Mr Candy's illness?' he resumed. 'The night of Lady Verinder's dinner-party was a night of heavy rain. My employer drove home through it in his gig, and reached the house wetted to the skin. He found an urgent message from a patient, waiting for him; and he most unfortunately went at once to visit the sick person, without stopping to change his clothes. I was myself professionally detained, that night, by a case at some distance from Frizinghall. When I got back the next morning, I found Mr Candy's groom waiting in great alarm to take me to his master's room. By that time the mischief was done; the illness had set in.'

'The illness has only been described to me, in general terms, as a fever,' I said.

'I can add nothing which will make the description more accurate,' answered Ezra Jennings. 'From first to last the fever assumed no specific form. I have had the presumption to occupy my leisure, for some years past, in writing a book, addressed to the members of my profession—a book on the intricate and delicate subject of the brain and the nervous system. My work will probably never be finished; and it will certainly never be published. It has none the less been the friend of many lonely hours; and it helped me to while away the anxious time—the time of waiting, and nothing else—at Mr Candy's bedside. I told you he was delirious, I think? And I mentioned the time at which his delirium came on?'

'Yes.'

'Well, I had reached a section of my book, at that time, which touched on this same question of delirium. I won't trouble you at any length with my theory on the subject—I will confine myself to telling you only what it is your present interest to know. It has often occurred to me in the course of my medical practice, to doubt whether we can justifiably infer—in cases of delirium—that the loss of the faculty of speaking connectedly, implies of necessity the loss of the faculty of thinking connect-edly as well. Poor Mr Candy's illness gave me an opportunity of putting this doubt to the test. I understand the art of writing in shorthand; and I was able to take down the patient's "wander-ings", exactly as they fell from his lips. Do you see, Mr Blake, what I am coming to at last?'

I saw it clearly, and waited with breathless interest to hear more.

'At odds and ends of time,' Ezra Jennings went on, 'I repro-duced my shorthand notes, in the ordinary form of writing—leaving large spaces between the broken phrases, and even the single words, as they had fallen disconnectedly from Mr Candy's lips. I then treated the result thus obtained, on something like the principle which one adopts in putting together a child's "puzzle". It is all confusion to begin with; but it may be all brought into order and shape, if you can only find the right way. Acting on this plan, I filled in each blank space on the paper, with what the words or phrases on either side of it suggested to me as the speaker's meaning; altering over and over again, until my additions followed naturally on the spoken words which came before them, and fitted naturally into the spoken words which came after them. The result was, that I not only occupied in this way many vacant and anxious hours, but that I arrived at something which was (as it seemed to me) a confirmation of the theory that I held. In plainer words, after putting the broken sentences together I found the superior faculty of thinking going on, more or less connectedly, in my patient's mind, while the inferior faculty of expression was in a state of almost complete incapacity and confusion.'

'One word!' I interposed eagerly. 'Did my name occur in any of his wanderings?'

'You shall hear, Mr Blake. Among my written proofs of the assertion which I have just advanced—or, I ought to say, among the written experiments, tending to put my assertion to the proof—there *is* one, in which your name occurs. For nearly the whole of one night, Mr Candy's mind was occupied with *something* between himself and you. I have got the broken words, as they dropped from his lips, on one sheet of paper. And I have got the links of my own discovering which connect those words together, on another sheet of paper. The product (as the arithmeticians would say) is an intelligible statement—first, of something actually done in the past; secondly, of something which Mr Candy contemplated doing in the future, if his illness had not got in the way, and stopped him. The question is whether this does, or does not, represent the lost recollection which he vainly attempted to find when you called on him this morning?'

'Not a doubt of it!' I answered. 'Let us go back directly, and look at the papers!'

'Quite impossible, Mr Blake.'

'Why?'

'Put yourself in my position for a moment,' said Ezra Jennings. 'Would *you* disclose to another person what had dropped unconsciously from the lips of your suffering patient and your helpless friend, without first knowing that there was a necessity to justify you in opening your lips?'

Without a moment's hesitation I told him the truth, as unreservedly as I have told it in these pages.

He started to his feet, and looked at me with breathless eagerness as I approached the leading incident of my story.

'It is certain that I went into the room,' I said; 'it is certain that I took the Diamond. I can only meet those two plain facts by declaring that, do what I might, I did it without my own knowledge—'

Ezra Jennings caught me excitedly by the arm.

'Stop!' he said. 'You have suggested more to me than you suppose. Have *you* ever been accustomed to the use of opium?'

'I never tasted it in my life.'

'Were your nerves out of order, at this time last year? Were you unusually restless and irritable?'

'Yes.'

'Did you sleep badly?'

'Wretchedly. Many nights I never slept at all.'

'Was the birthday night an exception? Try, and remember. Did you sleep well on that one occasion?'

'I do remember! I slept soundly.'

He dropped my arm as suddenly as he had taken it—and looked at me with the air of a man whose mind was relieved of the last doubt that rested on it.

'This is a marked day in your life, and in mine,' he said, gravely. 'I am absolutely certain, Mr Blake, of one thing—I have got what Mr Candy wanted to say to you this morning, in the notes that I took at my patient's bedside. Wait! That is not all. I am firmly persuaded that I can prove you to have been unconscious of what you were about, when you entered the room and took the Diamond. Give me time to think, and time to question you. I believe the vindication of your innocence is in my hands!'

'Explain yourself, for God's sake! What do you mean?'

In the excitement of our colloquy, we had walked on a few steps, beyond the clump of dwarf trees which had hitherto screened us from view. Before Ezra Jennings could answer me, he was hailed from the high road by a man, in great agitation, who had been evidently on the look-out for him.

'I am coming,' he called back; 'I am coming as fast as I can!' He turned to me. 'There is an urgent case waiting for me at the village yonder; I ought to have been there half an hour since—I must attend to it at once. Give me two hours from this time, and call at Mr Candy's again—and I will engage to be ready for you.'

'How am I to wait!' I exclaimed, impatiently. 'Can't you quiet my mind by a word of explanation before we part?'

'This is far too serious a matter to be explained in a hurry,

Mr Blake. I am not wilfully trying your patience—I should only be adding to your suspense, if I attempted to relieve it as things are now. At Frizinghall, sir, in two hours' time!'

The man on the highroad hailed him again. He hurried away, and left me.

CHAPTER VIII

How the interval of suspense to which I was now condemned might have affected other men in my position, I cannot pretend to say. The influence of the two hours' probation upon my temperament was simply this. I felt physically incapable of remaining still in any one place, and morally incapable of speaking to any one human being, until I had first heard all that Ezra Jennings had to say to me.

In this frame of mind, I not only abandoned my contemplated visit to Mrs Ablewhite—I even shrank from encountering Gabriel Betteredge himself.

Returning to Frizinghall, I left a note for Betteredge, telling him that I had been unexpectedly called away for a few hours, but that he might certainly expect me to return towards three o'clock in the afternoon. I requested him, in the interval, to order his dinner at the usual hour, and to amuse himself as he pleased. He had, as I well knew, hosts of friends in Frizinghall; and he would be at no loss how to fill up his time until I returned to the hotel.

This done, I made the best of my way out of the town again, and roamed the lonely moorland country which surrounds Frizinghall, until my watch told me that it was time, at last, to return to Mr Candy's house.

I found Ezra Jennings ready and waiting for me.

He was sitting alone in a bare little room, which communicated by a glazed door with a surgery. Hideous coloured diagrams of the ravages of hideous diseases decorated the barren buff-coloured walls. A book-case filled with dingy medical works, and ornamented at the top with a skull, in place of the customary bust; a large deal table copiously splashed with ink; wooden chairs of the sort that are seen in kitchens and cottages; a threadbare drugget in the middle of the floor; a sink of water, with a basin and waste-pipe roughly let into the wall, horribly suggestive of its connection with surgical operations—comprised the entire furniture of the room. The bees were humming among a few flowers placed in pots outside the window; the birds were singing in the garden, and the faint intermittent jingle of a tuneless piano in some neighbouring house forced itself now and again on the ear. In any other place, these everyday sounds might have spoken pleasantly of the everyday world outside. Here, they came in as intruders on a silence which nothing but human suffering had the privilege to disturb. I looked at the mahogany instrument case, and at the huge roll of lint, occupying places of their own on the book-shelves, and shuddered inwardly as I thought of the sounds, familiar and appropriate to the everyday use of Ezra Jennings' room.

'I make no apology, Mr Blake, for the place in which I am receiving you,' he said. 'It is the only room in the house, at this hour of the day, in which we can feel quite sure of being left undisturbed. Here are my papers ready for you; and here are two books to which we may have occasion to refer, before we have done. Bring your chair to the table, and we shall be able to consult them together.'

I drew up to the table; and Ezra Jennings handed me his manuscript notes. They consisted of two large folio leaves of paper. One leaf contained writing which only covered the surface at intervals. The other presented writing, in red and black ink, which completely filled the page from top to bottom. In the irritated state of my curiosity, at that moment, I laid aside the second sheet of paper in despair.

'Have some mercy on me!' I said. 'Tell me what I am to expect, before I attempt to read this.'

'Willingly, Mr Blake! Do you mind my asking you one or two more questions?'

'Ask me anything you like!'

He looked at me with the sad smile on his lips, and the kindly interest in his soft brown eyes.

'You have already told me,' he said, 'that you have never—to your knowledge—tasted opium in your life.'

'To my knowledge,' I repeated.

'You will understand directly why I speak with that reservation. Let us go on. You are not aware of ever having taken opium. At this time, last year, you were suffering from nervous irritation, and you slept wretchedly at night. On the night of the birthday, however, there was an exception to the rule—you slept soundly. Am I right, so far?'

'Quite right!'

'Can you assign any cause for the nervous suffering, and your want of sleep?'

'I can assign no cause. Old Betteredge made a guess at the cause, I remember. But that is hardly worth mentioning.'

'Pardon me. Anything is worth mentioning in such a case as this. Betteredge attributed your sleeplessness to something. To what?'

'To my leaving off smoking.'

'Had you been an habitual smoker?'

'Yes.'

'Did you leave off the habit suddenly?'

'Yes.'

'Betteredge was perfectly right, Mr Blake. When smoking is a habit a man must have no common constitution who can leave it off suddenly without some temporary damage to his nervous system. Your sleepless nights are accounted for, to my mind. My next question refers to Mr Candy. Do you remember having entered into anything like a dispute with him—at the birthday dinner, or afterwards—on the subject of his profession?'

The question instantly awakened one of my dormant

remembrances in connection with the birthday festival. The foolish wrangle which took place, on that occasion, between Mr Candy and myself, will be found described at much greater length than it deserves in the eighth chapter of Betteredge's Narrative. The details there presented of the dispute—so little had I thought of it afterwards—entirely failed to recur to my memory. All that I could now recall, and all that I could tell Ezra Jennings was, that I had attacked the art of medicine at the dinner-table with sufficient rashness and sufficient pertinacity to put even Mr Candy out of temper for the moment. I also remembered that Lady Verinder had interfered to stop the dispute, and that the little doctor and I had 'made it up again', as the children say, and had become as good friends as ever, before we shook hands that night.

'There is one thing more,' said Ezra Jennings, 'which it is very important I should know. Had you any reason for feeling any special anxiety about the Diamond, at this time last year?'

'I had the strongest reasons for feeling anxiety about the Diamond. I knew it to be the object of a conspiracy; and I was warned to take measures for Miss Verinder's protection, as the possessor of the stone.'

'Was the safety of the Diamond the subject of conversation between you and any other person, immediately before you retired to rest on the birthday night?'

'It was the subject of a conversation between Lady Verinder and her daughter—'

'Which took place in your hearing?'

'Yes.'

Ezra Jennings took up his notes from the table, and placed them in my hands.

'Mr Blake,' he said, 'if you read those notes now, by the light which my questions and your answers have thrown on them, you will make two astounding discoveries concerning yourself. You will find—First, that you entered Miss Verinder's sitting-room and took the Diamond, in a state of trance, produced by opium. Secondly, that the opium was given to you by Mr Candy—without your own knowledge—as a practical refutation of the opinions which you had expressed to him at the birthday dinner.'

I sat with the papers in my hand completely stupefied.

'Try and forgive poor Mr Candy,' said the assistant gently. 'He has done dreadful mischief, I own; but he has done it innocently. If you will look at the notes, you will see that—but for his illness—he would have returned to Lady Verinder's the morning after the party, and would have acknowledged the trick that he had played you. Miss Verinder would have heard of it, and Miss Verinder would have questioned him—and the truth which has laid hidden for a year would have been discovered in a day.'

I began to regain my self-possession. 'Mr Candy is beyond the reach of my resentment,' I said angrily. 'But the trick that he played me is not the less an act of treachery, for all that. I may forgive, but I shall not forget it.'

'Every medical man commits that act of treachery, Mr Blake, in the course of his practice. The ignorant distrust of opium (in England) is by no means confined to the lower and less cultivated classes. Every doctor in large practice finds himself, every now and then, obliged to deceive his patients, as Mr Candy deceived you. I don't defend the folly of playing you a trick under the circumstances. I only plead with you for a more accurate and more merciful construction of motives.'

'How was it done?' I asked. 'Who gave me the laudanum, without my knowing it myself?'

'I am not able to tell you. Nothing relating to that part of the matter dropped from Mr Candy's lips, all through his illness. Perhaps your own memory may point to the person to be suspected.'

'No.'

'It is useless, in that case, to pursue the inquiry. The laudanum was secretly given to you in some way. Let us leave it there, and go on to matters of more immediate importance. Read my notes, if you can. Familiarise your mind with what has happened in the past. I have something very bold and very startling to propose to you, which relates to the future.'

Those last words roused me.

I looked at the papers, in the order in which Ezra Jennings had placed them in my hands. The paper which contained the smaller quantity of writing was the uppermost of the two. On this, the disconnected words, and fragments of sentences, which had dropped from Mr Candy in his delirium, appeared as follows:

'. . . Mr Franklin Blake . . . and agreeable . . . down a peg . . . medicine . . . confesses . . . sleep at night . . . tell him . . . out of order . . . medicine . . . he tells me . . . and groping in the dark mean one and the same thing . . . all the company at the dinner-table . . . I say . . . groping after sleep . . . nothing but medicine . . . he says . . . leading the blind . . . know what it means . . . witty . . . a night's rest in spite of his teeth . . . wants sleep . . . Lady Verinder's medicine chest . . . five-and-twenty minims . . . without his knowing it . . . tomorrow morning . . . Well, Mr Blake . . . medicine today . . . never . . . without it . . . out, Mr Candy . . . excellent . . . without it . . . down on him . . . truth . . . something besides . . . excellent . . . dose of laudanum, sir . . . bed . . . what . . . medicine now.'

There the first of the two sheets of paper came to an end. I handed it back to Ezra Jennings.

'That is what you heard at his bedside?' I said.

'Literally and exactly what I heard,' he answered—'except that the repetitions are not transferred here from my short-hand notes. He reiterated certain words and phrases a dozen times over, fifty times over, just as he attached more or less importance to the idea which they represented. The repetitions, in this sense, were of some assistance to me in putting together those fragments. Don't suppose,' he added, pointing to the second sheet of paper, 'that I claim to have reproduced the expressions which Mr Candy himself would have used if he had been capable of speaking connectedly. I only say that I have penetrated through the obstacle of the disconnected expression, to the thought which was underlying it connectedly all the time. Judge for yourself.'

I turned to the second sheet of paper, which I now knew to be the key to the first.

Once more, Mr Candy's wanderings appeared, copied in black ink; the intervals between the phrases being filled up by Ezra Jennings in red ink. I reproduce the result here, in one plain form; the original language and the interpretation of it coming close enough together in these pages to be easily compared and verified.

'. . . Mr Franklin Blake is clever and agreeable, but he wants taking down a peg when he talks of medicine. He confesses that he has been suffering from want of sleep at night. I tell him that his nerves are out of order, and that he ought to take medicine. He tells me that taking medicine and groping in the dark mean one and the same thing. This before all the company at the dinner-table. I say to him, you are groping after sleep, and nothing but medicine can help you to find it. He says to me, I have heard of the blind leading the blind, and now I know what it means. Witty—but I can give him a night's rest in spite of his teeth. He really wants sleep; and Lady Verinder's medicine chest is at my disposal. Give him five-and-twenty minims of laudanum tonight, without his knowing it; and then call tomorrow morning. "Well, Mr Blake, will you try a little medicine today? You will never sleep without it." "There you are out, Mr Candy: I have had an excellent night's rest without it." Then, come down on him with the truth! "You have had something besides an excellent night's rest; you had a dose of laudanum, sir, before you went to bed. What do you say to the art of medicine, now?"'

Admiration of the ingenuity which had woven this smooth and finished texture out of the ravelled skein was naturally the first impression that I felt, on handing the manuscript back to Ezra Jennings. He modestly interrupted the first few words in which my sense of surprise expressed itself, by asking me if the conclusion which he had drawn from his notes was also the conclusion at which my own mind had arrived.

'Do you believe as I believe,' he said, 'that you were acting under the influence of the laudanum in doing all that you did, on the night of Miss Verinder's birthday, in Lady Verinder's house?'

'I am too ignorant of the influence of laudanum to have an opinion of my own,' I answered. 'I can only follow your opinion, and feel convinced that you are right.'

'Very well. The next question is this. You are convinced; and I am convinced—how are we to carry our conviction to the minds of other people?'

I pointed to the two manuscripts, lying on the table between us. Ezra Jennings shook his head.

'Useless, Mr Blake! Quite useless, as they stand now for three unanswerable reasons. In the first place, those notes have been taken under circumstances entirely out of the experience of the mass of mankind. Against them, to begin with! In the second place, those notes represent a medical and metaphysical theory. Against them, once more! In the third place, those notes are of *my* making; there is nothing but *my* assertion to the contrary, to guarantee that they are not fabrications. Remember what I told you on the moor—and ask yourself what my assertion is worth. No! my notes have but one value, looking to the verdict of the world outside. Your innocence is to be vindicated; and they show how it can be done. We must put our conviction to the proof—and you are the man to prove it!'

'How?' I asked.

He leaned eagerly nearer to me across the table that divided us.

'Are you willing to try a bold experiment?'

'I will do anything to clear myself of the suspicion that rests on me now.'

'Will you submit to some personal inconvenience for a time?'

'To any inconvenience, no matter what it may be.'

'Will you be guided implicitly by my advice? It may expose you to the ridicule of fools; it may subject you to the remonstrances of friends whose opinions you are bound to respect.'

'Tell me what to do!' I broke out impatiently. 'And, come what may, I'll do it.'

'You shall do this, Mr Blake,' he answered. 'You shall steal the Diamond, unconsciously, for the second time, in the presence of witnesses whose testimony is beyond dispute.'

I started to my feet. I tried to speak. I could only look at him.

'I believe it *can* be done,' he went on. 'And it *shall* be done—if you will only help me. Try to compose yourself—sit down, and hear what I have to say to you. You have resumed the habit of smoking; I have seen that for myself. How long have you resumed it?'

'For nearly a year.'

'Do you smoke more or less than you did?'

'More.'

'Will you give up the habit again? Suddenly, mind!—as you gave it up before.'

I began dimly to see his drift. 'I will give it up, from this moment,' I answered.

'If the same consequences follow, which followed last June,' said Ezra Jennings—'if you suffer once more as you suffered then, from sleepless nights, we shall have gained our first step.

We shall have put you back again into something assimilating to your nervous condition on the birthday night. If we can next revive, or nearly revive, the domestic circumstances which surrounded you; and if we can occupy your mind again with the various questions concerning the Diamond which formerly agitated it, we shall have replaced you, as nearly as possible in the same position, physically and morally, in which the opium found you last year. In that case we may fairly hope that a repetition of the dose will lead, in a greater or lesser degree, to a repetition of the result. There is my proposal, expressed in a few hasty words.'

'I understand perfectly. But I own I am puzzled on one point, which you have not made clear to me yet.'

'What is the point?'

'I don't understand the effect of the laudanum on me. I don't understand my walking downstairs, and along corridors, and my opening and shutting the drawers of a cabinet, and my going back again to my own room. All these are active proceedings. I thought the influence of opium was first to stupefy you, and then to send you to sleep.'

'I will try to answer you in a few words,' said Ezra Jennings. 'The action of opium is comprised, in the majority of cases, in two influences—a stimulating influence first, and a sedative influence afterwards. Under the stimulating influence, the latest and most vivid impressions left on your mind—namely, the impressions relating to the Diamond—would be likely, in your morbidly sensitive nervous condition, to become intensified in your brain, and would subordinate to themselves your judgment and your will—exactly as an ordinary dream subordinates to itself your judgment and your will. Little by little, under this action, any apprehensions about the safety of the Diamond which you might have felt during the day would be liable to develop themselves from the state of doubt to the state of certainty—would impel you into practical action to preserve the jewel—would direct your steps, with that motive in view, into the room which you entered—and would guide your hand to the drawers of the cabinet, until you had found the drawer which held the stone. In the spiritualised intoxication of opium, you would do all that. Later, as the sedative action began to gain on the stimulant action, you would slowly become inert and stupefied. Later still you would fall into a deep sleep. When the morning came, and the effect of the opium had been all slept off, you would wake as absolutely ignorant of what you had done in the night as if you had been living at the Antipodes. Have I made it tolerably clear to you so far?'

'You have made it so clear,' I said, 'that I want you to go farther. You have shown me how I entered the room, and how I came to take the Diamond. But Miss Verinder saw me leave the room again, with the jewel in my hand. Can you trace my proceedings from that moment? Can you guess what I did next?'

'That is the very point I was coming to,' he rejoined. 'It is a question with me whether the experiment which I propose as a means of vindicating your innocence, may not also be made a means of recovering the lost Diamond as well. When you left Miss Verinder's sitting-room, with the jewel in your hand, you went back in all probability to your own room—'

'Yes? and what then?'

'It is possible, Mr Blake—I dare not say more—that your idea of preserving the Diamond led, by a natural sequence, to the idea of hiding the Diamond, and that the place in which you hid it was somewhere in your bedroom. In that event, the case of the Irish porter may be your case. You may remember, under the influence of the second dose of opium, the place in which you hid the Diamond under the influence of the first.'

It was my turn, now, to enlighten Ezra Jennings. I stopped him, before he could say any more.

'You are speculating,' I said, 'on a result which cannot possibly take place. The Diamond is, at this moment, in London.'

He started, and looked at me in great surprise.

'In London?' he repeated. 'How did it get to London from Lady Verinder's house?'

'Nobody knows.'

'You removed it with your own hand from Miss Verinder's room. How was it taken out of your keeping?'

'I have no idea how it was taken out of my keeping.'

'Did you see it, when you woke in the morning?'

'No.'

'Has Miss Verinder recovered possession of it?'

'No.'

'Mr Blake! there seems to be something here which wants clearing up. May I ask how you know that the Diamond is, at this moment, in London?'

I had put precisely the same question to Mr Bruff when I made my first inquiries about the Moonstone, on my return to England. In answering Ezra Jennings, I accordingly repeated what I had myself heard from the lawyer's own lips—and what is already familiar to the readers of these pages.

He showed plainly that he was not satisfied with my reply.

'With all deference to you,' he said, 'and with all deference to your legal adviser, I maintain the opinion which I expressed just now. It rests, I am well aware, on a mere assumption. Pardon me for reminding you, that your opinion also rests on a mere assumption as well.'

The view he took of the matter was entirely new to me. I waited anxiously to hear how he would defend it.

'*I* assume,' pursued Ezra Jennings, 'that the influence of the opium—after impelling you to possess yourself of the Diamond, with the purpose of securing its safety—might also impel you, acting under the same influence and the same motive, to hide it somewhere in your own room. *You* assume that the Hindoo conspirators could by no possibility commit a mistake. The Indians went to Mr Luker's house after the Diamond—and, therefore, in Mr Luker's possession the Diamond must be! Have you any evidence to prove that the Moonstone was taken to

London at all? You can't even guess how, or by whom, it was removed from Lady Verinder's house! Have you any evidence that the jewel was pledged to Mr Luker? He declares that he never heard of the Moonstone; and his bankers' receipt acknowledges nothing but the deposit of a valuable of great price. The Indians assume that Mr Luker is lying—and you assume again that the Indians are right. All I say, in differing with you, is—that my view is possible. What more, Mr Blake, either logically, or legally, can be said for yours?'

It was put strongly; but there was no denying that it was put truly as well.

'I confess you stagger me,' I replied. 'Do you object to my writing to Mr Bruff, and telling him what you have said?'

'On the contrary, I shall be glad if you will write to Mr Bruff. If we consult his experience, we may see the matter under a new light. For the present, let us return to our experiment with the opium. We have decided that you leave off the habit of smoking from this moment.'

'From this moment?'

'That is the first step. The next step is to reproduce, as nearly as we can, the domestic circumstances which surrounded you last year.'

How was this to be done? Lady Verinder was dead. Rachel and I, so long as the suspicion of theft rested on me, were parted irrevocably. Godfrey Ablewhite was away travelling on the Continent. It was simply impossible to reassemble the people who had inhabited the house, when I had slept in it last. The statement of this objection did not appear to embarrass Ezra Jennings. He attached very little importance, he said, to reassembling the same people—seeing that it would be vain to expect them to reassume the various positions which they had occupied towards me in the past times. On the other hand, he considered it essential to the success of the experiment, that I should see the same objects about me which had surrounded me when I was last in the house.

'Above all things,' he said, 'you must sleep in the room which you slept in, on the birthday night, and it must be furnished in the same way. The stairs, the corridors, and Miss Verinder's sitting-room, must also be restored to what they were when you saw them last. It is absolutely necessary, Mr Blake, to replace every article of furniture in that part of the house which may now be put away. The sacrifice of your cigars will be useless, unless we can get Miss Verinder's permission to do that.'

'Who is to apply to her for permission?' I asked.

'Is it not possible for *you* to apply?'

'Quite out of the question. After what has passed between us on the subject of the lost Diamond, I can neither see her, nor write to her, as things are now.'

Ezra Jennings paused, and considered for a moment.

'May I ask you a delicate question?' he said.

I signed to him to go on.

'Am I right, Mr Blake, in fancying (from one or two things which have dropped from you) that you felt no common interest in Miss Verinder, in former times?'

'Quite right.'

'Was the feeling returned?'

'It was.'

'Do you think Miss Verinder would be likely to feel a strong interest in the attempt to prove your innocence?'

'I am certain of it.'

'In that case, *I* will write to Miss Verinder—if you will give me leave.'

'Telling her of the proposal that you have made to me?'

'Telling her of everything that has passed between us today.'

It is needless to say that I eagerly accepted the service which he had offered to me.

'I shall have time to write by today's post,' he said, looking at his watch. 'Don't forget to lock up your cigars, when you get back to the hotel! I will call tomorrow morning and hear how you have passed the night.'

I rose to take leave of him; and attempted to express the grateful sense of his kindness which I really felt.

He pressed my hand gently. 'Remember what I told you on the moor,' he answered. 'If I can do you this little service, Mr Blake, I shall feel it like a last gleam of sunshine, falling on the evening of a long and clouded day.'

We parted. It was then the fifteenth of June. The events of the next ten days—every one of them more or less directly connected with the experiment of which I was the passive object—are all placed on record, exactly as they happened, in the Journal habitually kept by Mr Candy's assistant. In the pages of Ezra Jennings nothing is concealed, and nothing is forgotten. Let Ezra Jennings tell how the venture with the opium was tried, and how it ended.

FOURTH NARRATIVE

Extracted from the Journal of EZRA JENNINGS

1849. June 25th, Monday.—The day of the experiment! It is five o'clock in the afternoon. We have just arrived at the house.

The first and foremost question, is the question of Mr Blake's health.

So far as it is possible for me to judge, he promises (physically speaking) to be quite as susceptible to the action of the opium tonight as he was at this time last year. He is, this afternoon, in a state of nervous sensitiveness which just stops short of nervous irritation. He changes colour readily; his hand is not quite steady; and he starts at chance noises, and at unexpected appearances of persons and things.

These results have all been produced by deprivation of sleep, which is in its turn the nervous consequence of a sudden cessation in the habit of smoking, after that habit has been carried to an extreme. Here are the same causes at work again, which operated last year; and here are, apparently, the same effects. Will the parallel still hold good, when the final test has been tried? The events of the night must decide.

While I write these lines, Mr Blake is amusing himself at the billiard table in the inner hall, practising different strokes in the game, as he was accustomed to practise them when he was a guest in this house in June last. I have brought my Journal here, partly with a view to occupying the idle hours which I am sure to have on my hands between this and tomorrow morning; partly in the hope that something may happen which it may be worth my while to place on record at the time.

Have I omitted anything thus far? A glance at yesterday's entry shows me that I have forgotten to note the arrival of the morning's post. Let me set this right before I close these leaves for the present, and join Mr Blake.

I received a few lines then, yesterday, from Miss Verinder. She has arranged to travel by the afternoon train, as I recommended. Mrs Merridew has insisted on accompanying her. The note hints that the old lady's generally excellent temper is a little ruffled, and requests all due indulgence for her, in consideration of her age and her habits. I will endeavour, in my relations with Mrs Merridew, to emulate the moderation which Betteredge displays in his relations with me. He received us today, portentously arrayed in his best black suit, and his stiffest white cravat. Whenever he looks my way, he remembers that I have not read *Robinson Crusoe* since I was a child, and he respectfully pities me.

Yesterday, also, Mr Blake had the lawyer's answer. Mr Bruff accepts the invitation—under protest. It is, he thinks, clearly necessary that a gentleman possessed of the average allowance of common sense, should accompany Miss Verinder to the scene of, what we will venture to call, the proposed exhibition. For want of a better escort, Mr Bruff himself will be that gentleman. So here is poor Miss Verinder provided with two 'chaperones.' It is a relief to think that the opinion of the world must surely be satisfied with this!

Nothing has been heard of Sergeant Cuff. He is no doubt still in Ireland. We must not expect to see him tonight.

Betteredge has just come in, to say that Mr Blake has asked for me. I must lay down my pen for the present.

Seven o'clock.—We have been all over the refurnished rooms and staircases again; and we have had a pleasant stroll in the shrubbery, which was Mr Blake's favourite walk when he was here last. In this way, I hope to revive the old impressions of places and things as vividly as possible in his mind.

We are now going to dine, exactly at the hour at which the birthday dinner was given last year. My object, of course, is a purely medical one in this case. The laudanum must find the process of digestion, as nearly as may be, where the laudanum found it last year.

At a reasonable time after dinner I propose to lead the conversation back again—as inartificially as I can—to the subject of the Diamond, and of the Indian conspiracy to steal it. When I have filled his mind with these topics, I shall have done all that it is in my power to do, before the time comes for giving him the second dose.

Half-past eight.—I have only this moment found an opportunity of attending to the most important duty of all; the duty of looking in the family medicine chest for the laudanum which Mr Candy used last year.

Ten minutes since, I caught Betteredge at an unoccupied moment, and told him what I wanted. Without a word of objection, without so much as an attempt to produce his pocket-book, he led the way (making allowances for me at every step) to the store-room in which the medicine chest is kept.

I discovered the bottle, carefully guarded by a glass stopper tied over with leather. The preparation which it contained was, as I had anticipated, the common Tincture of Opium. Finding the bottle still well filled, I have resolved to use it, in preference to employing either of the two preparations with which I had taken care to provide myself, in case of emergency.

The question of the quantity which I am to administer presents certain difficulties. I have thought it over, and have decided on increasing the dose.

My notes inform me that Mr Candy only administered twenty-five minims. This is a small dose to have produced the results which followed—even in the case of a person so sensitive as Mr Blake. I think it highly probable that Mr Candy gave more than he supposed himself to have given—knowing, as I do, that he has a keen relish of the pleasures of the table, and that he measured out the laudanum on the birthday, after dinner. In any case, I shall run the risk of enlarging the dose to forty minims. On this occasion, Mr Blake knows beforehand that he is going to take the laudanum—which is equivalent, physiologically speaking, to his having (unconsciously to himself) a certain capacity in him to resist the effects. If my view is right, a larger quantity is therefore imperatively required, this time, to repeat the results which the smaller quantity produced last year.

Ten o'clock.—The witnesses, or the company (which shall I call them?) reached the house an hour since.

A little before nine o'clock, I prevailed on Mr Blake to accompany me to his bedroom; stating, as a reason, that I wished him to look round it, for the last time, in order to make quite sure that nothing had been forgotten in the refurnishing of the room. I had previously arranged with Betteredge, that the bedchamber prepared for Mr Bruff should be the next room to Mr Blake's, and that I should be informed of the lawyer's arrival by a knock at the door. Five minutes after the clock in the hall had struck nine, I heard the knock; and, going out immediately, met Mr Bruff in the corridor.

My personal appearance (as usual) told against me. Mr Bruff's distrust looked at me plainly enough out of Mr Bruff's eyes. Being well used to producing this effect on strangers, I did not hesitate a moment in saying what I wanted to say, before the lawyer found his way into Mr Blake's room.

'You have travelled here, I believe, in company with Mrs Merridew and Miss Verinder?' I said.

'Yes,' answered Mr Bruff, as dryly as might be.

'Miss Verinder has probably told you, that I wish her presence in the house (and Mrs Merridew's presence of course) to be kept a secret from Mr Blake, until my experiment on him has been tried first?'

'I know that I am to hold my tongue, sir!' said Mr Bruff, impatiently. 'Being habitually silent on the subject of human folly, I am all the readier to keep my lips closed on this occasion. Does that satisfy you?'

I bowed, and left Betteredge to show him to his room. Betteredge gave me one look at parting, which said, as if in so many words, 'You have caught a Tartar, Mr Jennings—and the name of him is Bruff.'

It was next necessary to get the meeting over with the two ladies. I descended the stairs—a little nervously, I confess—on my way to Miss Verinder's sitting-room.

The gardener's wife (charged with looking after the accommodation of the ladies) met me in the first-floor corridor. This excellent woman treats me with an excessive civility which is plainly the offspring of downright terror. She stares, trembles, and curtseys, whenever I speak to her. On my asking for Miss Verinder, she stared, trembled, and would no doubt have curtseyed next, if Miss Verinder herself had not cut that ceremony short, by suddenly opening her sitting-room door.

'Is that Mr Jennings?' she asked.

Before I could answer, she came out eagerly to speak to me in the corridor. We met under the light of a lamp on a bracket. At the first sight of me, Miss Verinder stopped, and hesitated. She recovered herself instantly, coloured for a moment—and then, with a charming frankness, offered me her hand.

'I can't treat you like a stranger, Mr Jennings,' she said. 'Oh, if you only knew how happy your letters have made me!'

She looked at my ugly wrinkled face, with a bright gratitude so new to me in *my* experience of my fellow-creatures, that I was at a loss how to answer her. Nothing had prepared me for her kindness and her beauty. The misery of many years has not hardened my heart, thank God. I was as awkward and as shy with her, as if I had been a lad in my teens.

'Where is he now?' she asked, giving free expression to her one dominant interest—the interest in Mr Blake. 'What is he doing? Has he spoken of me? Is he in good spirits? How does he bear the sight of the house, after what happened in it last year? When are you going to give him the laudanum? May I see you pour it out? I am so interested; I am so excited—I have ten thousand things to say to you, and they all crowd together so that I don't know what to say first. Do you wonder at the interest I take in this?'

'No,' I said. 'I venture to think that I thoroughly understand it.'

She was far above the paltry affectation of being confused. She answered me as she might have answered a brother or a father.

'You have relieved me of indescribable wretchedness; you have given me a new life. How can I be ungrateful enough to have any concealment from *you*? I love him,' she said simply, 'I have loved him from first to last—even when I was wronging him in my own thoughts; even when I was saying the hardest and the cruellest words to him. Is there any excuse for me, in that? I hope there is—I am afraid it is the only excuse I have. When tomorrow comes, and he knows that I am in the house, do you think—?'

She stopped again, and looked at me very earnestly.

'When tomorrow comes,' I said, 'I think you have only to tell him what you have just told me.'

Her face brightened; she came a step nearer to me. Her fingers trifled nervously with a flower which I had picked in the garden, and which I had put into the button-hole of my coat.

'You have seen a great deal of him lately,' she said. 'Have you, really and truly, seen *that*?'

'Really and truly,' I answered. 'I am quite certain of what will happen tomorrow. I wish I could feel as certain of what will happen tonight.'

At that point in the conversation, we were interrupted by the appearance of Betteredge with the tea-tray. He gave me another significant look as he passed on into the sitting-room. 'Aye! aye! make your hay while the sun shines. The Tartar's upstairs, Mr Jennings—the Tartar's upstairs!'

We followed him into the room. A little old lady, in a corner, very nicely dressed, and very deeply absorbed over a smart piece of embroidery, dropped her work in her lap, and uttered a faint little scream at the first sight of my gipsy complexion and my piebald hair.

'Mrs Merridew,' said Miss Verinder, 'this is Mr Jennings.'

'I beg Mr Jennings's pardon,' said the old lady, looking at Miss Verinder, and speaking at *me*. 'Railway travelling always makes me nervous. I am endeavouring to quiet my mind by occupying myself as usual. I don't know whether my embroidery is out of place, on this extraordinary occasion. If it interferes with Mr Jennings's medical views, I shall be happy to put it away of course.'

I hastened to sanction the presence of the embroidery, exactly as I had sanctioned the absence of the burst buzzard and the Cupid's wing. Mrs Merridew made an effort—a grateful effort— to look at my hair. No! it was not to be done. Mrs Merridew looked back again at Miss Verinder.

'If Mr Jennings will permit me,' pursued the old lady, 'I should like to ask a favour. Mr Jennings is about to try a scientific experiment tonight. I used to attend scientific experiments when I was a girl at school. They invariably ended in an explosion. If Mr Jennings will be so very kind, I should like to be warned of the explosion this time. With a view to getting it over, if possible, before I go to bed.'

I attempted to assure Mrs Merridew that an explosion was not included in the programme on this occasion.

'No,' said the old lady. 'I am much obliged to Mr Jennings—I am aware that he is only deceiving me for my own good. I prefer plain dealing. I am quite resigned to the explosion—but I *do* want to get it over, if possible, before I go to bed.'

Here the door opened, and Mrs Merridew uttered another

little scream. The advent of the explosion? No: only the advent of Betteredge.

'I beg your pardon, Mr Jennings,' said Betteredge, in his most elaborately confidential manner. 'Mr Franklin wishes to know where you are. Being under your orders to deceive him, in respect to the presence of my young lady in the house, I have said I don't know. That, you will please to observe, was a lie. Having one foot already in the grave, sir, the fewer lies you expect me to tell, the more I shall be indebted to you, when my conscience pricks me and my time comes.'

There was not a moment to be wasted on the purely speculative question of Betteredge's conscience. Mr Blake might make his appearance in search of me, unless I went to him at once in his own room. Miss Verinder followed me out into the corridor.

'They seem to be in a conspiracy to persecute you,' she said. 'What does it mean?'

'Only the protest of the world, Miss Verinder—on a very small scale—against anything that is new.'

'What are we to do with Mrs Merridew?'

'Tell her the explosion will take place at nine tomorrow morning.'

'So as to send her to bed?'

'Yes—so as to send her to bed.'

Miss Verinder went back to the sitting-room, and I went upstairs to Mr Blake.

To my surprise I found him alone; restlessly pacing his room, and a little irritated at being left by himself.

'Where is Mr Bruff?' I asked.

He pointed to the closed door of communication between the two rooms. Mr Bruff had looked in on him, for a moment; had attempted to renew his protest against our proceedings; and had once more failed to produce the smallest impression on Mr Blake. Upon this, the lawyer had taken refuge in a black leather bag, filled to bursting with professional papers. 'The serious business of life,' he admitted, 'was sadly out of place on such an occasion as the present. But the serious business of life must be carried on, for all that. Mr Blake would perhaps kindly make allowance for the old-fashioned habits of a practical man. Time was money—and, as for Mr Jennings, he might depend on it that Mr Bruff would be forthcoming when called upon.' With that apology, the lawyer had gone back to his own room, and had immersed himself obstinately in his black bag.

I thought of Mrs Merridew and her embroidery, and of Betteredge and his conscience. There is a wonderful sameness in the solid side of the English character—just as there is a wonderful sameness in the solid expression of the English face.

'When are you going to give me the laudanum?' asked Mr Blake impatiently.

'You must wait a little longer,' I said. 'I will stay and keep you company till the time comes.'

It was then not ten o'clock. Inquiries which I had made, at various times, of Betteredge and Mr Blake, had led me to the conclusion that the dose of laudanum given by Mr Candy could not possibly have been administered before eleven. I had accordingly determined not to try the second dose until that time.

We talked a little; but both our minds were preoccupied by the coming ordeal. The conversation soon flagged—then dropped altogether. Mr Blake idly turned over the books on his bedroom table. I had taken the precaution of looking at them, when we first entered the room. *The Guardian*; *The Tatler*; Richardson's *Pamela*; Mackenzie's *Man of Feeling*; Roscoe's *Lorenzo de' Medici*; and Robertson's *Charles the Fifth*—all classical works; all (of course) immeasurably superior to anything produced in later times; and all (from my present point of view) possessing the one great merit of enchaining nobody's interest, and exciting nobody's brain. I left Mr Blake to the composing influence of Standard Literature, and occupied myself in making this entry in my Journal.

My watch informs me that it is close on eleven o'clock. I must shut up these leaves once more.

Two o'clock a.m.—The experiment has been tried. With what result, I am now to describe.

At eleven o'clock, I rang the bell for Betteredge, and told Mr Blake that he might at last prepare himself for bed.

I looked out of the window at the night. It was mild and rainy, resembling, in this respect, the night of the birthday—the twenty-first of June, last year. Without professing to believe in omens, it was at least encouraging to find no direct nervous influences—no stormy or electric perturbations—in the atmosphere. Betteredge joined me at the window, and mysteriously put a little slip of paper into my hand. It contained these lines:

'Mrs Merridew has gone to bed, on the distinct understanding that the explosion is to take place at nine tomorrow morning, and that I am not to stir out of this part of the house until she comes and sets me free. She has no idea that the chief scene of the experiment is my sitting-room—or she would have remained in it for the whole night! I am alone, and very anxious. Pray let me see you measure out the laudanum; I want to have something to do with it, even in the unimportant character of a mere looker-on.—R.V.'

I followed Betteredge out of the room, and told him to remove the medicine-chest into Miss Verinder's sitting-room.

The order appeared to take him completely by surprise. He looked as if he suspected me of some occult medical design on Miss Verinder! 'Might I presume to ask,' he said, 'what my young lady and the medicine-chest have got to do with each other?'

'Stay in the sitting-room, and you will see.'

Betteredge appeared to doubt his own unaided capacity to

superintend me effectually, on an occasion when a medicine-chest was included in the proceedings.

'Is there any objection, sir' he asked, 'to taking Mr Bruff into this part of the business?'

'Quite the contrary! I am now going to ask Mr Bruff to accompany me downstairs.'

Betteredge withdrew to fetch the medicine-chest, without another word. I went back into Mr Blake's room, and knocked at the door of communication. Mr Bruff opened it, with his papers in his hand—immersed in Law; impenetrable to Medicine.

'I am sorry to disturb you,' I said. 'But I am going to prepare the laudanum for Mr Blake; and I must request you to be present, and to see what I do.'

'Yes?' said Mr Bruff, with nine-tenths of his attention riveted on his papers, and with one-tenth unwillingly accorded to me. 'Anything else?'

'I must trouble you to return here with me, and to see me administer the dose.'

'Anything else?'

'One thing more. I must put you to the inconvenience of remaining in Mr Blake's room, and of waiting to see what happens.'

'Oh, very good!' said Mr Bruff. 'My room, or Mr Blake's room—it doesn't matter which; I can go on with my papers anywhere. Unless you object, Mr Jennings, to my importing *that* amount of common sense into the proceedings?'

Before I could answer, Mr Blake addressed himself to the lawyer, speaking from his bed.

'Do you really mean to say that you don't feel any interest in what we are going to do?' he asked. 'Mr Bruff, you have no more imagination than a cow!'

'A cow is a very useful animal, Mr Blake,' said the lawyer. With that reply he followed me out of the room, still keeping his papers in his hand.

We found Miss Verinder, pale and agitated, restlessly pacing her sitting-room from end to end. At a table in a corner stood Betteredge, on guard over the medicine-chest. Mr Bruff sat down on the first chair that he could find, and (emulating the usefulness of the cow) plunged back again into his papers on the spot.

Miss Verinder drew me aside, and reverted instantly to her one all-absorbing interest—her interest in Mr Blake.

'How is he now?' she asked. 'Is he nervous? Is he out of temper? Do you think it will succeed? Are you sure it will do no harm?'

'Quite sure. Come and see me measure it out.'

'One moment! It is past eleven now. How long will it be before anything happens?'

'It is not easy to say. An hour perhaps.'

'I suppose the room must be dark, as it was last year?'

'Certainly.'

'I shall wait in my bedroom—just as I did before. I shall keep the door a little way open. It was a little way open last year. I will watch the sitting-room door; and the moment it moves, I will blow out my light. It all happened in that way, on my birthday night. And it must all happen again in the same way, musn't it?'

'Are you sure you can control yourself, Miss Verinder?'

'In *his* interests, I can do anything!' she answered fervently.

One look at her face told me that I could trust her. I addressed myself again to Mr Bruff.

'I must trouble you to put your papers aside for a moment,' I said.

'Oh, certainly!' He got up with a start—as if I had disturbed him at a particularly interesting place—and followed me to the medicine-chest. There, deprived of the breathless excitement incidental to the practice of his profession, he looked at Betteredge—and yawned wearily.

Miss Verinder joined me with a glass jug of cold water,

which she had taken from a side-table. 'Let me pour out the water,' she whispered. '*I must* have a hand in it!'

I measured out the forty minims from the bottle, and poured the laudanum into a medicine glass. 'Fill it till it is three parts full,' I said, and handed the glass to Miss Verinder. I then directed Betteredge to lock up the medicine chest; informing him that I had done with it now. A look of unutterable relief overspread the old servant's countenance. He had evidently suspected me of a medical design on his young lady!

After adding the water as I had directed, Miss Verinder seized a moment—while Betteredge was locking the chest, and while Mr Bruff was looking back to his papers—and slyly kissed the rim of the medicine glass. 'When you give it to him,' said the charming girl, 'give it to him on that side!'

I took the piece of crystal which was to represent the Diamond from my pocket, and gave it to her.

'You must have a hand in this, too,' I said. 'You must put it where you put the Moonstone last year.'

She led the way to the Indian cabinet, and put the mock Diamond into the drawer which the real Diamond had occupied on the birthday night. Mr Bruff witnessed this proceeding, under protest, as he had witnessed everything else. But the strong dramatic interest which the experiment was now assuming, proved (to my great amusement) to be too much for Betteredge's capacity of self restraint. His hand trembled as he held the candle, and he whispered anxiously, 'Are you sure, miss, it's the right drawer?'

I led the way out again, with the laudanum and water in my hand. At the door, I stopped to address a last word to Miss Verinder.

'Don't be long in putting out the lights,' I said.

'I will put them out at once,' she answered. 'And I will wait in my bedroom, with only one candle alight.'

She closed the sitting-room door behind us. Followed by Mr Bruff and Betteredge, I went back to Mr Blake's room.

We found him moving restlessly from side to side of the bed, and wondering irritably whether he was to have the laudanum that night. In the presence of the two witnesses, I gave him the dose, and shook up his pillows, and told him to lie down again quietly and wait.

His bed, provided with light chintz curtains, was placed with the head against the wall of the room, so as to leave a good open space on either side of it. On one side, I drew the curtains completely—and in the part of the room thus screened from his view, I placed Mr Bruff and Betteredge, to wait for the result. At the bottom of the bed I half drew the curtains— and placed my own chair at a little distance, so that I might let him see me or not see me, speak to me or not speak to me, just as the circumstances might direct. Having already been informed that he always slept with a light in the room, I placed one of the two lighted candles on a little table at the head of the bed, where the glare of the light would not strike on his eyes. The other candle I gave to Mr Bruff; the light, in this instance, being subdued by the screen of the chintz curtains. The window was open at the top, so as to ventilate the room. The rain fell softly, the house was quiet. It was twenty minutes past eleven, by my watch, when the preparations were completed, and I took my place on the chair set apart at the bottom of the bed.

Mr Bruff resumed his papers, with every appearance of being as deeply interested in them as ever. But looking towards him now, I saw certain signs and tokens which told me that the Law was beginning to lose its hold on him at last. The suspended interest of the situation in which we were now placed was slowly asserting its influence even on *his* unimaginative mind. As for Betteredge, consistency of principle and dignity of conduct had become, in his case, mere empty words. He forgot that I was performing a conjuring trick on Mr Franklin Blake; he forgot that I had upset the house from top to bottom; he forgot that I had not read *Robinson Crusoe* since I was a child. 'For the

Lord's sake, sir,' he whispered to me, 'tell us when it will begin to work.'

'Not before midnight,' I whispered back. 'Say nothing, and sit still.'

Betteredge dropped to the lowest depth of familiarity with me, without a struggle to save himself. He answered by a wink!

Looking next towards Mr Blake, I found him as restless as ever in his bed; fretfully wondering why the influence of the laudanum had not begun to assert itself yet. To tell him, in his present humour, that the more he fidgeted and wondered, the longer he would delay the result for which we were now waiting, would have been simply useless. The wiser course to take was to dismiss the idea of the opium from his mind, by leading him insensibly to think of something else.

With this view, I encouraged him to talk to me; contriving so to direct the conversation, on my side, as to lead it back again to the subject which had engaged us earlier in the evening—the subject of the Diamond. I took care to revert to those portions of the story of the Moonstone, which related to the transport of it from London to Yorkshire; to the risk which Mr Blake had run in removing it from the bank at Frizinghall: and to the unexpected appearance of the Indians at the house, on the evening of the birthday. And I purposely assumed, in referring to these events, to have misunderstood much of what Mr Blake himself had told me a few hours since. In this way, I set him talking on the subject with which it was now vitally important to fill his mind—without allowing him to suspect that I was making him talk for a purpose. Little by little, he became so interested in putting me right that he forgot to fidget in the bed. His mind was far away from the question of the opium, at the all-important time when his eyes first told me that the opium was beginning to lay its hold on his brain.

I looked at my watch. It wanted five minutes to twelve, when the premonitory symptoms of the working of the laudanum first showed themselves to me.

At this time, no unpractised eyes would have detected any change in him. But, as the minutes of the new morning wore away, the swiftly-subtle progress of the influence began to show itself more plainly. The sublime intoxication of opium gleamed in his eyes; the dew of a stealthy perspiration began to glisten on his face. In five minutes more, the talk which he still kept up with me, failed in coherence. He held steadily to the subject of the Diamond; but he ceased to complete his sentences. A little later, the sentences dropped to single words. Then, there was an interval of silence. Then, he sat up in bed. Then, still busy with the subject of the Diamond, he began to talk again— not to me, but to himself. That change told me that the first stage in the experiment was reached. The stimulant influence of the opium had got him.

The time, now, was twenty-three minutes past twelve. The next half hour, at most, would decide the question of whether he would, or would not, get up from his bed, and leave the room.

In the breathless interest of watching him—in the unutterable triumph of seeing the first result of the experiment declare itself in the manner, and nearly at the time, which I had anticipated—I had utterly forgotten the two companions of my night vigil. Looking towards them now, I saw the Law (as represented by Mr Bruff's papers) lying unheeded on the floor. Mr Bruff himself was looking eagerly through a crevice left in the imperfectly-drawn curtains of the bed. And Betteredge, oblivious of all respect for social distinctions, was peeping over Mr Bruff's shoulder.

They both started back, on finding that I was looking at them, like two boys caught out by their schoolmaster in a fault. I signed to them to take off their boots quietly, as I was taking off mine. If Mr Blake gave us the chance of following him, it was vitally necessary to follow him without noise.

Ten minutes passed—and nothing happened. Then, he suddenly threw the bed-clothes off him. He put one leg out of bed. He waited.

'I wish I had never taken it out of the bank,' he said to himself. 'It was safe in the bank.'

My heart throbbed fast; the pulses at my temples beat furiously. The doubt about the safety of the Diamond was, once more, the dominant impression in his brain! On that one pivot, the whole success of the experiment turned. The prospect thus suddenly opened before me was too much for my shattered nerves. I was obliged to look away from him—or I should have lost my self-control.

There was another interval of silence.

When I could trust myself to look back at him, he was out of his bed, standing erect at the side of it. The pupils of his eyes were now contracted; his eyeballs gleamed in the light of the candle as he moved his head slowly to and fro. He was thinking; he was doubting—he spoke again.

'How do I know?' he said. 'The Indians may be hidden in the house.'

He stopped, and walked slowly to the other end of the room. He turned—waited—came back to the bed.

'It's not even locked up,' he went on. 'It's in the drawer of her cabinet. And the drawer doesn't lock.'

He sat down on the side of the bed. 'Anybody might take it,' he said.

He rose again restlessly, and reiterated his first words.

'How do I know? The Indians may be hidden in the house.'

He waited again. I drew back behind the half curtain of the bed. He looked about the room, with a vacant glitter in his eyes. It was a breathless moment. There was a pause of some sort. A pause in the action of the opium? A pause in the action of the brain? Who could tell? Everything depended, now, on what he did next.

He laid himself down again on the bed!

A horrible doubt crossed my mind. Was it possible that the sedative action of the opium was making itself felt already? It was not in my experience that it should do this. But what is experience, where opium is concerned? There are probably no two men in existence on whom the drug acts in exactly the same manner. Was some constitutional peculiarity in him, feeling the influence in some new way? Were we to fail on the very brink of success?

No! He got up again abruptly. 'How the devil am I to sleep,' he said, 'with *this* on my mind?'

He looked at the light, burning on the table at the head of his bed. After a moment, he took the candle in his hand.

I blew out the second candle burning behind the closed curtains. I drew back, with Mr Bruff and Betteredge, into the farthest corner by the bed. I signed to them to be silent, as if their lives had depended on it.

We waited—seeing and hearing nothing. We waited, hidden from him by the curtains.

The light which he was holding on the other side of us moved suddenly. The next moment he passed us, swift and noiseless, with the candle in his hand.

He opened the bedroom door, and went out.

We followed him along the corridor. We followed him down the stairs. We followed him along the second corridor. He never looked back; he never hesitated.

He opened the sitting-room door, and went in, leaving it open behind him.

The door was hung (like all the other doors in the house) on large old-fashioned hinges. When it was opened, a crevice was opened between the door and the post. I signed to my two companions to look through this, so as to keep them from showing themselves. I placed myself—outside the door also—on the opposite side. A recess in the wall was at my left hand, in which I could instantly hide myself, if he showed any signs of looking back into the corridor.

He advanced to the middle of the room, with the candle still in his hand: he looked about him—but he never looked back.

I saw the door of Miss Verinder's bedroom, standing ajar.

She had put out her light. She controlled herself nobly. The dim white outline of her summer dress was all that I could see. Nobody who had not known it beforehand would have suspected that there was a living creature in the room. She kept back, in the dark: not a word, not a movement escaped her.

It was now ten minutes past one. I heard, through the dead silence, the soft drip of the rain and the tremulous passage of the night air through the trees.

After waiting irresolute, for a minute or more, in the middle of the room, he moved to the corner near the window, where the Indian cabinet stood.

He put his candle on the top of the cabinet. He opened, and shut, one drawer after another, until he came to the drawer in which the mock Diamond was put. He looked into the drawer for a moment. Then he took the mock Diamond out with his right hand. With the other hand, he took the candle from the top of the cabinet.

He walked back a few steps towards the middle of the room, and stood still again.

Thus far, he had exactly repeated what he had done on the birthday night. Would his next proceeding be the same as the proceeding of last year? Would he leave the room? Would he go back now, as I believed he had gone back then, to his bed-chamber? Would he show us what he had done with the Diamond, when he had returned to his own room?

His first action, when he moved once more, proved to be an action which he had not performed, when he was under the influence of the opium for the first time. He put the candle down on a table, and wandered on a little towards the farther end of the room. There was a sofa there. He leaned heavily on the back of it, with his left hand—then roused himself, and returned to the middle of the room. I could now see his eyes. They were getting dull and heavy; the glitter in them was fast dying out.

The suspense of the moment proved too much for Miss

Verinder's self-control. She advanced a few steps—then stopped again. Mr Bruff and Betteredge looked across the open doorway at me for the first time. The prevision of a coming disappointment was impressing itself on their minds as well as on mine.

Still, so long as he stood where he was, there was hope. We waited, in unutterable expectation, to see what would happen next.

The next event was decisive. He let the mock Diamond drop out of his hand.

It fell on the floor, before the doorway—plainly visible to him, and to everyone. He made no effort to pick it up: he looked down at it vacantly, and, as he looked, his head sank on his breast. He staggered—roused himself for an instant—walked back unsteadily to the sofa—and sat down on it. He made a last effort; he tried to rise, and sank back. His head fell on the sofa cushions. It was then twenty-five minutes past one o'clock. Before I had put my watch back in my pocket, he was asleep.

It was all over now. The sedative influence had got him; the experiment was at an end.

I entered the room, telling Mr Bruff and Betteredge that they might follow me. There was no fear of disturbing him. We were free to move and speak.

'The first thing to settle,' I said, 'is the question of what we are to do with him. He will probably sleep for the next six or seven hours, at least. It is some distance to carry him back to his own room. When I was younger, I could have done it alone. But my health and strength are not what they were—I am afraid I must ask you to help me.'

Before they could answer, Miss Verinder called to me softly. She met me at the door of her room, with a light shawl, and with the counterpane from her own bed.

'Do you mean to watch him while he sleeps?' she asked.

'Yes, I am not sure enough of the action of the opium, in his case, to be willing to leave him alone.'

She handed me the shawl and the counterpane.

'Why should you disturb him?' she whispered. 'Make his bed on the sofa. I can shut my door, and keep in my room.'

It was infinitely the simplest and the safest way of disposing of him for the night. I mentioned the suggestion to Mr Bruff and Betteredge—who both approved of my adopting it. In five minutes I had laid him comfortably on the sofa, and had covered him lightly with the counterpane and the shawl. Miss Verinder wished us good night, and closed the door. At my request, we three then drew round the table in the middle of the room, on which the candle was still burning, and on which writing materials were placed.

'Before we separate,' I began, 'I have a word to say about the experiment which has been tried tonight. Two distinct objects were to be gained by it. The first of these objects was to prove, that Mr Blake entered this room, and took the Diamond, last year, acting unconsciously and irresponsibly, under the influence of opium. After what you have both seen, are you both satisfied, so far?'

They answered me in the affirmative, without a moment's hesitation.

'The second object,' I went on, 'was to discover what he did with the Diamond, after he was seen by Miss Verinder to leave her sitting-room with the jewel in his hand, on the birthday night. The gaining of this object depended, of course, on his still continuing exactly to repeat his proceedings of last year. He has failed to do that; and the purpose of the experiment is defeated accordingly. I can't assert that I am not disappointed at the result—but I can honestly say that I am not surprised by it. I told Mr Blake from the first, that our complete success in this matter depended on our completely reproducing in him the physical and moral conditions of last year—and I warned him that this was the next thing to a downright impossibility. We have only partially reproduced the conditions, and the experiment has been only partially successful in consequence. It is also possible that I may have administered too large a dose of laudanum. But I myself look upon the first reason that I have given, as the true reason why we have to lament a failure, as well as to rejoice over a success.'

After saying those words, I put the writing materials before Mr Bruff, and asked him if he had any objection—before we separated for the night—to draw out, and sign, a plain statement of what he had seen. He at once took the pen, and produced the statement with the fluent readiness of a practised hand.

'I owe you this,' he said, signing the paper, 'as some atonement for what passed between us earlier in the evening. I beg your pardon, Mr Jennings, for having doubted you. You have done Franklin Blake an inestimable service. In our legal phrase, you have proved your case.'

Betteredge's apology was characteristic of the man.

'Mr Jennings,' he said, 'when you read *Robinson Crusoe* again (which I strongly recommend you to do), you will find that he never scruples to acknowledge it, when he turns out to have been in the wrong. Please to consider me, sir, as doing what Robinson Crusoe did, on the present occasion.' With those words he signed the paper in his turn.

Mr Bruff took me aside, as we rose from the table.

'One word about the Diamond,' he said. 'Your theory is that Franklin Blake hid the Moonstone in his room. My theory is, that the Moonstone is in the possession of Mr Luker's bankers in London. We won't dispute which of us is right. We will only ask, which of us is in a position to put his theory to the test?'

'The test, in my case,' I answered, 'has been tried tonight, and has failed.'

'The test, in my case,' rejoined Mr Bruff, 'is still in process of trial. For the last two days I have had a watch set for Mr Luker at the bank; and I shall cause that watch to be continued until the last day of the month. I know that he must take the Diamond himself out of his bankers' hands—and I am acting on the chance that the person who has pledged the Diamond may force him to do this by redeeming the pledge. In that case

I may be able to lay my hand on the person. If I succeed, I clear up the mystery, exactly at the point where the mystery baffles us now! Do you admit that, so far?'

I admitted it readily.

'I am going back to town by the morning train,' pursued the lawyer. 'I may hear, when I return, that a discovery has been made—and it may be of the greatest importance that I should have Franklin Blake at hand to appeal to, if necessary. I intend to tell him, as soon as he wakes, that he must return with me to London. After all that has happened, may I trust to your influence to back me?'

'Certainly!' I said.

Mr Bruff shook hands with me, and left the room. Betteredge followed him out.

I went to the sofa to look at Mr Blake. He had not moved since I had laid him down and made his bed—he lay locked in a deep and quiet sleep.

While I was still looking at him, I heard the bedroom door softly opened. Once more, Miss Verinder appeared on the threshold, in her pretty summer dress.

'Do me a last favour?' she whispered. 'Let me watch him with you.'

I hesitated—not in the interests of propriety; only in the interest of her night's rest. She came close to me, and took my hand.

'I can't sleep; I can't even sit still, in my own room,' she said. 'Oh, Mr Jennings, if you were me, only think how you would long to sit and look at him. Say, yes! Do!'

Is it necessary to mention that I gave way? Surely not!

She drew a chair to the foot of the sofa. She looked at him in a silent ecstasy of happiness, till the tears rose in her eyes. She dried her eyes, and said she would fetch her work. She fetched her work, and never did a single stitch of it. It lay in her lap—she was not even able to look away from him long enough to thread her needle. I thought of my own youth; I thought of the gentle eyes which had once looked love at *me*. In the heaviness of my heart I turned to my Journal for relief, and wrote in it what is written here.

So we kept our watch together in silence. One of us absorbed in his writing; the other absorbed in her love.

Hour after hour he lay in his deep sleep. The light of the new day grew and grew in the room, and still he never moved.

Towards six o'clock, I felt the warning which told me that my pains were coming back. I was obliged to leave her alone with him for a little while. I said I would go upstairs, and fetch another pillow for him out of his room. It was not a long attack, this time. In a little while I was able to venture back, and let her see me again.

I found her at the head of the sofa, when I returned. She was just touching his forehead with her lips. I shook my head as soberly as I could, and pointed to her chair. She looked back at me with a bright smile, and a charming colour in her face. 'You would have done it,' she whispered, 'in my place!'

It is just eight o'clock. He is beginning to move for the first time.

Miss Verinder is kneeling by the side of the sofa. She has so placed herself that when his eyes first open, they must open on her face.

Shall I leave them together?

Yes!

Eleven o'clock.—The house is empty again. They have arranged it among themselves; they have all gone to London by the ten o'clock train. My brief dream of happiness is over. I have awakened again to the realities of my friendless and lonely life.

I dare not trust myself to write down, the kind words that have been said to me especially by Miss Verinder and Mr Blake. Besides, it is needless. Those words will come back to me in my solitary hours, and will help me through what is left of the end of my life. Mr Blake is to write, and tell me what happens in London. Miss Verinder is to return to Yorkshire in the autumn (for her marriage, no doubt); and I am to take a holiday, and be a guest in the house. Oh me, how I felt, as the grateful happiness looked at me out of her eyes, and the warm pressure of her hand said, 'This is your doing!'

My poor patients are waiting for me. Back again, this morning, to the old routine! Back again, tonight, to the dreadful alternative between the opium and the pain!

God be praised for His mercy! I have seen a little sunshine—I have had a happy time.

FIFTH NARRATIVE

The Story resumed by FRANKLIN BLAKE

CHAPTER I

BUT few words are needed, on my part, to complete the narrative that has been presented in the Journal of Ezra Jennings.

Of myself, I have only to say that I awoke on the morning of the twenty-sixth, perfectly ignorant of all that I had said and done under the influence of the opium—from the time when the drug first laid its hold on me, to the time when I opened my eyes, in Rachel's sitting-room.

Of what happened after my waking, I do not feel called upon to render an account in detail. Confining myself merely to results, I have to report that Rachel and I thoroughly understood each other, before a single word of explanation had passed on either side. I decline to account, and Rachel declines to account, for the extraordinary rapidity of our reconciliation. Sir and Madam, look back at the time when you were passionately attached to each other—and you will know what happened, after Ezra Jennings had shut the door of the sitting-room, as well as I know it myself.

I have, however, no objection to add, that we should have been certainly discovered by Mrs Merridew, but for Rachel's presence of mind. She heard the sound of the old lady's dress in the corridor, and instantly ran out to meet her; I heard Mrs Merridew say, 'What is the matter?' and I heard Rachel answer, 'The explosion!' Mrs Merridew instantly permitted herself to be taken by the arm, and led into the garden, out of the way of the impending shock. On her return to the house, she met me in the hall, and expressed herself as greatly struck by the vast improvement in Science, since the time when she was a girl at school. 'Explosions, Mr Blake, are infinitely milder than they were. I assure you, I barely heard Mr Jennings's explosion from the garden. And no smell afterwards, that I can detect, now we have come back to the house! I must really apologise to your medical friend. It is only due to him to say that he has managed it beautifully!'

At breakfast, Mr Bruff made no secret of his reasons for wishing that I should accompany him to London by the morning train. The watch kept at the bank, and the result which might yet come of it, appealed so irresistibly to Rachel's curiosity, that she at once decided (if Mrs Merridew had no objection) on accompanying us back to town—so as to be within reach of the earliest news of our proceedings.

Mrs Merridew proved to be all pliability and indulgence, after the truly considerate manner in which the explosion had conducted itself; and Betteredge was accordingly informed that we were all four to travel back together by the morning train. I fully expected that he would have asked leave to accompany us. But Rachel had wisely provided her faithful old servant with an occupation that interested him. He was charged with completing the refurnishing of the house, and was too full of his domestic responsibilities to feel the 'detective-fever' as he might have felt it under other circumstances.

Our one subject of regret, in going to London, was the necessity of parting, more abruptly than we could have wished, with Ezra Jennings. It was impossible to persuade him to accompany us. I could only promise to write to him—and Rachel could only insist on his coming to see her when she returned to Yorkshire. There was every prospect of our meeting again in a few months—and yet there was something very sad in seeing our best and dearest friend left standing alone on the platform, as the train moved out of the station.

On our arrival in London, Mr Bruff was accosted at the terminus by a small boy, dressed in a jacket and trousers of threadbare black cloth, and personally remarkable in virtue of the extraordinary prominence of his eyes. They projected so far, and they rolled about so loosely, that you wondered uneasily why they remained in their sockets. After listening to the boy, Mr Bruff asked the ladies whether they would excuse our accompanying them back to Portland Place. I had barely time to promise Rachel that I would return, and tell her everything that had happened, before Mr Bruff seized me by the arm, and hurried me into a cab. The boy with the ill-secured eyes took his place on the box by the driver, and the driver was directed to go to Lombard Street.

'News from the bank?' I asked, as we started.

'News of Mr Luker,' said Mr Bruff. 'An hour ago, he was seen to leave his house at Lambeth, in a cab, accompanied by two men, who were recognised by *my* men as police officers in plain clothes. If Mr Luker's dread of the Indians is at the bottom of this precaution, the inference is plain enough. He is going to take the Diamond out of the bank.'

'And we are going to the bank to see what comes of it?'

'Yes—or to hear what has come of it, if it is all over by this time. Did you notice my boy—on the box, there?'

'I noticed his eyes.'

Mr Bruff laughed. 'They call the poor little wretch "Gooseberry" at the office,' he said. 'I employ him to go on errands—and I only wish my clerks who have nick-named him were as thoroughly to be depended on as he is. Gooseberry is one of the sharpest boys in London, Mr Blake, in spite of his eyes.'

It was twenty minutes to five when we drew up before the bank in Lombard Street. Gooseberry looked longingly at his master, as he opened the cab door.

'Do you want to come in too?' asked Mr Bruff kindly. 'Come in then, and keep at my heels till further orders. He's as quick as lightning,' pursued Mr Bruff, addressing me in a whisper. 'Two words will do with Gooseberry, where twenty would be wanted with another boy.'

We entered the bank. The outer office—with the long counter, behind which the cashiers sat—was crowded with people; all waiting their turn to take money out, or to pay money in, before the bank closed at five o'clock.

Two men among the crowd approached Mr Bruff, as soon as he showed himself.

'Well,' asked the lawyer, 'have you seen him?'

'He passed us here half an hour since, sir, and went on into the inner office.'

'Has he not come out again yet?'

'No, sir.'

Mr Bruff turned to me. 'Let us wait,' he said.

I looked round among the people about me for the three Indians. Not a sign of them was to be seen anywhere. The only person present with a noticeably dark complexion was a tall man in a pilot coat, and a round hat, who looked like a sailor. Could this be one of them in disguise? Impossible! The man was taller than any of the Indians; and his face, where it was not hidden by a bushy black beard, was twice the breadth of any of their faces at least.

'They must have their spy somewhere,' said Mr Bruff, looking at the dark sailor in his turn. 'And he may be the man.'

Before he could say more, his coat-tail was respectfully pulled by his attendant sprite with the gooseberry eyes. Mr Bruff looked where the boy was looking. 'Hush!' he said. 'Here is Mr Luker!'

The money-lender came out from the inner regions of the bank, followed by his two guardian policemen in plain clothes.

'Keep your eye on him,' whispered Mr Bruff. 'If he passes the Diamond to anybody, he will pass it here.'

Without noticing either of us, Mr Luker slowly made his way to the door—now in the thickest, now in the thinnest part of the crowd. I distinctly saw his hand move, as he passed a short, stout man, respectably dressed in a suit of sober grey. The man started a little, and looked after him. Mr Luker moved on slowly through the crowd. At the door his guard placed themselves on either side of him. They were all three followed by one of Mr Bruff's men—and I saw them no more.

I looked round at the lawyer, and then looked significantly towards the man in the suit of sober grey. 'Yes!' whispered Mr Bruff, 'I saw it too!' He turned about, in search of his second man. The second man was nowhere to be seen. He looked behind him for his attendant sprite. Gooseberry had disappeared.

'What the devil does it mean?' said Mr Bruff angrily. 'They have both left us at the very time when we want them most.'

It came to the turn of the man in the grey suit to transact his business at the counter. He paid in a cheque—received a receipt for it—and turned to go out.

'What is to be done?' asked Mr Bruff. '*We* can't degrade ourselves by following him.'

'*I* can!' I said. 'I wouldn't lose sight of that man for ten thousand pounds!'

'In that case,' rejoined Mr Bruff, 'I wouldn't lose sight of *you* for twice the money. A nice occupation for a man in my position,' he muttered to himself, as we followed the stranger out of the bank. 'For Heaven's sake don't mention it. I should be ruined if it was known.'

The man in the grey suit got into an omnibus, going westward. We got in after him. There were latent reserves of youth still left in Mr Bruff. I assert it positively—when he took his seat in the omnibus, he blushed!

The man in the grey suit stopped the omnibus, and got out in Oxford Street. We followed him again. He went into a chemist's shop.

Mr Bruff started. 'My chemist!' he exclaimed. 'I am afraid we have made a mistake.'

We entered the shop. Mr Bruff and the proprietor exchanged a few words in private. The lawyer joined me again, with a very crestfallen face.

'It's greatly to our credit,' he said, as he took my arm, and led me out—'that's one comfort!'

'What is to our credit?' I asked.

'Mr Blake! You and I are the two worst amateur detectives that ever tried their hands at the trade. The man in the grey suit has been thirty years in the chemist's service. He was sent to the bank to pay money to his master's account—and he knows no more of the Moonstone than the babe unborn.'

I asked what was to be done next.

'Come back to my office,' said Mr Bruff. 'Gooseberry, and my second man have evidently followed somebody else. Let us hope that *they* had their eyes about them at any rate!'

When we reached Gray's Inn Square, the second man had arrived there before us. He had been waiting for more than a quarter of an hour.

'Well!' asked Mr Bruff. 'What's your news?'

'I am sorry to say, sir,' replied the man, 'that I have made a mistake. I could have taken my oath that I saw Mr Luker pass something to an elderly gentleman, in a light-coloured paletot. The elderly gentleman turns out, sir, to be a most respectable master ironmonger in Eastcheap.'

'Where is Gooseberry?' asked Mr Bruff resignedly.

The man stared. 'I don't know, sir. I have seen nothing of him since I left the bank.'

Mr Bruff dismissed the man. 'One of two things,' he said to me. 'Either Gooseberry has run away, or he is hunting on his own account. What do you say to dining here, on the chance that the boy may come back in an hour or two? I have got some good wine in the cellar, and we can get a chop from the coffee-house.'

We dined at Mr Bruff's chambers. Before the cloth was removed, 'a person' was announced as wanting to speak to the lawyer. Was the person Gooseberry? No: only the man who had been employed to follow Mr Luker when he left the bank.

The report, in this case, presented no feature of the slightest interest. Mr Luker had gone back to his own house, and had there dismissed his guard. He had not gone out again afterwards. Towards dusk, the shutters had been put up, and the doors had been bolted. The street before the house, and the alley behind the house, had been carefully watched. No signs of the Indians had been visible. No person whatever had been seen loitering about the premises. Having stated these facts, the man waited to know whether there were any further orders. Mr Bruff dismissed him for the night.

'Do you think Mr Luker has taken the Moonstone home with him?' I asked.

'Not he,' said Mr Bruff. 'He would never have dismissed his two policemen, if he had run the risk of keeping the Diamond in his own house again.'

We waited another half-hour for the boy, and waited in vain. It was then time for Mr Bruff to go to Hampstead, and for me to return to Rachel in Portland Place. I left my card in charge of the porter at the chambers, with a line written on it to say that I should be at my lodgings at half past ten, that night. The card was to be given to the boy, if the boy came back.

Some men have a knack of keeping appointments; and other men have a knack of missing them. I am one of the other men. Add to this, that I passed the evening at Portland Place, on the same seat with Rachel, in a room forty feet long, with Mrs Merridew at the further end of it. Does anybody wonder that I got home at half past twelve instead of half past ten? How thoroughly heartless that person must be! And how earnestly I hope I may never make that person's acquaintance!

My servant handed me a morsel of paper when he let me in.

I read, in a neat legal handwriting, these words—'If you please, sir, I am getting sleepy. I will come back tomorrow morning, between nine and ten.' Inquiry proved that a boy, with very extraordinary-looking eyes, had called, had presented my card and message, had waited an hour, had done nothing but fall asleep and wake up again, had written a line for me, and had gone home—after gravely informing the servant that 'he was fit for nothing unless he got his night's rest.'

At nine, the next morning, I was ready for my visitor. At half past nine, I heard steps outside my door. 'Come in, Gooseberry!' I called out. 'Thank you, sir,' answered a grave and melancholy voice. The door opened. I started to my feet, and confronted— Sergeant Cuff!

'I thought I would look in here, Mr Blake, on the chance of your being in town, before I wrote to Yorkshire,' said the Sergeant.

He was as dreary and as lean as ever. His eyes had not lost their old trick (so subtly noticed in Betteredge's Narrative) of 'looking as if they expected something more from you than you were aware of yourself'. But, so far as dress can alter a man, the great Cuff was changed beyond all recognition. He wore a broad-brimmed white hat, a light shooting jacket, white trousers, and drab gaiters. He carried a stout oak stick. His whole aim and object seemed to be to look as if he had lived in the country all his life. When I complimented him on his Metamorphosis, he declined to take it as a joke. He complained, quite gravely, of the noises and the smells of London. I declare I am far from sure that he did not speak with a slightly rustic accent! I offered him breakfast. The innocent countryman was quite shocked. *His* breakfast hour was half-past six—and *he* went to bed with the cocks and hens!

'I only got back from Ireland last night,' said the Sergeant, coming round to the practical object of his visit, in his own impenetrable manner. 'Before I went to bed, I read your letter, telling me what has happened since my inquiry after the Diamond was suspended last year. There's only one thing to be said about the matter on my side. I completely mistook my case. How any man living was to have seen things in their true light, in such a situation as mine was at the time, I don't profess to know. But that doesn't alter the facts as they stand. I own that I made a mess of it. Not the first mess, Mr Blake, which has distinguished my professional career! It's only in books that the officers of the detective force are superior to the weakness of making a mistake.'

'You have come in the nick of time to recover your reputation,' I said.

'I beg your pardon, Mr Blake,' rejoined the Sergeant. 'Now I have retired from business, I don't care a straw about my reputation. I have done with my reputation, thank God! I am here, sir, in grateful remembrance of the late Lady Verinder's liberality to me. I will go back to my old work—if you want me, and if you will trust me—on that consideration, and on no other. Not a farthing of money is to pass, if you please, from you to me. This is on honour. Now tell me, Mr Blake, how the case stands since you wrote to me last.'

I told him of the experiment with the opium, and of what had occurred afterwards at the bank in Lombard Street. He was greatly struck by the experiment—it was something entirely new in his experience. And he was particularly interested in the theory of Ezra Jennings, relating to what I had done with the Diamond, after I had left Rachel's sitting-room, on the birthday night.

'I don't hold with Mr Jennings that you hid the Moonstone,' said Sergeant Cuff. 'But I agree with him, that you must certainly have taken it back to your own room.'

'Well?' I asked. 'And what happened then?'

'Have you no suspicion yourself of what happened, sir?'

'None whatever.'

'Has Mr Bruff no suspicion?'

'No more than I have.'

Sergeant Cuff rose, and went to my writing-table. He came back with a sealed envelope. It was marked 'Private'; it was addressed to me; and it had the Sergeant's signature in the corner.

'I suspected the wrong person last year,' he said; 'and I may be suspecting the wrong person now. Wait to open the envelope, Mr Blake, till you have got at the truth. And then compare the name of the guilty person, with the name that I have written in that sealed letter.'

I put the letter into my pocket—and then asked for the Sergeant's opinion of the measures which we had taken at the bank.

'Very well intended, sir,' he answered, 'and quite the right thing to do. But there was another person who ought to have been looked after besides Mr Luker.'

'The person named in the letter you have just given to me?'

'Yes, Mr Blake, the person named in the letter. It can't be helped now. I shall have something to propose to you and Mr Bruff, sir, when the time comes. Let's wait, first, and see if the boy has anything to tell us that is worth hearing.'

It was close on ten o'clock, and the boy had not made his appearance. Sergeant Cuff talked of other matters. He asked after his old friend Betteredge, and his old enemy the gardener. In a minute more, he would no doubt have got from this to the subject of his favourite roses, if my servant had not interrupted us by announcing that the boy was below.

On being brought into the room, Gooseberry stopped at the threshold of the door, and looked distrustfully at the stranger who was in my company. I told the boy to come to me.

'You may speak before this gentleman,' I said. 'He is here to assist me; and he knows all that has happened. Sergeant Cuff,' I added, 'this is the boy from Mr Bruff's office.'

In our modern system of civilisation, celebrity (no matter of what kind) is the lever that will move anything. The fame of the great Cuff had even reached the ears of the small Gooseberry. The boy's ill-fixed eyes rolled when I mentioned the illustrious name, till I thought they really must have dropped on the carpet.

'Come here, my lad,' said the Sergeant, 'and let's hear what you have got to tell us.'

The notice of the great man—the hero of many a famous story in every lawyer's office in London—appeared to fascinate the boy. He placed himself in front of Sergeant Cuff, and put his hands behind him, after the approved fashion of a neophyte who is examined in his catechism.

'What is your name?' said the Sergeant, beginning with the first question in the catechism.

'Octavius Guy,' answered the boy. 'They call me Gooseberry at the office because of my eyes.'

'Octavius Guy, otherwise Gooseberry,' pursued the Sergeant, with the utmost gravity, 'you were missed at the bank yesterday. What were you about?'

'If you please, sir, I was following a man.'

'Who was he?'

'A tall man, sir, with a big black beard, dressed like a sailor.'

'I remember the man!' I broke in. 'Mr Bruff and I thought he was a spy employed by the Indians.'

Sergeant Cuff did not appear to be much impressed by what Mr Bruff and I had thought. He went on catechising Gooseberry.

'Well?' he said—'and why did you follow the sailor?'

'If you please, sir, Mr Bruff wanted to know whether Mr Luker passed anything to anybody on his way out of the bank. I saw Mr Luker pass something to the sailor with the black beard.'

'Why didn't you tell Mr Bruff what you saw?'

'I hadn't time to tell anybody, sir, the sailor went out in such a hurry.'

'And you ran out after him—eh?'

'Yes, sir.'

'Gooseberry,' said the Sergeant, patting his head, 'you have got something in that small skull of yours—and it isn't cotton-wool. I am greatly pleased with you, so far.'

The boy blushed with pleasure. Sergeant Cuff went on.

'Well? and what did the sailor do, when he got into the street?'

'He called a cab, sir.'

'And what did you do?'

'Held on behind, and run after it.'

Before the Sergeant could put his next question, another visitor was announced—the head clerk from Mr Bruff's office.

Feeling the importance of not interrupting Sergeant Cuff's examination of the boy, I received the clerk in another room. He came with bad news of his employer. The agitation and excitement of the last two days had proved too much for Mr Bruff. He had awoken that morning with an attack of gout; he was confined to his room at Hampstead; and, in the present critical condition of our affairs, he was very uneasy at being compelled to leave me without the advice and assistance of an experienced person. The chief clerk had received orders to hold himself at my disposal, and was willing to do his best to replace Mr Bruff.

I wrote at once to quiet the old gentleman's mind, by telling him of Sergeant Cuff's visit: adding that Gooseberry was at that moment under examination; and promising to inform Mr Bruff, either personally, or by letter, of whatever might occur later in the day. Having despatched the clerk to Hampstead with my note, I returned to the room which I had left, and found Sergeant Cuff at the fireplace, in the act of ringing the bell.

'I beg your pardon, Mr Blake,' said the Sergeant. 'I was just going to send word by your servant that I wanted to speak to you. There isn't a doubt on my mind that this boy—this most meritorious boy,' added the Sergeant, patting Gooseberry on the head, 'has followed the right man. Precious time has been lost, sir, through your unfortunately not being at home at half past ten last night. The only thing to do, now, is to send for a cab immediately.'

In five minutes more, Sergeant Cuff and I (with Gooseberry

on the box to guide the driver) were on our way eastward, towards the City.

'One of these days,' said the Sergeant, pointing through the front window of the cab, 'that boy will do great things in my late profession. He is the brightest and cleverest little chap I have met with, for many a long year past. You shall hear the substance, Mr Blake, of what he told me while you were out of the room. You were present, I think, when he mentioned that he held on behind the cab, and ran after it?'

'Yes.'

'Well, sir, the cab went from Lombard Street to the Tower Wharf. The sailor with the black beard got out, and spoke to the steward of the Rotterdam steamboat, which was to start next morning. He asked if he could be allowed to go on board at once, and sleep in his berth over-night. The steward said, No. The cabins, and berths, and bedding were all to have a thorough cleaning that evening, and no passenger could be allowed to come on board, before the morning. The sailor turned round, and left the wharf. When he got into the street again, the boy noticed for the first time, a man dressed like a respectable mechanic, walking on the opposite side of the road, and apparently keeping the sailor in view. The sailor stopped at an eating-house in the neighbourhood, and went in. The boy—not being able to make up his mind, at the moment—hung about among some other boys, staring at the good things in the eating-house window. He noticed the mechanic waiting, as he himself was waiting—but still on the opposite side of the street. After a minute, a cab came by slowly, and stopped where the mechanic was standing. The boy could only see plainly one person in the cab, who leaned forward at the window to speak to the mechanic. He described that person, Mr Blake, without any prompting from me, as having a dark face, like the face of an Indian.'

It was plain, by this time, that Mr Bruff and I had made another mistake. The sailor with the black beard was clearly not a spy in the service of the Indian conspiracy. Was he, by any possibility, the man who had got the Diamond?

'After a little,' pursued the Sergeant, 'the cab moved on slowly down the street. The mechanic crossed the road, and went into the eating-house. The boy waited outside till he was hungry and tired—and then went into the eating-house in his turn. He had a shilling in his pocket; and he dined sumptuously, he tells me, on a black-pudding, an eel-pie, and a bottle of ginger-beer. What can a boy *not* digest? The substance in question has never been found yet.'

'What did he see in the eating-house?' I asked.

'Well, Mr Blake, he saw the sailor reading the newspaper at one table, and the mechanic reading the newspaper at another. It was dusk before the sailor got up, and left the place. He looked about him suspiciously when he got out into the street. The boy—*being* a boy—passed unnoticed. The mechanic had not come out yet. The sailor walked on, looking about him, and apparently not very certain of where he was going next. The mechanic appeared once more, on the opposite side of the road. The sailor went on, till he got to Shore Lane, leading into Lower Thames Street. There he stopped before a public-house, under the sign of "The Wheel of Fortune", and, after examining the place outside, went in. Gooseberry went in too. There were a great many people, mostly of the decent sort, at the bar. "The Wheel of Fortune" is a very respectable house, Mr Blake; famous for its porter and pork-pies.'

The Sergeant's digressions irritated me. He saw it; and confined himself more strictly to Gooseberry's evidence when he went on.

'The sailor,' he resumed, 'asked if he could have a bed. The landlord said "No; they were full." The barmaid corrected him, and said "Number Ten was empty." A waiter was sent for to show the sailor to Number Ten. Just before that, Gooseberry had noticed the mechanic among the people at the bar. Before the waiter had answered the call, the mechanic had vanished. The sailor was taken off to his room. Not knowing what to do next, Gooseberry had the wisdom to wait and see if anything happened. Something did happen. The landlord was called for. Angry voices were heard upstairs. The mechanic suddenly made his appearance again, collared by the landlord, and exhibiting, to Gooseberry's great surprise, all the signs and tokens of being drunk. The landlord thrust him out at the door, and threatened him with the police if he came back. From the altercation between them, while this was going on, it appeared that the man had been discovered in Number Ten, and had declared with drunken obstinacy that he had taken the room. Gooseberry was so struck by this sudden intoxication of a previously sober person, that he couldn't resist running out after the mechanic into the street. As long as he was in sight of the public-house, the man reeled about in the most disgraceful manner. The moment he turned the corner of the street, he recovered his balance instantly, and became as sober a member of society as you could wish to see. Gooseberry went back to "The Wheel of Fortune" in a very bewildered state of mind. He waited about again, on the chance of something happening. Nothing happened; and nothing more was to be heard, or seen, of the sailor. Gooseberry decided on going back to the office. Just as he came to this conclusion, who should appear, on the opposite side of the street as usual, but the mechanic again! He looked up at one particular window at the top of the public-house, which was the only one that had a light in it. The light seemed to relieve his mind. He left the place directly. The boy made his way back to Gray's Inn—got your card and message— called—and failed to find you. There you have the state of the case, Mr Blake, as it stands at the present time.'

'What is your own opinion of the case, Sergeant?'

'I think it's serious, sir. Judging by what the boy saw, the Indians are in it, to begin with.'

'Yes. And the sailor is evidently the person to whom Mr

Luker passed the Diamond. It seems odd that Mr Bruff, and I, and the man in Mr Bruff's employment, should all have been mistaken about who the person was.'

'Not at all, Mr Blake. Considering the risk that person ran, it's likely enough that Mr Luker purposely misled you, by previous arrangement between them.'

'Do you understand the proceedings at the public-house?' I asked. 'The man dressed like a mechanic was acting of course in the employment of the Indians. But I am as much puzzled to account for his sudden assumption of drunkenness as Gooseberry himself.'

'I think I can give a guess at what it means, sir,' said the Sergeant. 'If you will reflect, you will see that the man must have had some pretty strict instructions from the Indians. They were far too noticeable themselves to risk being seen at the bank, or in the public-house—they were obliged to trust everything to their deputy. Very good. Their deputy hears a certain number named in the public-house, as the number of the room which the sailor is to have for the night—that being also the room (unless our notion is all wrong) which the Diamond is to have for the night, too. Under those circumstances, the Indians, you may rely on it, would insist on having a description of the room—of its position in the house, of its capability of being approached from the outside, and so on. What was the man to do, with such orders as these? Just what he did! He ran upstairs to get a look at the room, before the sailor was taken into it. He was found there, making his observations—and he shammed drunk, as the easiest way of getting out of the difficulty. That's how I read the riddle. After he was turned out of the public-house, he probably went with his report to the place where his employers were waiting for him. And his employers, no doubt, sent him back to make sure that the sailor was really settled at the public-house till the next morning. As for what happened at "The Wheel of Fortune", after the boy left—we ought to have discovered that last night. It's eleven in the morning, now. We must hope for the best, and find out what we can.'

In a quarter of an hour more, the cab stopped in Shore Lane, and Gooseberry opened the door for us to get out.

'All right?' asked the Sergeant.

'All right,' answered the boy.

The moment we entered 'The Wheel of Fortune' it was plain even to my inexperienced eyes that there was something wrong in the house.

The only person behind the counter at which the liquors were served, was a bewildered servant girl, perfectly ignorant of the business. One or two customers, waiting for their morning drink, were tapping impatiently on the counter with their money. The barmaid appeared from the inner regions of the parlour, excited and preoccupied. She answered Sergeant Cuff's inquiry for the landlord, by telling him sharply that her master was upstairs, and was not to be bothered by anybody.

'Come along with me, sir,' said Sergeant Cuff, coolly leading the way upstairs, and beckoning to the boy to follow him.

The barmaid called to her master, and warned him that strangers were intruding themselves into the house. On the first floor we were encountered by the landlord, hurrying down, in a highly irritated state, to see what was the matter.

'Who the devil are you? and what do you want here?' he asked.

'Keep your temper,' said the Sergeant, quietly. 'I'll tell you who I am to begin with. I am Sergeant Cuff.'

The illustrious name instantly produced its effect. The angry landlord threw open the door of a sitting-room, and asked the Sergeant's pardon.

'I am annoyed and out of sorts, sir—that's the truth,' he said. 'Something unpleasant has happened in the house this morning. A man in my way of business has a deal to upset his temper, Sergeant Cuff.'

'Not a doubt of it,' said the Sergeant. 'I'll come at once, if you will allow me, to what brings us here. This gentleman and I want to trouble you with a few inquiries, on a matter of some interest to both of us.'

'Relating to what, sir?' asked the landlord.

'Relating to a dark man, dressed like a sailor, who slept here last night.'

'Good God! that's the man who is upsetting the whole house at this moment!' exclaimed the landlord. 'Do you, or does this gentleman know anything about him?'

'We can't be certain till we see him,' answered the Sergeant.

'See him?' echoed the landlord. 'That's the one thing that nobody has been able to do since seven o'clock this morning. That was the time when he left word, last night, that he was to be called. He *was* called—and there was no getting an answer from him, and no opening his door to see what was the matter. They tried again at eight, and they tried again at nine. No use! There was the door still locked—and not a sound to be heard in the room! I have been out this morning—and I only got back a quarter of an hour ago. I have hammered at the door myself—and all to no purpose. The potboy has gone to fetch a carpenter. If you can wait a few minutes, gentlemen, we will have the door opened, and see what it means.'

'Was the man drunk last night?' asked Sergeant Cuff.

'Perfectly sober, sir—or I would never have let him sleep in my house.'

'Did he pay for his bed beforehand?'

'No.'

'Could he leave the room in any way, without going out by the door?'

'The room is a garret,' said the landlord. 'But there's a trap-door in the ceiling, leading out on to the roof—and a little lower down the street, there's an empty house under repair. Do you think, Sergeant, the blackguard has got off in that way, without paying?'

'A sailor,' said Sergeant Cuff, 'might have done it—early in the morning, before the street was astir. He would be used to climbing, and his head wouldn't fail him on the roofs of the houses.'

As he spoke, the arrival of the carpenter was announced. We all went upstairs, at once, to the top story. I noticed that the Sergeant was unusually grave, even for *him*. It also struck me as odd that he told the boy (after having previously encouraged him to follow us), to wait in the room below till we came down again.

The carpenter's hammer and chisel disposed of the resistance of the door in a few minutes. But some article of furniture had been placed against it inside, as a barricade. By pushing at the door, we thrust this obstacle aside, and so got admission to the room. The landlord entered first; the Sergeant second; and I third. The other persons present followed us.

We all looked towards the bed, and all started.

The man had not left the room. He lay, dressed, on the bed—with a white pillow over his face, which completely hid it from view.

'What does that mean?' said the landlord, pointing to the pillow.

Sergeant Cuff led the way to the bed, without answering, and removed the pillow.

The man's swarthy face was placid and still; his black hair and beard were slightly, very slightly, discomposed. His eyes stared wide-open, glassy and vacant, at the ceiling. The filmy look and the fixed expression of them horrified me. I turned away, and went to the open window. The rest of them remained, where Sergeant Cuff remained, at the bed.

'He's in a fit!' I heard the landlord say.

'He's dead,' the Sergeant answered. 'Send for the nearest doctor, and send for the police.'

The waiter was dispatched on both errands. Some strange fascination seemed to hold Sergeant Cuff to the bed. Some strange curiosity seemed to keep the rest of them waiting, to see what the Sergeant would do next.

I turned again to the window. The moment afterwards, I felt a soft pull at my coat-tails, and a small voice whispered, 'Look here, sir!'

Gooseberry had followed us into the room. His loose eyes rolled frightfully—not in terror, but in exultation. He had made a detective-discovery on his own account. 'Look here, sir,' he repeated—and led me to a table in the corner of the room.

On the table stood a little wooden box, open, and empty. On one side of the box lay some jewellers' cotton. On the other side, was a torn sheet of white paper, with a seal on it, partly destroyed, and with an inscription in writing, which was still perfectly legible. The inscription was in these words:

'Deposited with Messrs Bushe, Lysaught, and Bushe, by Mr Septimus Luker, of Middlesex Place, Lambeth, a small wooden box, sealed up in this envelope, and containing a valuable of great price. The box, when claimed, to be only given up by Messrs Bushe and Co. on the personal application of Mr Luker.'

Those lines removed all further doubt, on one point at least. The sailor had been in possession of the Moonstone, when he had left the bank on the previous day.

I felt another pull at my coat-tails. Gooseberry had not done with me yet.

'Robbery!' whispered the boy, pointing, in high delight, to the empty box.

'You were told to wait downstairs,' I said. 'Go away!'

'And murder!' added Gooseberry, pointing, with a keener relish still, to the man on the bed.

There was something so hideous in the boy's enjoyment of the horror of the scene, that I took him by the two shoulders and put him out of the room.

At the moment when I crossed the threshold of the door, I heard Sergeant Cuff's voice, asking where I was. He met me,

as I returned into the room, and forced me to go back with him
to the bedside.

'Mr Blake!' he said. 'Look at the man's face. It is a face
disguised—and here's a proof of it!'

He traced with his finger a thin line of livid white, running
backward from the dead man's forehead, between the swarthy
complexion, and the slightly disturbed black hair. 'Let's see
what is under this,' said the Sergeant, suddenly seizing the black
hair, with a firm grip of his hand.

My nerves were not strong enough to bear it. I turned away
again from the bed.

The first sight that met my eyes, at the other end of the room,
was the irrepressible Gooseberry, perched on a chair, and
looking with breathless interest, over the heads of his elders,
at the Sergeant's proceedings.

'He's pulling off his wig!' whispered Gooseberry, compas-
sionating my position, as the only person in the room who
could see nothing.

There was a pause—and then a cry of astonishment among
the people round the bed.

'He's pulled off his beard!' cried Gooseberry.

There was another pause—Sergeant Cuff asked for something. The landlord went to the washhand-stand, and returned
to the bed with a basin of water and a towel.

Gooseberry danced with excitement on the chair. 'Come up
here, along with me, sir! He's washing off his complexion now!'

The Sergeant suddenly burst his way through the people
about him, and came, with horror in his face, straight to the
place where I was standing.

'Come back to the bed, sir!' he began. He looked at me closer,
and checked himself. 'No!' he resumed. 'Open the sealed letter
first—the letter I gave you this morning.'

I opened the letter.

'Read the name, Mr Blake, that I have written inside.'

I read the name that he had written. It was *Godfrey Ablewhite*.

'Now,' said the Sergeant, 'come with me, and look at the man on the bed.'

I went with him, and looked at the man on the bed.

GODFREY ABLEWHITE!

SIXTH NARRATIVE

Contributed by SERGEANT CUFF

DORKING, Surrey, *July 30th, 1849.* To Franklin Blake, Esq.

Sir,—I beg to apologise for the delay that has occurred in the production of the Report, with which I engaged to furnish you. I have waited to make it a complete Report; and I have been met, here and there, by obstacles which it was only possible to remove by some little expenditure of patience and time.

As to your cousin's death, then, first.

It appears to be established, beyond any reasonable doubt, that he was killed (while he was asleep, or immediately on his waking) by being smothered with a pillow from his bed—that the persons guilty of murdering him are the three Indians—and that the object contemplated (and achieved) by the crime, was to obtain possession of the diamond, called the Moonstone.

The facts from which this conclusion is drawn are derived partly from an examination of the room at the tavern; and partly from the evidence obtained at the Coroner's Inquest.

On forcing the door of the room, the deceased gentleman was discovered, dead, with the pillow of the bed over his face. The medical man who examined him, being informed of this circumstance, considered the post-mortem appearances as being perfectly compatible with murder by smothering—that is to say, with murder committed by some person, or persons, pressing the pillow over the nose and mouth of the deceased, until death resulted from congestion of the lungs.

Next, as to the motive for the crime.

A small box, with a sealed paper torn off from it (the paper containing an inscription) was found open, and empty, on a table in the room. Mr Luker has himself personally identified the box, the seal, and the inscription. He has declared that the box did actually contain the diamond, called the Moonstone; and he has admitted having given the box (thus sealed up) to Mr Godfrey Ablewhite (then concealed under a disguise), on the afternoon of the twenty-sixth of June last. The fair inference from all this is, that the stealing of the Moonstone was the motive of the crime.

Next, as to the manner in which the crime was committed.

On examination of the room (which is only seven feet high), a trap-door in the ceiling, leading out on to the roof of the house, was discovered open. The short ladder, used for obtaining access to the trap-door (and kept under the bed), was found placed at the opening, so as to enable any person or persons, in the room, to leave it again easily. In the trap-door itself was found a square aperture cut in the wood, apparently with some exceedingly sharp instrument, just behind the bolt which fastened the door on the inner side. In this way, any person from the outside could have drawn back the bolt, and opened the door, and have dropped (or have been noiselessly lowered by an accomplice) into the room—its height, as already observed, being only seven feet. That some person, or persons, must have got admission in this way, appears evident from the fact of the aperture being there. As to the manner in which he (or they) obtained access to the roof of the tavern, it is to be remarked that the third house, lower down in the street, was empty, and under repair—that a long ladder was left by the workmen, leading from the pavement to the top of the house— and that, on returning to their work, on the morning of the 27th, the men found the plank which they had tied to the ladder, to prevent anyone from using it in their absence, removed, and lying on the ground. As to the possibility of ascending by this ladder, passing over the roofs of the houses, passing back, and descending again, unobserved—it is discovered, on the evidence of the night policeman, that he only passes through Shore Lane twice in an hour, when out on his beat. The testimony of the inhabitants also declares, that Shore Lane, after midnight, is one of the quietest and loneliest streets in London. Here again, therefore, it seems fair to infer that—with ordinary caution, and presence of mind—any man, or men, might have ascended by the ladder, and might have descended again, unobserved. Once on the roof of the tavern, it has been proved, by experiment, that a man might cut through the trap-door, while lying down on it, and that in such a position, the parapet in front of the house would conceal him from the view of anyone passing in the street.

Lastly, as to the person, or persons, by whom the crime was committed.

It is known (1) that the Indians had an interest in possessing themselves of the Diamond. (2) It is at least probable that the man looking like an Indian, whom Octavius Guy saw at the window of the cab, speaking to the man dressed like a mechanic, was one of the three Hindoo conspirators. (3) It is certain that this same man dressed like a mechanic, was seen keeping Mr Godfrey Ablewhite in view, all through the evening of the 26th, and was found in the bedroom (before Mr Ablewhite was shown into it) under circumstances which lead to the suspicion that he was examining the room. (4) A morsel of torn gold thread was picked up in the bedroom, which persons expert in such matters, declare to be of Indian manufacture, and to be a species of gold thread not known in England. (5) On the morning of the 27th, three men, answering to the description of the three Indians, were observed in Lower Thames Street, were traced to the Tower Wharf, and were seen to leave London by the steamer bound for Rotterdam.

There is here, moral, if not legal, evidence, that the murder was committed by the Indians.

Whether the man personating a mechanic was, or was not, an accomplice in the crime, it is impossible to say. That he could have committed the murder alone, seems beyond the limits of probability. Acting by himself, he could hardly have smothered Mr Ablewhite—who was the taller and stronger man of the two—without a struggle taking place, or a cry being heard. A servant girl, sleeping in the next room, heard nothing. The landlord, sleeping in the room below, heard nothing. The whole evidence points to the inference that more than one man was concerned in this crime—and the circumstances, I repeat, morally justify the conclusion that the Indians committed it.

I have only to add, that the verdict at the Coroner's Inquest was Wilful Murder against some person, or persons, unknown. Mr Ablewhite's family have offered a reward, and no effort has been left untried to discover the guilty persons. The man dressed like a mechanic has eluded all inquiries. The Indians have been traced. As to the prospect of ultimately capturing these last, I shall have a word to say to you on that head, when I reach the end of the present Report.

In the meanwhile, having now written all that is needful on the subject of Mr Godfrey Ablewhite's death, I may pass next to the narrative of his proceedings before, during, and after the time, when you and he met at the late Lady Verinder's house.

With regard to the subject now in hand, I may state, at the outset, that Mr Godfrey Ablewhite's life had two sides to it.

The side turned up to the public view, presented the spectacle of a gentleman, possessed of considerable reputation as a speaker at charitable meetings, and endowed with administrative abilities, which he placed at the disposal of various Benevolent Societies, mostly of the female sort. The side kept hidden from the general notice, exhibited this same gentleman in the totally different character of a man of pleasure, with a villa in the suburbs which was not taken in his own name, and with a lady in the villa, who was not taken in his own name, either.

My investigations in the villa have shown me several fine pictures and statues; furniture tastefully selected, and admirably made; and a conservatory of the rarest flowers, the match of which it would not be easy to find in all London. My investigation of the lady has resulted in the discovery of jewels which are worthy to take rank with the flowers, and of carriages and horses which have (deservedly) produced a sensation in the Park, among persons well qualified to judge of the build of the one, and the breed of the others.

All this is, so far, common enough. The villa and the lady are such familiar objects in London life, that I ought to apologise for introducing them to notice. But what is not common and not familiar (in my experience), is that all these fine things were not only ordered, but paid for. The pictures, the statues, the flowers, the jewels, the carriages, and the horses—inquiry proved, to my indescribable astonishment, that not a sixpence of debt was owing on any of them. As to the villa, it had been bought, out and out, and settled on the lady.

I might have tried to find the right reading of this riddle, and tried in vain—but for Mr Godfrey Ablewhite's death, which caused an inquiry to be made into the state of his affairs.

The inquiry elicited these facts:

That Mr Godfrey Ablewhite was entrusted with the care of a sum of twenty thousand pounds—as one of two Trustees for a young gentleman, who was still a minor in the year eighteen hundred and forty-eight. That the Trust was to lapse, and that the young gentleman was to receive the twenty thousand pounds on the day when he came of age, in the month of February, eighteen hundred and fifty. That, pending the arrival of this period, an income of six hundred pounds was to be paid to him by his two Trustees, half-yearly—at Christmas and Midsummer Day. That this income was regularly paid by the active Trustee, Mr Godfrey Ablewhite. That the twenty thousand pounds (from which the income was supposed to be derived) had every farthing of it been sold out of the Funds, at different periods, ending with the end of the year eighteen hundred and forty-seven. That the power of attorney, authorising the bankers to sell out the stock, and the various written orders telling them what amounts to sell out, were formally signed by both the Trustees. That the signature of the second Trustee (a retired army officer, living in the country) was a signature forged, in every case, by the active Trustee—otherwise Mr Godfrey Ablewhite.

In these facts lies the explanation of Mr Godfrey's honourable conduct, in paying the debts incurred for the lady and the villa—and (as you will presently see) of more besides.

We may now advance to the date of Miss Verinder's birthday (in the year eighteen hundred and forty-eight)—the twenty-first of June.

On the day before, Mr Godfrey Ablewhite arrived at his father's house, and asked (as I know from Mr Ablewhite, senior, himself) for a loan of three hundred pounds. Mark the sum; and remember at the same time, that the half-yearly payment to the young gentleman was due on the twenty-fourth of the month. Also, that the whole of the young gentleman's fortune had been spent by his Trustee, by the end of the year 'forty-seven.

Mr Ablewhite, senior, refused to lend his son a farthing.

The next day Mr Godfrey Ablewhite rode over with you to Lady Verinder's house. A few hours afterwards, Mr Godfrey (as you yourself have told me) made a proposal of marriage to Miss Verinder. Here, he saw his way no doubt—if accepted—to the end of all his money anxieties, present and future. But, as events actually turned out, what happened? Miss Verinder refused him.

On the night of the birthday, therefore, Mr Godfrey Ablewhite's pecuniary position was this. He had three hundred pounds to find on the twenty-fourth of the month, and twenty thousand pounds to find in February eighteen hundred and fifty. Failing to raise these sums, at these times, he was a ruined man.

Under those circumstances, what takes place next?

You exasperate Mr Candy, the doctor, on the sore subject of his profession; and he plays you a practical joke, in return, with a dose of laudanum. He trusts the administration of the dose, prepared in a little phial, to Mr Godfrey Ablewhite—who has himself confessed the share he had in the matter, under circumstances which shall presently be related to you. Mr Godfrey is all the readier to enter into the conspiracy, having himself suffered from your sharp tongue in the course of the evening. He joins Betteredge in persuading you to drink a little brandy and water before you go to bed. He privately drops the dose of laudanum into your cold grog. And you drink the mixture.

Let us now shift the scene, if you please to Mr Luker's house at Lambeth. And allow me to remark, by way of preface, that Mr Bruff and I, together, have found a means of forcing the money-lender to make a clean breast of it. We have carefully sifted the statement he has addressed to us; and here it is at your service.

Late on the evening of Friday, the twenty-third of June ('forty-eight), Mr Luker was surprised by a visit from Mr Godfrey Ablewhite. He was more than surprised, when Mr Godfrey produced the Moonstone. No such Diamond (according to Mr Luker's experience) was in the possession of any private person in Europe.

Mr Godfrey Ablewhite had two modest proposals to make, in relation to this magnificent gem. First, would Mr Luker be so good as to buy it? Secondly, would Mr Luker (in default of seeing his way to the purchase) undertake to sell it on commission, and to pay a sum down, on the anticipated result?

Mr Luker tested the Diamond, weighed the Diamond and estimated the value of the Diamond, before he answered a word. *His* estimate (allowing for the flaw in the stone) was thirty thousand pounds.

Having reached that result, Mr Luker opened his lips, and

put a question: 'How did you come by this?' Only six words! But what volumes of meaning in them!

Mr Godfrey Ablewhite began a story. Mr Luker opened his lips again, and only said three words, this time. 'That won't do!'

Mr Godfrey Ablewhite began another story. Mr Luker wasted no more words on him. He got up, and rang the bell for the servant to show the gentleman out.

Upon this compulsion, Mr Godfrey made an effort, and came out with a new and amended version of the affair, to the following effect.

After privately slipping the laudanum into your brandy and water, he wished you good night, and went into his own room. It was the next room to yours; and the two had a door of communication between them. On entering his own room Mr Godfrey (as he supposed) closed his door. His money troubles kept him awake. He sat, in his dressing-gown and slippers, for nearly an hour, thinking over his position. Just as he was preparing to get into bed, he heard you, talking to yourself, in your own room, and going to the door of communication, found that he had not shut it as he supposed.

He looked into your room to see what was the matter. He discovered you with the candle in your hand, just leaving your bed-chamber. He heard you say to yourself, in a voice quite unlike your own voice, 'How do I know? The Indians may be hidden in the house.'

Up to that time, he had simply supposed himself (in giving you the laudanum) to be helping to make you the victim of a harmless practical joke. It now occurred to him, that the laudanum had taken some effect on you, which had not been foreseen by the doctor, any more than by himself. In the fear of an accident happening he followed you softly to see what you would do.

He followed you to Miss Verinder's sitting-room, and saw you go in. You left the door open. He looked through the crevice thus produced, between the door and the post, before he ventured into the room himself.

In that position, he not only detected you in taking the Diamond out of the drawer—he also detected Miss Verinder, silently watching you from her bedroom, through her open door. His own eyes satisfied him that *she* saw you take the Diamond too.

Before you left the sitting-room again, you hesitated a little. Mr Godfrey took advantage of this hesitation to get back again to his bedroom before you came out, and discovered him. He had barely got back, before you got back too. You saw him (as he supposes) just as he was passing through the door of communication. At any rate, you called to him in a strange, drowsy voice.

He came back to you. You looked at him in a dull sleepy way. You put the Diamond into his hand. You said to him, 'Take it back, Godfrey, to your father's bank. It's safe there—it's not safe here.' You turned away unsteadily, and put on your dressing-gown. You sat down in the large arm-chair in your room. You said, '*I* can't take it back to the bank. My head's like lead—and I can't feel my feet under me.' Your head sank on the back of the chair—you heaved a heavy sigh—and you fell asleep.

Mr Godfrey Ablewhite went back, with the Diamond, into his own room. His statement is, that he came to no conclusion at that time—except that he would wait, and see what happened in the morning.

When the morning came, your language and conduct showed that you were absolutely ignorant of what you had said and done overnight. At the same time, Miss Verinder's language and conduct showed that she was resolved to say nothing (in mercy to you) on her side. If Mr Godfrey Ablewhite chose to keep the Diamond, he might do so with perfect impunity. The Moonstone stood between him and ruin. He put the Moonstone into his pocket.

*

This was the story told by your cousin (under pressure of necessity) to Mr Luker.

Mr Luker believed the story to be, as to all main essentials, true—on this ground, that Mr Godfrey Ablewhite was too great a fool to have invented it. Mr Bruff and I agree with Mr Luker, in considering this test of the truth of the story to be a perfectly reliable one.

The next question, was the question of what Mr Luker would do in the matter of the Moonstone. He proposed the following terms, as the only terms on which he would consent to mix himself up with, what was (even in *his* line of business) a doubtful and dangerous transaction.

Mr Luker would consent to lend Mr Godfrey Ablewhite the sum of two thousand pounds, on condition that the Moonstone was to be deposited with him as a pledge. If, at the expiration of one year from that date, Mr Godfrey Ablewhite paid three thousand pounds to Mr Luker, he was to receive back the Diamond, as a pledge redeemed. If he failed to produce the money at the expiration of the year, the pledge (otherwise the Moonstone) was to be considered as forfeited to Mr Luker—who would, in this latter case, generously make Mr Godfrey a present of certain promissory notes of his (relating to former dealings) which were then in the money-lender's possession.

It is needless to say that Mr Godfrey indignantly refused to listen to these monstrous terms. Mr Luker thereupon handed him back the Diamond, and wished him good-night.

Your cousin went to the door, and came back again. How was he to be sure that the conversation of that evening would be kept strictly secret between his friend and himself?

Mr Luker didn't profess to know how. If Mr Godfrey had accepted his terms, Mr Godfrey would have made him an accomplice, and might have counted on his silence as on a certainty. As things were, Mr Luker must be guided by his own interests. If awkward inquiries were made, how could he be expected to compromise himself, for the sake of a man who had declined to deal with him?

Receiving this reply, Mr Godfrey Ablewhite did, what all animals (human and otherwise) do, when they find themselves caught in a trap. He looked about him in a state of helpless despair. The day of the month, recorded on a neat little card in a box on the money-lender's chimney-piece, happened to attract his eye. It was the twenty-third of June. On the twenty-fourth he had three hundred pounds to pay to the young gentleman for whom he was trustee, and no chance of raising the money, except the chance that Mr Luker had offered to him. But for this miserable obstacle, he might have taken the Diamond to Amsterdam, and have made a marketable commodity of it, by having it cut up into separate stones. As matters stood, he had no choice but to accept Mr Luker's terms. After all, he had a year at his disposal, in which to raise the three thousand pounds—and a year is a long time.

Mr Luker drew out the necessary documents on the spot. When they were signed, he gave Mr Godfrey Ablewhite two cheques. One, dated June 23rd, for three hundred pounds. Another, dated a week on, for the remaining balance seventeen hundred pounds.

How the Moonstone was trusted to the keeping of Mr Luker's bankers, and how the Indians treated Mr Luker and Mr Godfrey (after that had been done) you know already.

I have ascertained that when he went abroad, on getting his five thousand pounds, he went to Amsterdam. There he made all the necessary arrangements for having the Diamond cut into separate stones. He came back (in disguise), and redeemed the Moonstone, on the appointed day. A few days were allowed to elapse (as a precaution agreed to by both parties) before the jewel was actually taken out of the bank. If he had got safe with it to Amsterdam, there would have been just time between July 'forty-nine, and February 'fifty (when the young gentleman came of age) to cut the Diamond, and to make a marketable commodity (polished or unpolished) of the separate stones. Judge from this what motives he had to run the risk which he actually ran. It was 'neck or nothing' with him—if ever it was 'neck or nothing' with a man yet.

I have only to remind you, before closing this Report, that there is a chance of laying hands on the Indians, and of recovering the Moonstone yet. They are now (there is every reason to believe) on their passage to Bombay, in an East Indiaman. The ship (barring accidents) will touch at no other port on her way out; and the authorities at Bombay (already communicated with by letter, overland) will be prepared to board the vessel, the moment she enters the harbour.

I have the honour to remain, dear sir, your obedient servant, RICHARD CUFF (late sergeant in the Detective Force, Scotland Yard, London).*

---

* NOTE.—Wherever the Report touches on the events of the birthday, or of the three days that followed it, compare with Betteredge's Narrative, chapters vi. to xi.

FINAL NARRATIVE

Contributed by GABRIEL BETTEREDGE

I AM the person (as you remember no doubt) who led the way in these pages, and opened the story. I am also the person who is left behind, as it were, to close the story up.

Let nobody suppose that I have any last words to say here concerning the Indian Diamond. I hold that unlucky jewel in abhorrence—and I refer you to other authority than mine, for such news of the Moonstone as you may, at the present time, be expected to receive. My purpose, in this place, is to state a fact in the history of the family, which has been passed over by everybody, and which I won't allow to be disrespectfully smothered up in that way. The fact to which I allude is—the marriage of Miss Rachel and Mr Franklin Blake. This interesting event took place at our house in Yorkshire, on Tuesday, October ninth, eighteen hundred and forty-nine. I had a new suit of clothes on the occasion. And the married couple went to spend the honeymoon in Scotland.

Family festivals having been rare enough at our house, since my poor mistress's death, I own—on this occasion of the wedding—to having (towards the latter part of the day) taken a drop too much on the strength of it.

If you have ever done the same sort of thing yourself you will understand and feel for me. If you have not, you will very likely say, 'Disgusting old man! why does he tell us this?' The reason why is now to come.

Having, then, taken my drop (bless you! you have got your favourite vice, too; only your vice isn't mine, and mine isn't yours), I next applied the one infallible remedy—that remedy being, as you know, *Robinson Crusoe*. Where I opened that unrivalled book, I can't say. Where the lines of print at last left off running into each other, I know, however, perfectly well. It was at page three hundred and eighteen—a domestic bit concerning Robinson Crusoe's marriage, as follows:

'With those Thoughts, I considered my new Engagement, that I had a Wife'—(Observe! so had Mr Franklin!)—'one Child born'—(Observe again! that might yet be Mr Franklin's case, too!)—'and my Wife then'—What Robinson Crusoe's wife did or did not do 'then' I felt no desire to discover. I scored the bit about the Child with my pencil, and put a morsel of paper for a mark to keep the place; 'Lie you there,' I said, 'till the marriage of Mr Franklin and Miss Rachel is some months older—and then we'll see!'

The months passed (more than I had bargained for), and no occasion presented itself for disturbing that mark in the book. It was not till this present month of November, eighteen hundred and fifty, that Mr Franklin came into my room, in high good spirits, and said, 'Betteredge! I have got some news for you! Something is going to happen in the house, before we are many months older.'

'Does it concern the family, sir?' I asked.

'It decidedly concerns the family,' says Mr Franklin.

'Has your good lady anything to do with it, if you please, sir?'

'She has a great deal to do with it,' says Mr Franklin, beginning to look a little surprised.

'You needn't say a word more, sir,' I answered. 'God bless you both! I'm heartily glad to hear it.'

Mr Franklin stared like a person thunderstruck. 'May I venture to inquire where you got your information?' he asked. 'I only got mine (imparted in the strictest secrecy) five minutes since.'

Here was an opportunity of producing *Robinson Crusoe*!

Here was a chance of reading that domestic bit about the child which I had marked on the day of Mr Franklin's marriage! I read those miraculous words with an emphasis which did them justice, and then I looked him severely in the face. '*Now*, sir, do you believe in *Robinson Crusoe*?' I asked, with a solemnity, suitable to the occasion.

'Betteredge!' says Mr Franklin, with equal solemnity, 'I'm convinced at last.' He shook hands with me—and I felt that I had converted him.

With the relation of this extraordinary circumstance, my reappearance in these pages comes to an end. Let nobody laugh at the unique anecdote here related. You are welcome to be as merry as you please over everything else I have written. But when I write of *Robinson Crusoe*, by the Lord it's serious—and I request you to take it accordingly!

When this is said, all is said. Ladies and gentlemen, I make my bow, and shut up the story.

THE END

WILLIAM WILKIE COLLINS

WILLIAM WILKIE COLLINS, the eldest son of William Collins the landscape painter and Royal Academician, was born in London on January 8th 1824. His mother had been a Miss Geddes, daughter of Andrew Geddes, A.R.A. The name Wilkie was given to him in honour of his father's friend Sir David Wilkie, R.A.

He was educated at a private school at Highbury and at the age of twelve he accompanied his parents to Italy where he remained with them for about three years. Rome made a deep impression on him. He stored up memories and made notes of his visit which became material for his first historical novel which he began writing secretly in 1841 while working as a clerk in the tea warehouse of Antrobus & Son in London.

His heart was not in the tea trade. Wishing to become a writer or a painter—he actually succeeded in having a painting of his exhibited at the Royal Academy in 1849—he chose the Law, as other potential writers had done before him and were to do in the future. He entered Lincoln's Inn in 1846 and was eventually called to the Bar in 1851, but he never practised as a barrister.

Meanwhile in 1847 his father had died and Wilkie set to work writing *Memoirs of the life of William Collins, R.A.* which was published the following year. The favourable reception accorded to the work encouraged him to continue with his historical novel which was published under the title, *Antonina, or the Fall of Rome* in 1850.

In 1851 he first met Charles Dickens, whose lifelong friend and companion he became. Dickens exercised some influence on Collins' early work, but in turn became influenced by him. At the time of their meeting, Dickens had just founded his periodical, *Household Words*, to which Collins became a regular contributor. In 1852 he published his next two novels, *Mr Wray's Cashbox*, and *Basil* in which he began to find his style as an author. The same year he began to take part in the private theatricals organised by Dickens at the latter's residence, Tavistock House, and to write plays for those performances, among them *The Lighthouse* (later publicly performed at the Olympic Theatre in 1857). In 1854 came a new work, *Hide and Seek*, a novel on the theme of deaf-and-dumbness.

In 1853 Collins accompanied Dickens on a tour through Switzerland and Italy, and again in 1856 he spent the winter with Dickens on the Continent, planning with him the story of *The Wreck of the Golden Mary* and writing *The Dead Secret*. In the intervening years he had published several more stories, but *The Dead Secret*, which was serialised in *Household Words* in 1857, proved his first important success. It was followed by a volume of stories called *The Queen of Hearts* (1859) serialised in Dickens' new periodical *All the Year Round*, and by *The Woman in White* (also first published in *All the Year Round*). The work achieved immediate and outstanding success. Seven editions appeared within six months of its publication in book form (1860). It brought its author much money and has established that he was practically the first English novelist to deal with the detection of crime. From then on Collins' books—in all he wrote close on thirty major works of fiction—had an eager public, and were immediately translated into French and other languages.

His next most famous works of that period were *No Name* (1862), *Armadale* (1866) and *The Moonstone* (1868). The latter was at one time considered the best detective story ever to have appeared in the English language.

In 1860 the ties with Dickens became even closer, when Wilkie's younger brother Charles Allston, a painter and author, married Kate, the younger daughter of Dickens. In 1867 Wilkie Collins collaborated with Dickens in the play *No Thoroughfare*,